A Serious Business

Roderick Hart

First published in 2013 by The Portable Press
Copyright © Roderick Hart 2013
First edition

This book is a work of fiction. Any resemblance to actual events, or persons, living or dead, is entirely coincidental.

The author asserts the moral right under the Copyright, Designs and Patents Act 1988 to be identified as the author of this work.

All Rights reserved. No part of this publication may be reproduced, stored in a retrieval system, or transmitted, in any form or by any means without the prior written consent of the author, nor be otherwise circulated in any form of binding or cover other than that in which it is published and without a similar condition being imposed on the subsequent purchaser.

ISBN: 1493625268
ISBN-13: 978-1-4936-2526-0

*With a friendly nod to Njal's Saga,
in which Njal is burned in his own home*

1

It happened once a year, the annual review. It was due at ten o'clock and he knew what to expect. She would rifle through her paperwork and ask questions from her checklist, but really what she wanted to know was why. Why was he still on the bottom rung of the ladder? Had he no ambition? Didn't he want to take it to the next level? There was a lot to be said for the lady, but she liked her colleagues to better themselves and she knew what better was. He combed his hair and ran up the stairs to Human Resources or, as it said on the door, Gemma A Laing.

'Take a seat', she said, indicating two chairs in front of her desk. She walked round and joined him as if to say, *There's nothing between us now, no desk, no rank, no status. We're in this together. We're equal.* Which was good technique and a mannerly thing to do, but her review of him was the one that mattered, his review of her wouldn't make the file.

'This isn't part of the annual review, Frank, but I go through contact details for everyone while they're here. You haven't changed your address, I take it?' No, though he needed to. 'And your next of kin is still your sister Flora. You haven't married since we last met?'

Gemma was short, auburn-haired and tidy, and had recently given up glasses in favour of contact lenses. Despite her professional qualification there was a faint hint of the unorthodox about her. In her attitude to stress, for example, a condition of which she was keenly aware. It didn't extend to incense, Tai Chi, or chill-out music on pan pipes, but she liked to play ocean surf in her office as she updated her files and worked on improvements to the staff welfare scheme.

'I'd better turn this off for now,' she said.

'Not on my account.'

But she turned it down anyway, to a barely audible watery white noise. This was, after all, a significant event. When the phone rang her voice-mail picked it up. There would be no interruptions.

'As you know, we now have feed-back from section managers ahead of these interviews.' Gemma glanced at her notes. 'Alastair obviously thinks highly of you.'

He knew that already but it was good to hear.

'We talked about your career progression last time round, have you given it any more thought?'

He had, but didn't feel able to share it with a woman so enamoured of marketable skills. Frank went where his interests took him, the market notwithstanding. And right now it was taking him to the natural sciences. He knew she wouldn't approve. It wasn't relevant.

'Well I hope you know that if you want to broaden your horizons we'd be happy to support you in any area of interest to you and of use to us.'

He wondered whether this was a plain statement of fact or if the lady's agenda was showing.

'Ms Laing, it would help me to know which areas might be of interest to you.'

She was worryingly ready with a suggestion. 'Computing.'

Alright, he was an electrician and computers used electricity – but apart from that, what was the connection? Why was she suggesting this? He could think of only one answer. Alastair was on the point of retiring: if they wanted to outsource maintenance this was the time to do it and he would be out of a job unless they moved him sideways. As for her suggestion, computing was already taken care of.

'Surely that's Preston's baby.'

'Indeed,' Ms Laing agreed, 'and two years on we're still waiting for its first word. A late developer, wouldn't you say?'

Ms Laing slid Alastair's report back in its folder.

'About the feedback from section heads, you may have a view on that. Concern has been expressed by the staff association.'

He knew why. It came close to measuring performance and those who didn't perform were apprehensive. If you're hiding in the shadows, the last thing you want is a woman with letters after her name going through the building with a flashlight.

'It's fine by me.'

'You're entitled to access these documents at any time, you just have to ask.'

He wondered if he should. He wasn't concerned about the contents, but Alastair said a principle was at stake. Rights, like bodies, should be exercised in case they withered on the vine. He was referring to the right to vote, for which he claimed to have fought and died – an interesting claim at an eccentric angle to the facts, but you could see what he was driving at.

'Just out of interest, Frank,' Gemma asked, when the formal proceedings were over, 'could you recommend anyone reliable for a domestic electrical job? I obviously mean by that anyone including you.'

'Would this be for yourself, Ms Laing, or someone else?'

Ms Laing looked slightly uneasy.

'For me. I know this isn't the most appropriate occasion to be asking but here we are, and I don't see you very often in the normal course of events.'

He did homers from time to time, provided he liked the person and the house was not too distant. Ms Laing was a down-to-earth person short of power points in her kitchen.

She lived within the city limits on a handy bus route. He'd be happy to help her out.

'So there isn't a Mr Laing you could sweet-talk into this one.'

Ms Laing was less than pleased.

'There is no Mr Laing and I fail to see why I should sweet-talk anyone.'

She rose and placed his folder in a hanging file.

'By the way, if you want to consider the computing side you should drop in on Pamela Ross while you're on this floor. There is no Mr Ross, but I think you'll find her competent nevertheless.'

As he stood to leave he registered the ocean waves. They'd been playing all along but he'd filtered them out. Why was it that when a wave approached a floating sea-gull it rose on the peak and vanished in the trough but wasn't carried closer to the shore? Was it something to do with wave motion, or were its little webbed feet paddling like mad to maintain its position, its folded wings and unruffled air concealing action beneath the surface? If so, stress relief was an illusion.

On his way to Pamela's office, he resolved to confine his small-talk to people he knew. Ms Laing didn't strike him as the touchy type so what was the problem? Maybe there had been a Mr Laing who died young of a fatal disease. Maybe there still was a Mr Laing but he had run off with an actress. Maybe Ms Laing was of lesbian persuasion. Or maybe she simply disliked personal remarks from relative strangers. He knocked on Pamela's door and entered.

'Hello, I'm looking for Pamela Ross?'

The girl behind the desk challenged him at once. 'And you are?'

'Frank Figures, maintenance. I don't wear my ID, it gets in the way when I'm working.'

'Don't tell me, you have it in one of your many pockets,' she said, giving his dungarees the once-over. 'Actually, I've seen you around.' He didn't remember seeing her. 'In the restaurant. I'm June, by the way.'

'And Pamela Ross?'

'Control room, one up.'

The seventh floor had always interested him. It was off limits to customers, who never had occasion to rise above the restaurant on floor six. The location of the restaurant was a particular joy to Hector Mowatt, grandson of the founder, since the accounts department was on the same floor. *Makes paying bills more palatable*, he would say with a twinkle. Either he was tickled by his own wit or the onset of old age had made his eyes watery. He was getting on a bit and it showed.

The meeting room, also on the seventh floor, was used for in-store training and meetings of the staff association. An overhead projector sat on a desk near the front not far from the flip chart. Next there was the boardroom, imposing in a tired sort of way, calling to mind a failing gentleman's club. And adjacent to that an activity room, available to members of staff for work-outs and weights.

But what intrigued Frank most about the seventh floor was the penthouse suite: a bedroom with en suite bathroom, galley kitchen, and small sitting room with television, mini-bar and phone. This was for the use of Hector or Alice Mowatt should they wish to stay over, and was now rarely used. As he passed, he caught sight of the PS sign Alastair had screwed to the door. Brevity wasn't his strong point as a rule, but he hadn't wanted to spell out what was, after all, a perk of ownership not open to the rank and file. Frank wouldn't have minded an afterthought like that, a tranquil environment where he could relax and read in peace.

Which left only three more doors: to the stair, the roof, and the control room. The door wasn't properly shut but he knocked anyway. Pamela saw his reflection in her screens as he entered: she was sitting at a table checking monitors and writing tape labels with a marker. The monitors provided most of the light in what seemed to him a seriously under-lit room.

'You're not short of channels.'

'They're all equally boring. Take a seat, Frank.' She still hadn't looked at him directly. 'Gemma said you might come.'

'I'm not sure why I'm here. She mentioned computing but we have a contract with the suppliers. If anything goes wrong, they fix it.'

Pamela pointed to a woman on monitor three. She was lingering beside a row of ladies' tops and looking to the left and right to see if anyone was watching.

'What do you make of her?'

'She looks like she's going to knock something off.'

'OK, so what do we do?'

Surely that was obvious: keep an eye on her. But it was less obvious to Pamela, who questioned whether she was what she seemed.

'I'm not sure where you're going with this, Miss Ross. It seems pretty clear cut to me.'

'Alright, she's acting suspiciously yet she knows there are cameras. Either she's unusually stupid, which is always possible, or she wants to be seen acting suspiciously. My name is Pamela, by the way, nobody calls me Miss Ross. So, Frank, why might she want to be seen?'

Good question, but he was toiling for an answer.

'She's hoping to be detained on suspicion of theft so she can sue us for false arrest?'

'With damages for embarrassment and humiliation.'

'Exactly.'

'I don't think so.'

According to Pamela, magicians attracted the eye with one hand so you missed what the other was doing. She left it to Frank to make the connection. He was being interviewed again, but this time by indirection.

'So if she's the hand that draws the attention, there must be another one. She's working with someone else.'

'That's the most likely explanation.'

She looked at him again, for too long, he thought. Not only interviewed but appraised. Alright, he wasn't handsome but he wasn't ugly either, and if his hair looked as if he'd cut it himself, so what? Who with a pair of scissors needed a barber?

He looked round the room. 'We could shed more light on the subject.'

'Ah,' Pamela replied, with mock solemnity, 'but would we see more clearly if we did?'

She had a neat face and tied-back blond hair, and he thought he detected the faint flickering of images on her cheek from the monitors. Till now, he had only seen her picture in the staff newsletter, a head-and-shoulders shot beside her column, Colleague of the Month.

He was caught by an involuntary smile. Before Preston joined the staff, the column had been called Member of the Month. When Preston recovered himself sufficiently, he wrote to the editor suggesting the title be changed to something more decorous.

'Care to share the joke?' Pamela asked.

'I was thinking about Preston.'

'I see,' she said. 'Well let me tell you something, I don't find him funny. Oh, and he doesn't compute.'

He appeared every day, sometimes on time, then disappeared into his office where he played with his toys. But as far as Pamela could tell, nothing came of it.

'Irregular time-keeping doesn't mean he isn't working.'

'The fact that someone's working doesn't mean he's achieving – like anything at all!'

She was referring to Preston Blair but in terms so general Frank felt included himself. Was this what Gemma felt, that he was underachieving? Was this what lay behind the pressure to move on?

'Look, Miss Ross, I haven't a clue what you and Preston do. The way you tell it, he doesn't either. So maybe I should put this computer business on the back burner for now.'

To his relief she agreed. She'd already written him off.

'Yes. Maybe you should.'

She wrote out a label, stuck it on the spine of a tape and looked back to the monitors.

'I've seen you many times,' she said with a smile, 'I'm sure I have you taped.'

'I'm sure you do.'

'I'll put a proposal together and pass it on to you. Something concrete. See what you think. No obligation.'

She was going through the motions knowing he would do nothing about it.

'Suck it and see.'

'Exactly.'

As he rose to leave, she moved away from the table and he saw the metallic gleam of her wheelchair for the first time. Till that moment he'd forgotten she used one.

'Nice to meet you, Frank.'

2

Frank's kitchen was to the back of the building looking out over what had once been a drying green. In the case of number six, the green was paved over, with weeds flourishing between the flagstones and a stunted elder in the middle. Only residents of the ground floor flats had access to this area and one of them, long gone, had used it to store refuse in black polythene bags – which left the residents above looking out over one of the worst views in the city. But there was nothing they could do about it since the rear door was locked and the key lost.

He was looking through the kitchen window when the phone rang. He walked to the hall and took the handset off its holder.

'Hi, Frank, it's me. I hope you're remembering.'

'Of course,' he lied, 'come right over.'

'Look out the window.'

He let the phone swing from its cord and walked through to the front room. There she was on the pavement opposite, casual in her cargo pants and jacket, smiling that knowing smile, her canvas bag over her shoulder, her mobile in her hand. He'd fallen for this one before, but with the Entryphone broken how else could she let him know she'd arrived? He heard her feet on the stair as he opened the door. She walked straight through to the kitchen, emptied the bag and loaded the washing machine. Flora was three years older than he was and behaved as though she owned the place.

'What's the problem, did he say?' Frank asked.

'No, but he's ordered spare parts, coming next week to fix it.' She looked at him and smiled. 'Listen. Hear that? Your phone's off the hook.'

Which was more than could be said for him. Unlike hers, his washing machine was working. She was welcome to use it, but he knew she'd use his TV as well.

'You're not watching *that*, are you?' she said. 'What is it?'

It was a documentary about forensic detection. Why did Mrs Griswold poison her daughter systematically over a period of years? There was no financial benefit so the gain had to be elsewhere, deep in her damaged psyche where even the woman herself couldn't find it. Maybe he'd missed a programme or two, but he couldn't recollect a case where a sister had poisoned her brother.

'Tea or coffee?' Flora asked.

Apart from a tell-tale rectangular shape her bag was empty, she'd brought chocolates to soften him up. With her washing taken care of she took his remote and selected a soap. As far as he could see, most of the characters aspired to change partner, either out of naked desire or to get back at someone else. It was, he thought, an artful compilation of heated confrontation and soft-focus sex, yet Flora still found time to ask him how things were at work and how much longer he could stand living in 'this hell-hole.' She was sympathetic though, she really was.

'I'd let you move in with me, but I might be entertaining.'

Entertaining, as Flora used the word, meant having someone round to her flat with a view to a chat which might, or might not, lead to sex. As far as Frank could tell, the chat part of it amounted to a verbal test of indeterminate construction containing trick statements and trickier questions. If her guest failed, the coffee turned out to be exactly that. Which confirmed Frank in his view that conversation was an ordeal best avoided.

He admired his sister's social skills. Her job took her to a succession of different events in various parts of the country so she was constantly working with strangers. Apart from customers, whom he rarely met, Frank saw the same people every working day. Over a period of time he'd sussed them out, based more on observation of their behaviour than how they appeared or even what they said. As for social gatherings, he never knew what to say to people he'd just met.

'No wonder you're so reluctant to take holidays, Frank. How many days leave have you built up now? The only friends you have are people at work!'

Nearly, but not quite. There was always his friend Archie, who'd gone on to greater things as a lawyer.

'So what's been happening in your life lately?' Flora asked, sitting down in one of his two upholstered chairs. And Frank said nothing much, apart from his little spot of bother with Gemma Laing.

'She was sounding me out about staff development again as if I didn't have enough on my plate.'

He thought of his father. Voluntary severance they called it, a fitting description since he had been severed not only from employment but from the exercise of his skills. Maybe if he didn't sign up to something soon he was on his way out.

'Perhaps she fancies you,' she said, taking her shoes off and wriggling her toes, 'ever thought of that?'

'She wants some wiring done.'

'Right. That's what they all say. A ruse to get you round there, if you ask me. Flex those biceps and you're off!'

Given his sister's wayward take on Gemma, he kept his encounter with Pamela to himself.

'My next job, and thank you for asking,' Flora said, as the closing titles rolled, 'is the opening of that new adventure centre I told you about. It's got the lot: climbing arena, mountain bike trail, white water kayak course and a state-of-the-art health club. I'll be away for a week.'

So that's what this was about. She wanted him to drop by once a day to water the plants and feed the cat. As she made to wash the dishes, Frank stopped her. She had clothes to fold. They were still damp but her tumble drier was working, the one he had ducted through her kitchen wall.

'Your windows could do with a clean.'

Frank wasn't minded to wash them, especially at the back. Seeing a pile of black polythene bags was bad enough but seeing them clearly was worse.

'Appearances matter, you know. The impression you create.'

She looked round, slowly, for effect. 'You have several areas of wall in this place and not a thing on any of them. Not a painting, not a print, not a photograph. Not even a calendar. What does that tell people about you? Let me rephrase that. What would it tell them if they ever set foot over the threshold? You live in your own head too much, Frank. How could you bring a girl round here?'

'You may have a point,' he conceded, lamely enough to arouse the suspicion that he didn't really mean it.

Before she connected with her shoes and left she gave him a book, Art and the Currents of Life, by Hsieh Chao-cheh. So much for the chocolates! As her heels clattered down the stairs he glanced at the cover. It seemed the author wrote from the perspective of the San He school of Kan Yu. The contents had been culled from his famous book, Three Jars of Pot Pourri, in which he showed 'an unsurpassed insight into the effective disposition of household effects'. He wanted to think it was a wind-up but this was the woman who, he reminded himself, had used a compass to align the top of her bed with north, referring in the process to the effect of the Earth's magnetic field on everything from the navigation of homing pigeons to the condition of the soul. The result was a bed at thirty degrees to the wall.

It wasn't late when he finished washing the dishes and prepared for bed, but he was starting early and had nothing better to do. His radio alarm was next to the pillow, permanently tuned to a talk radio station, its digital display glowing in the dark. What was the topic tonight: the glass ceiling for female executives, the decline of pop music, fat cat salaries, the surveillance society, Third World poverty? None of the above. Tonight's burning issue was the increase in sexually transmitted diseases among the young, and the studio guests were having a disputatious time of it since one of their number was a paid-up member of the 'Just Say No' campaign. But if they gave up sex, the presenter asked, what would they turn their attention to instead? Not clubbing and popping Es, if that's what you're implying, she answered, they're into that already. He scented his opening at once. You have first hand evidence of that, do you? Heavily into the club scene, Sister Agnes? Apparently not. But there was anecdotal evidence. Many of the young persons contacting her organisation...

As Frank was considering these matters, he nodded off in the direction of a good night's sleep till he became aware of noise from the flat below. The Gnome, as was his custom, had started work in the evening. Getting up before noon might have helped, but the Gnome had an aversion to daylight and claimed his best work was done when everyone else was asleep. Into public art in three dimensions at least, he had assembled a lathe, a milling machine and turning equipment in his front room. He had welding gear too, and used it to light cigarettes when they were actually in his mouth. Those who had seen this had the impression it was The Gnome at his most offhand and cool. A studied performance, part of the image. The trick was to light the cigarette without melting his face.

It might have been Frank's imagination, but the noise from below grew steadily louder as the hours of darkness wore on. Phoning to complain wasn't possible since the Gnome had no phone. Getting up, going downstairs and knocking on his door would have wakened him up so much that he wouldn't have fallen asleep again afterwards. And the problem was compounded by the Gnome's habit of working to a background of heavy metal ranging through the decades from Captain Beefheart to Metallica.

As the night progressed, both the music and the metalwork grew louder by degrees. It was not clear that the Gnome actually liked heavy metal, but it suited his image and his end-product. The effect of the music and metal-work combined, wafting up through the floor with the cigarette smoke, called to mind the activities of dwarves in the nether regions, hammering away at shoes for winged horses and swords fit for heroes against a background of roaring furnaces, burning water and flying sparks.

The Gnome had invited him into his flat two months before: he hadn't noticed one of the letters left behind the main door was actually for Frank. Fair enough. Seeing through his glasses must have been difficult at the best of times.

'I'm The Gnome, by the way. Everyone calls me that.'

Frank followed him through the hall to his front room. From what he could see of it through the pall of smoke it resembled a workshop, except for a small table with a flower pot doubling as an ashtray, a threadbare sofa, a goldfish bowl, and some old books. Two of the window panes were covered with plywood patches where the glass had been broken. The Gnome saw him taking this in and volunteered a partial explanation.

'Difference of opinion with the opposite sex. Making a point without words. No future in replacing the glass.'

He didn't say why, but the implication was that, if he did, the new glass would go the way of the old. Frank was glad he lived on the upper floor.

The Gnome liked wearing black. Everything was black, from his sweatshirt to his ankle socks, except for the silver Thor's hammer on a leather thong round his neck. He was missing a trick in the eye-ware department though, Frank thought, the transparent frames of his glasses emphasising the thickness of the lenses without contributing the least bit of gloom. And whatever colour his hair had once been or really was, it was now dyed black, grown to some length and tied in a pigtail. The overall effect was of a sombre Scandinavian with oriental tendencies.

'Ah, here it is,' he said, handing Frank a monthly statement from his bank. 'Opened it before I realised. Sorry.' He glanced at the bottom line. 'You could be better off.'

Frank spotted some drawings on the table pushed against the wall to make room for the machines. They didn't look too bad. The one on top showed two figures in a hall playing dice with groups of spectators looking on, one behind each player. The spectators were armed to the teeth.

'What's this,' Frank asked, 'a contest of some kind?'

'That,' the Gnome said, as if it must be self-evident, 'is King Olaf Haraldsson of Norway playing King Olaf Ericsson of Sweden for the farm at Hising.'

'Of course, it would be, yes.' Frank smiled. 'A game of two Olafs.'

'You think it's funny,' the Gnome said, pounding his fist on the table so hard the ashtray jumped up and clattered back down.

'Not funny, no. Archaic, maybe.' Frank stepped back a bit, out of harm's way.

'Archaic!' It appeared the Gnome was on the point of bursting a blood vessel. 'It's a perfectly sensible proceeding. Take Kashmir.'

'What about it?' Frank was listening.

'It's a dispute about which side controls a piece of land. Okay, so Kashmir's bigger than a farm, but the same principle.'

'Right,' Frank said, in a 'with you so far' tone.

'So it's obvious, isn't it. General Musharraf sits down with Prime Minister Singh and they settle it by throwing dice.'

'That's hardly likely to happen though, is it.'

'Exactly my point, friend. They'd rather have a million men glaring at each across the line of control, nukes at the ready. Dice would be quicker, safer and cheaper and, let's not forget this, result in a decision. My God, that's only what we've been waiting for these last sixty years!' The Gnome looked down at his sketch and shook his head. 'This game took place in 1020 so we haven't learned much in the last thousand years, have we?' He sighed at the futility of it all.

'I suppose not.'

'Might as well tell you. Why not. I'm illustrating scenes from the Heimskringla. You're looking at the first.'

'Right.'

'A major undertaking. We're talking eighteen Norwegian kings here. In due course I'll work up some of these sketches into 3D metal panels.'

'If you live that long,' said Frank, looking at the broken windows.

'It's all proportionate. She'll only take it so far.'

Well that was good to know. Frank took a closer look at the technology.

'You're into industrial archaeology, I see,' he said, casting an eye over an old milling machine.

His host was offended. 'What do you mean by that?'

'No CNC.'

The Gnome's mood changed from outrage to superiority in an instant.

'Let me tell you, my friend, nothing creative has ever been done by computer. If it's art you want, do it yourself. Art is an expression of the personality. The artist chooses the settings and exercises total physical control of the machine. He doesn't turn it over to a computer. Enter numeric control, exit art.'

Frank looked round the room and it occurred to him, for the first time, that one of the Gnome's machines was so large it couldn't possibly have come in through the door.

'How did you get that thing in here?'

'Let's just say a fair amount of dismantling was involved.'

'It's okay to use it in a domestic environment, is it? You don't need a licence or something?'

'What, like a street trader? Don't think so somehow.'

Whatever else he was, the Gnome would not be confused with a street trader.

'I was thinking more of an application to the Planning Department.'

But whether through fatigue, alcohol, drugs or tobacco, the Gnome's attention was beginning to wander. He was yawning and bleary-eyed. Perhaps any reference to officialdom had that effect on him. If so, Frank thought, he wouldn't be the first. He excused himself and left.

His visit had helped at the time but it wasn't helping now. When the noise from below reached a level where he couldn't block it out with mental filters alone, he reached for his headphones. Ear-enclosing, sealed, they reduced ambient noise by thirty decibels. Or so it said on the box. Well they weren't doing it for him, not tonight. He couldn't take much more, something would have to give. If the past was anything to go by, it would probably be him.

3

Preston Blair drove to work in a customised Ibiza 1.4 Sport which had cost a lot second hand but had a certain appearance and was thought, by the man himself, to add to his attraction. He knew this was a costly way to do it compared to an artfully placed tattoo which might attract the female eye without the heavy overheads of capital depreciation, insurance, road tax, maintenance and fuel. But adornment of the body conferred less status: everyone was into it. Everyone did not go to work in a classy glacier-blue number like his.

Other colleagues arriving in the car park took the lift from the basement to the appropriate floor, but here again Preston went his own way. He left the building entirely, sauntered round to the front and entered through the imposing hardwood doors thick with the varnish of the ages. He could have walked swiftly through cosmetics, past jewellery, and straight up to his office, but chose to take his time and it was Pamela, following his movements from the control room, who realised that Preston, far from making a grand entrance, was passing through a portal to possible joy in one of the many games he confused with life.

Preston was fascinated by the cosmetics department, in its array of counters with sophisticated French-sounding products of which customers expected so much: Clinique, Givenchy, Lancôme, Garnier, l'Oreal. He would have given it to them straight. *No madam, we cannot delay the onset of age nor repair the ravages of time. Sorry, but there you are.* And then there was the aroma, not a simple scent but a heady confection of many. The air was thick with chemicals and he wasn't sure he approved. Plainly they did your lungs no good but they were, after all, a powerful medium of sexual communication. He'd read an article on pheromones in Men's Health. He knew the score.

All of this set the scene for Preston's real interest, the beautifully turned-out ladies with brand-name sashes who knew everything there was to know about fragrances, foundations, moisturisers, night creams and anti-wrinkle preparations. One of them in particular had caught his eye, a dusky beauty with a film-star physique and luminous dark brown eyes. He would quarter the department, stealing views of her from one angle or another, moving when she moved to keep her in sight. Sometimes he ogled her through several panes of glass and sometimes admired not the woman herself but her reflection: which struck Preston as uncommonly subtle, the store detective as suspicious, and Pamela as pathetic.

He was still considering the best course of action when the first ads for Mother's Day appeared. His time had come. He made his way to cosmetics and checked himself over in one of the mirrors. He had no grounds for concern: a fine head of black hair, neatly styled, and not a trace of recession even at the temples. Good skin quality and not too pallid a complexion. Reasonably attractive brown eyes, though nothing to compare with the object of his interest. As he was checking his shoulders for stray hairs he realised she was finally available, so he approached her in what he hoped was a casual manner.

'Hello, Anita,' he said, quickly scanning the name on her badge.

'Hello Preston,' she replied, doing the same thing. 'How can I help you?'

He had a problem with Mother's Day. He'd bought her flowers last year so that was out, leaving perfume or jewellery. Anita was an accomplished sales person and treated Preston no differently from her other customers, which entailed undivided attention and full eye contact. He felt she was hanging on his every word but did not consider how easy that was. And as for those eyes, he was surely about to melt, leaving a pool on the floor for the contract cleaner.

'There's always a meal out, especially if your mother cooks a lot.'

'That's true. And I could give her a gift during the meal.'

'What fragrance does your mother prefer?' Anita asked. 'We carry an exceptionally wide range.'

Preston hadn't the faintest idea and glanced around with controlled anxiety at the products nearby. An atomiser caught his eye. He'd seen his mother use one to spray a fine mist of water over potted plants. So that wasn't much use, she had one already. Anita smiled. She'd seen it many times before.

'Maybe you can't remember. That's not a problem. Really. You're here every day: make discreet inquiries and let me know. I'm sure we can work something out.'

His alarm subsided, his spirits lifted. This was easy. Human chess. If you had a setback you turned it to your advantage. His ignorance had set him up with a second chance to talk to this girl so where would knowledge get him?

'Anita,' he said. 'That's quite a common name here as well.'

'I *am* here,' she replied, 'you're talking to me.'

'By "here" I mean in this country, in this culture.'

Even as he said it he knew he was getting in deeper. She would tell him she *was* in this country, which was clearly the case. This time he would pay for his mistake. She would add an extra charge. But she didn't. In her department surfaces were always impeccable, regardless of what was going on beneath them.

'Anita is also a name in Hindi,' she said. 'Maybe you didn't know that.'

But her beautiful brown eyes were surely a shade less warm.

Preston made his way to the lift with mixed emotions. Yes, he had a cast-iron reason to talk to her again but he hadn't done well with her name. He'd only mentioned it by way of breaking the ice, but that was not the effect he had achieved. The temperature had dropped. When he reached his office he found SAMITA'S GUIDE TO INDIAN NAMES. The web never ceased to amaze him. As he did so, Kathy arrived at Anita's counter and Anita affected not to know her, as she'd been trained to do.

'Yes, madam,' she asked, 'can I be of assistance?'

'I wonder if you could help me. I'm looking for a quality night cream. Something which actually does what it says on the label.'

'Well that's a tall order, but in my experience the secret lies in the active ingredients.'

'Yes, I suppose it would,' said Kathy. 'And while we're on the subject of secrets it would help me to know what Mr Blair was up to. I can promise you it won't go any further.'

Anita looked surprised but played along. 'A lot of our clientèle go for a twelve hour multi-active night cream,' she said, then added, looking round. 'Not a lot. Mother's Day, and the fact I'm an alien.'

'Some alien. You could be a Bollywood star!'

'No Kathy. An alien as in foreigner. You know, a stranger to these shores.'

Kathy wondered who had come up with the crazy idea that the same word could have two different meanings. Meanwhile Anita had produced an expensive-looking tube.

'This is a good product without breaking the bank.' She handed it to Kathy.

'Antioxidant vitamins A, C, E plus pro-vitamin B5.'

There was so much more on the tube she was reminded of her brief battle, fought and lost, with the periodic table of the elements. She wondered what pro-vitamins were, but decided not to ask in case she found out. There was only so much a store detective needed to know.

Several floors above Preston was studying SAMITA'S GUIDE when a grey-haired man in overalls knocked on the door and walked in. Preston ignored him but he didn't go away
'And you are?' he asked, without looking up.
'Alastair Geddes, maintenance. You wanted some work done.'
'I did?' Preston slapped his forehead with the palm of his hand. 'Of course, yes. Trunking.'
Preston already found the interruption tedious. He felt as if it were keeping him from his beloved – even though he didn't have one and it wasn't. Alastair produced a piece of paper.
'The thing is, Mr Blair, you failed to submit it on the appropriate form.'
What was this guy, a maintenance man or a superannuated bureaucrat? But Preston was only listening with half an ear: he'd just tracked down Anita.
'Couldn't lay my hands on one at the time.'
'I appreciate that, Mr Blair. You'd just have to fill in this requisition as per standard procedures.'
Preston looked blank. He knew nothing about requisitions and even less about standard procedures. He had no recollection of the subject being covered at his induction and no, he had not been given a copy of the staff handbook.
'Dear me,' said Alastair, 'there's something amiss there.'
But the only miss who interested Preston was Anita whose name, in Hindi, meant 'full of grace'. Amazing. How did her parents know what an accurate description it would turn out to be? Full of grace really hit the mark. He felt like a gambler whose number had come up.

Alastair produced a pad and began to takes notes for his own reference: two computers, two monitors, two speakers, a web cam, a printer, a flat-bed scanner, and a digital camera. Producing a metal rule he jotted down some measurements. He also noted a large black Pro Tour (Limited Edition) sports bag on the floor beside the bin.

'I see you have shelves here,' he said, eyeing several software manuals and a large ring binder with STAFF HANDBOOK on the spine. And then a small device caught his eye. He thought he had a handle on small devices but this one was new to him.

'If you don't mind me asking, Mr Blair, what's this little fellow here?'

'Ah,' said Preston proudly, 'that's my GPS handset.'

Alastair picked it up and examined it but he was still none the wiser.

'Global positioning system. Using satellite technology, this little gismo will tell me exactly where I am anywhere on the planet to within about two metres.

Alastair had heard of the global positioning system. As an ex-navy man, he could see how useful it might be. Also as an ex-navy man, he couldn't see what use it could be to Preston.

'You're a sailor', he said, with the faintest suggestion of disbelief.

'No way. You wouldn't catch me on a boat.'

'A mountaineer then?'

'You've got to be joking. Neither of the above. No,' Preston remarked with apparent conviction, 'I just like to know where I am.'

When Alastair left, Preston's thoughts lingered with Anita for a while, but even her image couldn't blank out for long the tasks which lay ahead. He looked at a pile of documents, recently collected, all you'd ever need to know about beds, futons, mattresses, valances and duvets. Since all these items were available at Mowatts they clearly should appear on their website. He reached for the nearest leaflet, sighed, and put it on the scanner – the Derby Divan. Oh joy!

And so he occupied himself from day to day with small-scale manageable tasks which had to be pieces of the jigsaw, of that he was sure. But in everyday life as lived, for example, at stately pace in retirement homes for the elderly, a jigsaw came in a box with a picture on the front. You didn't need to get the picture, you were given it on a tray with your morning coffee. And as an added bonus, all the pieces you needed were in the box. Chance would be a fine thing, Preston thought, suddenly feeling envious of the old.

When he'd worked for an hour and couldn't take any more he backed up his files, shut down his computer, and pulled a sweatshirt and shorts from his bag. He usually took the lift to the Activity Room. By rights he should have used the stairs for added exercise, but since a room was reserved for activity, he reserved activity for the room and, in so doing, constrained himself within a description.

The brain-child of Gemma Laing, the activity room boasted exercise bikes, rowing machines and resistance equipment. The latest improvements, following a short campaign by the staff association, were a water tower and full length wall-mounted mirrors. Preston approved of the mirrors. Taped to one of them, a series of print-outs drew colleagues' attention to the concept of body mass index and the selection of heart zones. For those members of staff arithmetically challenge, fitness guru Lynn had attached to the wall a large-button, multi-coloured pocket calculator straight from the children's range. Isn't maths fun!

Lynn was hot on stretching and so was Preston, but his hamstrings were unusually tight.

'Hm,' Lynn told him when she first noticed, 'a common problem with the male of the species.' And Preston felt better about it then, even more male than he had been before. He took Lynn's simple statement and inflated it into a sliding scale: the tighter a man's hamstrings, the more male he was. By that reckoning Preston was very male indeed. Preston was a god.

His favourite mode, circuit, allowed him to compete with the machine. He programmed his bike to fifteen miles an hour knowing full well he could cruise at sixteen himself. And then, as the circuit progressed, had the pleasure of seeing on the display a representation of himself gradually pull away from his opponent. There was never a head wind. It never rained. There was never a collision. His chain never came off. He never had a puncture. He always crossed the line first. He always won. And though he knew how he'd done it, his victory gave him pleasure every time.

Kathy took the lift to the seventh floor and entered the control room with two plastic cups of coffee, a packet of chocolate fingers and a desire to chat.

'You've been watching Preston,' Pamela said.

'You've no idea how much time that boy spends in cosmetics.'

'He's after the Body Beautiful.'

'I know that now but I had to be sure. Actually, it was a little tricky. Anita wanted to know why I was asking about him, so I said it was a routine check. But I knew she didn't believe me so I said, which everyone knows, that Preston has a bit of a reputation as a ladies' man. I sort of gave her the impression I was making sure she wasn't being harassed.'

'That's a bit dodgy isn't it? What if it gets back to him?'

But Kathy wasn't having that. Preston logged on to pornographic sites, everyone knew that. If not outright porn, then glamour at the very least. His hard disc was groaning with pics of scantily clad women in compromising poses. He whiled away his days making serial advances in chat rooms. He was heavily into cyber sex. And all of that in company time.

'You have evidence of any of this?' Pamela asked hopefully.

'He's a sleaze-ball. Come on, Pam, what evidence do you need?'

'Hey, look. Sadie's back.'

'Dammit, I've just started my coffee!' Kathy raced from the room to the lift. When the doors opened at the third floor, Frank was waiting to go up.

'Catch you later, big boy,' she said as they shut.

Alastair and Frank usually met mid afternoon for a break, when they brewed up, exchanged information and compared notes. Alastair thought highly of Frank but considered him untidy.

'You know me lad, everything ship-shape and Bristol fashion.' Frank suspected this was the affectation of a man who liked to consider himself a seafarer of the old school. No crumpled flags of convenience in his day, Alastair ironed them all. 'I mean, just look at your hand, lad. Have you ever considered writing on paper or hasn't it been invented yet?'

'You can mislay paper. You can't mislay hands.'

'The skin's porous. Must be.'

'What makes you think that?'

'All these face creams and lotions they sell downstairs – if the skin was waterproof they wouldn't work, they wouldn't sink in.'

Frank wasn't fooled. 'They don't work. They don't sink in. They just smear the surface.'

'Tell that to the ladies and see where you get. They swear by them.'

'The triumph of hope over experience. Doesn't prove a thing.'

If Frank said anything to the ladies it would probably have been, 'You can't improve on nature,' something he often said as an untested article of faith.

'You know that Preston Blair chap?' Alastair asked. 'He has a GPS handset in his office.'

Frank was surprised. 'Why?'

'Says he likes to know where he is.' Alastair rinsed his mug and made for the door. 'Ah well, it takes all sorts I suppose. Don't overdo it.'

Left to himself, Frank's mind went back to the handset. Preston liked to know where he was, but how could he possibly know that? The handset would give him his position on the planet. But the planet was rotating, so his actual location was changing by the second. On top of that, the Earth was orbiting the sun. In addition to which the spiral arm containing the solar system was spinning round the centre of the galaxy. And as for the galaxy, since the universe was expanding it was also on the move, blown outwards with the rest of the debris from the Big Bang. Not to mention bends in the space-time continuum. How could anyone hope to know where he was? Preston should settle for where he appeared to be.

4

Frank didn't exactly come out and grab you. Maybe he was so busy dealing with objects he had no time left for people. Maybe he had little interest in dealing with people to start with, in which case his career prospects weren't good. People were weak. People needed attention, treatment. Anyone who neglected human weakness would remain on the ground floor. But maybe that was where he preferred to be. Too many maybes, Pamela thought. She phoned him and Alastair answered.

'He's here. We're shuffling job cards.'

'Please ask him to wait, Mr Geddes. I won't be a minute.'

Alastair was leaving when she arrived so he held the door open for her.

'Duty calls. Have to love you and leave you, I'm afraid.'

'What is it this time?'

'Ah,' he said, 'that would be telling.'

She'd never been to the maintenance office before, which was just as well: there was hardly room to move for the able-bodied. Frank pushed a chair under the table then moved them both to one side, leaving just enough space for her to wheel herself in. She looked round in amazement: no windows, no ventilation, dingy in the extreme.

'This isn't an office, it's a glorified cupboard. No one should have to work in a place like this!'

No one did. They just dropped by to keep track of the paperwork, check the answering machine, brew up. They had a workshop in the basement. She noticed him checking her out. His gaze seemed to centre on her waist so it took in her chair as well. Was that what interested him? Probably. It was, after all, a mechanical device.

'I sent you an e-mail a week ago and you haven't replied. Now I see why.'

Maintenance was supposed to have a computer. They'd been offered one but there was no place to put it in their office and the network didn't extend to the basement. They were used to it, he explained. Alastair called them the Cinderella Service. Hardly surprising they were lukewarm about computing.

'Frank,' she said, with a quizzical smile, 'there's something needing fixed in my office. Have you twenty minutes?'

'Have you a job card?'

She smiled. 'Charm. Opens doors everywhere I go.'

They left the office and made their way to the lifts. Quite a few customers were there already, most of them making their way to the sixth floor: women wanting an early coffee before they got down to business, mothers heading for the crèche with children, and a few well-organised people looking for Accounts to pay in person and leave with a receipt. When the lift arrived and the door opened several people, seeing Pamela, got out to leave her room. They were smiling and helpful. Acting on an impulse which he instantly regretted Frank grabbed the wheelchair, pushed it into the lift and pressed button six. He bent down and whispered an apology into her ear. As he did so he noticed how good Pamela smelled. Clean as a whistle, like a cat. Music was playing in the lift, probably from the album Wallpaper 3, he thought, (not available in the shops). Pamela let him push her out onto the sixth floor and watched the customers disperse.

'Training as a carer?' she asked.

He'd taken her out of her own control because some thoughtful customers made space and waved them in. Stimulus, response. Simple as that.

'Hey, lighten up. Don't let it get to you,' Pamela said, seizing her push-rims and propelling herself down the corridor. 'I won't.'

Pamela shared an office with June, though they were seldom in it at the same time. She would create an account for him on her own computer, which he could use whenever she was in the control room. June wouldn't mind him being there provided he kept his hands off her biscuits. He rolled June's chair over and joined her. She had just created his account when the phone rang. Pamela reached over and picked it up.

'Mr Gibson,' she said, with excess warmth and a knowing look at Frank. 'No, June's not here at the moment, can I help?' She held the phone a little away from her ear and grimaced. 'A discrepancy? Surely not! So let me get this straight, you want her to check the restaurant rota for the week ending . . . I'll make a note of that, Mr Gibson. I'll ask her to call you back.'

Frank read Pamela's message. An ad hoc group was being set up to advise management on aspects of IT. The first meeting would convene in the boardroom, seventh floor.

'I know nothing about IT.'

'It's not just about IT.'

'It says here . . .'

'It says that to sweeten the pill. For me, the point is to nail Preston, for you it's a chance to make your mark. So what do you think?'

'Do I have to tell you now?'

'You can sleep on it if you like, but the way I see it we only have one life. Better to follow your instinct and have done. What's your instinct, Frank?'

Being on an ad hoc committee wasn't the best offer he'd ever had and he wasn't impulsive by nature, so he surprised himself when he accepted on the spot. Pamela was right. Besides, she'd been waiting a week already and what did he have to lose? Nonetheless, he wondered afterwards how he would square it with Alastair. Meetings took time and their services were in constant demand. In the event, he surprised himself again by implying he'd been drafted. Alastair would accept any new development given a sufficiently exalted point of origin.

'So let me get this straight,' Alastair asked, looking impressed, 'the word came from Upstairs?'

That was where the CEO had her office, Alice Mowatt. And Hector, on the few occasions he put in an appearance, headed straight for the seventh floor too. If he hadn't known otherwise, Alastair would have assumed the existence of executive toilets to which the family alone had the keys and a private lift all the way to the top.

Replacing June's seat, Frank took a peek in her drawer. Quite a cache, and not just biscuits. A couple of black cherry yoghurts and a banana. Apparently she'd warned Pamela off, and more than once. Strange. Pamela didn't look the guzzling type. You couldn't put your hands round her waist but she was trim in that department nonetheless. Maybe she was flattered by the cut of her slacks, but he didn't think so. And he was struck again by her neat blond hair, tied at the back by a single band and not a trace of deception at the roots. The genuine article alright.

It may have been his distracted look, but it seemed to her he wasn't entirely happy. Perhaps he felt she'd bounced him into it.

'Frank, we can talk about this, you know. It's a decision we can make.'

Frank looked surprised. 'That's what we've been doing.'

Was he serious? Apparently he was.

'I don't think so. We've talked about what you might do, okay, but not why you would do it. You wouldn't go along with this out of politeness, would you, or because it came from Gemma?'

Or because it was coming from her, strange she wasn't mentioning that.

'The thing is,' he said, sitting down again, 'I don't normally do heart-on-the-sleeve stuff.'

They were facing each other, separated by desks largely taken up with office technology. June had a tiered set of document holders groaning under bits of paper and, as he now knew, a drawer full of goodies. On Pamela's desk a Flaming Katie with numerous small red flowers looked in need of dusting and a little more water. And more daylight, Frank thought. That would do no harm.

'You've spoken to Gemma.'

Pamela nodded. Gemma sometimes confided in her, knowing it wouldn't go any farther. Like everyone else, she needed someone to run her ideas past. Fair enough. But as far as Frank was concerned, his life was an open book anyway. Open but boring. Every time he picked it up it opened at the same page. Nothing happening, nothing taken forward.

'She thinks you have more to offer. Is that so bad?'

'The way I see it, the plan is either to move me out of maintenance or move me out of Mowatts altogether.'

Pamela was amazed. Gemma was showing him the door to advancement and what was he doing? Walking through the door to disaster. He failed to realise, it seemed, that moving on involved management, and management called for certain skills.

June's phone rang and Frank ignored it. The call wasn't for him. When it stopped, Pamela's started.

'A group hunt,' she explained, 'June first, then me. If I don't pick up, it diverts to the control room.'

'What if no one answers there?'

Pamela grinned. 'Mr Gibson gets it,' she said, making it sound fatal. She lifted the phone and listened. 'I'm afraid June isn't in the office right now but I'll ask her to call you back.' She wrote a message on a post-it, leaned forward and left it on June's desk beside several others.

'You could have e-mailed her,' Frank said, thinking of the trees.

Pamela gave him a hard look. 'And you could challenge yourself, but left to your own devices you won't. And you know what the trouble with that is? Circumstances change.' She paused for maximum impact. 'When Alastair retires the job will be advertised.'

Frank was shocked. 'What's the point? I know it inside out.'

'The point,' Pamela said, adopting the tone of a weary teacher addressing a backward child, 'is explained in the recent policy document on recruitment agreed between management and the Staff Association.'

'Comes as news to me.'

'It would. It was circulated by email, not your fault you haven't seen it.'

Frank made for the door. The job wasn't his for the taking after all, he'd have to jump through management hoops, compete with golden-tongued applicants from the outside world who would think on their feet and create an impression. Unless, of course, he side-stepped the whole thing. He could sit on his hands and smile, watch the candidates sweat in their suits while he relaxed in tired overalls. And once again evasion would do the trick.

'I wouldn't have to apply. I could carry on in my present position, stick with what I'm good at.'

'You're right, you could stay in the slow lane all your life, but where would that get you?'

The answer was obvious: nowhere fast. He was reminded of a film, a comedy, where the robbers in their getaway car were overtaken by an old lady on a bicycle. An old lady not unlike Alice Mowatt.

'What's so bad about getting ahead? What are you afraid of, Frank?'

She moved to June's desk, opened her drawer and borrowed the biscuits.

'Comfort eating. The way I see it we have to adapt or die.'

'So what you would do?'

'Let's put it this way, sunshine – if I could run, I wouldn't run on the spot.'

By the time Frank left, Pamela's screensaver had taken over, with added sound. Bubbles. From the mouths of aquarium fish. Preston claimed that another version was available, where the bubbles still came from the fish but not from their mouths. She'd looked for it once but failed to track it down. How sad was that?

5

Frank walked into the boardroom not knowing what to expect and ten minutes earlier than anyone else. Then Mr Gibson arrived with a folder of work from his in-tray which he intended to expedite as the meeting progressed. Time was money and he didn't waste either. Nothing of value ever came from a committee. The effectiveness of a committee was in inverse proportion to the number of people attending. The greatest achievements were those of individuals able to see the way forward and follow it single-mindedly, without distraction. Everything he saw in life confirmed him in this, even lovers walking along the street. Particularly lovers. Intertwined as they were, arms around each other's waists, he overtook them easily and left them trailing in his wake.

'Everything prepared I take it,' he said when he saw Frank, who realised at once that as a mere mechanical he was not expected to remain.

Next to arrive, Gemma Laing in an elegant grey trouser-suit headed straight to a seat with her back to the window. More sensitive to glare than before, she didn't care for light in her eyes, even with the sun behind a cloud.

'Still okay for tonight Frank?' she asked, with the hint of a smile.

Mr Gibson was appalled, he was scandalised, and slightly redder in the face than usual, accentuated by his neat black hair parted with precision on the left. Did she have to be so blatant about her extra-curricular activities? He'd heard about women who liked a bit of rough. No doubt muscles came into it. And sweat. And staying power. It didn't bear thinking about.

Miss Mowatt and Pamela entered the room together, and Frank pulled a chair from the boardroom table as Pamela eased into the space.

'Done your homework?' she asked, smiling.

Alice sat beside Gemma.

Seeing them together Frank caught a fleeting whiff of collusion, too subtle to bottle but in the air nonetheless.

'So,' Alice said, 'who are we waiting for?'

'No one.'

Because Mr Gibson seldom set eyes on Preston he never gave him a thought.

'Mr Blair,' Gemma said, 'and we can hardly start without him.'

'Okay,' Alice said, 'Gemma has kindly agreed to minute our proceedings, so while we're waiting let's whittle down the agenda. I'm assuming telephony won't be involved.' Then she noticed that Frank was still standing. 'Unless you have a medical reason for remaining on your feet, Mr Figures?'

Five minutes into the meeting Mr Gibson was still finding ways of challenging Frank's presence. It was his understanding that the maintenance of IT equipment was subject to an external contract. Was everyone present directly concerned with IT? But this promising topic was overtaken by the continued absence of Preston Blair. Gemma phoned Kathy and asked her to track him down. Frank saw Pamela write *he's chickened out* on her pad, which she angled in his favour.

'The question of tele-working has been raised,' Alice said, hopelessly.

'Beyond our purview I would have thought,' Mr Gibson said. 'Customers come to the store on the reasonable assumption that it's staffed. Unless I'm missing something,' he added, with a rhetorical flourish of his pencil.

'I suppose it may be worth looking into at a later date,' Alice said. 'Oh, and by the way, Mr Gibson, I considered your suggestion very seriously but I don't feel we can go down that route. Not in today's society. Not the way things are. I do hope you understand.' She glanced at Gemma. 'No need to minute that of course.' So Gemma knew what Alice was talking about even if no one else did.

It may have been the bunched up way that Alice wore her hair and her attractively upturned nose that reminded Frank of Wilma Flintstone, though her hair was more grey than red. People often reminded Frank of cartoon characters who, he assured his sister, were based on real people, their mannerisms drawn from life and often very well. Anyone could see that. To which Flora replied with a flounce that in that case she must be blind and wasn't it time he grew up?

Kathy was on the first floor when the call came through. This was one of the places she favoured since it was dense with small, high-value items. A pilferer's paradise. She phoned Preston's office. No reply. She phoned June in the control room and asked her to keep her eyes peeled. She contacted the car park attendant. Yes, his car was still there. Then she saw him in cosmetics.

'She likes Amerige.'

Anita looked surprised. 'You asked her? She's bound to know why.'

'I asked her dressing table and there it was, large as life and twice as expensive.'

Anita was on the point of replying when she noticed Kathy rushing over. What was it with this Mr Blair? What was he up to?

'Found you at last,' Kathy said, taking up position beside him at the counter. 'Do you realise how many people are searching for you right now?'

Preston looked blank. 'No. What's the problem? Can't it wait?' He cast an eye over her heaving chest. 'You seem a bit out of condition for a security person.'

'The problem,' Kathy gasped, 'is that you're supposed to be at a meeting in the boardroom. It started ten minutes ago.'

Preston looked at his watch. 'My God, so it did.'

'Sorry Anita,' Kathy said, 'Mr Blair has a prior engagement.'

'That's okay,' Anita replied. 'I'm sure he knows where to find me.'

'I'm sure he does,' Kathy said with a knowing smile as Preston dashed for the lift.

Anxious to make up lost time Preston, in one fluid movement, knocked on the door as he opened it. The boardroom table was actually two large rectangular tables pushed together to form a square. Alice and Gemma were sitting on one side, Pamela and Frank on another. Mr Gibson was sitting by himself on the side nearest the door and there was no way Preston was joining him, so he pulled out a chair on the remaining side and made his apologies. His watch was running slow. No one would believe him but he didn't care.

Even as he sat he realised his notes were in his office. They were lying on his desk, he could see them in his mind's eye, but what use was that? He couldn't arrive late then rush off for his paperwork. Beads of sweat sprang up on his scalp. Unless he got himself under control they'd run down his face. In an effort to compose himself he studied the coat of arms on the wall opposite. The same coat of arms graced the outside wall of the building and very impressive it was. But what did it really amount to? The nouveau riche kidding themselves they'd arrived. He began to feel better again. He was on the attack. The sweat was starting to subside.

'So Mr Blair,' Alice said, 'what's your take on this IT business?'

Feeling more at ease, Preston told them. Talk was cheap. IT enabled communication between staff, communication between their business and other businesses such as suppliers, it offered a new and improving channel of communication between the store and its customer base, and there were certain other areas where it could plainly be of greater benefit which, in his view, had yet to be properly addressed.

'We could form a working agenda from these points,' Alice suggested to Gemma.

'Perhaps you could enlighten us on the areas yet to be addressed,' Mr Gibson said.

'Sounds like a good idea.' Pamela was doodling while she listened, not expecting to hear anything specific.

'Well, okay, how about the in-store security system? VCRs are on the way out and the monitors hardly conform to our environmental policy.'

'As far as I'm aware,' Alice said, 'we don't have an environmental policy. Gemma?'

'It's high on our to-do list,' Gemma said, 'we really should have one. So, Preston, what's wrong with the monitors?'

'They use too much power, cost too much too run.'

Gemma was already having trouble with her notes.

'What would you advise, Mr Blair?'

As always, Preston felt free to spend other people's money.

'A completely digital system replacing the lot, with LCD displays.'

'Any other thoughts on this?' Alice asked, looking round the table over her glasses. 'Frank?'

'Yes, Mr Figures,' Mr Gibson said, still on the attack, 'any blinding shafts of light?'

This was not what Frank had expected. The discussion had strayed into an area he knew about, but it was clearly a ploy on Preston's part: he was taking the heat off himself.

'This has nothing to do with the price of fish. It's totally off-topic.'

'Indulge us for a moment, Frank,' Alice said. 'You have, after all, a working knowledge of electrons.'

What an artful woman! Alastair had told him once not to be fooled by the twin-set and pearls or the greying hair. How right he was.

'VCRs can't be described as obsolete just because an alternative does the same thing. As for the monitors, Preston's right. But suppose you junk the lot, you have to ask if that's environmentally friendly either.'

Mr Gibson was puzzled. 'I don't see why.'

So was Preston. 'Neither do I.'

Frank sighed, the cares of the world on his shoulders. It took energy to make these machines. That energy was still at work. Junk them and it wasn't. Then there was the energy needed to make replacements. People were forever up-grading things these days. The waste was unbelievable.

'And if all that stopped, Mr Figures, the global economy would collapse overnight! A colossal inventory overhang would cast a giant shadow over commerce.' Mr Gibson was working himself up, as was his custom when provoked. 'Is that really what you want? Are you some sort of greener than green anti-Christ!'

'Ms Mowatt, I'm sorry, there's no way I can minute this.'

'I believe Mr Gibson meant to say *anarchist*,' Alice said helpfully.

'Exactly. Of course. That's what I said.'

'Well,' Alice said, 'this is exciting, isn't it. Anyway, looking ahead to our next meeting, since he's clearly given the matter some thought I would ask Mr Blair to prepare a brief paper outlining his proposal for improving our security system. And I would ask Mr Figures to prepare a document outlining the issues for us here at Mowatt's concerning the environment. And now if I may, taking the areas identified by Mr Blair in his opening remarks, I think we should turn our attention to IT as it affects the customer. When all's said and done, the customer is what we're about. Mr Blair, you're the expert here, I believe.'

The moment of truth had arrived. Preston looked uncomfortable but knew he had to be convincing, so he described Mowatts website as he'd found it when he came. Functional, reasonably good to look at and easy to use, which wasn't surprising given its limited applications. The historical section was excellent, as was the section on working at Mowatts, the types of job available, staff benefits and recruitment procedures. As far as the customer was concerned, however, there wasn't a great deal: the advantages of the Mowatts account card and advance information about sales and promotions.

'I understand you're developing this side of things,' Alice said.

'I'm setting up a system to allow existing and potential customers to register. We'll be able to send them promotional material at a fraction of the current cost and they'll be able to settle their accounts on-line. A two-way street, you might say.'

Mr Gibson didn't believe it. 'I checked ahead of this meeting: there was nothing like that to be seen.'

'I'm leaving the existing set-up unchanged till the new one's ready. You'll find it at www.newmowatt.com. But please remember it's still under construction.'

'A hard hat area,' Alice suggested. 'We enter at our peril?'

'Not at all, visitors welcome. Just be aware that one or two glitches remain to be ironed out.'

'How do we ensure we don't keep mailing people after they register?'

'Good question, Mr Gibson,' Preston admitted. He hadn't thought of that, not his job as he defined it.

'So what's the good answer?'

Alice asked Preston to outline his plans for selling, which he did. And the more he explained the more he was questioned. Gemma needed to know that client confidentiality would be assured. Alice was concerned about stock control. Suppose a customer ordered, say, a juicer – a big seller just now – only to find the model she wanted wasn't in stock? And Mr Gibson was concerned about credit card details provided in good faith by customers. Would they be secure from hackers? Or a dishonest member of staff, come to that?

Alice affected shock. 'Mr Gibson!'

'I'm sorry, Miss Mowatt, but it's not beyond the bounds of possibility.'

Gemma looked up from her notes. 'We cover this angle, Mr Gibson. It's an integral part of our interview procedure. It features on the application form too.'

'You ask applicants if they're honest?'

'Not in so many words but yes, we do.'

'Don't tell me, let me guess. They all say yes.'

'Most of them, though a few admit to minor indiscretions.'

'What a relief. I can't tell you how reassured I am.'

'You should be, Mr Gibson. It's not just what they say, it's how they say it. You know, what we reveal when we conceal.'

'I believe Gemma is referring to body language,' Alice said. She was about to move on to psychometric testing when the sound of a trolley was heard in the corridor and a lady from the restaurant came in with tea, coffee, a selection of biscuits, and jam doughnuts sprinkled with sugar to choke the unwary.

'If you could excuse me for a moment or two,' Gemma said, and everyone assumed she was heading for the ladies. Except Pamela.

'Did you notice that?' she whispered to Frank. 'She left with her notes.'

After pouring himself a coffee and balancing some biscuits on his saucer, Preston joined Pamela and Frank.

'What do you make of the coat arms, phoney or what?'

'It's harmless enough,' Frank said.

'No, it's what it represents. The hired help do the work, the owners rake it in. And don't tell me times have changed, they're still at it today.'

'It's a point of view,' Pamela said, it being her policy never to give Preston anything more useful than the time of day, and sometimes not even that. But Preston didn't notice, engrossed as he was in sounding negative notes.

'That was some fancy footwork, suckering us into writing those papers. Management are paid to come up with the ideas, so what do they do? Ask us to write them down and hand them over. Brilliant in its simplicity! Breathtaking in its effrontery!'

'I like Alice,' Pamela said.

'You can afford to. No paper being screwed out of you.'

'I don't have your expertise,' Pamela said, knowing he'd swallow it whole.

'There is that, I suppose.' He turned to Frank. 'I don't believe this praise of old technology, by the way. We've moved on since the 90s, or were you looking the other way?'

'He was. Peering regretfully through a fog of nostalgia,' Pamela said. 'Right Frank?'

'Right, Pamela. And if you play your cards right I'll get you a biscuit.'

'The bourbon creams are pretty good,' Preston said.

Pamela smiled. 'Royalty has its good points then.'

When the meeting reconvened, Alice thanked Preston for his remarks and asked for comments. She didn't seem surprised when Gemma spoke.

'I've just visited the site Preston has been telling us about. I searched for items of stock in the departments he's dealt with so far and I wasn't disappointed. Full descriptions accompanied by illustrations.'

Preston tried to hold back a smile and failed. Gemma glanced at her handwritten notes.

'I tried a juicer – thanks for that one, Alice. Several models came up. I checked sofa-beds and found five, some in a choice of colour scheme. I tried fridge freezers and chest freezers, and there they all were. My problems only began when I tried to register.' She rose and distributed a sheet of paper. 'I didn't have long, but the first time I tried I failed. However, when I submitted the same information a second time, I got the message on this sheet.'

'How annoying,' Alice said.

'Yes', Gemma agreed, 'when you go through the whole rigmarole twice and your application fails due to error number 637187 your patience wears thin.'

Alice read from the sheet. 'Error number 637187. CONTACT YOUR ADMINISTRATOR. How do you know who your administrator is? How do you contact him?'

'Aren't we the lucky ones,' Mr Gibson said. 'We're privileged to have him among us. The man himself. In person.' And as he spoke the sun appeared, flooding the room and everyone in it. But Preston didn't feel fairly treated. The light fell on everyone but the heat was only on him.

'As I said earlier, there are still one or two glitches but I'm working on them.'

'I'm sure you are, Mr Blair. For the record,' she added, indicating Gemma, 'when can we expect to have them fixed?'

6

Mr Gibson entered the food hall in search of Alastair and found him talking with Pat Greig at frozen foods – Breaded Haddock: Special Offer While Stocks Last. This was not a reference to dwindling stocks of haddock in the North Atlantic and such a thought would never have entered his mind. Mr Gibson believed in maximising profit within the law. He had once suggested to Pat, as an experiment, that she select certain items – chocolate bars, for example – and promote them on the basis Two for the Price of Three. He was sure there would be takers. Pat unconsciously corrected his suggestion, pointing out that they did this already. But the superior smile on Mr Gibson's face caused her to replay the tape. Surely this man needed treatment!

'I don't think that would be right, Mr Gibson.'

'So long as the offer is fairly described. A fool and his money, as they say.'

'I'm sorry, but I really don't think we should be taking advantage of people.'

'Take a good look round this Temple of Mammon, Mrs Greig. Retail distribution depends on people buying goods they don't need at prices they can't afford. On credit, as often as not. Strip away all that and the enterprise fails.'

'People need food, Mr Gibson. People need to eat. You probably eat yourself.'

On this occasion, though, food was far from his mind. He was a man on a mission and was determined to keep pleasantries to a minimum.

'So how are we today, Mrs Greig? Any special offers I should know about?'

'You could do worse than our back bacon: half price for a twin pack.'

'Unsmoked?'

'Both. And rindless, of course.'

'I would expect nothing less from your counters, Mrs Greig. Not a loss-leader, I trust.' Mr Gibson disapproved of losses however they were incurred.

'Not this time, Mr Gibson, our suppliers had a problem with excess stock. We were happy to help them out.'

Mr Gibson beamed. 'Excellent.'

Alastair waited patiently, complete with clip-board, clearly a prop to give the impression of work underway.

'Actually,' he turned and looked at him while talking to Pat, 'I was hoping to borrow Mr Geddes here for a moment or two.'

'Be my guest,' Pat said, with a feeling of a relief and a cheeky parting smirk at Alastair.

'The thing is, Mr Geddes, there's been a suggestion that our security system be upgraded so I thought I'd seek your advice. I tried consumer electronics but all I could get out of that McCandless fellow was digital is better.'

Mr Gibson had taken a dislike to Colin McCandless on several counts. His self-confidence irritated him, since it wasn't justified by the facts. He always had a slightly crumpled air caused, he suspected, by an over-reliance on drip-dry shirts which he never ironed and machine-washable slacks which he never pressed. But it was only after some months that he was able to add the final charge to the sheet: McCandless, too lazy to think these things out for himself, bought shirt and tie combinations from menswear. For those with eyes to see it was obvious. He castigated himself for failing to notice sooner.

Mr Gibson shivered. They were standing between two rows of freezers. So he guided Alastair to the fruit and vegetables, trying as he did so to sneak a look at the papers on his clipboard.

'Your side-kick, Frank, questions the wisdom of buying new when the existing equipment still works.'

'Frank's not one to fall for marketing hype.'

Mr Gibson knew that already and was about to say so when a customer approached him for the whereabouts of the organic bread.

'I'm afraid I don't work here, madam,' he replied, meaning the food hall.

The woman looked at the Mowatts ID card with mug-shot on a plastic chain round his neck.

'What do you call that then, a pensioner's bus pass?'

Alastair pointed her in the right direction and Mr Gibson, now slightly redder in the face, made one last request for clarification and Alastair decided, on balance, that digital had it over analogue by a short nose, but Frank was the man to come up with more accurate odds. He was, after all, an electrician.

Following Alastair's directions, Mr Gibson threaded his way out the food hall and headed for the basement. Pausing at the foot of the stairs he looked round the underground car park, an unprepossessing and draughty environment of bare breeze blocks, concrete, painted lines and signs. If he remembered Alastair's directions correctly, the workshop was at the far end to his right. Walking past rows of cars, he couldn't help noticing some of the stickers which he found so offensive. WINDSURFERS DO IT STANDING UP. Was this supposed to be funny? Did we really need to know that? On the rear of a clapped-out Metro, a sticker from a home-working company: I'VE UPPED MY EARNINGS – UP YOURS! Dear me, toilet humour was no way to advertise a business, not in his opinion. And then, rounding a column, he found himself gazing at Preston's car: JESUS SAVES – HE COULDN'T ON MY SALARY! He was overcome with a desire to obliterate these words by smashing the windscreen, but that was too noisy an option and there was no crow-bar to hand. Despite his principles, thoughts of bent wing mirrors and twisted aerials crossed his mind. Preston Blair had to be dealt with. The question was how.

Locating the workshop door, Mr Gibson knocked but there was no reply, so he swung it open and walked in. Frank was standing at a workbench behind which, on a large rack on the wall, various tools were located in an orderly, Alastair-like manner. A place for everything, everything in its place. There was also equipment of one sort or another on the workbench itself and on the floor. The lighting was harsh and not improved by reflecting off dull grey walls. Frank was examining an electrical device and listening to the radio. Mr Gibson paused before speaking. Surely not, there had to be some mistake. He preferred the Baroque himself, but whatever the young man was listening to seemed pleasant enough in a burbling sort of way. Then it stopped. 'The soloist in Franz Krommer's concerto in Eb for clarinet and orchestra was Emma Johnson who, as regular listeners will recall . . .'

'I'm sorry to interrupt,' Mr Gibson said, 'but I did knock.'

Frank turned in surprise. Visitors didn't beat a path to the workshop door. They didn't know where it was. He turned the radio off.

'Sorry Mr Gibson, didn't hear you.' He reached for some sheets of paper and quickly looked through them. 'No, we don't seem to have anything outstanding for you here. An emergency, I take it.'

'Not at all. Before we continue, I should perhaps explain that I've already approached Mr Geddes on this matter. Protocol has been observed.' Frank looked perplexed. What was the man talking about? 'Which is to say,' Mr Gibson explained, helping him out, 'that I have the permission of your line manager to consult you on this. We don't want to tread on anyone's toes, do we?'

Mr Gibson was having trouble deciding the best way forward. The current system had been in place for some time. On the other hand, as Frank himself had pointed out, it did the job, and since it was his responsibility to ensure that any expenditure was justified he had to take that into account. But if Mr Blair was correct the new technology, once bought, would cost less to run. It seemed to him there were no clear grounds for comparison.

'I mean,' he said, with signs of exasperation, 'everyone keeps telling me digital is better but they don't say why!'

Frank realised that Mr Gibson was under some strain. Why not begin by taking the weight off his legs, he suggested? He reached for a stool and brushed some sawdust off it with his sleeve. Pulling it to the workbench, he grabbed a newspaper and spread it out over the seat. Mr Gibson's suit wasn't cheap. He was grateful and sat down, but not without comment.

'You don't read *that*, surely?' He was referring to Alastair's tabloid.

Alastair was into the pictorial coverage of events, he explained, indicating shots of the scantily-clad D-list celebrities Mr Gibson was about to sit on.

'The thing is,' Frank said, 'I don't think you can say one is better than the other. It depends what you want it for.' He explained analogue recording to Mr Gibson, from source to tape.

'Well I must say, that seems quite straight-forward.'

But he wasn't so happy with digits, unexpected given that arithmetic was his stock in trade. His eyes glazed over as Frank took him through quantisation levels and sampling frequencies. So Frank drew a sketch of voltage levels and an incoming sine wave, and Mr Gibson reached into the inside pocket of his jacket for his polished metal spectacle case which Frank, for one hopeful moment, mistook for a hip flask.

'Of course,' Frank pointed out, 'there'd be a lot more levels than that'.

'When you say a lot more, how many are you talking about?"

'Thirty-two thousand or more.'

'That's a bit excessive, wouldn't you say?' One of Mr Gibson's guiding principles was moderation in all things.

'The more levels the better.'

'I see.'

'And the more samples per second the better.'

'But what's the point?' Mr Gibson asked. 'When you already have the wave in its entirety, why make do with bits of it?'

Frank was astonished to hear Mr Gibson asking this question. How would they answer it in Consumer Electronics, he wondered? Probably with reference to digital being 'future-proof', whatever that meant. They used the term a lot. He knew. He'd heard them. *The beauty of this product, madam? It's future-proof. It's just a matter of time before analogue transmissions are switched off. Five years. Ten at most. Digital could be described as tomorrow's technology today.* Colin McCandless frequently peddled the line that a step-change was underway. There was nothing analogue which would not, in the next few years, be replaced by its digital equivalent, and this was a prospect he appeared to relish.

'Strangely enough, Mr Gibson, I would say the answer lies in your area of expertise.' Mr Gibson allowed himself a faint smile. He was rarely credited with anything, let alone expertise. 'When you've made your measurements you have a set of numbers, and there isn't much you can't do with them.

Add, subtract, multiply, divide. Makes for easier editing and efficient transmission. And,' he added, as an afterthought, 'digital's a numeric code, you know. It doesn't occur in nature. So really, when you come right down to it, God is analogue.'

Mr Gibson felt in the presence of a blinding light, a powerful illumination. Unfortunate that he had once referred to Frank, albeit by a dreadful slip of the tongue, as the Antichrist and now it turned out that this improbable individual, despite his laid-back temperament, dishevelled appearance and tree-hugging tendencies, was on the side of the angels. Perhaps his presence on the committee, unaccountable at first blush, was justified after all.

'There's a rumour going the rounds, Mr Figures, that you have been identified as possible management material.'

Frank had heard this suggestion, but only from Pamela Ross. 'I hardly think so, Mr Gibson. Not the type, I would have thought.'

'Well,' Mr Gibson said, thoughtfully, 'I would have to agree with you there, and I mean no disrespect when I say that. I don't consider myself management material either.'

'But surely,' Frank asked, 'you're part of the management team yourself?'

'That may be the perception but it's erroneous I assure you. They consult me, of course. They ask for analyses, projections and so on. But really, my role is to facilitate management and that's the way I like it. Managers these days spend half their time looking over their shoulders. Employees take days off at the drop of a hat, and when they do turn up they're late or the worse for wear. And what do management do? Invite them into the office. Sit them down with a cup of coffee, de-caffeinated of course. They're probably high on drugs but let's protect them from caffeine! Then they ask them what the problem is. They offer them support. What they don't do is sort them out. And you know the reason why?' Frank had no idea. 'They're fire-proofing themselves against the possibility of an industrial tribunal. It's a lawyer's paradise, Mr Figures, which is always a sign, in my view, that civil society is unravelling. Not for me thanks. Count me out.'

Frank was struck by the depth of feeling underlying these remarks, as if Mr Gibson had bottled up his outburst for months, perhaps even years and no one, not even Mrs Gibson, knew what was weighing so heavily upon him. What emotions he had were strangled. The conventions of life as he lived it, represented by his tightly fitting collar and discreet but expensive tie, had him firmly by throat. The strange thing was that the main target of his ire, apart from most of the workforce and the whole of the legal profession, was the innocuous Gemma Laing. Gemma was too naïve altogether. Gemma didn't see it as it was.

'If you're the sort of person I take you for', Mr Gibson added, 'I'd give this management business a body-swerve. Assist them by all means, but farther down the road, if and when it comes to it, don't join the club. The dues are too high.'

'But you must know more about the business than they do themselves,' Frank suggested, implying that Mr Gibson, despite his protestations, was up there with the best of them.

'Well that's certainly true of Hector. Every now and again he comes up with some hare-brained scheme he's borrowed from the FT but, that aside, he's living in the past. Alice is a different matter.'

'You like her.'

'Affection doesn't come into it, Mr Figures, but I do hold her in high regard, yes. She persists in the view that all she has to do is work hard and lead from the front. Where she goes, others will follow. An admirable trait,' he conceded. 'She embodies certain antiquated virtues and I admire her for that, but she fails to appreciate that people now, in the main, are in it for what they can get. An unsatisfactory state of affairs, but there we are.'

Mr Gibson waved his hand as if to say 'Enough of that'. He may have felt he was giving too much away, or again, that he had strayed off topic. The existing equipment had seen better days, which suggested to him that if it wasn't replaced by choice today, it would be replaced of necessity tomorrow.

'You're a technical type, Mr Figures. I'm sure you would agree with me when I say that all the products of man tend to entropy. Witness the device you're working on now.'

Frank nodded in agreement. 'True'. It was an extractor fan, still working but rasping like a blender crunching nuts. 'Mind you', he added, putting down his screwdriver, 'we tend to entropy ourselves. You wear reading glasses, Mr Gibson.'

Mr Gibson shrugged. 'Hardly to be wondered at. Time steals a march on us all.'

'Exactly. Everything breaks down and dies.'

Mr Gibson disagreed. He disputed this vigorously on theological grounds.

'Okay,' Frank conceded, 'with the exception of the Deity, everything breaks down and dies. How's that for size?'

'Considerably better, Mr Figures, there's hope for you yet. Concerning the costs of manufacture and disposal,' he added, 'you have facts and figures, no doubt?'

'Not in my inside pocket, no, but I have them in the office somewhere.'

'Pursuant to your eagerly awaited paper on our environmental policy'.

'That's it'. Frank smiled. 'What can I say? I'll copy them to you tomorrow.'

'By the way, I've been meaning to ask you, what do you make of Preston Blair? My enquiries suggest his qualification is in graphic design rather than IT.'

Frank admitted he didn't know what to make of him. No doubt his training included web design, and the look of the thing was important. It had to be attractive, well laid-out. As far as he could tell the jury was out. There wasn't much to go on.

'Yes,' Mr Gibson said, 'and that may be significant in itself.'

7

She was still in her slippers, her hair in disarray, when she opened the main door, but seeing how heavy the postman's bag was she held it open for him as he entered.

'Thanks,' he said, sifting through the mail for no 6. 'Nothing for you today, Miss Hamilton.'

As Jenny went back upstairs again she heard the delayed click of the main door shutting and the postman knocking on the Gnome's door. Being relatively early in the morning, the Gnome was in. In his flat and in his bed. He'd heard voices, but whose? He knew it could be the postman, but what if it wasn't? The last thing he wanted was to open the door and get his jaw rattled, his lip split or his nose flattened. Apart from the pain, his appearance was not so wonderful that he could live with further blemishes and be at peace with his mirror.

'Postman, Mr Dvergurinn.'

The Gnome, who always slept in yesterday's T-shirt, got out of bed and put his jeans on. 'Just slip it under the door,' he shouted, looking for his shoes.

'Can't do that, I'm afraid. Need a signature for this one.'

When the Gnome finally opened the door the postman saw at once that he had shoes on but no socks, which confirmed his impression of a young man in the last stages of dilapidation. That and the crude reinforcement of the door, which covered a perfectly useful letterbox. He held out his pad for signature.

'Sorry about this but the item's tracked.'

The Gnome signed and took the letter inside. He felt well disposed towards the postman for being the real thing, but the letter seemed light. He opened it with a screwdriver. It contained a single sheet of paper, folded twice, with nothing on it. Not a word. Who in their right mind would waste a stamp on that? He took it to the kitchen, put it on the table and switched on the light, but no matter which angle he inspected it from there wasn't a trace of a dubious substance. He knew what to look for. Anthrax or ricin. Was ricin white? Probably. He brought his head to within an inch of the paper and was about to sniff when it occurred to him. Not everything was visible. Not everything had an odour. Viruses, for example. Bacteria He wouldn't want a dose of meningococcus up the left nostril. He straightened up sharply. This was no way to start the day. Stress, anxiety, and he hadn't had a cigarette yet!

As the postman left the close a girl came in with a pushchair, no one he knew. She waited till the main door closed and knocked on the Gnome's front door. She knocked quietly, in a civilised manner. The last thing she wanted was to attract attention. Though the other downstairs flat had lain empty for months, she knew the upstairs flats were occupied.

The Gnome, who had just lit up and was savouring his first drag of the day, made his way from the kitchen to the hall. The postman had obviously forgotten something. Or maybe it was that Jenny Hamilton, he thought he'd heard her voice. He was reaching for the key when caution overtook him.

'Who is it?' He waited a moment, expecting a reply, but whoever it was said nothing and knocked again.

'Who's there? Identify yourself.'

A normal, law-abiding person would surely have answered by now. Unlikely as it was so early in the morning, he assumed the worst and shot the security bolts he had recently installed at the top and bottom of the door. No point having safeguards if you didn't use them. And Barbara, hearing the bolts, knew her plan had failed.

'It's me. Open up. We have to talk.'
'So talk. I can hear you.'
'Open the door you rat, you stinking bag of shite!'
'Get lost. Go away.'
'You'd like that, wouldn't you? Open the door, you bastard, or you'll fry!'

By now the Gnome was accustomed not only to threats but attempts to carry them out. The only way into his flat was through the front door, secured by a five-lever mortice lock and security bolts, all of case-hardened steel. Following her previous attempt on it with a four pound felling axe – where had she laid her hands on that? – he'd also screwed to the outside face a large panel of thick marine ply which had the added advantage of preventing an unhinged individual like Barbara screaming at him through the letter box or pushing anything unpleasant through it. And in case she turned up with tools, which wasn't out of the question as her violence sometimes took a practical turn, he'd counter-sunk the screws deeply enough to give her grief. He knew he was safe. All he had to do was sit tight.

Barbara reached down to the tray under her daughter's push-chair, picked up a container of paraffin, opened it, and splashed its contents high over the hard-board panel, watching as it turned the wood dark and streamed down to the floor. Going to the main door, she pulled it open and wedged it with the push-chair. The child was still sleeping, the pom-pom from her pink woollen hat over her left shoulder. There was no way her daughter would be in danger. She returned to the Gnome's door, took out a book of matches and lit one. Standing well back, she threw the match at the door, but the rush of air extinguished the flame before it arrived. She tried again and the same thing happened. She lit three in a bunch, but that didn't work either. There was nothing for it but to risk a singe or two.

She approached the door and held a match to it. The explosion of fire was immediate, and upwards rather than out. She walked quickly to the push-chair and rolled it into the street. Apart from the roar of traffic from the main road nearby, everything was peaceful. People going about their business as she was going about hers. And as she crossed to the other side the Gnome went into his kitchen, where he found a mug half filled with cold, dark brown liquid. Coffee he hadn't drunk yesterday. He opened the microwave and put it in. Waste not, want not. He wasn't made of money. And because of the noise from the oven and the smell of his cigarette, he didn't notice his front door was burning.

Jenny couldn't explain why she thought something was wrong. Perhaps it was the crackling noise when the fire began to take, perhaps she smelt paraffin through the pall of cigarette smoke in the stair well. But the second she went out onto the landing she knew there was a problem and rushed downstairs. The Gnome heard her shouting, assumed it was Barbara upping the ante and ignored her. The coffee tasted better than expected. But when he finally picked up on the word 'fire', he ran through to the hall and saw smoke coming under the door.

'For Christ's sake, I've got years of work in here!'

'I'll phone the Fire Brigade!' Jenny shouted. He could just make her out.

She ran back upstairs to make the call and the Gnome considered his position. The fire had been started on the outside of the door and that was where it should be tackled, but opening the door wouldn't be a good move. It would provide more oxygen for combustion, and it was obvious Barbara was trying to flush him out. That was the point of the exercise. She'd be standing on the other side with a frying pan or pick-axe handle ready to do him in. He ran to the kitchen, filled a jug with water and rushed back to the door. The wetter it was the better. Too bad he hadn't a bucket.

He turned on his heel, searching for a larger container, and spotted the goldfish bowl. God almighty – Oskar! He grabbed it, raced into the kitchen splashing as he went, and opened the window. Because of the basement below there was a ten foot drop to the garden. He pulled his duvet cover from the laundry bin where it had lain for weeks, put the bowl inside, leaned out the window and lowered it carefully to the ground. But that was the best he could do. He couldn't re-use the cover without taking the bowl out, and he couldn't do that without being with it on the ground.

The flames were louder now. He ran back into his front room, wrapped his sketches together with masking tape, sprinted through to the kitchen, put his cigarettes in his pocket, and despite a twinge of anxiety about his work in progress sat on the edge of the window and jumped out. The impact was hard but his work was safe and so was he. No one had a key.

Jenny waited in her flat till the fire brigade arrived. As one of the firemen pointed out to her later, not the smartest thing to do when the fire was on the ground floor and she was on the first. But she could assure them that the flat opposite had only one occupant and Mr Figures always left early for work and hadn't been in when the fire started.

The firemen made short work of dousing the flames engulfing the Gnome's door and wooden facings and quickly smashed their way through the smouldering remains into the flat. A search revealed there was no one at home, which gave Jenny something more to worry about.

'There has to be,' she said, 'he was there. I heard him. He doesn't get up till noon!'

'A member of the leisured classes, this Mr Dvergurinn?' Was this merely a wry aside from the fireman or did he consider leisured persons not worth saving? 'A student perhaps.'

'Everyone calls him the Gnome. He's insistent on that.'

A second search revealed nothing either. Mr Dvergurinn wasn't in the house. But when one of the firemen looked out the kitchen window into the yard he saw a small figure with a goldfish in a bowl sitting with his back to a stunted elder tree. He was sporting a creased Metallica tee-shirt, a pair of black jeans, scuffed shoes and a black woollen hat. Seen from above he looked even shorter than normal, even more wizened.

'You'll be the garden gnome then.'

'Very funny.'

'If you could spare us a few moments . . .'

'Door's locked. No way back in.'

The Gnome did his best to look apologetic.

The officer came back with a ladder and lowered it through the kitchen window to the ground. To his surprise, the Gnome risked life and limb by clambering slowly upwards rung by rung clutching his sketches. It might rain. He couldn't risk several months' work. He went back for the goldfish, which the fireman took from him and placed on the kitchen table. And then a policeman arrived.

'I understand the fire was started deliberately.'

'No question about it. Clear signs of accelerant. You can probably smell it.'

'Oh, and I thought the unpleasant odour was our friend here,' the policeman said, indicating the Gnome, who was sitting on one of his two kitchen chairs.

'You've met him before, I take it,' the fireman said.

'I've had that dubious pleasure.'

'Wait a minute,' the Gnome shouted, looking round his devastated flat, 'I'm the injured party here.' He turned to the fireman. 'Did you have to use so much water? The place is swimming.'

A second fireman came in looking serious and shaking his head.

'I'm afraid we'll have to ask you to pack a few things and leave for the time being, Mr Dvergurinn. Until we know it's safe.'

'What about my gear. What about my work. Anyone could walk in here and take the lot.'

Since his front door had been largely demolished by fire and axes, he was quite right. Anyone could walk in. But what would they take? Dirty dishes? His extensive selection of distressed casual clothes? Oskar? The policeman looked round the flat and his eye fell on the Bridgeport machine in the middle of the living room floor. Charles Atlas couldn't move that, it weighed a ton, and as for the work, well, he wasn't into art. As far as he was concerned the Gnome couldn't pay him to take it. As he filled in a form he tried to reassure him.

'We'll keep an eye on the place, don't worry.'

The firemen who'd found him watched Mr Dvergurinn throw some clothes and toiletries into a hold-all and then, after some frantic casting around, ease the goldfish bowl carefully into a carrier bag and make his way outside. But the Gnome wasn't happy. He wanted to know how long this inconvenience would last, when he would get back into what was, after all, his own house. It was blatantly obvious that apart from smoke and water damage, the only serious problem was the front door and he could fix that himself. There was nowhere else he could stay. Did he look the sort of person who could afford a hotel?

'Not without your wallet, sir,' the policeman said, joining them on the pavement and handing it to him. 'Better check it's all there.'

'The thing is,' the Gnome explained, checking his paper money, 'I have one or two acquaintances in this area but nobody I could impose on for the night. I'm not from these parts.'

The fireman and the policeman exchanged a look. Where was he from, the look seemed to say – Middle Earth?

'We start from where we are, Mr Dvergurinn.' The policeman held his hand out, palm upwards. 'It's beginning to rain. I'll take you to the station and we can sort it out there. As I'm sure you appreciate, we'll need to ask you a question or two anyway. But for now I have to give you this.' He handed the Gnome a piece of paper. 'An incident information form. You'll notice the incident number and today's date. That will be essential in the event of an insurance claim. I also have to ask you if you want to tick this box,' the officer said, indicating the section concerning the victim support service. 'We can safely say you've been at the receiving end of heavy aggravation here.'

'No thanks. I believe I can walk these next few steps without crutches.'

The Gnome looked round, realising for the first time that he was a small centre of attraction surrounded, or so it seemed, by two massive fire engines completely blocking the road. To judge by their angry gestures, some of the bystanders thought he was the cause of the snarl-up, that he had set fire to his own flat. He'd fallen asleep while smoking in bed, and we weren't talking tobacco here. Or maybe he'd set fire to those soiled, sun-faded curtains of his while working with a flame-thrower on a sculpture for the Central Bar.

One of them, a heron standing on one leg peering down into imaginary water, graced the bar's display window. The resident wits had it that the Gnome chose the heron as his subject to avoid the work entailed by a second leg, to which the Gnome replied that getting the balance right on one leg was a lot harder than two. And when he challenged them to try it themselves none of them could hold the position for more than a second and alcohol wasn't the only reason for that. They were, he insisted, shamefully out of condition and carrying too much fat, especially round the gut. In fact, he claimed, they were in a permanent state of unstable equilibrium such that their only recourse was following their paunches the way they were going or parking the whole shebang on bar stools.

As he slid onto the back seat of the police car a fireman spoke to the policeman.

'We have serious issues with this guy. We'll send someone over to talk to him later, if that's okay with you.'

8

The interview room was sparsely furnished and drably decorated, so apart from the absence of an ashtray the Gnome felt at home. There was a recorder for evidence purposes, but DC Thomson had no intention of using it.

'Okay if I light up?' the Gnome asked, hopefully. 'This has taken a lot out of me you know.'

'Sorry. The best I can do is caffeine. Tea or coffee, the choice is yours.'

'Coffee thanks. The stronger the better.'

'Make yourself comfortable,' she said, producing a notebook and flicking through it. The Gnome thought her very attractive. He was especially impressed by her hair, dark brown, close to black, lustrous and glossy, kept in good order by the discreet application of kirby grips. There was an opening here, a niche as they called it in marketing circles. Anglo-Saxon grips, Norse skewers, ethnic African clamps for the fashion-conscious woman. High value work which wouldn't take a lot of raw material. A nice little side-line. As usual with the Gnome's money-making schemes, it hadn't occurred to him that anyone else had got there first.

'I've been talking to my colleagues. It seems we've been called to your address several times before but never by you, always by neighbours or members of the public. Why would that be, Mr Dvergurinn? How do you account for that?'

'I've been attacked several times.'

'But never seen fit to report it. And now the violence has escalated to the point where other people's lives have been put at risk. This has got to stop.'

'I'm with you there.'

'You suggested to my uniformed colleague that your assailant got into the close by waiting for the postman. We found a letter in your flat, recorded delivery signed for today.'

'Ah, yes, typical of her. You'll notice the paper was folded twice.'

DC Thomson wondered whether this unlikely looking man was an eccentric, which she could just about tolerate, or winding her up, which she could not.

'Go on, Mr Dvergurinn. I'm on the edge of my seat as you can see.'

'It's obvious, isn't it? A sheet of paper folded twice is divided into three sections.'

Hearing this, said with a straight face, the detective concluded that the Gnome was a head-case and attempted to provoke him to whatever point he imagined he was making.

'Right, so what are you saying? You've been targeted by the Triads? Some people might think you're off your trolley!'

The Gnome sprang to his feet in anger. 'Listen, I know what I'm talking about here. She's into allusion. Big time. Why do you think she tried to burn me out?'

DC Thomson took him by the shoulder and eased him back onto his seat.

'We both know the answer to that. You wouldn't open the door.'

The Gnome slumped against the back of the chair. Being attacked in his own home was bad but not being taken seriously was worse.

'Okay,' DC Thomson sighed, 'you referred to a woman. Why don't we talk about her.'

To her surprise the Gnome complied, only refusing for reasons to do with the chivalric code of honour, to divulge her address. He told her about Barbara, her daughter, and

Barbara's claim that he, the Gnome, was Karen's father. 'I mean,' he asked, 'does that seem likely to you?'

Glancing at the threadbare and down-at-heel Mr Dvergurinn as he sat in the chair with a calloused hand wrapped round a polystyrene coffee cup, the detective found it hard to imagine anyone engaging in sexual congress with him. But her imagination was frequently trumped by reality so she knew it was possible. She could hardly contain her distaste.

'She wants you to get back together,' she suggested, in her driest tone.

The Gnome laughed, slapping his thigh with his free hand. 'Don't be ridiculous. There's no way I'd get back with her. You've seen what she's capable of. Setting fire to the door wasn't an accident, you know.'

'I don't suppose it was.'

'Everything she does refers to something. Remember what happened to Njal? That was no accident either.'

'Another case of wilful fire-raising, I take it.'

'Exactly. And the paper you found, in three sections? In honorem trinitas, no doubt about it. She's never content with one cross round her neck, it's always two or three. And she bears them all, I can tell you.'

'She suffers.'

The Gnome looked up, impressed. 'There's hope for us yet. You're starting to think the way she does. You're entering her mind. With her it's Easter all year round.'

'So if she doesn't want a reconciliation . . .'

'It's maintenance, isn't it? She knows perfectly well I'm not the father but she wants to bleed me dry.'

'You're not the father. You're sure.'

'She was seeing someone else at the time. I'm counting back nine months here from Karen's birthday. Blond hair, same colour as Karen's.'

'In which case, all you need is a DNA test. That would put an end to this one way or the other.'

'I don't believe in new technology. It's leading us up a blind alley, a dead end. Dolly the Sheep, six years old when she was born! What sort of a life is that?' The Gnome paused for breath. The weaker his case the more he talked. 'And don't think you can get round me with this butter-wouldn't-melt-in-your-mouth routine. What happens to these DNA samples? They end up on a national database. You can't spit without your co-ordinates being broadcast by your mobile phone even when it's off!'

'You refuse to take the test.'

'That's a fair summary.'

'Even though, if your suspicions are correct, it would put you in the clear.'

'It's a matter of principle. If you're not legally obliged to do something, you shouldn't do it. If you agree, you're extending the scope of the law by your own volition and it covers enough ground already. Too much!'

'But Mr Dvergurinn, really, if we only did what we were legally obliged to do we wouldn't get up in the morning, would we?'

A smile spread across the Gnome's face, a good argument ruined by a bad example. He scratched his head through his woollen hat.

'You don't get up in the morning.'

'Not if I can help it.'

Another officer knocked and entered. 'Sorry Stella, Dr Girdwood has just arrived.'

'Stella, very nice, suits you. And just when we were getting somewhere,' the Gnome complained. 'But I'm fine. Really. Never felt better. No need for a quack.'

'If you'll accompany this officer we'll make sure you're thoroughly checked over.'

'What about Oskar?'

'The doctor's expertise doesn't extend to fish.'

DC Thomson left for the other interview room, where Barbara was waiting with Karen. The child was sitting at the table drawing.

'Barbara Gunnarsdóttir, I have reason to believe you set fire to Stephen Dvergurinn's premises with the intention of causing him grievous bodily harm.'

'His name isn't Dvergurinn, it's Smith. He changed it to be in keeping.'

'Oh well, that's alright then.'

Barbara was happy to talk and she too wanted to light up but, as Stella pointed out, she'd done enough lighting up for one day. She had, she insisted, and despite Stella recommending it, no need of legal representation. Anything she had done was the result of provocation. Stella considered asking what the door had done to her, but knew very well that humour didn't translate.

'You've no idea what he's like. Totally bone-headed. Lives in the past. That's how I met him. Claimed to be doing research. I suppose he was. He's into those historical recreation things. Makes his own chain mail. Iron links. Forges them in his front room. Would you believe it? He wears that woollen hat in bed. He never takes it off. You know why, of course.' Barbara glanced at Stella's notebook, assuming the answer must be in it. But since it wasn't, she obliged.

'According to him, it delays the onset of baldness by keeping the follicles warm. Did you know that more heat is lost from the top of the head than any other part of the body? Of course not. You're normal. The thing is, as one woman to another, he never washes it. Never. Well he can't, can he. He'd have to take it off to wash it and he never takes it off. Why don't you buy another, I asked him? He wouldn't hear of it. So what happens when that one wears out? He didn't want to know. See what I mean? He just won't listen.'

Stella showed her some pieces of paper.

'Friendly little notes from you to him. We found them in his tea caddy.' Barbara shrugged and Stella said, 'God knows what they were doing there, but nothing surprises me any more. *Pay up, you bastard.* I wouldn't call that a reasoned argument, would you? Or how about this: *Take the test, you arsehole, you turd, you fritter of excrement.*'

Stella was reminded of something the Gnome had said with a strangely pained expression in his list of complaints against Barbara. 'She uses bad words.' It seemed to bother him a lot, and certainly more than the fact she attacked him in his lair with fire, as if a bad word was worse than a bad action. Perhaps he was so behind the times he didn't hold with the fair sex sullying themselves with profanities. She looked back at the notes.

'Choice language, I'll give you that. And then we have *Glass breaks, so do legs.* Your address was on that one. Very helpful for us as it turns out. I don't know what they would make of that where you come from, but I would call it threatening.'

'So would I. I wrapped it round a stone.'

'You threw it through his window. You don't deny it then?'

'Of course not. He's the one in denial, not me.'

As DC Thomson paused to add another entry in her notebook she noticed that Karen had wandered off the paper the sergeant had thoughtfully provided and was now drawing on the desk to an accompaniment of humming sounds.

'Want me to arrest her as well?' she asked, indicating the girl.

Barbara glanced at her daughter, lifted her arm by the sleeve and slid the paper back under her hand with what sounded like an encouraging remark in a foreign language.

'Like the crucifix, by the way,' Stella said.

'Which one?'

'The larger of the two. The silver one. Has a good solid look.'

Barbara's fingers strayed to the chains round her neck, and from those to her hair.

'For the record, your full name?'

'Barbara Aðalbjörg Gunnarsdóttir'.

'And you are a citizen of the Republic of Iceland.'

'Correct.'

'Your daughter' name?'

'Karen Guðrún Stefánsdóttir.'

'Right,' Stella said, 'so you're naming Karen after Stephen.'

'That is the custom.'

'Well, yes, except in this case you're attributing paternity where none is admitted. What if the father is actually this other individual Mr Dvergurinn has referred to, the one with the blond hair Karen is said to resemble?'

'I don't know what they teach in your schools,' Barbara answered, 'but in ours we are led to believe that pregnancy results from sex, not the lack of it.'

'But you do admit setting fire to the door.'

'As I said . . .'

'He's the one in denial, yes. My problem, apart from the fact you committed a criminal act, is that other people were put at serious risk.'

'I understand they are safe.'

'No thanks to you. And just for the record, Miss Jennifer Hamilton, her partner, and a Mr Frank Figures are now temporarily homeless, three people having nothing to do with your dispute.'

She leafed back through her notes, 'Mr Dvergurinn appears to believe this is not the first time you've resorted to these tactics. Another name has been mentioned.'

'This is news to me.'

'So tell me about Neil.'

'Neil?'

Stella looked back to her notes and corrected herself. 'Sorry, Njal.'

For the first time Barbara looked surprised, then she smiled.

'You can't blame me for that. Don't even try. I wasn't there at the time.'

'You can prove that.'

'It shouldn't be difficult.'

She asked her about the accelerant, which turned out to have been paraffin sold at a local DIY outlet for use in greenhouse heaters, and as she noted these facts she wondered what the doctor was making of the Gnome.

Dr Girdwood, being a general practitioner, saw all sorts anyway, so he was not disconcerted by the Gnome and his protestations of health. He was given to wearing three-piece suits, even at the height of summer, and often resorted, as now, to taking his jacket off and hanging it on the back of a chair. So when the Gnome saw him for the first time, in his waistcoat with his slightly too long slicked-back hair, he was reminded more of a thirties spiv than a medical practitioner. But the Gnome had been attacked so a report was required. In any case, Dr Girdwood maintained, it was better to be safe than sorry. The effects of smoke inhalation could be insidious. However, as the examination proceeded, he became increasingly concerned.

'I have to tell you, Mr Dvergurinn,' he said, laying his stethoscope aside, 'your breathing sounds less than excellent. It may be the smoke has affected you more than you realise. If you could breathe into this for me please.'

The Gnome looked at the doctor's hand-held device and jumped to the wrong conclusion.

'You won't catch me out with that one, doc. I haven't touched a drop.'

'This isn't a breathalyser, Mr Dvergurinn, it's a spirometer. State-of-the-art. It will allow me to assess the condition of your lungs.'

'State-of-the-art, eh?' the Gnome gasped, after he had breathed into it twice. 'So that's where our taxes go.'

'If only,' the doctor sighed as he studied the display. 'I bought this little beauty myself.'

'Very public-spirited. So what does she have to say for herself?'

'She wants to know how many you smoke.'

'Not many. I roll my own.'

'Yes, well I would guess from these readings that you do rather a lot of rolling. Your total lung capacity is less than I would like, your vital capacity is far from impressive and as for your inspirational capacity, well, I have to say it's very poor indeed.'

To the Gnome, who considered himself not only creative but inspired with it, this was a serious insult.

'I've had enough of this medical mumbo jumbo. I take it we're finished here.'

'Not quite. We like to check blood pressure as a matter of course.'

'And none of this stuff ends up on police records.'

'Patient confidentiality is assured. Believe me, if it wasn't I wouldn't get very far with junkies and winos, would I?'

'For all I know, you're a junkie yourself. Easy access to the stuff. Write your own prescriptions.'

Dr Girdwood affected not to hear this, inflated the cuff and took his readings.

'You, Mr Dvergurinn, are clearly a smoker. 164 over 92. Far too high for a man of your years. And if I may say so, your resting pulse is nothing to write home about either.'

'I don't mean to be personal doc, but your bedside manner leaves a lot to be desired. Why do I suddenly have the feeling I'm at death's door?'

'Hey, it's not all doom and gloom,' the doctor enthused. 'There are things you can do, actions you can take.'

'Like what? Giving up the weed?'

'That would help. And as far as the lung capacity goes, take up a wind instrument. The trombone or euphonium. You'll be amazed at the improvement.'

The Gnome looked at Dr Girdwood with disbelief.

'What are you on? I have enough trouble with neighbours as it is. Practising the bone would be the last straw. Couldn't afford one anyway.'

'Ah yes, but Mr Dvergurinn, from what I hear you're a man of considerable talent where metalwork is concerned. Make your own. As wind instruments go, the trombone's easy. No keys. None of these tricky valves to consider. Just one tube inside another and a bell to let the sound out.'

The Gnome was on the point of dismissing the idea out of hand for the lunacy it was when the dangerous words 'why not' entered his mind. He'd always liked the look of trombones, though it had never occurred to him to play one. And if he succeeded, if he got the design right, what he had made for himself he could make for others. And being hand-made one-offs, they would be much more valuable than those mass-produced Japanese efforts. Just what he needed, a new income stream. The Dvergurinn signature bone.

He would require a brand name, of course. Something striking, arresting, original. And it came to him in a blinding flash

— *The MetroGnome* —

engraved in a flowing serif typeface on the bell.

'I don't know if they told you,' the doctor said, but there's a gentleman from the fire service waiting for a word.' He took his jacket from the chair and snapped shut his medical bag. 'I'll ask him to pop in on my way out. Don't hesitate to try the scales,' he said, indicating the old-fashioned device with metal balancing arm in the corner. 'Good scrap metal there, I would think.'

The fire officer came in as the doctor left.

'Good morning, Mr Dvergurinn, I'm John Sanderson, Fire Brigade. I deal with questions of fire safety. The doc tells me you suffered no side-effects from smoke inhalation or fire.'

'That would be the doc who told me to give up smoking.'

'He tells everyone that, Mr Dvergurinn, just as we tell everyone to fit smoke alarms.'

'Ah, right,' the Gnome now knew what was coming. 'I've been meaning to install one for some time.'

Sanderson shook his head. He'd heard it too often before.

'They do say the road to hell is paved with good intentions. But in this case a smoke detector is the least of my concerns. In checking your flat our officers found welding gear including an oxygen cylinder, an acetylene cylinder, plus a third cylinder which I take to contain flux. So they contacted me.'

'It's not on a commercial scale. Just a bit metal sculpture.'

'Mr Dvergurinn, the gases in question are unstable in fire conditions and must be considered explosive. They are, after all, stored under pressure.'

'You don't expect a fire, though, do you. It's not an everyday occurrence.'

The fire officer had taken some shots of the Gnome's flat. He wanted the Gnome to pay particular attention to the cylinders and hoses. As the Gnome could see, there was no way of securing the cylinders when cutting or welding. And another thing, he added, pushing a shot of the Gnome's rug under his nose, a number of burn and scorch marks were clearly visible. The Gnome looked and couldn't deny it, though he did point out in mitigation that the rug was second-hand and of no value. In fact, there were so many burn and scorch marks that Mr Sanderson had taken the liberty of examining the Gnome's welding tips and there was no getting away from the fact that his orifices were badly in need of cleaning. Which brought him to his next point. If the Gnome had tip cleaners on the premises they were very well hidden.

'You're foreign, aren't you?' the Gnome asked. 'Where are you from?'

'Newcastle,' Mr Sanderson replied. But he wasn't to be deflected. He couldn't stress enough the importance of scraping off the encrusted slag, and not only in the interior of the tip. The exterior was almost as important and he strongly advised polishing it with a piece of steel wool.

'For heaven's sake,' the Gnome said, 'what is this? I don't care if it looks good, I just want it to work. You'll have me black-leading the grate next!'

'You have a licence for home welding, I take it?'

The Gnome blanched, his face looking even paler than usual against his black hat and T-shirt. He could almost have passed for a Goth.

'I wasn't aware a licence was required.'

Mr Sanderson smiled grimly. 'It should be, but it isn't. It would be in the States.' He paused a moment, wondering how best to proceed. 'Mr Dvergurinn, do you mind if I ask you something – it's been puzzling me.'

'Be my guest. What have I got to lose?'

'When you first realised there was a fire, you removed your goldfish from the flat but left your welding gear behind.'

'The fish is a living thing. It was at risk.'

'What from – smoke inhalation?'

'Well, no, of course not.'

'Water evaporating from the bowl?'

'You're being ridiculous now.'

'So you removed a fish which was perfectly safe and left potentially explosive canisters of gas at the scene of the fire.'

'Look, I see where you're coming from here, but in the heat of the moment so to speak . . . call me sentimental if you will, it was a split-second decision. I mean, with the benefit of twenty-twenty hindsight I might have done it differently. But there we are. What's done is done.'

The fire officer rose to leave, handing the Gnome some leaflets.

'Welding comes under the aegis of the Health and Safety Executive: you might find some of their leaflets useful. Also, I have to say that if you're engaged in home welding and haven't so informed your insurance company, you're likely to find they are not liable for any accident which occurs.'

Normally the Gnome, being argumentative by nature, would have challenged this statement, but dealing with a succession of firemen, police officers and doctors had depleted his reserves. Nonetheless, as the door closed and he was left in peace for a few moments he couldn't help thinking of the Vikings. They insured nothing. The monks, on the other hand, renewed their policies every day in prayer and plainsong, and where did it get them? Nowhere. The Vikings still torched their cloisters and used their sacred texts to light their pipes. Insurance was a mug's game. Definitely not for him.

Mr Sanderson poked his head back round the door.

'Almost forgot. Before you resume your operations, obtain a fire extinguisher. Anyone engaged in welding, cutting and brazing should have one to hand. Even metal sculptors such as yourself.'

As he was making to leave Dr Girdwood was intercepted by Stella for what she hoped would be a short case review, but Dr Girdwood felt he had little to contribute; code, in Stella's view, for a wish to leave the building as quickly as possible.

Which left her with two problems. The more serious was Barbara and whether it was safe to release her. On balance she felt it was, regarding what Barbara had done with paraffin and matches as the result of an imperative to communicate, unreasonably blocked by a non-certifiable lunatic, but a lunatic nevertheless. And there was Karen to consider, a little girl who needed her mother. If Barbara was under lock and key, Karen would be looked after by the social work department, there being no relative available locally, placed for the time being either in a home or with foster parents.

Barbara was alarmed by these options. She had read articles in newspapers.

'Children are sexually abused in care homes.' She referred to several cases, including a long-running story from Wales.

'It has been known to happen, but not often.'

'That's not what I have read. And foster parents only do it for money. They don't care about the children. They leave them in front of television sets and give them sugary drinks and junk food from the microwave.'

'You read that as well, I take it.'

'There have been studies. And documentaries. Flies on the wall. You can never be sure what will happen when a child is taken into care.'

Okay, so it wasn't a desirable outcome if it could be avoided, but hearing Barbara's gloomy view of care Stella realised that, finally, she had serious leverage if she hit her with it straight. Barbara was already in danger of having her daughter taken into care: one more offence and it would certainly happen. Was that what she wanted? Evidently not.

'This is not what I want,' she said.

Her icy composure, thick enough to skate on, was at last showing signs of cracking.

'It may not be what you want,' Stella replied, 'but it may be what you'll get.'

Since Barbara showed so little concern for the consequences of her actions on others the best way forward, in Stella's opinion, was ramming home the impact they might have on herself.

'You probably don't want to be deported either, but that's what will happen if you commit any further criminal act.' She had no idea if this was true, but neither did Barbara and there was no lawyer present. It sounded plausible enough to make her think twice before buying a box of matches with her morning paper. 'And if that happens Mr Dvergurinn will be off the hook. Permanently. Is that what you want?'

'This is also not what I want.'

'Good. We'll have to charge you, of course, but provided you're willing to sign a statement declaring you'll have no further recourse to violence, then I'll consider allowing you to leave.' Stella knew that such a statement, even if signed and witnessed, would have no status in law, but that wasn't the point. If Barbara felt bound by it, it would do the job. Provided precautions were taken. 'However,' she added, 'We shall be keeping an eye on Mr Dvergurinn's flat and I shall advise him to apply for an interim interdict prohibiting you from setting foot in Kirk Loan and its immediate environs. Also,' she added, 'I shall require you to hand over your passport until this matter is resolved and report to this police station at regular intervals.'

'I don't know about these things,' Barbara said, 'but I can tell you that Stephen doesn't take advice.'

'The question we're considering here, Miss Gunnarsdóttir, is whether *you* take advice.'

9

'He's here. Come straight up.'

June put the phone down and looked across her desk at Frank, who'd spent much of the morning researching the pros and cons of disposable dishes. What could the boys in blue possibly want with a lad like him?

The door opened and Kathy showed a policeman into the office.

'Mr Figures?'

'That would be me,' Frank said. 'What's it about?'

The constable looked uncomfortable and glanced at June.

'Don't mind me, I've heard it all before,' she said, her eyes on the screen, her ears on the conversation.

'There's been a fire in the flat below yours.'

'Bloody hell!'

On their way down Leith Walk they passed the usual attractions: theatres, cinemas and tall metal giraffes. But Frank registered none of it, his mind was elsewhere. Mr Gibson had approached him that morning in a state of high excitement. He believed he could help Frank with his project and was already collating figures. No doubt, being of religious disposition, Mr Gibson's favourite book of the Bible was Numbers. And didn't we all have to account for our life on earth when we passed to a better place? Of course we did. Looked at clearly, accounting principles underpinned the moral philosophy.

'Here we are then,' the officer said, drawing up as near the door as the one remaining fire engine allowed. 'Not a pretty sight, I'm afraid. We can only allow you a few minutes to collect some personal effects, Mr Figures.'

The damage to the Gnome's door was obvious, the little that was left of it lying in charred splinters, but the havoc was largely confined to the artist's flat, a blackened, water-logged, foul-smelling mess with two firemen sitting on kitchen chairs ready to damp down any new outbreak of smouldering. Excepting the firemen and their water, Frank thought, as he took in the outline of the Gnome's heavy gear in the gloom, it wasn't so far removed from its usual condition.

'So what's the problem?' he asked.

'I only know what I've been told,' the policeman said. 'There's some concern about the utility supplies.'

Both gas and electricity ran in metal conduits along the top of the close wall just below the ceiling. Where they passed above the entrance to the Gnome's flat they were heavily stained with smoke but Frank couldn't detect any sign of buckling. It was highly unlikely the insulation was affected, and as for the gas there'd been no explosion and there was no noxious odour. But there wouldn't be, would there, the supply had been cut till the integrity of the pipe was assured.

The policeman followed Frank's gaze as he surveyed the damage. 'We're waiting for the gas board and the power company to check them out. The water people have been. A structural engineer's on his way.'

Frank looked round his flat as he gathered his things, a basic place for a basic person, but given the aggravation from below the rent was money wasted. As long as the Gnome remained in residence there was no hope of a peaceful life. Even if his lunatic girlfriend never set foot in the building again, and there was no guarantee of that, there was the noise to contend with. He knew he'd have to move and this was a push in the right direction.

He found a battered case and filled it with clothes, underwear, shirts, socks, and headed to the bathroom. All he'd need was his electric razor, toothbrush, and paste. And deodorant might be a good idea. No one could say when residents would be allowed back, but owing to the deliberation of the bureaucratic process he might need a bed for two nights at least, maybe more. He was about to leave when he noticed his current assignment on the kitchen table: Living Without Oil: Chemistry for a Sustainable Future. He liked the sound of that. The less accelerant the better.

Back on the street he phoned his sister. He had nowhere else to turn.

'Frank, hi, look, I'm in the middle of something right now.'
'I have a problem.'
'I've known that for years.'
'I need a bed for the night. Tell you why.'
She was busy so he kept the explanation short.
'Well that's a bit tricky, young man. I'm entertaining tonight and it's looking good going forward. I really need my privacy on this one. Try dad, why don't you. Take a break. Use some of that accrued leave you were telling me about. Tide you over for a day or two till they let you back in. There you are. Nothing to it. Problem solved.'

Frank was stunned. Visiting his father was a round trip of over three hundred miles, a long way to go for a bed for the night. Longer still if you didn't have a car. She'd be singing a different song if she wanted her cat looked after.

June was gone and Pamela back at her desk when he returned to Mowatts. She looked up as Frank came in with his bag. In his haste to leave when the policeman came for him he'd left his file on screen.

'It seems to me,' she said, before he had even sat down, 'that you're attempting to cover too many angles here. It can't be done.'

'So what do you suggest?' he asked, sitting at June's desk and sliding his bag alongside it, 'packing it in?'

She referred to the screen. 'Okay, a water management system to regulate cistern flow is a great idea, but how much water would it save? You don't make that clear.' Frank didn't seem to be listening. 'So where were you? Alastair's been asking.'

When he told her she was furious. 'Why didn't anyone tell me? Why didn't June leave a note? My God, imagine it, sitting here sounding off while you're burned out of house and home – I can hardly believe it! This is awful. Where are you going to stay?'

She wheeled herself round to where he was sitting and put her hand on his arm. She was concerned. What a change of state, what a woman to contain such extremes of intellect and emotion. She struck him full on in his moment of weakness: neat, attractive, seductively perjink. Despite his predisposition for the uncomplicated life, he was affected. But he couldn't say he had nowhere to go, so he told her he'd be staying at Flora's and instantly wondered why. He was ashamed to admit that his sister wouldn't help him in his hour of need? He didn't wish to appear unwanted?

'You could stay with me. You'd be very welcome, I hope you know that.'

He was astonished. His sister, who should have known better, had given him the brush-off yet Pamela who was, on the surface, every bit as brusque, had offered to take him in.

'That might not be a good idea.'

'You don't have to like me, Frank. I can live with that. Anyway, the offer stands.'

He was appalled: this was not what he had meant.

'It's not that at all. I like you. I like you a lot.'

'But?'

'We hardly know each other.'

'And that's a problem, is it?'

'Not right now, but it could be later.'

'I see.'

Frank often felt, as now, at the mercy of his mouth, as if his unconscious intervened to overcome his reticence. Not to say his inhibition. Alright, his downright repression. Could that be it? A built-in safety mechanism without which he'd be doomed to a solitary life lived in adequate but austere surroundings owned by someone else? What sort of a life was that? Not exactly fulfilling. So perhaps his habit of unpremeditated disclosure was a blessing in disguise, a valve releasing the pressure when it grew too great. In fact, Pamela had no sense that Frank had spoken on impulse but she did wonder what lay beneath their words. She could picture two children in a school playground, one saying 'I like you' and the other replying I 'like you too.' Charming no doubt, but this was not the feeling she had. They were adults.

When Alastair came in he had the impression, fleeting though it was, that he had interrupted something. Frank and Pamela appeared to be communicating wordlessly by gazing at each other, and were they holding hands? Surely not, but that's how it seemed. Whatever they were up to his arrival put a stop to it. He'd just heard. It was unbelievable. Was there anything he could do? Frank should take the rest of the day off. Apart from the cleaners there was nothing pressing.

To his relief, Frank declined his offer. He seemed strangely relaxed for a man burned from his own home.

'Well, if that's the way you really feel,' Alastair said. He sounded reluctant but Frank knew he was relived: he'd been hoping to finesse an early exit.

'I'll get the cleaning rota,' Alastair said, 'just make sure the angles are covered. Annie's still off with her back.' He left the office, but before they could say anything he popped his head back round the door. 'You'd be welcome to stay with us, you know. Mrs Geddes could have the spare room spruced up in no time. And there's beer in the fridge.'

Pamela smiled. 'I don't stand a chance, do I, with all this competition to take you in?'

Beer in the fridge, whisky in the mini-bar. A plan was beginning to form and Frank had a question. There were no cameras on the seventh floor, why was that? It concerned him since anyone could come and go unnoticed. What was to stop a member of the public venturing up from the sixth floor regardless of the STAFF ONLY BEYOND THIS POINT signs and stealing something?

Pamela laughed. What were they going to steal, a flip chart? No great loss. An exercise bike? Far too heavy. Mr Gibson had completed a cost/benefit analysis at the time and it wasn't worth extending the surveillance system to the seventh floor. His figures proved it conclusively.

'Speaking of figures,' Frank said, 'I've forgotten the code for the penthouse suite.'

Like every other room, it had to be checked.

'AD one nine two one.'

Frank took a pen from the desk and noted it on the back of an envelope. He was considering what to write beside it by way of identification when Pamela explained that the code was Hector Mowatt's year of birth, Anno Domini 1921, so that was what he wrote.

Asking her to save his file he went down to the food hall for supplies. Pamela didn't want anything so he was buying for himself: one ham sandwich, wholemeal brown, one egg mayonnaise sandwich, also wholemeal brown, and a bottle of water. If he worked out as well he'd exemplify the healthy life. But he preferred to exercise the mind more than the body, though what would come of that remained to be seen.

Earlier that day Pamela had read through his notes on the sustainable approach to the retailing of foodstuffs, recalling a bygone age when biscuits were sold without the wrapping which oppressed them now and the cheerful grocer sliced through cheese with wire and wrapping weighed portions in grease-proof paper. There had been few wasteful practices then, but where did that get him when there was no going back? And if it got him nowhere, why mention it? Here was a man who required protection from himself. He had a contribution to make, but not from the front. Frank wasn't leadership material, and that was probably true of his personal life as well. Left to himself he would initiate nothing, so if anything were to happen he would have to be encouraged. Or surprised into action, caught off balance at the psychological moment.

As Frank sat in the maintenance office later that evening with his sandwiches and juice, he leafed through a newspaper Alastair had left behind. He claimed he bought it for the racing section – he had accounts with William Hill and Joe Coral and placed the occasional bet – but really he read it for the gossip about celebrities, their parties, orgies, indiscretions, affairs, break-ups and break-downs. Dreary stuff, Frank thought, as his eye wandered to the astrology column, written by a local lady masquerading under the name of Renata Abendroth. 'Venus moves into your relationship zone today, thus heralding a new time of greater emotional warmth and security.'

He put the paper in the bin and rose. So what were the cleaners up to? Only one way to find out. And they were just finishing floor seven when he got there. Jessica was parking the floor polisher in the cleaning cupboard and Juanita, from sunny down-town Manila, was cleaning the mirrors in the exercise room. Mr Gibson believed Juanita was an illegal immigrant, his evidence consisting solely of her name. But June confirmed that she paid her national insurance and had even attempted to fill in the form for a tax credit, her income being low.

'We don't often see you up here,' Jessica said, as she made for the stairs.

'Spreading my wings,' Frank replied, 'soaring heavenwards on a thermal from the lift shaft.'

She looked at him doubtfully. 'We'll leave you to it then.'

And when they did, he toured the floor room by room, ending with the penthouse suite. He sat in an easy chair and switched on the television. It was restricted to free-to-air channels but it worked. He rose and opened the minibar. Orange juice, bottled water and yes, there they were, whisky miniatures. Though the room was not in regular use, there were towels in the bathroom, and toilet roll, and in the wardrobe a few abandoned articles of clothing with a Hector Mowatt look to them. The bed was made up and very tempting, but he knew he couldn't use it. The cleaners would notice it had been slept in.

He was still wondering exactly what to do as he went down to the sixth floor office, drawn by June's biscuits and the lingering effect of his recent conversation with Pamela. He sat at her desk wishing she was still there. He trusted her judgement. She told it as it was.

He felt an urge to contact her, but he knew he couldn't, not without running the risk of seeming to take her up on her offer. If it hadn't been for that, he assured himself, he'd call. He wanted to speak with her, hear her voice, picture her at the other end of the line. But when you'd drawn it yourself so many years before, stepping over the line was always going to be the hard part.

10

You don't think on your feet Frank, his father told him, you'll never make a boxer. Well, Frank had thought at the time, thank God for that. He'd seen graphics of what happened when the opponent, usually black and panther-like, with enormously strong muscles rippling to a rhythm of their own, landed punches to the head. It all added up to the vegetative state. He'd be even less capable of thinking on his feet if he took up the noble art.

Unused to making moves himself, Frank was thrown when anyone else did. It was thoughtful of Pamela to invite him round but if he said yes, which he wanted to, he'd have to respond by inviting her to his place and that wasn't such a good idea. He'd already notified the letting agent he was leaving and only had two weeks left. And they were going to be busy. To reclaim his deposit he had to leave the place as he'd found it, which would involve cleaning and some retouching of paintwork. And how would he get her upstairs? Carry her then go back down for the chair? The close still bore the scars of the fire. She'd be less than impressed. Yet having no solutions to any of these problems he accepted her invitation and met her in the car park after work.

'This is yours, then.'

He was referring to her VW, neat and compact like herself. He was impressed by her technique in transferring from the chair to the driver's seat. She could safely stand if she had something solid to lean on. As he folded the chair and put it in the back he wondered how she handled that on her own. No doubt she had her methods. He noted the hand controls.

'I can brake, if that's what you're worried about.'

'My life in your hands.'

'You wouldn't have it any other way,' she smiled. She didn't walk much but she was always one step ahead.

As she drove him to her flat he regressed into a pleasingly passive frame of mind. He'd started life as a passenger being driven by his parents which meant, if he thought about it, that he was leaving both the route and destination to them. And nothing had changed. Since he hadn't learned to drive he was always the passenger, never the driver: Flora most often, the police most recently, and now this young woman who had acquired a skill he lacked. A 'life skill', as Gemma Laing would have it, leaving yet another box unchecked on the thin file with his name on it.

'Have you ever wondered,' Pamela asked, after some minutes of silent travel, 'if we have anything in common other than where we work, anything else to talk about?'

'Why do we have to talk? Why can't we just exist in the same place at the same time?'

He was thinking of two dogs he'd seen stretching out together in the sun with their tongues hanging out, their chests rising and falling, close to each other but not quite touching. They could have lain apart but chose not to. What was that about if not fellowship, silent communion? Very peaceful. Much to be admired.

'Silence may not be enough.'

Frank was puzzled. 'Enough for what?'

'To understand the person you're with.'

'But surely,' Frank said, 'we understand people best from what they do, not from what they say. Sometimes we can't find the right words. We even say things we don't really mean. Communication's harder than particle physics.'

'Frank,' Pamela said, stopping at a junction and looking round, 'I'm danger of losing my way here, but it seems to me that speech is a form of behaviour.'

Of course it was. But what people said was difficult to interpret, and sometimes they left things unsaid.

'Well now,' Pamela said, checking her rear view mirror before turning into her street, 'and who does that remind us of?'

Pamela's house was part of a small terrace, ground floor, with a ramp and hand-rail leading to the front door. The rent was reasonable she added, without saying what it was, and there was a concierge service in the event a problem arose, like a leaking tap or a faulty lock. Frank understood that she was telling him this for a reason. There was a resident caretaker. She wasn't lining him up for his practical skills and she wanted him to know that. Fair enough, but these were the only skills he was known to have.

'It's customary for a visitor to accept a drink at this point whether they want one or not. What would you like?'

'Water would be fine.'

'Water! You're really into the high life then.'

'Alcohol doesn't do much for me. I like a glass of wine with a meal, though.'

'You're worried drink will lower your guard.'

'I'm hoping it will lower my guard, that's what these are for,' he said with his best attempt at a wry smile, tapping the box of chocolate liqueurs he had brought. But alcohol wasn't a factor in the complex equation which described what was going on. Drink was a relaxant, reducing the drinker's inhibitions, and he had plenty. But he was no match for Pamela so the question didn't arise. How could you lower a guard you didn't have?

She powered through to the kitchen and as she poured him a glass of water he noted through the doorway that she filtered it from the tap. Then he heard the clink of ice.

'Make it yourself?'

'I don't bring it home in bags if that's what you're asking. By the way', she said, handing him his water, 'I take it you're in the eat to live category – none of this live to eat, every mushroom traced to its source, got to be extra virgin olive oil nonsense.'

'That would be me, yes.'

'That's a relief. I can cook but I'm nothing to write home about. I rely on prepared meals and the micro-wave quite a lot.'

Which meant she was popping too much salt, sugar, preservatives, colouring agents and trans fatty acids for a woman in her condition. Whatever her condition was. She hadn't mentioned it and he hadn't asked. But the longer that went on the larger it would loom. Like an iceberg in the night, he thought, with a sinking feeling.

'I'm the same,' he said. 'It's likely to be that way when you live on your own.'

'Good. Well I hope you'll be alright with Plaice Florentine, potatoes and cauliflower.'

'Followed by?'

'Don't push your luck, Frank,' she said, with apparent seriousness. Had she taken his question as sexual innuendo? He hadn't meant it that way. Evidently not, she was smiling. 'Chocolate mousse from a six-pack. You can have two if you like. Three even.'

'Sounds good to me.'

She declined his offer of help and he wandered round the flat as she worked in the kitchen. He liked the colours, some of them pastel, which made the rooms seem warm compared to his own. No doubt they had names like magnolia, lemon grass and autumn sunset. Evocative sells. He admired the artful way the prints were hung at a variety of heights, all of them lower than usual on the wall.

The contents of the living-room bookcase were sensibly arranged, with the smallest books on the top shelf and the largest just above her waist height seated. There were also family photographs, including one of her, a school shot against an artificial sky. She was seated and her tie was fashionably loose. Trying to look serious, she wasn't quite bringing it off.

The bathroom was fitted with hand-rails at strategic points near the toilet, the shower and the bath, but as soon as he saw it he went to the medicine cabinet. Detectives did this in films and always learned something. But it contained nothing out of the ordinary: a bottle of eye-drops, pain-killers available over the counter, sticking plasters in assorted sizes, and a tube of Deep Heat for aching muscles. As he shut the cabinet door he caught a view of his waist in the mirror where his face should be. The bulge wasn't large but it was discernible and he'd never noticed it before.

'Low level mirrors have their uses.' Pamela had appeared in the doorway, silently, no footstep to give away her approach. 'Would the gentleman care to come through?'

Pamela didn't use a table, preferring to balance her tray on her knee. There was a coffee table, but too low to be of use to guests, so they sat with trays as well. Frank noted a small potted plant balanced on top of the set. He could picture her attending to it while the TV was on and water getting through the ventilation grills with explosive results. It didn't bear thinking about, but he knew this wasn't the time to mention it, not while they were enjoying the meal.

'This is delicious,' he said, slicing through a piece of plaice with his fork, 'excellent.'

'Reflects no credit on me.

After they'd finished the main course Pamela asked him to collect the chocolate mousse from the fridge and when he sat down again she asked him what he thought of the flat. He liked it. Nicely fitted out and brightly decorated, it was well designed for a wheelchair-user. It felt more spacious than it was, though he hadn't seen the bedroom. She smiled when he said that since she knew he was simply stating a fact.

'I'm sure we can put that right.'

'I wasn't suggesting . . .'

'I know that, Frank' she said, 'I'm worryingly safe with you. So, tell me, why do I need a place like this? What's my problem? And what's yours? Why have you never asked?'

'I assumed you'd tell me when you were ready.'

'I'm ready now. You've a right to know what you're getting into. Are you comfortable with that?' He nodded. 'Okay, so it wasn't a skiing accident or a car crash. It's a genetic defect that affects the legs. It won't get any better. It might get worse, though in my case there's a good chance it won't. Oh, and I'm not likely to offend Mr Gibson.'

'What's he got to do with it?'

She laughed. 'There's no way I could do it standing up.'

This was very neat, Frank thought, implying she could do it lying down and wanting him to know. He might have gone on to wonder if her problem impaired her ability to conceive, but children were not on his wish-list.

'It has a name, this condition?'

'Does HSP mean anything to you?'

She told him how it affected her, though he already had an idea. There was no cure, though being genetic in origin her condition might benefit from gene therapy one day, but physiotherapy and exercise helped. That was why she didn't use a powered chair, she needed heart and lung work as much as anyone else. Maybe more. She also needed strength in her arms. But she had to work her legs as well and did that in the pool.

When they had demolished two chocolate mousses each – after all, they weren't large – Pamela gathered up the plates, the four plastic cartons and the cutlery on her tray and wheeled them through to the kitchen.

'Give you a hand?' Frank asked, pulling a dishtowel from its home on the oven handle.

'I don't think so. Apart from the fact you're a guest I'm making coffee, not washing up. The dishes can wait till tomorrow.'

'But I won't be here tomorrow,' he said, before he knew whether he would be or not.

Pamela turned round to see him more clearly. 'So much for my planned night of bliss. When do you want me to drive you home? No, don't tell me, you've come with a bus pass and no toothbrush.'

Apart from the chocolates he'd come unprepared. No toothbrush. He wouldn't have presumed. You couldn't take people for granted. They didn't like it. Over coffee Pamela made a suggestion. She would tell him how she saw things and he would tell her. And Frank agreed, provided he could go first. For a start, it hadn't crossed his mind that she would drive him home though, yes, he never went anywhere without his bus pass. Anyway, as far as he could tell he fancied her for a number of reasons, some too embarrassing to mention.

'Let's begin with those then,' Pamela said, 'get the tricky stuff out of the way.'

'Well I can't speak for blind people,' he said, 'God knows how they get by, but for the likes of me it all starts with how you look. Men are at the mercy of their eyes. Visual stimuli.'

'How romantic.'

Frank had heard this word many times and had a whiff of its function. Like make-up, it attempted to obscure by improving on reality. What was romantic about roses, earrings, perfumes, candles, valentine cards? As far as he could see, men used these things to get round women, compensating for shortfalls in more meaningful areas such as affection, consideration and fidelity. Some of them were free with their gifts till the marriage took place, less so afterwards. As for women, they weren't faultless in this area either, attaching too much importance to rings, or to the wedding as an end in itself rather than a door to a room which, if lived in at all, would require regular attention. What was the point, he wondered, in having albums full of pictures of the happy day, not to mention a video or DVD of the ceremony, if you failed to maintain your relationship.

'That would require a touch of oil, would it?' Pamela asked, 'and reference to the workshop manual.' She toyed with her cup. 'I believe you mentioned appearance.'

This was difficult for Frank, which was why she had to remind him. Without looking at her directly, he admitted that when he first saw her he was affected by her figure which seemed, somehow, to be accentuated by her close-fitting slacks and tidy posture in the chair. I mean, he said, you have a neat waist, which just draws attention to the rest of you. We're talking hour-glasses here. Or acoustic guitars.

'Acoustic, wow!'

'Also,' he added, 'when I've been close to you, like behind you, I've noticed you smell really good. Clean as whistle. Like fresh air.'

'So,' Pamela said, 'the sight and smell of me fills you with lust from head to toe. You can't wait to get your hands on me, both above and below my neat waist.' Frank looked abashed. 'It's okay to say yes,' she said, 'if that's how you feel.' But Frank wasn't sure he could agree to that without putting himself in a bad light. 'Frank, really, you have natural impulses, that's all. Why would I think less of you for that? I have them too. Everyone does.'

He noticed a movement out the corner of his eye. It was himself reflected in the television screen, the shadowy action of a man with appetites. While he didn't deny he had desires, what he really wanted was the simple uncomplicated life, a long term relationship where his partner was also his friend. That would work for him. He couldn't prop up the bar every night knocking back beer and talking football, so he'd be talking with her. They would have to get on.

Pamela could tell from his strained expression that Frank needed a break. He had, after all, broken the habit of a lifetime and uttered several consecutive sentences concerning himself.

'Okay Frank, but could I start by mentioning something I don't want. I don't want a carer. I look after myself quite well and I intend to carry on doing that. It keeps me active, keeps me fit. The last thing I need is someone doing everything for me. It wouldn't work.'

'Fair enough.'

'You can live with that?'

'Yes.'

'I agree with what you said though. I would like to think my partner was my friend.'

He stood up and held out his hands. He helped her to her feet but she wasn't entirely steady till he hugged her. If he needed one, that was his excuse. Even as he did it he noticed her chair roll back as her calves pushed against it. The brakes hadn't been on. If this was a move they were committed to it.

'I like this,' he said, one hand behind her head, the other low down on her back. He could feel her against him all the way from the head to the knees. It was a good fit. It felt right. His nose was in her hair. She smelled so good, so wholesome. He had a strong impulse to move the hand on her back lower down to those lovely hind-quarters, so often seen but never felt. When she kissed him he took his chance.

'You know where you're hand is now,' she said. He withdrew it instantly. 'I'm not complaining,' she said, moving it back to where it had been, 'it's just that I've seen your eyes flitting in that direction from time to time.' True, though he'd always tried to disguise it. 'Just as well you're not a bosom man, you'd only have eyes for June.'

Frank knew some men liked big breasts but he wasn't one of them. Not only did they do nothing for him, he also had the impression that as the years went by they would be harder to maintain, having a tendency to deflate and sag. Whatever supported the young large breast would be unequal to the task over the decades. And if that support was provided by an external agency such as a bra, then the muscles which should be doing the job would surely atrophy through lack of use. His instinct was to prefer the smaller model which, he liked to think, would remain upstanding and pert into middle age and beyond. Like Pamela's would.

After a while in the standing position, pleasing though it was, Frank felt his arms growing tired and Pamela beginning to sag. Just a little, but enough to take her mind off the job.

'You'll have to put me down somewhere.' That would be the chair or the bed. But when the phone rang he lowered her carefully onto the nearer of the two, the chair, and she propelled herself to where it sat, constantly recharging, on the window ledge.

'There is a Good News team in my area . . . why do I want to know that? You realise,' she said, grinning at Frank, 'I stepped out of the shower to take this call?'

By the way, she wondered, hanging up, did he remember at the meeting, when Alice had refused a request from Mr Gibson and Gemma had agreed not to minute it? Mr Gibson had requested that formal meetings begin with a prayer. Everyone stood to benefit from guidance, and none more so, he had suggested, than those who thought they didn't need it. Given what he knew of Mr Gibson, Frank wasn't surprised.

Later, after another coffee and too many chocolate liqueurs, they made it to Pamela's bedroom, which seemed to Frank almost as austere as his own except for the dressing table with obligatory mirror though, in this case, no chair since Pamela wheeled her knees under the table top.

'You don't go in for make-up much,' Frank said, noting little in the way of tubes, jars and atomisers.

'You think I could do with more?' she said.

'You don't need any at all.'

It wasn't a single bed but it wasn't a king-sized double either. Maybe four foot six across, Frank guessed. It wouldn't do if you weren't getting on well together, though sharing it might leave you no alternative. They lay there for a long time, talking, cuddling, getting to know each other in the glow of the single bed-side light. It occurred to Pamela that they resembled a couple of young teenagers, having a good time without going the whole way, until she remembered stories about teenage pregnancies and girls of eleven having babies one minute and doing their home-work the next.

'I'm not on the pill,' she said.

'Glad to hear it,' Frank said. 'You shouldn't mess with your hormones if you don't have to.'

'You're sort of assuming I don't have a constant stream of importunate suitors knocking at my door,' she said. 'Am I really so unattractive?'

'You're attractive alright, but you're also a woman of character,' he said. 'You don't encourage competition among your admirers.'

'I'm fastidious like you,' she said, leading him on.

He was always reserved in everything he did, an engine requiring an external stimulus before it could function, like a car and its starting motor. And it didn't always work. She was reminded of pressing the lift button at Mowatts and wondering when, if ever, anything would happen, then hearing it glide past her floor without stopping. The lift in flight, as the Otis man would have it. If Frank were the economy, commentators would use expressions like 'kick start' and 'pump prime'. And that was fine to get things going. But suppose you invested your energy in starting the machine or priming the pump and it was never enough to keep it running? What if Frank was by nature a consumer and she was a supplier? She couldn't keep pushing it out year after year while he sat back and absorbed. She spoke in Frank's ear.

'I hope you don't feel I've been coming on too strong.'

'I did wonder sometimes, when you were putting me through my paces in the control room. It felt like you were out to get me by the throat.' And there had been something of the interrogation about it, just a hint of aggression not only then but since.

'I was trying to wake you up.'

At the moment she said this his right arm was going to sleep under her weight. He raised her head a little with his left hand and rescued his arm, stretching it out along the pillow, waiting for the unpleasant tingle of returning blood.

According to June, some couples went at it with abandon, ripping each other's clothes off in public parks, motor vehicles and aircraft toilets and getting down to business as if their lives depended on it. But let's forget about them, Pamela said, everyone wasn't like that. Some women liked being taken which, as far she could tell, came close to being ravished by consent while others, more in the femme fatale mould, were never happier than when seducing the object of their interest out of his honourable intentions.

Of course, she said, she was talking women here because that's what she knew, and Frank was male, but surely the same range of behaviour applied to males, just tending more to the extremes. Well, she had formed the impression that left to himself Frank would do nothing, that meeting him half way wasn't an option because when she got to the halfway point he wouldn't be there. So he was right, she had been out to get him. It was the only way to meet. But she wanted him to know this didn't make her a seductress, a siren, or a scarlet woman. Even, she added, giving him a heavy nudge in the ribs, if that's the sort of woman he was hoping for.

There's something else, she said. Listen, you've got to face this. She sounded serious.

'You're pregnant with another man's child,' he said, in an attempt to deflect her and lighten the mood.

'Frank,' she said, grabbing his head between her hands, 'cut it out! When you look at me you see my disability, you think to yourself, okay, there it is, I know what's wrong with her. But really I'm the same as everyone else. I have my faults and weaknesses.'

He tried to dispute it, she was perfect, but she covered his mouth with her hand.

'What I'm saying is look past the chair, don't let it kid you my legs are the only problem.'

As she released his head he felt a slight airy feeling of de-compression, which made made him realise how strong propelling a wheelchair had made her. He wouldn't want to pick a fight with Pamela.

'That's it,' she said lightly, kissing him on the end of nose, 'I've told you now, I'll never mention it again.'

What was this kissing the nose business, he wondered? Perhaps a mating ritual, like gannets on the Bass Rock, or maybe a greeting related to the traditional Maori hongi or the custom practised by the Inuit on the icy wastes of the north. Yes, that would be it. He kissed her nose in return. And then, suddenly transported to the Arctic, saw the kiss freezing, the salivary amylase denatured by the chill, and the end of the nose going black as frostbite set in. But the image was entirely visual, aesthetic almost, with no negative emotion, no emotion of any sort. Not by way of a portent then, nor a sign of anxiety breaking the surface like a harp seal through a blow-hole. Strange how the mind worked, freely associating to no obvious end. What was going on? Where was he at? Wherever it was, he'd be the last to know.

She asked him how things were going at his flat and he told her about the clean-up, what he had done and what he still had to do. Messy though it was, he was sleeping there again till he finished. He'd already moved some of his belongings to Flora's but, though he didn't say so, that was a temporary measure. Her flat wasn't so large it could take his gear on a permanent basis and, even if it had been, what would be the point since he wouldn't be living there himself. With two weeks to go a solution was not yet in sight.

Pamela reached back with one hand, removed a light plastic grip from her hair, and rather than wriggle round and place it on the bedside table, threw it across the room. What the hell, she said, but she didn't want to let go of Frank or do anything else which might contradict the mood. Her hair fell down, partly covering her face, allowing Frank the luxury of brushing it aside. Caressing a blond on her own bed, he could hardly believe it.

'If it doesn't work out with your sister, what will you do?' she asked.

'Don't worry, I'll think of something.'

She started to take off her top, which wasn't so easy, intertwined as she was with him and lying on part of it.

'Give you a hand?' he asked.

Well, there was a question. How to deal with a man like that?

She put her mouth to his ear and whispered. 'Give me two if you like.'

And when they'd wrestled it off and she was down to her bra she realised that without a formal invitation that's where the action would stop. What did he need, a job card?

'I have a sweatshirt somewhere in one of these drawers,' she said.

'You do?' Frank said, now assuming she intended to replace one top with another, not the impression he had a moment before when her lips were brushing his ear.

'I bought it in one of those print shops. Impulse buy.'

'Right,' he said, sensing a punch but knowing where it would come from. 'What does it say?'

'It says,' she said, guiding his hand to the clasp, 'JUST DO IT'.

11

Despite his interest in Anita, it would never have occurred to Preston Blair to search the top shelf of his local newsagent for Burmese Babes or Thai Hard Kore. He was sufficiently in touch with reality to realise that images, however suggestive the come-on smile, were no substitute for the real thing. Women's magazines were of no interest to him either. He only set eyes on them in the waiting room at his local medical practice as he fought off the fungal infection attacking his toe nails.

While he was waiting for his name to be called, he came across an article in Good Housekeeping. Why spend a fortune on fragrances, the author asked, when you can cook them up for a fraction of the price in your own home? All you needed, she claimed, was a few simple ingredients and a little patience. Under the snappy title INVENT A SCENT, she explained how to do it, threw in two handy recipes and listed some useful sources and contact numbers. Surely this was it, the entry he'd been looking for? A shared interest. A common pursuit. What do you think of this, he would say to the smouldering Anita, producing a dinky little bottle of Eau de Blair? Made it myself.

A dispute in the children's play area gave him the chance to tear out the article and slip it in his inside pocket. No one could hope to remember so much detail so it was wasted in the waiting room anyway. The door opened and his name was called, but not by Doctor Duncan. The practice operated a rotating door policy for medics and patients alike. This one was Chinese and petite with it. Chinese Chicks.

Preston was reluctant to discuss certain things with his mother. Money problems he felt as free to raise as she did to remedy, but he was reluctant to share details of his private life with her, however embryonic it might be. So, for the production of fragrances, he avoided communal areas such as the kitchen and bathroom and assembled the necessary ingredients in his bedroom, intending to keep his enterprise secret. She would have wanted to know why, and he didn't want to tell her about Anita, not until there was something definite to tell.

Ada had given up cigarettes many years before but she still bought an occasional packet of cigars. Produced with ladies in mind they were long, slim, and could be held as an accessory with an elegant inclination of the wrist. This appealed to Ada, who had standards to maintain. But it failed to impress her son, who could always tell when she'd smoked one, even if she'd committed the crime in the garden an hour before he arrived. What a nose! What a superb instrument! Just what was needed to perfect a world-class fragrance. That his nose was inherited didn't occur to him, and not long into his experiments his mother knew something was going on.

Using the stolen article as a guide, Preston visited an outlet specialising in alternative therapies and, sure enough, Herb's Place contained a wide range of essential oils from several suppliers. What struck him most, apart from the prices of what were, after all, very small bottles, was the width of the selection. Spoiled for choice, he didn't know which to select and asked an assistant for advice. But though she knew about the uses of various oils in the hands of experienced practitioners, her knowledge of perfumery was non-existent.

'Experienced practitioners?' he asked, hoping for a clue.

'You know,' she said, 'qualified aromatherapists. Why don't you check the ads?'

And there, to the left of the door going out, was a large notice-board fully supported by the alternative community. Philip Goodfellow advertised cognitive behavioural therapy on a one-to-one basis; a support group for arthritis sufferers meeting in the local church hall offered an introduction to balneotherapy; a night class in neurolinguistic programming was available at a further education college; acupuncture, aromatherapy and reflexology were to be had, at a modest price, in the Chinese holistic medicine centre. And technology could solve your problem if you were into magnetic insoles, ionised wrist bands, low level laser therapy, ultrasound or hyperbaric oxygen treatment. One woman, left behind by these developments, still sought to interest the public in yoga. Not that Preston remembered much of this later, but now he knew it was out there, all of it. Whatever you were looking for. Seek and ye shall find.

In an effort to make sense of essential oils Preston surfed, which was what he should have done in the first place. Some sources not only listed the various oils but guided the prospective buyer as to their qualities. Comparing this data with the information from Good Housekeeping, Preston placed his order with a reputable supplier and a carefully packed box arrived three days later. What might this be, his mother wondered when she opened the door to the delivery man and signed for it? Preston assured her it was computer sundries, samples, nothing of interest, and so saying took them upstairs to his room. They were carefully packed in tissue paper and bubble-wrap, six small bottles of essential oils. An artist in the making, he placed them in a row on his bedside table: lavender, bergamot, juniper, jasmine, patchouli, sandalwood. He wasn't motoring yet but he would be soon.

Later that day, along with his lunchtime sandwiches, he almost bought a half bottle of gin before remembering it had an odour of its own and opted for vodka instead. He wasn't into spirits, but according to his recipes alcohol was required. Ready and waiting for it when he got home was an empty coffee jar, washed out several times and labelled ETHANOL in his own neat hand. And in case his mother spotted the jar he boldly inscribed CH_3CH_2OH beneath the name. Surely that would fool the old girl, whose work as a teacher of French and German didn't equip her to translate something so symbolic. And when she asked what the substance was for he would tell her it was used, with cotton buds, to clean computer keyboards.

These precautions were not successful. Ada noticed the empty vodka bottle in the glass recycling bin and the discarded wrapping from Eve's Essentials lurking in the rubbish. As she used to say, she wasn't born yesterday, though the phrase had fallen out of favour the first time Preston, ever the diplomat, had looked her up and down and agreed.

Ada kept a close eye on her son, though she did it from a safe distance. A suspicion aroused would lead to concealment and she preferred to know. Her concerns were the usual ones, alcohol or substance abuse, pornographic magazines under the mattress, flavoured condoms in his jacket pocket. Because of her job she got home earlier than some, especially on a Friday afternoon, and since Preston wasn't given to arriving early for work (flexi-time, mum, you know how it is) he always felt obliged to put in a full afternoon and then some, since by working on he could avoid the worst of the evening rush hour and give his car a run for its money. He wasn't to know that in his absence Ada checked his room and drew her conclusions. The first, that he was remarkably tidy for a young man: socks in the sock drawer, shirts on hangers, jerseys folded, shoes lined up under the bed. The second, that he was making perfume.

The signs were everywhere. Six small bottles of essential oils in the top drawer of his chest, plus the article lodged among the papers he kept in an orderly pile on the dressing table. Invent a scent, indeed! There were also two small artist's brushes, no obvious explanation for those, and the ethanol – which troubled her a bit, but not for long. Her friend from the science department soon set her straight.

'Indeed Mrs Blair,' Mr Braunschweig said, looking up from his crossword, 'ethanol may be used for cleaning purposes. It may also be used in the manufacture of perfume, though there are other ways.'

But when she mentioned the brushes, more as a matter of narrative colour than anything else, he wasn't impressed.

'We know the boy has artistic tendencies, Mrs Blair, but it appears to me most likely,' he said with a frown, 'that your son is using them to transfer liquid from one container to another. I do not consider this good practice. On the contrary, it would difficult to conceive of anything less exact.'

So saying, he returned to his crossword. But Mrs Blair was agreeably surprised when he entered her room at the end of the day when the final bell had rung.

'I have for your son,' he said, 'something useful.'

This turned out to be two pipettes and some tips.

'If your son might begin to take this subject seriously, he should feel free to consult with me.'

Ada thanked him for his trouble, but she was left with a problem: to intervene or not and, if so, how. She couldn't say to Preston during the evening meal, 'by the way, Preston, I have a couple of pipettes and some tips for you', without giving away the fact that she'd been prying. After some deliberation she decided to speak. Why not?

'I couldn't help noticing, dear,' she said one evening over lemon cheesecake, 'that you're dabbling with fragrances.'

Preston looked startled. He'd been so discreet. 'I mean,' she said, trying to reassure him, 'you can't open one of those bottles without the scent permeating the atmosphere. And when I was changing the sheets the other day, well, I was in the room, wasn't I . . . I couldn't help it, my nose started twitching.'

In more ways than one, he thought. There was no point in denying the obvious, but what reason could he give? He was about to claim he was cooking up something special for her birthday when she saved him the trouble.

'Who could blame you starting an enterprise of your own with the future so uncertain. It may begin as a side-line but who knows where it will lead? As Confucius used to remark, a journey of a thousand miles starts with a single step. You could be head of your own multi-national company twenty years down the line. And by the way, Mr Braunschweig has kindly given me a couple of pipettes to help you out. I'll let you have them after tea.'

Confucius! She was really losing it. Where had she got that one, a Christmas cracker? And what did this Braunschweig character have to do with it? What were pipettes?

'Thanks mum. That's great. But let's face it, you can't start a business without capital.'

'Well,' she replied, 'you won't have long to wait, will you?'

She was referring to the twenty-year endowment his loving parents had taken out in his name, looking ahead to the time he might need some ready cash. A good idea, but they hadn't thought of it till he was five, so it wasn't due to mature till his twenty-fifth birthday. She'd explained this to him several times over the years but the concept of a with-profits policy proved strangely elusive. A great cost to herself, his mother had kept up the premiums when his father had fled the scene.

As usual, Preston rushed headlong into his latest project, trying various combinations of oils, binding them with vodka, shaking vigorously, and leaving them to stand. It was three weeks before he achieved anything resembling a result, and he could hardly wait to waft Blair No 1 under his mother's experienced nose. Unfortunately, he had no choice since, on the evening of his first major breakthrough, his mother was attending a French film season. 'Les Soeurs Fâchées,' she said, hitting him with the full accent. She'd been wanting to see for it ages. She'd always been an Isabelle Huppert fan. Fine mum, though Preston suspected that there was a touch of professional interest at work. Not at all, his mother protested, she could name half a dozen French actresses she didn't like nearly so much. But Preston knew what these French films were like. Arty. Cultural. Dialogue so strange it was either deep or meaningless. How would you know, his mother had asked, you haven't seen any? Maybe not, but he read the reviews and he'd seen a Godard film once. Never again. Life was too short.

On the night of this, his first success, his mother came home full of the joys. An excellent film, she maintained, unexpected hidden depths. 'Right,' Preston said when she finally had her coat off and a coffee in her hand, try this for hidden depths. He produced a bottle and wafted it under her nose. His mother sniffed, looked at him, and sniffed again.

'This really is quite good,' she said, 'though the French do it better of course.'

'Of course. But you like it?'

'Oh yes, it has a certain something, no doubt about that. What's in it?'

This was the obvious question. He'd begun his experiments in an orderly manner, but as failure followed failure his impatience had grown, his speed had increased and his record-keeping fallen by the wayside. He had a only rough idea of what had gone into Blair No 1, and even then he knew at once, when his mother asked, that he couldn't recall the quantities. He felt like an alchemist who'd created the elixir of life but couldn't remember the ingredients. Perhaps it would be possible, under hypnosis, to reconstruct his moves. Or maybe if he sent a sample to a lab they would analyse it for him. But that would cost, and he realised with dismay that both of these approaches would reveal his recipe to a third party. This was a disaster. It was back to the drawing board but this time with painstaking records.

Reluctantly, he went to his room and opened a spreadsheet for no better reason than it came ready-made with columns. He reserved the first for essential oils. Something might spring to the eye when he entered his figures. All the authorities agreed that top notes evaporated most quickly, so maybe a perfume relying too much on bergamot wouldn't be a good idea. But how long were the ladies out there anyway, expecting a fragrance to work its magic? Given the amount they drank of an evening in wine bars and clubs, two hours at least. And two should be enough for your average painted Jezebel to make an impact on the male of the species. Of course, they always claimed they wanted to smell good for themselves, just as they wore low cut tops and short skirts for their own benefit. They wanted to give themselves a good view of their own breasts and sheer thighs? He didn't think so somehow. They could accomplish that quite easily in private with their own bedroom mirrors.

But already his mind was wandering from his task. And as he realised that, a message appeared on the screen. It was Janice, who saw from his amended profile that he was now experimenting with perfume-making. Did he want to chat? He did. Any distraction was welcome. Good to be in contact again, she wrote. Certainly is, he replied. I guess it's worth mentioning quantities, she said. What about them, he asked? Well, she replied, prices of oils being what they are, I would use very few drops of each. Like VERY FEW. If it works out and you want to make a usable quantity, just multiply by 10 or 20. Whatever. Saves a lot of money when you're playing around.

It was so obvious, such a good point, and it had never crossed his mind. Janice wanted to know if he was still there. He was. Okay, she replied, just thought I'd mention that. Signing off now. Thanks Janice, he typed, very useful. He knew that Janice, aged twenty-three, might actually be Harold aged fifty-seven, but provided useful tips kept coming his way he didn't really mind. He headed three more columns, one for alcohol, one for water, and a third for a carrier oil in case he ever got round to that. And then called up a picture Janice had sent him of herself. Or somebody else. She had dark hair, parted in the middle, and wore glasses. He suspected it was genuine. A girl wanting to appear glamorous wouldn't have sent this particular image. If librarians had a look, this would be it. And as he looked he warmed to her. She could be a great help. He'd sent her a shot of himself, what harm could it do?

As the weeks went by, Preston plodded on at work and continued to experiment at home, but when he socialised with his friends from the badminton club the subject of perfume never came up. As far as he could tell the girls used it, though any subtle effects it might have had were masked by deodorants which sporty types always used. Sweat patches under the arms were fine, if you played you perspired, but offensive smells from the same place were out of the question. He would love to have checked their kit bags, but entering the female changing area wasn't an option. Still, he felt he was making progress till his mother came home one night with Mr Braunschweig.

'There's a do at the school tonight,' his mother told him, 'for the visiting party from Alsace, so we can't stay long. We've just popped in for a coffee and a freshen up,' she explained. 'The home economics people always put on an excellent spread. Finger buffet, wine, you name it. Excuse me a moment, Anton.'

'Yes,' Mr Braunschweig said, by way of light conversation after she had gone, 'the key to the whole thing is repeatability, don't you agree?'

'It is?' Preston said.

'Oh yes, certainly. It's all very well producing a successful perfume on one occasion, but if you cannot replicate your product then, I submit, you are no further forward.'

'I suppose that's true,' Preston admitted. He would know.

'And the way to achieve success is precision in everything we do. For example,' he said, 'there is little point transferring five drops of a given solution if, the next time you do it, the drops are not of the same size. We might mention calibration in this context. If the size of drop varies from one occasion to the next then the product will also vary from one occasion to the next. It is a question of quality control.'

'In what sense would that be?' Preston asked.

'That would be where ingredients are concerned,' Mr Braunschweig explained, placing a large folder and a book on the dining table. 'We may,' he said, 'use oils from natural sources, but oils produced in this way will vary since Nature herself varies. It is for this reason,' he said, 'that we in the industry synthesise our ingredients. It is the only way to ensure that our product is free from impurities and also does not change in character from one batch to the next. If I may say so,' he said, 'you have set yourself an exceedingly difficult task for one lacking both a background in chemistry and a laboratory of any sort.'

If Mr Braunschweig had stopped at that point, Preston would have felt like topping himself. But he didn't.

'Of course,' he added, 'you may yet be successful pursuing what one might term the artistic approach. But only for small quantities, I'm afraid. Only for small quantities.'

Preston looked glum under what felt like a frontal assault. He didn't beat about the bush, this Braunschweig fellow who, even as his mother came in with the coffees, was taking papers from his folder.

'I have taken the liberty,' he said, 'of bringing with me notes which I use with my students. You will find, among other things, instruction on the use of pipettes illustrated by line drawings. You may be surprised to learn that evaporation is of considerable significance here.'

Preston accepted the notes with less enthusiasm than the coffee.

'So, mother, what's going down tonight, speeches, entertainment, the usual?'

'That sort of thing,' she replied, smiling towards Mr Braunschweig. 'Our visitors include a choir, so I expect we can look forward to a song or two.'

'Wonderful,' Preston said, spreading his hands in a generous gesture, 'you've got it made.'

And so had he because, now he thought about it, all he needed was a small quantity, a liquid key to the door. It was a hard trick, no doubt about that but, Mr Braunschweig notwithstanding, he only needed to work it once.

'You'll find some individual meals in the freezer, Preston. You won't starve.'

After they'd gone he sat at the table and glanced through the notes. Heavy stuff, he wasn't cut out for this sort of thing. Too rigorous. Too demanding. But following what Mr Braunschweig had described as the artistic approach, following as it were, his nose, and with a bit of luck, success could yet be his. That's what these scientists never took into account. Luck. They eliminated chance by the dogged application of method. But who could deny that luck was a factor in life, and wouldn't it take a clever scientist to calibrate that? So these boffins, these chaps in white coats, they didn't have all the answers.

His mood was improving by the minute. He picked up the book Mr Braunschweig had left and glanced at the title.

'La Mélodie Française de Berlioz à Duparc.' The book was in French but he could tell at a glance it was gripping stuff. He was putting it back on the table when he noticed the copy was inscribed. 'Dear Ada,' it read, 'in grateful thanks for your many acts of kindness over the years and looking forward to whatever the future may bring, Anton.'

This raised a question in his mind. Over the years? She'd only mentioned him recently. Was something going on here? Could it be that his mother, deserted by her husband a decade before, was finally lining up a replacement, looking to the future? Very interesting. Had something been discussed, tentative arrangements made? If you sell your place, Anton, and move in here, we could afford to retire and live in comfort.

His coffee was lukewarm but he drank it anyway. The idea had its attractions. When it came to the elderly and infirm stage they could look after each other, taking the strain off him.

As these thoughts were running through his head, it didn't occur to Preston that he should have been upset by the thought of his mother and Mr Braunschweig having sex. He'd read Hamlet at school, he'd had no choice, and he'd heard of Oedipus and his complex, but overly serious people had never interested him much, too busy agonising to butter the toast. As long as the freezer contained an individual meal such matters would never concern him.

12

The following day found Preston remarkably buoyant. He would have arrived at work earlier than usual had he not returned to Herb's Place for some small amber bottles in which to store his most likely confections while they matured.

'Will ten millilitre bottles be large enough for you, sir?'

'Absolutely,' he replied, and watched with pleasure as the assistant packed them. In his mind's eye they were already full.

He was reminded of his primary school class, where each pupil had a hyacinth bulb in a jam jar full of water. Miss Redford kept them in a dark cupboard yet, when she opened the door to let her charges check for progress, shoots were sprouting in the dark. How could that be? Yet it was. And so it would be with his range of fragrances.

When he reached his office his mood was even better because on his way in he glimpsed Anita, smiling as she listened to a customer, melting ice with a glance. But it began to dissipate almost at once. That interfering bungler of a man, Alastair Geddes, was working in his office installing Intelligent Trunking.

'The latest thing, Mr Blair. Very clever stuff this,' he said, brandishing a length of intricate-looking uPVC, 'keeps power and signal runs separate in the same housing. We'll have you sorted in no time.'

As Preston put down his package of bottles he noticed a post-it on his screen. Apparently his presence would be appreciated in Ms Laing's office, and could he possibly make it before twelve? The matter was urgent! The note was from Gemma herself, so she'd been in his office too. He took a tie from the top drawer of his desk and the jacket he always left on the back of his chair to imply his presence in the building. Best to look the part.

When he walked into Human Resources, Gemma was sitting near her desk and someone he had never seen before was behind it with a lap-top. She was younger than Gemma, wore her dark hair short and sported an artfully cut trouser suit with a mild pin-stripe. Gemma smiled. She seemed genuinely pleased to see him, but that was her way. Preston had been fooled before but he wasn't now.

'Glad you could make it, Preston, she said, 'I'd like you to meet a colleague of mine, Astrid Bonthrone.'

Astrid looked up. 'Gemma has filled me in on your work, Mr Blair. Pleased to meet you.'

'Likewise,' he said. He considered the single word reply polite but businesslike.

'Astrid works for Henderson McQuarrie LLP. You may have heard of them? She specialises in commercial and media work. We've been looking at your site and a number of points have arisen. Astrid?'

Astrid looked up. 'Yes, well Mr Blair, the first thing that strikes me is how wonderfully unfussy your web pages are. I usually find myself drowning in a welter of images all clamouring for attention at once. What you have produced here has a most attractive simplicity of style.'

Preston agreed with every word but knew this was a sucker punch and so extravagant with it that a knock-out blow was on the way.

'Your college course will have covered legal aspects of web design,' Astrid said, still very pleasant.

'Yes.' She raised an eyebrow. She wanted more. 'For example,' he said, straining to remember, 'our tutors emphasised the law of copyright. And if I could just say, I've gone to great lengths to ensure I have the necessary agreements for all the images used.'

'That's excellent, isn't it Astrid?' Gemma said. 'We were going to ask about that.'

'So,' Astrid said, 'you have clearances either in written or electronic form.'

'For most but not all. There have been times when people just haven't replied.'

'But you can show you contacted them?'

'I can show I tried. June typed the letters and sent them out, I assume she has copies.'

'June, yes,' Gemma explained, 'most methodical. She'll have copies on file.' She smiled reassuringly at Preston. 'You can see what we're doing here, I'm sure, enlisting Astrid's expertise to plug any legal loopholes.'

Preston could see what they were doing all right, and the nicer they were the more worried he became.

'A technique we sometimes advise our clients to use, in extremis,' Astrid said, 'is to send a follow-up letter to non-respondents stating that, since they have not replied to our previous letter seeking the necessary permissions, we shall assume these permissions granted unless we hear from them to the contrary. It's not water-tight, obviously, but it does demonstrate our bona fides in attempting to do everything by the book.'

'A bit like inertia selling,' Preston said.

'Inertia, yes,' Astrid said, 'selling, no. We would, after all, offer to buy if the need arose and the price was right.'

Astrid Bonthrone, with her dark hair, dark suit and glasses seemed somewhat menacing to Preston, like an undertaker preparing him for burial. He might have revised his opinion a little if he'd known that her glasses were non-prescription, for effect only, to add an edge to the severe and learned look.

The frames, however, were designer and far from cheap, so the effect was bought at a price, though given her hourly rate the cost was nothing to her.

'Tell me,' she said, starting to screw down the lid, 'how would you characterise your approach to the revised EU distance selling directives?'

Preston began to panic, this was it, and when he panicked his sweat glands went into overdrive. He'd never heard of the EU distance selling directives. If he pretended he had she'd catch him out. If he admitted he hadn't, he was confessing to ignorance of a subject which, by the sound of it, was important. She had him either way. But he tried. What else could he do.

'My intention was to complete a full draft first. Total content, text and graphics.'

Ms Bonthrone removed her glasses and let them hang from one hand in a gesture which seemed to say, I'm letting you dangle boy, I'm hanging you out to dry. Then she looked him full in the face and let him have it.

'In less than half an hour,' she said, 'Gemma and I have found three major infringements of the latest directive in the work you have done so far. Your site, while aesthetically pleasing would, if published, cost this company a fortune in claims it couldn't hope to defend.'

'As I say,' he said, but did not have the chance to continue.

'To take one example,' she said, picking up a piece of paper and waving it in his direction. 'The customer must be told how to identify and correct input errors. If a customer finds that she has inadvertently ordered the same item twice, it must be crystal clear from the site not only that she has done so but also how she can rectify this before she places her order. And I have to tell you, Mr Blair, that failure to comply with this last commitment gives the consumer an unlimited period to cancel the contract. Furthermore,' she said, with a hardening tone to her voice, 'trading standards officers have powers to serve "Stop Now" notices against traders in breach of these regulations. Which you clearly are, and to some tune.'

'As I say,' Preston said, 'my intention was to complete a full draft first then check it against the directives point by point.'

'In that case,' Ms Bonthrone said, rather sharply he thought, 'I'd better have sight of your copy of the regulations. I will then be able to certify to Ms Laing that your sources are up-to-date. Or not, as the case may be.'

'Yes Preston,' Gemma said, looking worried, 'this is something we really need to know.'

'And Mr Blair,' Astrid added, 'be sure to include your copy of the e-commerce directives as well. They're just as important.'

He was wondering how to get out of this trap when, with the softest of knocks, Alice came in. His first instinct was to rise, which he rapidly repressed on the grounds that Miss Mowatt was his employer, not royalty, and was due no special deference. But though the interruption gave him thinking time it soon became clear that her arrival was expected. She stopped suddenly, half way across the room, and held a hand to her ear in a deliberately pantomime gesture, her pearls bouncing against her blouse as she came to a halt. His eye was drawn to the silver broche on her jacket. Jensen, a name to conjure with. Quality on display.

'I do miss your soothing tones,' she said, presumably referring to Gemma's ocean waves lapping the shore. So do I, Preston thought, but no doubt Gemma had stopped the CD when the hardened professional arrived, her hired hit-woman. Hard men were bad enough, but hard women were worse, over-compensating as they felt they must for the imagined softness of their sex.

'We've dealt with the legal stuff, I take it?' Alice asked.

'I certainly hope so, it's all a bit beyond me,' Gemma admitted.

'Good, well for my part I conducted an experiment along the lines suggested by Mr Gibson and, do you know, he was right. I logged on as an existing customer and ordered a top-of-the-range fridge-freezer. It all worked very smoothly, I must say.'

Of course it did, Preston thought, you superannuated old bat.

'I'm pleased to hear it,' he said.

'The trouble is, the customer in question lives in Orkney. Do you have any idea, Mr Blair,' Alice asked, 'how much it would cost to transport a top-of-the-range fridge-freezer to South Ronaldsay?'

Preston felt sick. 'Not off the top of my head, Miss Mowatt.'

'Bearing in mind,' she added, 'that our vans go no further afield than fifty miles in any direction from this location. It would certainly be more than the twenty pounds charge for delivery of white goods indicated in your billing page. Freight charges on the ferry alone . . . you see where I'm coming from, I'm sure.'

'Absolutely, Miss Mowatt.' He wondered why an Orcadian would have an account with Mowatts in the first place, but knew that asking would reveal his ignorance and he couldn't afford to do that.

'You have to remember them, you know' Alice explained, 'our far-flung customers who order smaller items, often of great value, which we mail out in the usual way. Jewellery, cosmetics, gifts, monogrammed linen handkerchiefs. For some, there is a certain cachet in dealing with an old-established concern such as ours.'

Okay, there was a problem here, he hadn't picked it up and that was his job. But the directives business was worse, a legal minefield he had wandered into without knowing. No warning signs, no skull and cross-bones. Taking the two together, they were hitting him with both barrels, whether by accident or design didn't really matter much. He was shot full of holes. Sweating profusely, he unbuttoned his jacket and loosened his tie. He had to do what he could to limit the damage and he didn't have much time.

Astrid rose and handed some papers to Gemma and Alice. 'I've listed the major areas where Mr Blair fails to comply. Any one of them could spell serious trouble for your business. It will take a major revision to bring this site into line. I'm sorry,' she said to Alice, 'as I explained to Gemma I have to leave now for another meeting. If we had started sooner,' she said, referring to Preston's late arrival, 'we'd have covered the ground.'

When she left, without a backward glance, he rose to follow her out.

'I'd better raise my copies of the directives now, as you requested,' he said to Gemma, 'if that's alright with you.' His plan was simple. He would track them down on the web and save them to disc. If they asked for hard copy he would claim that he referred to the regulations on screen, but he'd be happy to print them out if that's what they wanted. They'd know he was making it up but they wouldn't be able to prove it, and so he would live to fight another day. Keep the money coming in, that must be his objective till something better came along.

Alice and Gemma were happy for him to leave, they had notes to compare.

'He hadn't a clue what Astrid was talking about,' Gemma said, as Alice sat down, 'but admitting it is something else. Men don't as a rule, can't be seen to lose face.'

'He hadn't a clue what I was on about either. So what do we do?'

Gemma sighed. She wasn't nasty by nature. 'Give him a month to come good. Tell him if he doesn't we let him go.

Use that month to find someone competent then contract out the work. Payment by results, no more strain on the payroll. We can't afford it.'

'Do you want me to tell him?' Alice asked.

'My job, I'll do it. But you should be there to witness what's said.'

Safely out of the room, Preston headed straight for the swing doors and dashed down the stairs to the floor below. If sliding down the banister would have got him there sooner he'd have done it, but like most solutions to his problems a suitable banister didn't exist. As he approached his office he noticed the door was open. Alastair was still there. Too bad. He'd ask him to leave and come back later. Something urgent had come up, which was no more than the truth. But when he entered he found the head of maintenance sitting on the corner of his desk, one foot on the floor, one leg swinging, relaxed in holiday mode. He was drinking tea from a polystyrene cup.

'Slight hold-up, I'm afraid. Shouldn't be long though.'

'What's the problem?' Preston asked, clocking some clutter and several bare wires.

'Waiting for Frank to restore the power.'

'Restore it yourself, you cut it. '

'Not as simple as that, I'm afraid. Frank's the electrician. Must be done by a qualified man.'

'So where is he, waiting in the basement for you to check the plumbing?'

Alastair could tell Preston was rattled.

'Now then, Mr Blair, no need to take that tone. Frank's being interviewed by a precognition officer.' Preston looked blank so Alastair helped him out. 'In connection with the fire.'

'Preston tore off his tie and put it back in the drawer. 'I don't know what you're talking about.'

'It was in the papers.'

'I'm sure it was.' Preston didn't read papers, took too long.

'The fire where he lives. A girl's been charged with wilful fire-raising.'

Was Preston listening? He didn't seem to be.

'Arson', Alastair said loudly. 'Arson!'

'Ah, Mr Geddes, Mr Blair,' Alice said, arriving at the door, 'I thought you'd detected a fire for a moment there. Miss Laing will be here shortly.'

'Just sorting out Mr Blair in the wiring department,' Alastair said.

'That's right,' Preston said, suddenly sensing a way out. 'Power's down, I'm afraid, can't print a thing right now.'

He offered Miss Mowatt a seat and sat down himself with a feeling of relief, which lasted till Frank knocked and entered with his tool box.

'Sorry about the delay, the law moves in mysterious ways.'

'And performs no wonders, I fear,' Alice said.

'Miss Mowatt,' he said, acknowledging the executive presence.

'How soon can you sort us out here, Frank?' she asked.

He checked. 'Five minutes tops should do it.'

Preston suggested they re-convene in an hour but Alice wasn't having it.

'It's always interesting,' she said, from her chair at Preston's desk, 'to see the world from someone else's perspective, don't you think?'

She was surveying the battery of equipment and the shelf of software manuals in their ring binders, which confirmed her in her view that the only resource which counted, when the chips were down, was staff. Any equipment he'd asked for had been supplied. Any software too. He couldn't claim he hadn't had support. It wasn't the wiring in the room that needed sorting, it was the wiring in his head.

'If you're asking me, Miss Mowatt,' Alastair said, 'I have to agree with you there. When you've sailed the seas like I have, you see the old country in a different way.'

'I'm sure you do, Alastair,' she said, but she was looking at Preston.

When Gemma arrived Alastair took it as his cue to leave. The room was overflowing, the temperature rising, the oxygen fast depleting. There was an atmosphere and it wasn't comfortable.

'I'll just remove these off-cuts then,' he said, scooping them up and making his escape.

Preston stood and offered Gemma his chair but she declined.

'Never lie when you can sit,' she said, 'never sit when you can stand, never walk when you can run, never take the lift when you can use the stairs.'

'That would be part of your fitness regime,' Frank suggested, emerging from under a counter with a screwdriver.

'It would be,' Gemma said, 'if I stuck to it.'

'I'll need to tidy up but I can do that later. You have the power,' he said, adding on impulse, 'use it wisely.' Thinking he had gone too far with Alice in the room he apologised. 'Sorry. Couldn't resist it.'

When Frank had gone, Alice spoke. 'You've never heard of the distance selling directives, have you, Mr Blair?'

'That sort of thing was always going to be farther down the road.'

'So far down you couldn't see it, didn't know it was there.'

Preston knew he was trapped. He couldn't show them paper copy and his computer was sitting there, staring at him blankly, just waiting to be switched on. But with both ladies present he couldn't conduct a search without them noticing.

'Okay,' Preston admitted, 'I hadn't got round to the legal side of it yet.'

Alice looked at leaflets on his desk. 'Some very interesting information about wardrobes here. Were you planning to ship those to Orkney as well?'

'That's different,' Preston said. 'Local customers will want to browse our stock, all of it, and compare it with other retailers before they decide to come in. We can't exclude wardrobes because of one account-holder in South Ronaldsay.'

'Yes Preston,' Gemma said, 'but that account holder has to know what she can order and what she can't. It has to be clear.'

'Beyond peradventure,' Alice said. She was quoting Hector, who had borrowed the phrase from the UN High Representative for Bosnia and Herzegovina.

'I realise the site has a few shortcomings,' Preston began, but Alice cut him short.

'Mr Blair, in the light of Miss Bonthrone's analysis which, I have to say, gives us cause for concern, we have agreed the way forward. Gemma?'

'It gives me no pleasure to say this, Preston, but we are prepared to give you one month from today to sort things out. In view of the time you've had already we both feel this is reasonable. If, at the end of one month, your website has changed from the hazardous hard-hat area it is at present to something which is both fully functioning and legally complaint, then we will review the position again. I'll put all this in writing, of course, so there can be no misunderstanding.'

'And if it's deficient in any respect, however small?' Preston asked, already feeling aggrieved.

'In that event we reserve the right to contract the project out and re-negotiate your employment with this firm. Furthermore, we reserve the right to determine whether or not a deficiency is small.'

'So that's it then.' Preston sighed. 'I have been working at this you know.'

'We know, Mr Blair,' Alice said, 'but to little effect. We have to judge your work as we would anyone else's, not by good intentions or hours put in, but by results. You must realise that, surely.'

Preston didn't have the stomach to go straight home that night, driving instead to a place he seldom visited, the shore, where he parked at the end of one of the many windswept streets leading to the promenade and sat behind the wheel looking morosely out to sea. A variety of sea birds, all of them toiling to make a living, flew in and out of his field of view, but he didn't know one from another. So industrial fishing was killing the sand eels, what did he care if they starved? Who needed sea birds anyway?

By the time he got home his mother had left the house, leaving him a note concerning food in the oven. All he needed to do was reheat it. Perhaps it was force of habit that she still felt responsible for him, or maybe she liked having someone at home. No doubt she felt more secure. He understood his mother, but she didn't understand him. How could she? There were too many things she didn't know because he kept them to himself.

His life was staring to contract. He had to escape, but how was he going to do it? He had a strong desire, almost a need, to talk with Janice, whoever she was, though he felt he knew. She wasn't on line at first, though her absence was probably due to the time difference. She would still be at work. He imagined her in a large institution where customers filled in request slips at the front desk, having no direct access to the shelves, a youthful librarian hurtling round the stacks on roller blades retrieving requests, a waitress in a café of the mind.

Then she arrived. He asked her how she was and she was fine. As he had hoped, she asked him the same thing. And he told her, just a little. Problems at work, no doubt she knew how it was. As he filled in the picture bit by bit, always with reluctance and at her request, never threatening her sympathy threshold, he called up her picture and parked it at the edge of the screen. If she took her glasses off Janice could be quite a looker.

A hierarchy might help a person in your situation, she suggested. Like you could start with what's achievable most easily and list your way down, then start at the top of the list and knock items off it one by one. That way you'd know you were achieving, your self-esteem would grow. I intuit it's low right now, she observed, though he'd pretty much told her that himself. The thing of it is, Preston, if something can't be done don't waste your effort. Relax, let it go. Hey, it's gone! Doesn't that feel good? He told her it did. It felt good. It felt great.

You have a web cam, Preston, Janice asked? He had one at work, not at home. You're at home then. That's right, he replied. Just an idea, she said. A good one, he replied.

He looked at her picture again. He'd been right. This was the girl herself or she wouldn't be planning to let him see her live.

13

In the days following the show-down with Astrid Bonthrone, it was clear that Gemma's ultimatum to Preston was not having the desired effect. If anything, his effort had diminished. Always in transit between his office and other departments, he resembled a space probe which lacked sufficient energy of its own and so employed the slingshot effect about a powerful gravitational attraction to reach its destination. And the sultry Anita was very attractive.

He travelled to white goods via cosmetics, furniture via cosmetics, consumer electronics via cosmetics, the toilet via cosmetics. And he made these journeys so frequently it was clear he was losing it in more ways than one. Pamela had heard from June, who'd overheard Mr Gibson on the phone, that Preston's job was on the line, but she only believed it after Preston told her himself.

'You'll be happy now,' he said, when they met by chance in the lift. 'You've had it in for me from day one.'

'I beg your pardon?'

'Don't pretend you don't know, going for the sympathy vote with that chair of yours.'

'What the hell are you talking about, Preston!'

He took a letter from his pocket and waved it in front of her.

'They have no idea how complicated it is. None! So if they think I'm toiling away to complete it in a month they've got another think coming. I've got better things to do with my time!'

When the lift doors opened on the fifth floor Pamela impeded his exit.

'You were going to your office, right?'

'Where else,' he said. 'My empire, my world.'

Boy what bitterness was there, she thought, then the doors shut and the lift continued to six.

'The restaurant,' she said, 'we need to talk.'

'Never go there. Don't use it,' he said.

'You do today. My shout. You've some explaining to do.'

As usual the place was packed but they found a table at the edge of the seating area, still covered with empty mugs and crumb-laden plates. Pamela suggested they claim it anyway.

'I know you said it was your shout but obviously,' Preston said, 'that's a bit impractical here.'

'You think I can't handle it?' she asked. 'What would you like?' Then, in an afterthought, 'I'm talking snacks here, by the way, not a three course meal.'

Preston wasn't aiming high, a coffee would be fine. Filter, latte, cappuccino? He didn't care. Okay then, he said, a cappuccino with a light sprinkling of chocolate. Preston had some difficulty imagining how Pamela could hold a tray with two coffees on it and push her chair at the same time, she didn't have two pairs of hands. But she returned with nothing and a smile. She'd paid, she explained, their order would follow in a minute.

'You've got it made,' Preston complained, 'how do you do it?'

'Well the first thing I do is ask politely,' she said, 'and if that doesn't work I refer to the Disability Discrimination Act.'

'Fine for some.'

He should know, she thought, disabled as he was between the ears.

'So show me the letter.' He handed it to her and she read it, then a second time more carefully. 'Okay, so when you say you have a month you actually have two.'

Preston looked surprised. 'How do you make that out?'

'This doesn't give you notice. It says that if you don't come good in a month, then they'll give you notice.'

'You're right, but where does that get me? My time would be better spent lining up interviews, testing the waters.'

She gave him back the letter. 'Preston, this is your first job.'

'I realise that.'

'So anyone else you approach will want a reference. If you don't get one from Gemma you won't get one at all. So try earning your money, do your level best or you're dead in the water. Oh, and by the way, that would be the water you're testing.' Preston looked sick. He hadn't considered that.

'Remember you said you'd better things to do with your time?' He nodded. 'Well you don't. Now,' she said, 'what the hell did you mean by that cheap shot about the sympathy vote, and remember you're drinking my coffee.'

'I shouldn't have said it,' Preston admitted, as close as he came to looking abashed.

'I know, but you did.' She was angry. 'Why was that?'

He didn't know himself so he guessed.

'I was just lashing out. Frustration really. I mean, Pamela, damn it, I'm having my throat cut here by your bosom buddy Gemma and that hit-woman friend of hers, Astrid what's her name, the lawyer with the legs. Not to mention our leader, dear sweet Alice. Butter wouldn't melt in her mouth – yeah, right! And while we're at it,' he said, taking a second sheet of paper from his pocket, this time a folded memo, 'How about this!'

Headed VEHICULAR INGRESS AND EGRESS, it had Alastair written all over it. Space in the car park would, in future, be reserved for customers. The only exceptions would be senior management and disabled badge holders.

'Absolutely unbelievable,' Preston said, taking it back and hitting it with his fist.

'Comes as news to me,' she said. 'When did you get it?'

'Today. It was left on my desk. You'll have a copy yourself.'

'I assure you I don't. First I've heard of it.'
'You didn't have a hand in it? You weren't consulted?'
'No.'
'It's still discrimination though, isn't it, against the able-bodied? You'll come waltzing in here of a morning, into your designated parking bay, and hell mend the rest of us.'

Pamela wasn't as astonished as she should have been.

'Preston,' she said, 'you're accusing me of waltzing when I can hardly walk. I expect to be the last person off the plane, the last person leaving the burning building. And you know why?'

'No.'

'In case I prejudice the safety of normal people like yourself,' she said, using her index fingers to place inverted commas round normal, 'yet you grudge me a parking space!'

She was right, he did, but he couldn't admit it. He was about to complain about something else when she stopped him, pointing out that the memo was undated.

'So what?' Preston asked, in a belligerent tone.

So it probably hadn't been released yet, it was a draft. The chances were Alice hadn't seen it, nor Gemma.

'Right enough,' Preston said, 'that Geddes man is a jumped-up jackass, an officious buffoon.'

Pamela admitted this was a point of view, and though she couldn't explain how the memo had landed on his desk it was obvious to Preston. He was about to explain it to Pamela when Bertrand appeared behind him with a tray in one hand and an extravagant flourish in the other.

'Bonjour mes amis, how are the tricks?'

'Bog off, Bertrand, there's a good lad,' Preston said, without turning round, 'and take your cod French with you. The adults are talking here.'

'Now wait a minute, Preston,' Pamela said, appalled by his rudeness, 'Bertrand has kindly brought us our coffees. As a favour, right Bertrand?'

'Mais oui,' Bertrand said, placing them carefully on the table. 'Exactement.'

Preston groaned. 'Oh God, I don't know how much more of this crap I can take.' But Bertrand didn't hear him. He'd already cleared the table and gone, with a deft flick of his cloth to disperse the crumbs.

'He's a fraud, you know that don't you, he comes from Motherwell.'

'I've heard it said.'

Bertrand amused her and he plainly wasn't stupid. He'd figured out long ago that the best way to counterfeit French origins was a base of French phrases lightly garnished with eccentric English. I am doing this, he would say to his kitchen colleagues, as fastly as I can. Or again, these young persons are causing, how you say, the commotions.

'That Astrid woman . . .'

'Never met her.'

'She praised my design and now she's flushing me down the pan!'

'It looks good,' Pamela agreed, 'it looks great, but it doesn't work.' In that respect it was an accurate reflection of himself. 'You started the job without a plan and you've kept on doing it that way ever since. You have never, not once, sat down and analysed what really needed to be done. Most people, when they're lost, ask for directions.'

'Well if you really want to know,' Preston said, 'the last thing I need is directions. I always know exactly where I am!' He was referring to his GPS hand-set, but before he could say so a better put-down occurred to him. 'I'm going to ask advice from someone who applied for the job and wasn't good enough to get it? I don't think so! What really gets me,' he said, abruptly changing the subject, 'is that he expects people to fall for it.'

'Who?'

'Bertrand. He actually thinks all it takes to get one past us is a few French phrases.'

Now that was an interesting observation, Pamela thought. It often seemed to her that Bertrand was openly playing a part. His audience knew he was acting and therein lay his pleasure. Contrast that with Preston, raging against the injustices of the world. Preston was also playing a part, that of the competent web designer, but the game was up when his audience saw through the act.

'Pamela, hello!' Preston snapped his fingers in front of her nose to bring her back. He was reading from the memo. 'And who the hell does he mean by board level and above. The Monarch? The Deity?'

Pamela shrugged. She didn't know. 'It's just the way he puts things.'

'Or maybe it's that Frank chap. He seems to have risen well above the basement where he belongs.'

This was Preston at his worst. She felt like asking him where, in his estimation, he belonged himself but decided against it when she saw Mr Gibson arriving for his lunch. She resolved to make her escape while he was still in the queue, which might have worked if he had joined it.

'Ah, there you are, Miss Ross, I've been looking for young Frank. Is anyone sitting here?' he asked, indicating one of the two empty chairs.

Preston leaned forward and studied it closely. 'Unless my eyes deceive me, Mr Gibson, no one is sitting there.' He prodded the space above the seat with his free hand. 'No, not a soul.'

Mr Gibson ignored him and sat down.

'Excuse me,' Preston said, 'but the lady and I are having a private conversation.'

'If that is your objective, Mr Blair,' Mr Gibson said, 'you would be well advised to conduct it in a private place. This restaurant is a public facility. I thought Mr Figures might be interested in these,' he said, taking a bundle of car stickers from his inside pocket and handing one to Pamela.

'Why would you think that, Mr Gibson, surely you know he doesn't drive?'

'Indeed I do, Miss Ross. I was thinking more of the windows at his flat. Not to mention,' he added, 'the magnum opus he is presently engaged on. I think you'll agree that this message is relevant to that?'

Preston craned round to read it and saw the words WHAT WOULD JESUS DRIVE?

'We start from the premise,' Mr Gibson said, 'that the Lord who created all thing wishes harm to none. From that I think we can safely infer that Jesus would select a vehicle with the least damaging exhaust emissions. He would therefore avoid a gas guzzler, or indeed a showy but impractical model such as yours, Mr Blair. And if I may say so, this sticker would be much more to the point than the one you presently display which, to those of the faith, is not in good taste.'

Given the fact that he might soon be unemployed, Preston decided his current sticker was irreverently to the point and declined Mr Gibson's offer. Pamela took one for herself and asked for another.

'Dear me, Miss Ross, I hadn't put you down as a two-car person.'

'Look on the bright side, Mr Gibson,' Preston said, with a smile, 'she can't drive both of them at once. You have trouble driving one of them at once, don't you Pamela?'

'One for the car, one for the chair,' she said, taking her stickers.

'I would have said, Mr Blair, that Miss Ross does very well. She's an example to us all in the consistently cheerful way she triumphs over adversity.'

'Oh come on, Mr Gibson, lighten up! It was a just a bit of black humour.'

'Black it may have been, humour it was not.'

As Mr Gibson rose to leave, Colin McCandless arrived, several creases visible on his shirt. Without betraying his disapproval, Mr Gibson offered him his seat.

'What is this, musical chairs?' Preston protested. 'You don't get a moment's peace in this place, even during a break!'

'Come off it, Preston,' Colin said, sitting down, 'your working day is one long break from start to finish. I've been to your office three times already today and you weren't there.'

'Sanctimonious bastard,' Preston said.

'What?'

'Not you. Gibson. Can't stand the man. Takes his pulpit wherever he goes. Anyway, leaving him to one side . . .'

'I've checked those pages of yours, Preston. First time I'd seen them, by the way.'

'And?'

'There's no way we're selling TV sets from a website.'

'Why not? Other people do.'

'Large organisations maybe, not us. TVs have to be installed, which nowadays means getting them to talk to other equipment – satellite boxes, cable boxes, Freeview boxes, VCRs, DVDs, surround-sound systems. A lot of my time is already spent on the phone taking customers with problems through these procedures. If we start moving this stuff in bulk through a web site we couldn't cope. And another thing,' he added, 'TVs aren't like frying pans or curtains rails, they can malfunction and they do. What happens then?'

'Customers send them back?'

'Preston, have you any idea how heavy a large TV set can be? What's the customer supposed to do, pop it in a giant jiffy bag and take it round to the post office?'

'Won't be my problem,' Preston said, 'not for much longer.'

'Is there something we should know?' Colin asked, sensing a breaking story.

'No,' Preston said, glaring at Pamela, 'though I can reveal I'm working on another project at the moment, and if it takes off the sky's the limit.'

Pamela assumed this was hot air, which it was since Preston was referring to his experiments with fragrances and his mother's fond fantasy of success on a commercial scale.

'Other irons in the fire, eh?' Colin said, with a wink at Pamela. 'Another string to your bow.'

Pamela smiled sweetly. 'He'd have to have a string in the first place.'

Preston rose so quickly his knee caught the table and spilled what was left of his coffee.

'I don't have to take this from a pair of inadequates like you.'

To Colin he said he would get back to him within five working days, to Pamela that he would take the question of car parking right to the top and, if that failed, to judicial review. He made recourse to law sound cost-free to himself and threatening to everyone else.

'He doesn't take kindly to criticism, does he,' Colin said.

'If he wants to play with the grown-ups he'll have to learn.'

Back in his office Preston came to two decisions. He would leave the site in the best condition possible before the month was out. Then any reference they provided would have some positives at least. No doubt they would damn him with faint praise, but faint was better than none at all. While he was downloading the EU distance selling directives he composed a short e-mail to Pamela thanking her for her advice, telling her he was acting on it, and adding that she shouldn't take seriously his remarks about the chair, they were simply part of the cut-and-thrust of office politics. His second decision was to plan his revenge.

Of course it might not come to that, they might retain his services. But he doubted it, and when they hit him he would hit back. Where it hurt. In the reputation department. He glanced round his office as regulations poured from his printer. He didn't have much to lose, it wasn't exactly a palace. And when his eye fell on his camera past impressions flooded back. For what were eyes but cameras, saving their files to the deeper levels of the brain. Retrieval could be a problem, everyone knew that, it wasn't guaranteed, but association usually worked the trick as it had now.

He left the printer to its own devices, picked up the camera, put it in his hold-all and walked out of the office, locking the door behind him. He met no one he knew on the lift, which took him silently to the seventh floor. Anyone seeing him would assume he was heading for the activity room, why else would he be carrying a Pro Tour (Limited Edition) sports bag? Exiting the lift, he walked along the corridor to the meeting room. The door was shut, but putting his ear to it he couldn't hear a thing, no clink of tea cups, no rustle of papers, no one droning on. It was empty. As was Alice's office, though that was a harder call. He'd heard that she liked to work with the door open so, since it was shut, she probably wasn't behind it.

It was all happening in the activity room, where a plump sales assistant from menswear was working an ab-frame and a girl with an iPod was cycling flat out to music he couldn't hear. The man saw him, the girl did not. He put down his bag and removed his camera and towel. Not so much a bag as a symbol of a man in his prime and, given the supple black leather, handy side pockets, and smooth-as-silk easy-glide zip, a functional work of art. His intention was to wear the towel round his neck and hide the camera under it.

He waited outside the boardroom door and listened. Nothing. Not a squeak. So he entered and shut the door behind him. The room was empty, but his memories of it weren't good: the lather of late arrival, Gibson's sarcastic remarks, Alice out of the blue asking him to write a paper and, worst of all, Gemma Laing slipping from the room to set him up. That should have put him on his guard, alerted him to the possibility they might be planning to shaft him. But it hadn't. He still had a lot to learn about manoeuvring in the workplace. No doubt there was a chapter in the staff manual entitled the Mowatt Machiavelli. If there wasn't, there should be.

He studied the coat of arms on the wall. This was a subject he knew nothing about but detested anyway, representing as it did a social order where rank and status lorded it over ability. As far as he knew. none of the Mowatts still living was titled, nor had any title ever been mentioned in connection with Archibald Mowatt, the founder of the business, not in his hearing anyway. Perhaps a title wasn't a required for this feudal flummery, but it was worth looking into.

He switched on his camera and removed the lens cap. Since the bearings in question included a motto, he focused on that, pressing his up and down buttons till the letters were totally crisp in his viewfinder, then took three shots of the complete coat of arms. *Hic habitat felicitas*, what the hell did that mean? His mother would probably know, she was into languages, and if she didn't she'd know someone who would – a Latin teacher fighting to control a class of three sixth year girls buying social advancement at a private school with turrets set in several acres of its own grounds.

Leaving the boardroom, he shut the doors behind him and wandered back towards the lift, passing the room marked PS. He'd noticed it earlier but this time it was slightly ajar, an open invitation to get past its keypad entry device. Feeling like a safe-cracker with no need for drills or explosives, he pushed it open farther and walked in.

Preston was now in the penthouse suite, which he had never seen before, and he was impressed. It reminded him of a hotel room, but better. The living area was reasonably spacious with a three piece suite, television set, coffee table, mini-bar and commercial prints which, if they did nothing else, broke up the monotony of the walls. There was only one window, but a large one, looking out over the city.

He picked up a book from the table and glanced at the title: A Brief History of British Cooperation from the Fenwick Weavers to the Present Day. That's what these historians did, he realised now, selected a juicy period and squeezed it dry. The tome had over six hundred pages. Given the dated appearance of the cover, the present day probably meant 1935 or thereabouts. Plainly the choice of an insomniac, he put it down with relief.

A quick look in the small galley kitchen revealed wall cabinets with plates, cups, saucers, and an encouraging variety of glasses. Cooking would be minimal given a hob and microwave but no oven. The cutlery drawer, he was pleased to see, contained a bottle opener and a cork screw. But kitchens had never interested him much and he moved swiftly on to the bedroom. Large wardrobe, good-sized double bed, and laid out on top of it a uniform: a dark green tunic with black facings, a freshly pressed pair of dark green trousers and a Balmoral complete with regimental badge and a single long feather. Someone, it seemed, was going to a fancy dress ball.

He took two shots of the outfit, one with flash, and left to check the bathroom expecting the full works, including a jacuzzi. But before he got there he heard the cistern flush and the sound of running water. He should have reacted more quickly but he hadn't made it to the door when old

Hector Mowatt appeared, towel in hand. To Preston's amazement, he didn't seem in the least surprised to see him.

'Good afternoon, young man,' he said, finishing off his hands. He spotted the camera on its lanyard round Preston's neck. 'You have your camera I see.'

'Yes Mr Mowatt, I'm taking shots of the store for a report I'm writing. I'd just visited the boardroom when I spotted the open door and came in. Hope you don't mind.'

'Not at all,' Hector said, 'why would I mind? Take a seat,' he said indicating the sofa.

Many years before, Hector had grown a moustache to compensate for loss of hair on the head, and he appeared to be wearing remarkably wide Black Watch braces. Preston was reminded of officers he'd seen in pictures of the First World War.

'So which department are you in?' he asked, though he should have known since he was at the interview. 'I see you have an ID card but I can't read the damn things unless I change my glasses. Tried bifocals, can't stand them. A complete waste of money if you ask me.'

'I suppose you could say I'm in a department of one,' Preston replied. 'Preston Blair, I'm designing the new web site.'

'What can I offer you?' he asked, waving vaguely in the direction of the mini-bar. 'Just had it re-stocked. A soft drink, beer, whisky? I can even stretch to salted peanuts!'

The old buffer seemed pleasant enough but then, Preston thought, he could afford to be.

'A soft drink, thanks. Orange, if you have it.'

Hector brought two glasses from the kitchen, poured himself a whisky and an orange for his guest. It was seeing the drinks which gave Preston the idea.

'To your continued good health, Sir Hector,' he said, raising his glass.

'Oh no, dear me, definitely not,' Hector said. 'Plain Hector Mowatt will do me fine.'

14

Looking out their dining room window was always a joy, especially on a sunny day, since all they could see was their own ground stretching into the distance complete with lawns, cropped grass verges, flower beds, shrubs, trees, and the wide gravel path which ran along the front of the house to the garage where Alice kept her bicycle. A spacious garden, it was popular with birds, who were always welcome, and Tweed, Hector's golden retriever. What a lovely animal, he would think to himself, as he ambled past.

Hector liked to talk at the breakfast table while leafing through the paper, and might have done the same at his evening meal had Alice allowed it.

'I see that woman's installing surveillance cameras now,' he remarked, 'her neighbours are complaining again.'

'If you were as famous as she is, you'd do the same,' Alice replied. 'Fame comes with a price like everything else. Recognised wherever you go, photographed by all and sundry. I couldn't stand it.'

There was a short silence, broken by Hector crunching toast. He hadn't been photographed lately, but he had been talking to a man with a camera.

'Bumped into that Blair chap in the suite. Said he'd just come from the board room. Claimed to be taking photographs.'

'How did he get in?'

'Ah,' Hector said, turning a page, 'bit of a confession there. I'd left the door open.'

'And what was he doing,' Alice asked, looking at him over her half-moon reading glasses, 'with his camera?' He had her attention now.

'Claimed he was checking security, some paper he was writing. Gave me the impression he was doing it for you. Did wonder at the time. Seemed a bit unlikely.'

Very unlikely, Alice thought, that a man whose job depended on the successful completion of one project would be wasting time on another. She couldn't escape the feeling that something was going on.

'So what did you talk about, yourself and Mr Blair?'

'Not a lot really. The history of the store, mostly. The family, that sort of thing.'

'If you'll excuse me,' she said, rising from the table, 'I have a phone call to make. I may have to go in.'

'You work yourself far too hard, you know,' Hector said, not in the least concerned.

'I realise that, father,' she replied, 'but it keeps me off the streets.'

She left immediately, making good time through the traffic. Alice cycled to work on an old bone-shaker with outbreaks of visible rust and a tired wicker basket slung from the handlebars, the same bike she had used as a schoolgirl. She'd considered buying a new one, but apart from its heavy frame her machine had everything she wanted and an appearance so antique no one in his right mind would steal it.

When she arrived she took it to her office using the service lift, then headed to the boardroom and looked round. There was nothing there worth photographing, so Preston had been spinning her father a line. She moved quickly on to the penthouse suite, entered the code and walked in. As far as she could see, nothing was missing. The towels were still in the bathroom, the bed still neatly made and Hector's spare trousers, jackets and suits hanging in the wardrobe. The uniform was no longer there, but that was now at home.

Being in this room, looking into the wardrobe and seeing these articles of male clothing reminded her of another life, a life which might have been had things turned out differently. Why had she never married? She'd been asked this question often over the years and her reply had always been the same. She had nothing against the idea, and no doubt a satisfactory man had been out there, but their paths hadn't crossed. With a slight tinge of regret, nothing more, she shut the wardrobe doors and left the bedroom. Which left one last thing to check, the mini-bar. But everything appeared to be in place. It certainly hadn't been raided. Whatever Preston was up to didn't involve theft.

On her way to check in with Gemma she visited the restaurant. She liked to drop in when it was busy, partly to see how her staff were coping but also because a crowded restaurant was a successful restaurant and she enjoyed being part of it. In previous years she would have ordered a latte, but being more conscious of her health her new drink of choice was green tea which, Lynn assured her, was rich in flavonoids, an argument she also used to justify her fondness for red wine. All the tables were occupied and the noise was considerable, much of it coming from ladies she thought of as matrons, though some were younger than she was. She sat at one of the bar stools ranged round the counter which separated the restaurant from other areas of the sixth floor. It was then she noticed it, a Guzmania dying from lack of water. Really, how ridiculous was that! She poured what was left from her cup onto the dry, parched soil, hoping it would help, and pushed through the swing doors to the back shop.

'Good morning, Miss Mowatt.'

Who was that? She couldn't remember her name. 'Good morning. I'm looking for Bertrand.'

The girl pointed him out but he had had already seen her.

'Bonjour Miss Mowatt,' he said. 'As you can see, 'I am busy with the all day breakfasts.'

He glanced at her head, which wasn't covered. 'Are we remembering our hat?'

'For heaven's sake, Bertrand, I'm just popping in for a moment. I think the regulations can cope with that.' Alice looked round at the bustling kitchen staff. 'I can see you're busy, this won't take long. I was wondering about the plants.' Bertrand paused for a second, his fish slice stalled in mid air above a hot plate.

He looked blank. 'The plants?'

'You know,' Alice said, 'the plants in the restaurant area. Who's supposed to water them?'

'Strictly entre nous,' he said, 'I haven't the clue. I cook plants. For me, that's as far as it goes.'

Gemma was pleased to see her, as always, but Alice was surprised to find three young people in her office.

'Ah,' Gemma said, 'what excellent timing. This,' she said to the visitors, 'is our chief executive, Alice Mowatt. What that means, basically, is that she runs the business.'

'What,' said a sulky-looking girl with high-gloss lipstick and a light pink cap at a raffish angle, 'all of it?'

'Not single-handedly, of course, she does have help.'

Chloe looked Alice up and down, her sneer suggesting that Alice would need it.

'Ms Mowatt,' Gemma said, 'allow me to introduce Chloe, Sarah and David.'

Chloe, Sarah and David were on the YES scheme, Gemma reminded her – say 'YES' to youth – and would be assigned to departments within the store for six weeks on a part-time basis. They'd been specially selected by their schools. Alice didn't doubt it for a moment, the main criterion being desperation to get rid of them for a while. Alice had known about this, she'd agreed to it three months earlier, but in the interval had forgotten all about it. The Youth Enterprise Scheme, giving children from under-privileged backgrounds a taste of working life was, Gemma had assured her, a very worthwhile initiative.

'So Chloe,' Alice said, 'what would that object be glittering in your navel? We wouldn't want it setting off the alarms!'

Sarah and David grinned. Chloe shot them a filthy look and eyeballed Alice closely.

'Ears, belly buttons, same difference. You pierce one, I pierce the other.'

'I trust it's galvanised,' Alice said, thinking of rust.

'Stainless steel, if you must know,' Chloe said. 'Right, Sarah?'

'Right.'

Faced with such confident native intelligence Alice fell back on asking Chloe which department she'd be in. She wasn't sure so Gemma checked her paperwork. The salon and cosmetics. Chloe was into streaked hair and painted toe-nails.

When they headed off to their respective destinations Alice leafed through their forms. She wasn't surprised to read that Chloe's interests were boys, clubbing, fashion, hair and beauty. Contraception wasn't on the list, but she trusted Chloe had covered that angle too. David's interests were confined to sport and cars. He'd been assigned to white goods in the hope that his interest in technology might extend to washing machines and cookers. Sarah, Alice was amazed to read, wanted to be a plumber. Her careers teacher had told her there was a shortage of plumbers and happened to mention how much a plumber could earn. She'd be working with Alastair.

'Good God,' Alice said, 'he agreed to that?'

'He was hostile to the idea at first. To be perfectly honest, he made a number of sexist remarks which I won't repeat here. He's totally unreconstructed, you know. Anyway, he changed his mind when he met her. She has winning ways, that one. I think she'll go far.'

'I trust Mrs Geddes won't get to hear of this.'

'Not if Alastair has anything to do with it. She looks great in overalls, apparently.'

'You couldn't make it up,' Alice said. 'There was something I was hoping to discuss but I can see,' she said, looking at the files on Gemma's desk, 'that you have rather a lot on your plate.'

Alice took her through the business with Hector, the penthouse suite, and Preston's interest in the Mowatt family history. And the camera. What was going on there? He admitted having come from the boardroom and claimed to be working on his paper concerning security.

'You think he's up to something and can't imagine what.'

'Exactly,' Alice replied.

'Ask Kathy. She keeps a close eye on Preston.'

'Now why am I not surprised to hear that?' Alice asked.

Alice took the escalator to the first floor where she saw Kathy pretending to take an interest in gifts: presentation sets of china thimbles, tie pins with clan crests, gift boxes of single malt whiskies complete with two leaded crystal shot glasses and a guide to the distilleries.

'Can I help you, madam?' Alice asked, appearing out of nowhere on her blind side.

'Well yes,' Kathy replied, when she realised who it was, 'if I send these thimbles to a relative in Canada do I have to pay VAT or do they?'

'I'm glad you asked me that,' Alice replied, having no idea what the answer was. 'Now, about Preston.'

'Oh,' Kathy said, 'don't get me started on him!'

But Alice had no choice. And so she discovered that Preston used his computers to access dubious material.

'You have evidence of any of this?'

'Not yet, Miss Mowatt, but I'll tell you one thing, he's really furious about the memo.'

'Memo? My goodness,' Alice said, her eye caught by a rail of ties, 'what a price!'

'He bent Pamela's ear on the subject for half an hour. Called her for everything.'

'Kathy, what memo are we talking about here?'

'I've seen a copy. Pamela has it. Staff won't be allowed to park here any more.'

It was one of these days when nothing was going to plan. Alice had come in to investigate one problem only to discover another. She went to the nearest sales point and phoned Alastair.

'Hello, maintenance,' said a young female voice.

'I was hoping to speak to Mr Geddes,' Alice said.

'He told me if anyone called he'd be back in a minute.'

'Please tell him Alice phoned, she's on her way up, she's started her stop watch, and his minute will be up in sixty seconds.'

In fact, Alastair made it back to his office before Alice and was spreading his purchases on the table as Sarah tried to tell him what Alice had said.

'Did she sound annoyed?' Alastair asked.

'Probably,' Alice said as she walked in.

'Ah, Miss Mowatt, allow me to introduce my glamorous assistant.'

And she was attractive in her overalls, very fetching, her hair tied back in two short pigtails secured with rubber bands. Or were they washers? Maybe the girl had gone native already. Equally interesting was the table, which Alastair had covered in clean papers towels on which he had placed a colourful assortment of Danish pastries and other iced cakes.

'Sarah and I have met, and if I may say so, young lady, you seem to have your head screwed on the right way.' If only the same could be said of Alastair. Alice sat down on one of the two chairs.

'Feel free to sample the wares, ladies,' Alastair said.

'Oh we do, don't we, Sarah?' Alice said.

But Sarah looked wary. Something was going on and she wasn't sure what it was. Perhaps Alice and Mr Geddes... but the thought of two wrinklies getting their kit off and going at it on the table was too much. They'd be covered in icing and cream. Raisins everywhere.

'So where did you park this morning, Sarah, the staff car park?'

Sarah looked nonplussed. 'I came by bus.'

'That's probably just as well,' Alice said, 'what with our new policy coming in.'

'Yes, I've been meaning to up-date you on that,' Alastair said, believing he was being chivvied. 'It may not seem that way, but I've given it a lot of thought. Actually, I've completed a final draft which I can run past you any time you like. Reads pretty well, though I say so myself.'

'Now would be fine,' Alice said, gesturing Sarah to have a seat.

Alastair tracked down a copy of his policy and gave it to Alice. Finding he had nowhere to sit, he stood awkwardly while she read it, glancing at the kettle and the empty mugs. She was certainly taking it seriously; he had the impression that when she reached the bottom of the page she went right back to the top and read it again.

'Obviously,' Alastair said, 'I wouldn't go public on this without your say-so.'

'But Alastair,' Alice said, 'this document is already in the public domain.'

Alastair couldn't believe that Preston had a copy. The only contact he'd had with him lately was when he'd installed some trunking in his room. He hadn't mentioned parking, and even if he had, that wouldn't explain how Preston came to have a copy of the memo. Alice asked him to think back, had he taken any paperwork with him? A job sheet, perhaps, the manufacturer's instructions?

He had. That's what must have happened. When he'd picked up the paperwork from the table he'd taken a copy of the memo without noticing and left it in Preston's office by mistake. It sounded likely to Alice.

'If only you'd taken the precaution of covering your table with Danish pastries on that occasion,' she sighed, 'but your glamorous assistant hadn't joined us then.'

'I'm sorry about this, Miss Mowatt,' Sarah said, thinking she was implicated by the sudden outbreak of bakery products.

'Oh no, Sarah, you have nothing to apologise for. And neither does Alastair. It was an honest mistake. It could have happened to anyone. But now that it has we deal with it. Alastair,' she said, 'I think our guest could do with something hot and wet to go with her pastry.'

As she left, Alastair followed her out. 'So what do you think, Miss Mowatt? Would you say I've covered the angles? I did take soundings preparatory to writing it. As I'm sure you know, I like to keep my ear to the grindstone.'

'I'm sure you do,' Alice said, with a faint smile, 'though I would say, Alastair, that if we're going to tempt our colleagues into accepting this proposal we'll have to come up with something better than a one-off ex-gratia payment of five pounds.'

When she came to Preston's office she removed a set of keys from the quick-release clip attached to her belt, selected the correct one at the second attempt and let herself in.

Sitting at his desk behind his computer, Alice tried to enter Preston's mind. The room was small. Being windowless, it was easy to imagine it was airless as well, though Alastair assured her there was adequate ventilation. There were several other devices in evidence, but apart from a printer she had no idea what they were. She opened the top drawer of Preston's desk. It was crammed with leaflets from cosmetic companies and print-outs from their websites. She had never seen so much information about perfumes in one place at one time. Well, this was a move in the right direction; selling small, high value items through the site had to be a good idea.

She switched on Preston's computer, hoping to learn something, anything, from checking his files, but she was stopped in her tracks by a request for a password. Feeling less than hopeful she tried PRESTON. Asked if she wanted a clue she chose YES. The clue provided was 'full of grace', so she tried 'graceful' and then, though she wasn't of the faith herself, 'Our Lady'. Really, this was quite frustrating. She lifted Preston's phone and tried the control room. No Reply. But Pamela was in her office. I know you must be busy, Alice said, but I'm going to pay you a visit. Shouldn't take long.

As always, Pamela was pleased to see her, but Alice went straight to June's chair and collapsed on it with a heavy sigh.

'I was supposed to be at home with Hector today, but since I've come in it's been one thing after another, pillar to post, achieving absolutely nothing. Gemma's swamped with YES scheme trainees and associated paperwork, Kathy's fighting crime on the ground floor, or so she would have us believe, Alastair's setting up a bakery stall in his office – don't ask – and Preston's room is a shrine to technology, most of it unnecessary as far as I can see.'

Pamela didn't know what Preston's password was and, as she explained to Alice, the possible permutations of twenty-six letters, ten numbers and numerous symbols were inconceivably large. Trial and error was out of the question. Alice glanced round the room. Pamela cared for her plants, but she could hardly ask her to water the restaurant's as well.

'It seems a bit cool in here,' Alice said.

'June keeps turning the heating off at the valve. It's the latest craze, the Keep Cool Weight Loss Programme. You've probably heard of it, it's in all the magazines just now.' Alice didn't read that type of magazine so Pamela took her through it.

'The body loses heat more quickly in a colder environment so, if we keep a bit cooler, and provided we don't compensate by eating more, we start burning energy stored as fat to keep warm. That's it in a nutshell, as I understand it.'

Alice looked bemused. 'And who came up with this one?'

'Jefferson P Dangerfield, an America vet. You'll find his recent best-seller in June's drawer beside the biscuits: The Keep Cool Weight Loss Program, Homeostasis and Health.'

'A vet! I've heard it all now.' Alice shook her head. 'At increasingly frequent intervals I'm troubled by a desire to resign from the human race and I don't think it's age, though that may be a factor.'

Alice was starting to sound like Frank, who regularly voiced similar sentiments, accusing the species of piracy, pillage and plunder on a planetary scale, but Pamela knew she had come for other reasons.

When Alice had gone Pamela phoned Frank, who was on top of a ladder with a paintbrush. Hoping it wasn't an advertising call, he clambered down to answer the phone.

'Hello young man, how's it going? Are you okay to talk?'

'Hold on a second,' he said. He went to the kitchen, turned the radio down, brought back a stool and put it beside the phone. 'Okay.'

'It's all happening here,' Pamela said, 'you could stir it with a stick!' He could tell she was excited. 'Alice just left. She's found out about Alastair's memo. She's also heard about my run-in with Preston. Probably from Gemma, she's the only person I've told, apart from you.'

'I didn't tell her, if that's what you're thinking.'

'She asked me to confirm what she'd heard, which I did, in a watered down version.'

'Expletives deleted.'

'I don't believe in kicking a man when he's down.'

'Kicking isn't your strong point,' Frank agreed.

'Watch it, or I'll come round and sort you out.'

'Can't wait.'

'Anyway, it seems Hector found Preston in the penthouse suite with a camera and Alice thinks he's up to something. Any ideas? No one else has, apart from Kathy, who believes – wait for it – he's bugging the place!'

'Why would he do that?'

'Good question. Listen, how's it going?'

'Slowly.'

'What will you do for lunch?'

'Cross the road,' he said, meaning the Central Bar.

'Phone me when you've finished?'

What did she have in mind? It could range from simply hearing his voice, which he knew she liked, to going round for a meal and staying the night, which she probably liked as well, though other factors were involved. Sharing the same bed was easy but sharing it overnight needed forward planning. What shirt would he put on the following morning, which socks? And should he keep a supply of these items in her flat? Life before Pamela had been simple, the only aspect of it he regretted.

He was about to climb the ladder again when someone knocked at the door. It could only be Jenny or the postman, but he opened the door to the Gnome, his black and wizened look enhanced by a Berzerker Dissimulate T-shirt showing darkly under his black leather jacket.

'Greetings,' he said, walking past him into the hall. 'Saw the light on. Thought I'd see how you were doing. You know, Frank, you're the only person in the area with a creative bone in his body, someone I can talk to and hope to be understood.' This came as news to Frank: despite some of his wiring solutions he didn't consider himself the least bit creative. 'Though having said that,' the Gnome remarked, looking into the living room, 'you can take creativity too far.'

The Gnome was the last person Frank had expected to see. His popularity, never high, had reached new depths since the fire. Strictly speaking, and in the eyes of the law, it hadn't been his fault yet locals, knowing the woman was not only volatile but foreign, assumed he'd provoked her and might as well have set the blaze himself.

Frank caught up with his uninvited guest appraising the walls in the living room. Prior to letting the flat the owner had painted them white, but two years on some of them weren't as white as they had been. Stains had appeared here and there and usually Frank had no recollection of the cause. But what had started out as a re-touch job was turning into a major redecoration. Dilute his emulsion as he might, painting out the marks left new areas of paint which, even to a casual glance, stood out against the old.

'Yes,' the Gnome remarked, stroking his stubble thoughtfully, 'there's an abstract artist turns out stuff like this. What's her name again?' He couldn't remember. 'Never liked her work. A total lack of impact, for my money, anyway.'

'You don't have any money,' Frank said.

'Good point,' the Gnome admitted. 'You haven't lost that edge, I see.' Then, noting that Frank was working in several places at once, the Gnome caught up. 'You're planning to leave.'

'End of next week.'

'Nothing to do with me, I hope,' the Gnome said. And he appeared to mean it.

'Nothing at all,' Frank said, 'if we exclude noise in the small hours and nearly being burnt to a cinder.'

'That wasn't so funny for me either, you know. At least they've let you back in. I can't get back till the landlady fixes things up and she's dragging her heels. Serious argument with the loss adjuster, he claims she was under-insured. That's her story, anyway. Not a thing's been done. It's still a burnt out shell. I come back from time to time to move things out. A temporary measure, you understand.'

Maybe the landlady thought that if she dragged her heels long enough her troublesome tenant would move on. The Gnome walked over to the window.

'Nice view you have here, Frank, from the upper deck so to speak.' But Frank noticed he was looking up and down the street with some unease.

'Hear that,' the Gnome said, as his watch chimed the hour, 'lunch time. Game for a quick one over the road?'

Frank knew what he was up to. The Gnome was looking for protection in case Barbara was in the vicinity, lurking in a doorway or hidden behind a car. But what did he have to lose? His work wasn't going well and he could do with a break.

The Central Bar had its good points especially if, like the Gnome, you preferred a working man's pub where smoke from years gone by still seeped from the woodwork. In the not-so-distant past the floor had been covered in sawdust and dented metal cuspidors had been provided for the clientele, all male and, to a man, devotees of darts and dominoes. The walls displayed old photographs of the city in bye-gone days. Great Junction Street, 1908. Leith docks, 1911.

Settling down with a beer and a filled roll, the Gnome asked Frank where he'd be going when he left number six. Frank wouldn't have told him even if he'd known. He'd already moved out most of his belongings, some to his sister's and some to the basement workshop. He could live at Flora's but only when she wasn't there and had yet to decide where to stay when she was. As for Pamela, she didn't know he still had a problem. He had yet to tell her.

His thoughts returned to the penthouse suite. It would be ideal but too dangerous. Someone would notice. Cleaners would realise the bed had been slept in, however well he made it when he rose. Feeling on the verge of something without knowing what, he told the Gnome what he told everyone else.

'My sister's, till I find another place.'

Fuck the System sounded from the Gnome's jacket pocket, though not many people knew it. What's that, they would ask? Total Chaos, he would reply with a smirk, leaving them to figure it out.

'Sorry about this,' he said, and fished out his mobile. From what Frank could make out someone was offering to display a few of his pieces for four weeks definite, maybe even five.

'Someone taking your work?' Frank asked.

'Tearoom. Unlikely place, but you never know. Might move something. Stranger things have happened. It just takes one interested party. God knows I could do with the cash.'

The Gnome pocketed his phone and rose to leave.

'I know it's my round and all that, but I have to get there quickly. Finalise the deal before she changes her mind.'

He took a cautious look outside, waved, and left.

The TV was showing the news as a silent movie, an explosion at a plastics factory, workers by the roadside cut and bleeding, an ambulance leaving the scene. He'd dealt with someone last week. A customer on the first floor had cut herself opening a blister-wrapped pack. Could he get there as quickly as possible? He arrived to find her pressing a wad of paper towels against the index finger of her right hand, the sludge green of the paper showing a spreading patch of red.

Blood was oozing from the wound. Colin had a sympathetic arm round her shoulder but his mood didn't match.

'As I say, I'd have been only too happy to tell you. All you had to do was ask. Ah, Frank, Miss Venning here, a nasty-looking cut.'

'Okay, if you'll come with me we'll see what we can do.'

The medical room was on the fourth floor, the theory being that it was at an approximate mid-point in the building. Frank could tell his patient wasn't impressed by her surroundings as he parked her in one of the chairs.

'I'll just be a moment,' he said, as he washed his hands. 'Now then.'

'What are you doing?'

'Oh these,' he said, referring to the surgical gloves he was pulling on, 'I have to wear them when blood is involved. Company policy.'

'You think I have aids!' Miss Venning was outraged.

'Gloves work both ways, Miss Venning, I'm protecting you from direct contact with my hands. Now let's see what we're dealing with here.'

The cut was just above the first joint in her right index finger. He asked her to pull her chair closer to the sink and hold her finger under running water. While she was doing that he opened the cabinet and took out some supplies. The wound was clean and not very serious. He stopped the bleeding with a gauze pad, cleaned the area, and applied some antiseptic cream. As he was cutting a section of sticking plaster she cast back her mind to the incident.

'My boyfriend asked me to get replacement connectors.'

'He did?' Frank said, applying the plaster.

'He gave me the old ones. SCART to something or other. All I had to do was get the same, but I couldn't tell which was which through the packaging and I cut myself opening it.'

He asked her to wait while he completed an accident report, but she'd lost too much time already. She had to go.

'I'll sign it,' she said, 'you can fill it in later.'

When she left, he sat down and breathed easy again. Dealing with objects was one thing, dealing with people another. The room was fitted out sparely but in keeping with its size: a bed, two chairs, a sink with lever taps, a medicine cabinet, a cupboard, a locker and a stainless steel pedal bin for disposing of medical waste. All very businesslike, as was the décor; an institutional pale green.

A bed. A cupboard. A sink. Strange it was occurring to him now when it hadn't struck him before. Okay, the bed was of the medical variety and somewhat hard. So what? One floor above, they called a firm bed orthopaedic and marked up the price. Its movement was manual crank, it wasn't motorised. Again, so what? He didn't need movement anyway. Furthermore, he was a designated first-aider, no surprise to see him entering and leaving. On top of which he was maintenance, and maintenance went everywhere. Maintenance, as Mr Gibson put it, had a finger in every pie.

All he needed was the sleeping bag his sister had taken to Glastonbury and T in the Park. It would benefit from dry-cleaning but he knew where it was and she didn't use it any more. Sleep, rise, fold the bag and stow it in the cupboard. What could be easier than that? No disturbed sheets to give the game away. As for the penthouse suite, it would have its uses: television room, eating area, view out over the hill. Just till he found somewhere else, somewhere reasonable, somewhere that didn't cost an arm and a leg. Just till he was sorted.

15

It was late and Preston's mother had gone to bed. He raided the kitchen for a handful of biscuits and climbed to his room in the hope of a message from Janice or, better yet, finding her on line. She'd left a message, wanting to know if his site was coming good. It was. No fair-minded person could deny that. Having tracked down the directives referred to by the bitch Bonthrone, he had spent a good part of the afternoon listing the safeguards needed to comply with their requirements. How boring was that? But he was also growing weary of unproductive hours spent with essential oils, alcohol, small bottles and pipettes.

He had slowed down, taken the time to be methodical, filled in his spreadsheet for every new theme and variation, and still had failed to improve on Blair Number 1, a formula he could no longer replicate from those first impulsive days. That couldn't be right. Virtue should never go unrewarded: if it did, it lost what little attraction it had. In any case, all he had been looking for was a way in, an entrée. The effort he was expending to open the door was out of all proportion to the prospect beyond.

So what were his options? Giving up was one, or trying another approach. Tempting, but he couldn't think of any. And that left cheating, which appealed to him a lot. He could buy a fragrance from a reputable manufacturer, fill a bottle with it and pass it off as his own. An attractive idea but risky considering the recipient was in the trade. One whiff and he'd be rumbled. And then there were her friends, the cosmetic coven. What they didn't know wasn't worth knowing.

A Serious Business

Suppose she passed it round, Blair Number 2. One of them would surely sniff out his little secret. Unless, a much better idea, he adapted a quality product and made it his own. Such as Amerige.

He took off his shoes and padded along the corridor to the bathroom. Switching on the ceiling light activated a noisy extractor fan, so when he came in late he always used the shaving light above the mirror, a quiet click when the cord was pulled. About to open the medicine cabinet, he turned instead to the glass shelves on each side of the basin. They were loaded with an intimidating array of products: instant boost skin cleanser, hot cloth cleaner, soothing eye lotion, intensive nourishing treatment, revitalising moisturiser, eight hour cream skin protectant, lip fix cream, smoothing line serum and, last but not least, daily eye repair. His mother was concerned with laughter lines round the eyes, which was strange because she didn't laugh much. Mr Braunschweig didn't laugh much either. Life was a serious business for them both.

There were always odours in the bathroom, and those no longer included air fresheners since Mr Braunschweig had persuaded his mother to dispense with them.

'You must understand, Ada,' he had said, that all you are doing is releasing a chemical cloud into the air which, because you breathe, you then inhale. Have you any idea what these chemicals are?' Ada had no idea. 'From which it must follow, must it not, that you have no idea what effect they might be having on your lungs, blood-steam, tissues and vital organs?'

Ada was obliged to agree with this assessment.

'Is it any wonder,' Mr Braunschweig continued, not expecting an answer, 'that so many people suffer from asthma nowadays when they behave in this way?'

Preston found these arguments persuasive, but strange coming from a man who smoked a pipe. And that was what had been bothering him, a smell additional to the usual perfumes, after-shaves and less attractive human odours – the distinctive smell of Mr Braunschweig's tobacco which always made him think of marshmallow, though it might have been vanilla. Mr Braunschweig had been visiting tonight. Maybe he was still on the premises. Preston had a strong urge to tip-toe along to his mother's room, open the door and take a peek. But her curtains were heavy and lined. He wouldn't see a thing and he could hardly put on the light. Better to search for clues downstairs.

He looked in the sink for dirty dishes, cups and glasses, but it was empty. The pedal bin was more promising, but rummaging through it was distasteful and oil from discarded lettuce leaves proved hard to remove from his hands. He pulled the living room curtain aside to check for an alien car in the drive, but only his mother's modest jalopy was there in its usual place, and his own car, no longer glacier blue but pitch black in the dark. All in all, he thought, the likelihood was Mr Braunschweig had come and gone. Only the morning would tell.

Back in his room, Preston checked his mail. He'd forgotten how many messages he'd sent, but it must have been several. He'd posted a query to a newsgroup for Latin scholars and had several replies, not all of them complimentary. Publius took him to task for trying to get help with his homework. Agricola pointed out that his question concerning the use of Latin mottoes on coats of arms should have been directed to a heraldry group, it had ABSOLUTELY NOTHING to do with the Latin language per se. Claudian's lengthy reply was probably very interesting but, being entirely in Latin, there was no way of knowing. Then there was Dale. Dale was of the view that you could do what you liked with a Latin motto because no one in his right mind gave a toss anyway. Dale claimed to be fourteen years of age. If so, Preston thought, he was wise beyond his years.

A Serious Business

Two of his ex-colleagues from the graphic design course had responded to his query about the coat of arms itself, which he had sent as an attachment. Gail thought the whole thing 'altogether too flat,' and offered to re-draft it complete with ground plane and vanishing points. Alexander believed it had something to do with the Lord Lyon King of Arms, whose duty it was to regulate such things. A search along those lines might help. Preston glanced up at his newly installed web cam, the unblinking eye of the age, and winked. It didn't wink back. But Alexander might be on the money here. Surely the Lord Lyon was the bloke Miss Brodie went on about in the book, not that it did her much good.

His train of thought was interrupted by a flashing icon. Janice had noticed he was on-line. Okay to chat, she wondered? It was. Always okay to chat with you, he replied. Janice would be encouraged by that. She asked how things were going and he told her he'd taken her advice. You know, he reminded her, according to your hierarchy idea. Excuse me for asking, but when you said you worked at a medical centre – what do you do there, are you a doctor? Research student, pharmacology, she replied. Sounds interesting. It was. What are you doing at the moment? Chatting to you. Well, either she was one hundred percent literal or she had a sense of humour. He hoped it was the latter. Actually, she said, if you really want to know ... I do, he replied ... I'm working on an aliquot study comparing two drugs, how effective they are relative to their side-effects. Did you bring that web cam home? He had. So we could see each other right now.

It wasn't the best resolution, the lighting in her room was none too good, but when he had her picture in front of him, small but live action, it was exciting. Janice, a research student with dark lustrous centre-parted hair and glasses. When she reached up to adjust them it was with that fluid movement some women have, that slight outward turn of the hand with out-stretched fingers. No doubt when she ran, her feet described ellipses at thirty degrees to the ground. Women often ran like that, to catch a bus, to get out of the rain. She was wearing a cardigan over her top with small reflective buttons. Not at the fore-front of fashion then, but attractive nevertheless. For some reason, a problem at her end or his, they couldn't hear each other, but that could always be sorted.

If you don't mind a suggestion, she said. This customer safeguards thing, would it be an idea to check out existing sites and model your pages on these? Preston was impressed. You can type a lot faster than I can, he wrote, and you don't make mistakes. Why thank you, Preston, she replied, but it's no big deal. Typing's one thing, finding a soul mate's something else. Janice was telling him she hadn't yet found the love of her life, and she was telling him for a reason. In her own quiet way, and okay, she was doing it from a safe distance, Janice was coming onto him. It was well into the small hours but he'd never felt more awake.

When Ada rose later that morning, she enjoyed a leisurely breakfast leafing through holiday brochures. She hadn't heard him but knew Preston was in. The front door couldn't bolt itself. She was expecting Mr Braunschweig for lunch but that was some time off. Preston appeared two hours later and headed straight for the Frosties, though Ada remained to be convinced they did a body much good. You'd be better with fruit, she would say. Yes mother, he would reply, pouring himself a generous bowlful.

'You remember Mrs Linton, the one who does Latin crosswords, she confirmed to me yesterday that "hic habitat felicitas" means here dwells happiness. And I must say, Preston,' she added, 'your new-found interest in language is most encouraging.'

'It doesn't stretch to German.'

'Be that as it may, he's coming round for lunch.'

'He was here last night,' Preston said. 'He should have stayed over, saved himself the trouble of coming back.'

She looked at him uneasily.

'I could smell tobacco in the bathroom.'

'But he left the fan on for ages!'

'It'll take more than that, mum. It's a strong smell. It lingers in the curtains and towels.'

'Anyway' Ada said, 'we're thinking of taking a break in Germany this summer. A week or two.'

'That's what these brochures are about,' Preston said.

'Yes', his mother replied, but by now Preston was smelling more than stale tobacco. Perhaps Mr Braunschweig planned to introduce his mother to his relatives for their approval.

Ada left him to his breakfast and went upstairs. Was the odour of Anton's tobacco so pervasive? If it was, he might have to indulge his habit outdoors. On her way to the bathroom she passed Preston's room. She entered and opened the curtains. Why did he never do that for himself? On her way out she noticed a piece of paper on his desk and picked it up. She recognised the image at once and clattered downstairs.

'I hope you don't mind, dear, I couldn't help noticing this.'

Preston glanced at the picture. 'Yes, took it myself. God knows what it is. Fancy dress costume, straight from the joke shop.'

'Not this one, Preston.'

'You know what it is?'

He couldn't believe his luck, but everyone had to have some.

'Oh yes,' his mother replied, 'certainly. It's the Royal Company of Archers.'

Mr Braunschweig arrived at twelve forty-five, the appointed hour, and rapped on the door. There was a bell with pleasant chimes but Mr Braunschweig preferred the cast iron lion's head with the hoop in its mouth. Surprisingly, it was Preston who let him in and followed him to the kitchen. He usually made himself scarce when Mr Braunschweig arrived, not because he didn't like him, though he wasn't especially likable, but because Mr Braunschweig tired him out.

'Mum says she'll be with you in a minute,' Preston said. 'Please have a seat.'

Mr Braunschweig noticed at once the holiday brochures still on the kitchen table and wondered what had passed between the boy and his mother.

'I'd never thought of Germany as a holiday destination,' Preston said.

Mr Braunschweig was astonished. 'Bavaria? The Black Forest? Berlin? Our many centres of cultural excellence?'

'Yes, but compared to France or Spain no one I know goes there.'

'I freely concede,' Mr Braunschweig said, 'that if your objective is to lie on a beach and smear yourself with oil then Germany is not the destination of choice.'

'There's something I've been meaning to ask you,' Preston said.

Mr Braunschweig looked wary and stiffened despite himself: the delicate subject of his relationship with Ada was about to come up. He'd been expecting this for some time.

'What does aliquot mean?'

The boy was full of surprises. What was he up to now, looking things up in books to test the extent of his knowledge? Or had he been floored by this question in a pub quiz the previous night?

This was a difficult subject and Mr Braunschweig felt the need of drugs before venturing into it. Since Preston's social graces didn't extend to making coffee for his mother's guests, coffee was not on the horizon. Mr Braunschweig reached into his jacket pocket, took out a tin of tobacco and placed it on the table. The tin was resolutely black and white and pictured above the text what looked like a cathedral. Presbyterian Mixture. My God, Preston thought, even when smoking the man was making statements.

'Would that be what you were smoking last night?' Preston asked, to let him know he'd noticed.

'Actually, no. Last night I indulged myself with Davidoff Blue. I do that from time to time. You may have detected the aroma. Most people consider it very pleasant.'

'Very pleasant,' Preston agreed.

'I will, of course, repair to the garden before lighting up.' Mr Braunschweig had been warned of Preston's sensitivities on this subject. You might care to join me.'

Deliberately misunderstanding, Preston replied that he didn't smoke. That should wrong-foot the Teutonic bastard, he thought. And he was right. It did.

Ada's lawns, both front and back, were closely cropped, kept that way by Preston at her request. The borders were packed by the lady herself with colourful flowers: pansies, begonias, polyanthus. In the middle of the lawn to the rear, accessed through the kitchen door, was a lavatera which looked wonderfully full of flowers at the height of the season, though not so many were showing yet.

'Well,' Mr Braunschweig said, exhaling a cloud of smoke as if to ward off mosquitoes, 'the word aliquot opens the door to a range of issues from the tuning of pianos to mathematical theory. But then again,' he said, seeing Preston's expression, 'we should better begin by establishing the nature of your interest.'

'A friend of mine happened to use the word yesterday.'

'From which we may infer that he knew what it meant.'

'I didn't have the presence of mind to ask her at the time. Stupid, really.'

'Not at all. Entirely understandable. Who among us can safely say that he has never let an opportunity pass him by.'

Preston thought he detected a personal tone creeping in, a wistful note amid the purely analytic. Perhaps there had been a woman in the past and he was not going to make the same mistake again.

'However that may be,' Mr Braunschweig said, removing his pipe from his mouth and using it to point at an imaginary blackboard, 'we might say that an aliquot is an exact divisor of an integer, other than the integer itself.'

Preston looked blank. He didn't know what an integer was. He had no use for the term.

'Okay,' Mr Braunschweig said, helping him out, 'taking the number six, we find that we can divide it by one, two and three.' Seeing that Preston had now caught up, Mr Braunschweig continued his exposition, circling the lavatera as he talked and expecting Preston to keep up with that as well. 'And when we look further into this subject and examine aliquot sequences, we discover the existence of what we term amicable numbers. Not having been given prior notice of your question I can only advise you of two such numbers at this time, though you should be aware that there are others.'

'Really!' Preston said, astounded that anyone could consider a number friendly.

'Indeed,' Mr Braunschweig said, 'it so turns out that the sum of the divisors of 220 equals 284, while the sum of the divisors of 284 equals 220!'

'That's amazing,' Preston said, as an arithmetic chasm opened beneath his feet like an expanding zero lying in wait for the innumerate, 'though I have to admit I'm not too hot on maths.'

'In which case,' Mr Braunschweig said, stopping his progress round the shrub, 'you are one of a very large group, but I ask you to consider,' he said, looking slightly unstable because he had stopped so abruptly, 'that in your area of graphic design you undoubtedly rely on computers and, further to that, the processors of these computers employ floating point mathematics to produce the results you require. You use us but ignore us, and so the prophet goes unregarded in his own land.'

It hadn't occurred to Preston that Presbyterians might have prophets, associating them as he did with bearded gentlemen trudging round Galilee in days gone by in second-hand sandals from charity shops uttering resonant words of doom.

'What I don't see,' Preston said, ignoring this cry from the heart, 'is what this has to do with medical research.'

Mr Braunschweig frowned. 'You realise Preston,' he complained, 'that you have not before mentioned medical research in this context.' Preston apologised. 'I think you will find that aliquot here may refer to samples, for example, of known quantities of drugs, or samples taken from patients for analysis. But this is not my field. You will remember, I hope, my earlier remarks about calibration.' He was thinking of Preston's attempts to make perfume. 'Well, I have recently come across manufacturers of aliquot pipettes which will, by definition, ensure great accuracy if used correctly. These are clearly intended for use in the medical sphere.'

Mr Braunschweig wasn't stupid, not even in the ways of the world. If Preston's friend had referred to aliquots Preston could have asked her what she meant. Instead he was asking him. Here was a boy who didn't want to reveal his ignorance, a boy who wanted to impress someone. He'd been through that stage himself, he knew what was going on. With any luck Preston would be well disposed towards someone like him, willing to expend time and effort on his behalf. Not a father figure, he wouldn't presume to be that, more of a walking encyclopaedia available for instant reference.

Hearing voices, Ada looked out her bedroom window and saw them, Anton and Preston, deep in conversation in the garden. No doubt they were talking about the proposed trip to Germany and possibly discussing, in a round-about way, the nature of her relationship with Anton. Good to see they were getting on so well. If only she could hear what they were saying, but opening the window would attract their attention and that wouldn't do at all.

Gathered round the kitchen table, all three of them, Ada boosted the new man in her life as best she could.

'It isn't well known, is it Anton, but your tobacco was favoured by the first Earl Baldwin?'

'Who on earth was the first Earl Baldwin?' Preston asked.

'Stanley Baldwin. They cover him in history surely? Prime Minister during the General Strike.'

'So he was the one who shafted the workers?'

Though work was not his strong point, Preston always felt for the working man and, as a corollary, liked to traduce what he termed the establishment, all of whom, he was sure, enjoyed the products of others' labour without doing a hand's turn themselves.

'I'm sure it's not as simple as that,' his mother said.

'I wouldn't know, it's a bit before my time,' Preston replied. 'Before your mother's too, I would have thought,' Mr Braunschweig said, smiling coyly at Ada and managing to look sagacious without his pipe, which he'd left outside on the window sill to cool before putting it back in his pocket. If only he'd left his ardour in the same place, Preston thought. They could surely conduct their love-in without an audience, as befitted two persons of mature years. Mr Braunschweig still had his tin of Presbyterian Mixture however, and toyed with it on the table as he spoke.

Memories of primary school came flooding back, when Preston and his classmates had come home with their tins and every day with another added word. He'd always opened his tin whenever he got back to the house and looked through his collection, spreading it out on the kitchen table: HOUSE, DOG, DUCK, SOCK, SHOE. This was the closest he had ever come to treasure. An excitement, a freshness had gone from the world since then.

It occurred to him, for the first time, what the origin of his aversion to tobacco smoke had been, a young boy opening his tin of words made real only to be hit by the smell of stale tobacco. His grandfather had provided the tin and his grandfather smoked. Some of the boys and girls of primary one had been luckier, having relatives who bought boilings in tins or, if they were prone to sore throats, liquorice and glycerine pastilles.

'Yes,' Ada said, 'Anton may have told you we were thinking of the Hanover area as a destination.'

'I still have family there,' Anton said, confirming Preston's suspicions.

'We were thinking one week definitely,' his mother said, 'though two would be better. I don't like leaving you on your own for so long.'

'I don't see what the problem is,' Preston said. 'You're entitled to a holiday. You deserve one. It's not as if I can't look after myself.'

'I'd leave plenty of food in the freezer,' his mother said.

'Hey,' Preston said, 'we have a food hall at work, and a restaurant. I'll be fine.'

When Preston was talked out, which never took long, he excused himself and retired to his room, and with him safely out of earshot Ada and Anton reviewed their situation. It seemed to Anton that Preston had no problem with their relationship. Ada couldn't help wondering whether that might change if Anton stayed overnight but it seemed that Preston displayed no signs whatsoever of what might be termed a hang-up.

'Does he never ask why his father left?' Anton asked. And Ada had to say that he didn't. He seemed quite happy to exist in the world as he found it, untroubled by what had been.

Anton wasn't a psychiatrist, but in his opinion Preston would only be troubled if the relationship affected him adversely in some practical way, such as finding the bathroom door locked when it would otherwise have been open. Ada took exception to this analysis. Surely her son was not so superficial as Anton was suggesting?

'But my dear Ada, saying that is to miss the point,' Anton answered. Her son was happily free of those psychological complications which afflicted so many young people today. In a word, Preston was well adjusted, for which his mother must take a great deal of credit.

'But Anton,' Ada said with a smile, 'it's because he doesn't concern himself with the minutiae that he's so happy and relaxed, carefree even. Surely you realise that?'

Anton wasn't convinced. He couldn't accept that laziness might have its advantages. That would not be the case in a well ordered world.

16

Frank was checking his worksheets for the day when the phone rang. It wasn't eight o'clock yet. Someone was keen.

'Frank, I know there's never a good time, but could you pop up and see me. Shouldn't take long.'

'Give me five, Miss Mowatt and I'll be with you.'

Alice was seated at her desk with an isotonic drink to the right of her notes. Lynn Marshall had persuaded her that she would benefit greatly from the electrolytes, not to mention the carbs. Alice hadn't asked her what electrolytes were, nor carbs, assuming they were something like the quads and pecs Ms Marshall mentioned from time to time. And this despite the fact that Lynn had given her clues.

'The thing is, Miss Mowatt, I've seen it so often.'

'Seen what?'

'Old people in homes. They're plunked down in easy chairs and that's it. They're not strapped in or anything, but when they sink into that chair they don't have the strength to get up again. They're trapped till a member of staff comes along and helps them. But if we work on our quads and take our drink on board we won't be put upon like that. We shall rise like Aphrodite from the cushions!'

'Oh, I don't know,' Alice had said. Then Lynn offered to mix it for her.

'Mix it?' This was more like it, a cocktail!

'Yes,' Lynn said, 'it comes in powder form, in a can.'

'Add alcohol to taste,' Alice suggested.

Lynn was shocked. 'Certainly not Miss Mowatt, we're talking health here! Add filtered water in the correct proportion as specified on the label.'

Lynn had come with a supply of Growling Dog which, to Alice's ears, did have a cocktail ring to it. Unfortunately, she also brought an exercise which anyone could do, without equipment, to bulk up their quads.

'It's easy,' she said, 'why don't I show you?'

And without waiting for an answer she strode, in her rangy way, to the nearest wall, stood with her back to it, and slid down it till she was sitting on a chair which wasn't there.

'Now it's most important,' Lynn said, with no sign of strain or discomfort, 'to have your upper legs horizontal to the floor and to hold this position as long as you can.'

But when Alice tried it she found that though she could slide down the wall alright she couldn't slide up it again and had to be helped back into the upright position.

'Come in,' Alice said, when Frank knocked. 'Ah, the man of the moment. Something's come up. We've had a request to mount an exhibition in the restaurant – nothing large scale, twenty watercolours, local artist, Helen someone. Flowers in a vase, bowls of fruit, dead-eyed fish on a plate. You know the sort of thing.' Frank believed he did. 'If you could be there when the artist's putting them up, just to be on the safe side? We don't want the woman hammering a picture-hook into a live wire.'

On his way back to his office, Frank dropped in on the girls. June was changing her shoes.

'Always drive in these,' she said, throwing them under her desk. 'Had an accident once with heels. Nothing serious, but I paid for it big time in the body shop.' She gestured round the room. 'She's not here yet.'

'So I see.'

A Serious Business

June took the weight off her feet, which she allowed to breathe for a while like a bottle of newly opened red, though with less welcome effect.

'Left before her, did you?'

She wanted to know if they'd spent the night together and he wasn't going to tell her. Though they had never discussed it, Pamela set the limits as to what aspects of their relationship made it to the public domain. In social matters, she was the boss, the alpha female. Which is why she'd subjected him to the occasional dominance and submission routine. She'd been brusque and abrasive. Rude even. So, as far as the world was concerned, nothing had changed, no one would guess at their growing closeness. But in private, sometimes on the sofa, sometimes in bed, all that dropped away. Though she preferred not to advertise the fact, Pamela had a soft side. But he'd give the subject more thought when he finished his draft policy document which Pamela, stifling a yawn, had promised to look over if he ever managed to complete it.

When Preston arrived later that morning his mood was up-beat, the way forward clear. He was determined to press on with his work and show the doubters what he could do knowing that, in the meantime, his requests for information were out there and replies would be forthcoming, some curt, some beside the point, but a few would come up with the goods and that was all he needed to fight back. Because he couldn't help feeling that even if his efforts bore fruit an unholy alliance of women would find a way of showing him the door. They'd down-size him so much he could be posted through the letter box, his work would be out-sourced so aggressively it would be completed in Calcutta or the Western Isles.

When he sat down to switch on his computer he found he didn't have to. It was slumbering but it was on. Strange.

Suspicious. He always shut down and switched off. Someone had been checking his work, or trying to. And when he realised that, his plan for the day fell apart. Under the pressure of indignation and the need to ventilate his feelings, he stormed from the room and headed upstairs to Pamela's office.

'What's the big idea?' he demanded, bursting in with such vigour that several sheets of paper were blown from her desk.

'Good morning, Preston,' Pamela said, 'who are you asking, me or June?'

'You. Who else? You're the one who's twisting the knife.'

June rose from her chair and walked towards Preston: she was holding a staple gun. With obvious deliberation she invaded his comfort zone and threatened him full on. Menaced by mammaries, as he later described it, Preston stepped back a pace or two fearing for his unblemished cheek, his sculptured nose and, fleetingly, his paternal prospects.

'Listen, Buster,' June said, 'if you don't want your ear stapled to the wall you'll back off my friend.'

Intimidated, Preston stepped back and eyed her up and down.

He was no match for June, the punch she packed had weight behind it and there was still the staple gun to consider.

'Someone's been at my computer!'

'And you think it was me.'

'Who else?'

'I can think of a few.'

Back in his office after the most ungracious of apologies, Preston considered the possibilities. Okay, it hadn't been Pamela, bloody stupid idea that had been. He'd queered his pitch with her all over again. And he ruled out June, another girl who knew what she was doing. Eventually, he narrowed it down to Alastair or Frank. They were always in his office messing about with trunking, wires, hacksaws and screwdrivers. And neither of them used computers much, they didn't even have one in their office. Alastair might have been playing with the toys, he was stupid enough. But Frank was the one with the motive, the one they were grooming for a management role, the one who was friendly with Pamela. Worksheet in one hand, spanner in the other, Frank could always come up with a plausible reason for being anywhere. The perfect cover. But short of dusting his gear for dabs then finger-printing the suspect he hadn't a hope of nailing his man, so why bother trying?

Ignoring the information he'd painstakingly collected on perfumes, colognes and after-shaves, Preston checked his mail. Nothing on the Royal Company, but one response to his questions on heraldry. From a Mr Anderson, it went to the heart of the matter. Noting the supporters, he stated that those were only granted to peers and certain orders of knights. But he could discount peers since the helm appropriate to a peer would be silver, not steel, and would show 'five bars or facing dexter', which this one did not.

Or what, Preston wondered – he did not then know, and never found out, that 'or' referred to gold – what was the man trying to say? Mr Anderson concluded that the armiger was a knight, in this case, a Knight of the Thistle, of which there were only sixteen at any one time. He ended his reply with some helpful suggestions concerning public registers. Signing off with 'yours aye', he wished Preston good fortune in his searches.

At last he was getting somewhere, the net was closing in. When he'd addressed the old man as Sir Hector he'd denied it at once. Either he was excessively modest or he wasn't a knight, and if that was the case it was hard to see how the arms could be genuine. Preston suffered from a sudden impulsion to drop everything and follow the matter up. He was confirmed in this by the discovery that the documents referred to by Mr Anderson were held in Register House, a few hundred yards from where he was sitting. Fate was smiling upon him. If this wasn't an omen, what was? He printed Anderson's message, took some sheets of paper from the printer, stuffed them in a folder and rushed from his office. Anita saw him as he sped from the building. She smiled. He smiled back.

If he and Anita were an item, he'd have arrived. Accepted by a Beautiful Person he would become a Beautiful Person. Beauty rubbed off. Not that he wasn't good looking anyway, but the stamp of Anita's approval would make it official. Like hallmarking silver. Increasingly, too, he wanted Janice, which intrigued him since it was out of character. If anything, he wanted her for herself, or as he perceived her to be. He knew he didn't know her, but already he knew her better than Anita, with whom he had yet to have a meaningful conversation. With Janice, genuine communication was taking place. There was no one he met in the flesh to whom he had revealed so much. But all that was unfinished business, it could wait. He was riding the wave. Natural forces were at work. If he didn't go with the flow he'd go nowhere at all.

The flow took him a short distance along Princes Street, but despite a widening of the pavement it was thick with people so he opted for West Register Street instead, cold and draughty though it was, and soon found himself standing near the statue of Wellington, looking up the impressive flight of steps to Register House. It struck him that the building had been buffed up lately, looking in much better shape than he remembered. The statue, too, had clearly received attention. Even the pigeon droppings were less extensive than a stationary general on a horse had any right to expect. The magnificent animal high on its plinth, rearing on its hind legs, was purely for effect of course, the old myth of the Iron Duke bravely leading his men from the front. Preston wasn't into great men and even less into rank and titles. Wellington was probably driven everywhere by a staff chauffeur or, if he'd played his cards really well, a staff chauffeuse who doubled as a mattress, though the job probably wasn't open to women in those benighted days.

A man nearby asked if he wouldn't mind taking a photograph of himself and his wife. The happy couple, both short, posed in front of the statue. There was something about them which reminded Preston of chipmunks, the fixed expression as they stood motionless waiting for the shutter, reinforced perhaps by the maple leaves on their backpacks. But however he framed the shot other people were in it, ducking in front of them, strolling behind them. And the further he retreated, hoping to include Wellington's name, the worse the problem became. Suppressing an urge to give up, he took three shots and handed the camera back.

'We're going on a Trainspotting Tour this morning,' the wife explained.

'Really,' Preston said, 'good for you.' He pointed across the street in the direction of the Waverly Steps. 'The station's over there.' Was he making fun of them? They weren't sure.

Arriving at the top of the stairs and entering the reception area he found he had come to the wrong building.

'This is General Register House, sir. The building you want is New Register House, just round the corner off Gabriel's Road. It's well signed. You can't miss it.'

How long had lived in this city, how often had he passed this spot? And here he was in the wrong building. Or the wrong part of the right building. As for Gabriel's Road, he'd never heard of it. But then it was pedestrian only and he drove a car, which was why he hadn't noticed the work in progress either. His eyes had been otherwise engaged.

Entering reception, he was alarmed to see a large notice about security passes. So far and no farther. The gentleman behind the desk asked him what he wanted, was he working on his family tree, did he require access to parish records? Preston professed an interest in coats of arms.

'In that case, sir, it's up the stairs and through the door on your left. I'll phone up and tell them you're coming.'

This was more like it, treated with the respect he deserved.

And once through that door, he had arrived. The inner sanctum. The spiritual home of the landed gentry, not to mention those and such as those who could trace their ancestors back through the generations, yea even unto Cináed mac Ailpín.

He looked down the long corridor with rooms giving off, took in the books and the display case full of colourful old documents written in fine hands. Seeing his reflection in the glass, he realised his hair had been disturbed by the wind and smoothed it down with his palm. That was the advantage of a car, it took you from one place to another without upsetting your style. But he was here for the documents: his gaze had to penetrate the glass, not stop at its surface. He studied the papers on display. Okay, so this wasn't calligraphy as the Chinese would understand it, but some of it was well done nonetheless. There was an artistic side to the subject which had its attractions. Next thing he knew he'd be wanting a coat of arms himself. But he had no intention of lowering his guard. He would be vigilant.

There was no one at the desk so he rang the small handbell. How quaint. Hadn't they heard of buzzers? Someone could muffle the clapper in a handkerchief and make off with it no trouble at all! Trainspotters, for example, they'd be into that. The redistribution of wealth. The lady who answered his summons was helpful and friendly. He didn't feel good about enlisting her help in his scheme, it seemed an underhand thing to do, but it couldn't be helped and surely he had every right to seek the information he sought. I'm afraid we don't lend books but you're welcome to have a look through these, she said, handing him a selection of texts in his area of interest. There's a little room at the end of the corridor, she told him, you're welcome to use it. Just leave these on the counter when you go.

The little room was excellent, with a large table and an expansive view over the entrance he'd just come in. What he was seeing now he'd never seen before, a totally fresh viewpoint. The scene was bathed in weak sunlight. He felt a water colour coming on and he hadn't felt that since his last year at school. He spread the books on the table and removed some sheets of paper from his folder. Imagine having a room like this, in the still centre of things, where you were free to pursue your interests at leisure without having targets to meet, expectations to fulfil.

At first his reading led him nowhere. A detailed description of the Knights Chapel didn't help, nor did a history of the order. It was nearly an hour before he came across a reference to a member who might still be in the land of the living: The Rt. Hon. The Earl of Graham and Aberuthven KT, GCVO, PC. Apparently this gent had been elevated to the order in 1996.

But Preston knew he couldn't stay much longer in this haven of rest, his absence would be noted by one or more of the people out to get him: Pamela, who didn't land the job; Frank, the unlikely man of the moment; Alastair, who plainly didn't like him; and that interfering busybody, Kathy Reid who, he had begun to feel, was keeping a closer an eye on him than she was on the criminal classes.

And behind these minor figures, these midgets, the people who really counted: Gemma Laing, always out to help, like help him through the door, for his own good of course and in the nicest possible way; the lovely but lethal Astrid Bonthrone, never take looks as a guide to character; and Alice Mowatt, spinster of this parish, who wouldn't hurt a fly but would shaft you as soon as look at you. Yes, he would have to return to the hectic world of retail distribution before he was missed.

As he put his papers back in their folder and gathered up the books, perhaps because of these new surroundings, an island of tranquillity in the sea of times past, he remembered Hector. Hector had found time to talk, he'd taken an interest. As far as he could tell the old man was completely benign. He'd actually quite liked him. But really, come on, if he'd ever had any to start with he'd outlived his usefulness. He ought to stop trying and retire. He should read his morning paper in a room like this, bathed in sunlight, glass in hand. Two glows for the price of one. How retail could you get?

He rang the bell at the counter and the assistant reappeared, complete with helpful smile.

'I didn't like to leave these lying,' he said. 'You never know.'

'Did you find what you wanted?' she asked, taking the books and laying them to one side.

'I made a good start. Tell me,' he asked, 'if you want to check someone's coat of arms I'm assuming this is the place to do it.'

'It is' she agreed, 'though there's a fee for each search you undertake.'

This wasn't good news. 'So if I was researching the Knights of the Thistle that would be sixteen fees.'

'More, if you included the supernumerary members. I believe there are three or four.'

'So how much is the search fee,' he asked, 'or do I need a mortgage?'

The assistant laughed. Wasn't this young man a card! It turned out that looking at the index was free, but after that there was a set fee per page. So he might shell out the money only to be told he'd done a great job and his employment was secure after all. How sick would he be then?

He became aware of voices behind him. People were continually dropping in to check out the action. Yes, it was all happening at Register House. My forbears came from Drumlanrig, and I was wondering . . . As a member of the Clan Mackay who can trace his ancestry back several generations . . . This may seem somewhat academic I'm afraid, but I'm conducting a spot of research into feudal baronies . . .

On his way out, Preston took a wrong turn and found himself in a room he couldn't believe: perfectly circular, it rose to a great height, finishing in a large dome. People were working at desks on ground level, and he counted four large circular galleries, one above the other, all of them full of records – births, marriages, deaths. No doubt the record of his mother's birth was there, and her marriage to his father. What a mistake that had been! And they never let you bury a thing like that, these people. Probably all his grandparents' lives were here too, barring the death of his grandmother, who still lingered on in a rest home to no great point.

How far did he want to go back? Not a week, not a month, not a year. He lived in the present, for the present, changing direction whenever the mood took him and often on a whim. But the look of this place was something else. For a second he wished he'd hung on to the tourists' camera, but he knew there was no way of capturing an interior like this. The best you could do was a section here, a section there, or make do with the false perspective of the fisheye lens. And who with any standards would settle for that?

17

It wouldn't have happened so soon if Frank hadn't answered the phone when Pamela was in the shower. Who is this, the caller wanted to know. So he told her. Was he the concierge? Not exactly. The caller was not impressed: either he was or he wasn't. Could she speak to Pamela please, at once? She could, yes, but not without soaking the phone. He'd ask Miss Ross to return the call. Who should he say was calling?

He put the phone down and opened the bathroom door. The shower was in the corner beside the bath with a custom-built wet floor, handrails, low controls and stool. He felt he was privileged, the sole witness to a come-on scene in a thriller or a bathroom fittings commercial, where the alluring female form under the shower is saved from the censor by water vapour condensing on the panels or, as in this case, streaming down a semi-transparent curtain, a lively affair with playful dolphins cavorting in a translucent light-blue sea.

'Are you okay in there?'
'Yes.'
'Someone just called. I'd said you'd call back later.'
'Who was it?'
'Flossie.'

Until that call Pamela's mother hadn't known Frank existed. She wanted to know what was going on. What was she hiding, why was she being so secretive? But Pamela wasn't hiding anything, she was merely protecting her privacy as grown-up offspring usually do. She wasn't ashamed of Frank but she didn't feel like showing him off either. Not yet. Explaining that to Flossie without putting her nose out of joint wouldn't be easy.

'You could say,' Frank suggested, 'that our relationship's like a new plant. It needs care and protection till it's established. She'll understand that.'

Pamela laughed. 'You're something else. You're on another planet if you think she'll buy that.'

'Flossie,' Frank said, 'sounds like a pet rabbit.'

'We'll see how adorable you think she is when you meet her.'

'Meet her?'

'She won't rest till she checks you out. You may as well start the clock. We're talking tomorrow here, we don't have long.' Pamela pulled the curtain open and the bathroom mirror steamed up. 'Hand me that towel would you?' she said, pointing to the hook behind the door.

Being wet, her hair looked longer than usual and drops of water stood on her skin, some friction of the flesh helping them defy gravity for a moment or two, probably those short blond hairs so difficult to detect. Her skin had a healthy glow Frank found irresistible.

'Flossie's not her real name, you know.'

'That's a relief. What is it?'

'Florence. Everyone's always called her Flossie. Don't know why, but it stuck.'

They would meet tomorrow for lunch. Sunday. Flossie would drive down from Errol and meet them at the Gallery. What does she do, your mother, Frank wanted to know? No point explaining, Pamela said, she'll tell you herself. Give the pair of you something to talk about. Frank guessed it was her picture on the bookcase and it was, all dolled up with nowhere to go in a silver Rennie Mackintosh frame. She was sitting with a dog, a border collie with one ear up and the other down. Very appealing.

They arrived in good time and parked in a bay for the disabled. Pamela knew the only way to reassure her mother was allowing her to satisfy herself that Frank was acceptable and safe with it. If she liked him too so much the better, but she'd need an opportunity to suss him out.

'So I've brought a note-pad. I'm working on a report. Didn't know that, did you? It's due on Alice's desk first thing Monday morning. When I know what it's about myself I'll tell you. You two can leave me scribbling in a sheltered spot for a while and go for a walk.'

'She won't fall for that.'

'Of course not, but it will suit her to go along with it.'

They were interrupted by a sudden rap on Pamela's window. Flossie had arrived.

'Have you any idea,' she asked, 'how difficult it is driving through this city? I've never seen so many road works in my life!' She looked across Pamela to Frank. 'You must be Mr Figures.'

As they strolled round the building to the restaurant, Frank knew that Flossie was sizing him up. Though he could have been more stylish, he had made an effort. By his usual standards he was neatly turned out. He'd cleaned his shoes before they left.

'This is where I say I've heard a lot about you,' Flossie said, referring to Frank but looking reproachfully at her daughter, 'but I didn't know you existed till yesterday.'

Frank detected an edge to her voice. He had the feeling he was in the middle of a contest and it wasn't round one. By his standards it was remarkably full on.

'I *am* your mother you know.'

When they arrived at the French windows Pamela stopped.

'This isn't going to work unless you dump your aggrieved mother routine.'

Not liking troubled waters, Frank took out his oil can.

'Inside or out, Mrs Ross, which do you prefer?'

It was a nice enough day, no prospect of rain and very little wind. Flossie opted for one of the outside tables, perhaps to make life easier for her daughter.

'If you two grab a table,' Frank said, in a weak attempt at an escape bid, 'I'll check the menu and tell you what's cooking.'

'Not on my account,' Pamela said. 'A coffee and a sandwich will do me fine.'

'I wouldn't say no to a bowl of soup,' Flossie said, 'as long as it's not minestrone.' She pulled a chair from a table so Pamela could wheel herself in. 'Ham and pea, carrot and coriander, something like that.' She looked at Frank and smiled. 'And a sandwich?'

'Consider it done.'

'Thank goodness it's not raining,' Flossie was saying, as he made his way inside.

Being midday the queue was long and slow. Normally Frank would have found this tiresome but today it came as a relief. The lady in front was afflicted by the constant changing of young minds. But I thought you said you wanted banana cake? And what does Megan want, has she said? What a relief, watching someone else's problems while yours were talking outside. With any luck, peace would have broken out by the time he made it back out there with a tray.

'So Frank,' Flossie said, as he handed her a bowl of tomato and pepper soup, 'Pamela tells me you're a practical man.'

'So they say.'

'You could make a fortune up our way. Certain trades are in very short supply.' She inspected the sandwich. 'Egg and cress, excellent.'

'That's Frank,' Pamela said, 'tuna and mayo or egg and cress.'

'Oh, I'm sure there's more to him than that,' Flossie said.

Nothing to it, Frank thought. Daughter implies a criticism, mother leaps to his defence. His acceptance had begun. Pamela knew the moves. Three pigeons touched down, heads bobbing on their necks as they walked about searching for crumbs. One of them landed on the table.

'Remarkably forward, these creatures,' Flossie said.

'They're into recycling.'

'That's all very well, Frank,' Flossie said, 'but I haven't finished yet!'

She offered to buy coffees and anything else they might want. An angel cake perhaps, a gypsy cream? But Frank wouldn't hear of it. She'd come a long way: the least they could do was top up her tank. When he returned, after another decent interval, he could tell the discussion had continued.

'Pamela tells me she's working on a report.'

'If I'd known you were coming,' Pamela said to her mother, in the tired tone of one whose hands were tied, 'but it's due tomorrow first thing.'

'I hear you're in the throes yourself, Frank.'

He had her sympathy. Apparently there was writing to be done at Flossie's clinic, a constant stream of paperwork. They spent so much time proving they were working efficiently they'd less time to be efficient, a mark of modern management.

'I job-share now you know, I'm not sure if Pamela told you.'

'I don't believe she did,' Frank said.

Pamela put on a sainted look. 'So if you two could give me, say, half an hour?'

They left her parked at her table leafing through the notepad she was pretending to draft her report in. Their destination was the Landform, a sculpture in earth and water to the front of the gallery.

'I understand you were turned out of your previous flat.'

'That would be *burned* out, Mrs Ross. Not literally, but there was a fire. It was the last straw really, I'd had enough by that time anyway.'

'It must have been quite traumatic for you.' She hesitated, but she needed to know. 'I don't mean to pry but I get the impression you stay with Pamela from time to time.' The word 'overnight' hung on the air, unspoken but unmistakeable, like the subtle scent of magnolia.

'It has been known. But really Mrs Ross, you don't have to worry. I'm not looking for an excuse to move in. I have a new place now, less central but more affordable.'

He was renting a room in Sighthill. The flat was on the fourth floor and there wasn't a lift so visits from Pamela were out, but he wouldn't want her going home on her own anyway, especially at night. That was his story and he'd told it to Pamela as well. And Flora. He believed he had covered the angles. And the flat existed. It belonged to Archie, an old school friend, now a lawyer, who found the whole thing entertaining, a touch of cloak and dagger to lighten his life.

Flora might be a problem, though. If she ever insisted on visiting he'd have to come up with an excuse to put her off. But the most critical issue was his treatment of Pamela: he hadn't told her the truth. If she'd worked anywhere else he would have, but there was always the risk she would let something slip, probably by mischievous public remarks that only he would understand, showing him the edge but not quite pushing him over. Till the day she did by mistake.

Pamela liked dangerous living. She'd go too far, someone would put the pieces together and everyone would discover he sometimes slept at work.

But the intriguing pattern of the landform wasn't uppermost in Flossie's mind.

'Listen Frank,' she said, 'I'm not stupid. I realise Pamela's set this up, but given where I live we might not have many chances to talk.'

'You want to check out my prospects.'

'For heaven's sake, is that how I come across? No,' she said, 'but relationships have dynamics. I mean,' she said, 'they can be fraught at the best of times but when one of the parties has a disability . . . interests can be very hard to read.' She could tell from Frank's expression he'd no idea what she meant. 'Has Pamela mentioned John?'

'No.'

'Well John was interested in her. And Pamela liked him at first, but the more time they spent together the more controlling he became. As if she couldn't make decisions for herself.'

Frank laughed. 'He picked the wrong girl there.'

'Didn't he just!'

They found a bench and sat down.

'Pamela thinks I'm over-protective. I probably am. It wasn't always like this, but after John my first question now is what's in it for him? Why is he going for my daughter when there are able-bodied girls out there with fully functional legs and provocative walks?'

She opened her handbag and offered him a mint. Frank was slow to answer. If he couldn't explain it to himself, how could he do it for her? Pamela was lovely, but what did that mean? When he caught sight of her unexpectedly sometimes, and got an eyeful of that trim figure, or when they were relaxing in bed and her hair, normally pinned back, fell from her head and framed her face, then he knew. She might not be aware of him at the time, her mind might have wandered, but no one else saw Pamela in her natural state, relaxed, at peace with the world and herself.

'Have you ever had a recurring dream, Frank?'

He sometimes dreamt he was flying, and in his dream he

was remarkably proficient, possessed of astonishing control, swooping to within an inch of the ground before climbing back up to a great height. Nowhere near as high as migrating geese, but high enough.

'No. Why do you ask?'

'I'll tell you what my greatest fear is, my greatest anxiety.'

'Okay.' She was going to tell him anyway.

'I'm afraid she'll be signed up by a total inadequate, someone who'll make himself indispensable as a carer to compensate for other qualities he should bring to the relationship but can't, the sort of boy who thinks a disabled girl won't leave him because she's nowhere else to go.' She looked at him intently, waiting for a reaction – a word, a gesture – to confirm or allay her fears. 'A boy who needs her wheelchair more than she does.'

'And you're afraid that's me.'

'Till I know any different.'

'Well it's true,' he said, 'you've marked my card alright. I'm inadequate. My sister's strong on that. I'm deficient in social skills and I lack ambition. Show me the greasy pole and I want to slide down it. And that's just reading from the top of the list. But I don't need Pamela's wheelchair. If someone came along and said take up thy chair and walk . . .'

'You'd be delighted.'

'Yes.'

She looked doubtful. She wished to be persuaded.

'I know I leave a lot to be desired,' he said, 'and I'm probably not what you had in mind, but I'm not your greatest nightmare either. Really!'

Flossie looked a little more relaxed. Concede the lesser point to gain the greater. Who had recommended that, his father? Whoever it was it seemed to be working. She was coming round. Then she caught him off balance with a sudden change of tack.

'You two go at it hammer and tongs, I take it.'

'Mrs Ross!'

'I work in a hospital. You learn to be direct.'

'Right, well, okay . . . we have our moments.'

'And you're taking precautions, of course.'

Frank smiled. 'You don't want to be a granny.'

'Not yet, thank you very much. I'm only forty-nine.'

Frank was distracted by a man offering a piece of his sandwich to a squirrel.

'Tell me,' Flossie said, 'when you look at me do you think, My God, that's how Pamela will look twenty years from now?'

'You look fine to me, very elegant.'

And Flossie was attractive in her slacks and two-tone jacket, and though her blond hair was laced with grey she hadn't bothered to dye it. Another plus. Vain people tired him out.

'You were probably expecting an old battle-axe with her hair in a bun or done up in ear phones. The complete twin-set and pearls.'

Frank's phone rang. Pamela thought they'd probably had long enough, she was really curious to know how it was going and fancied another coffee. She could go and get one easily enough but things were really hotting up at the café. If she left their table they'd lose it.

'Pamela, I take it,' Flossie said, 'thinking we should have covered the bases by now.'

'You must be telepathetic,' Frank said.

'Don't you mean telepathic?'

'I was quoting my boss. He has a way with words.'

'Yes, I heard he was getting on a bit.'

Maybe she was more interested in his prospects than she was willing to admit.

'Aren't we all,' Frank replied.

'But Frank', Flossie said, as they headed back to the café, 'come on, compared to me you're in the first flush of youth.'

Frank spent the rest of their stroll back to the café explaining his view that young people aged faster than their elders. If you waited long enough the babe in arms ended up a pensioner like her mother.

'Well,' Flossie said, 'you've certainly given me something to think about.'

'Ah, there you are dear,' Flossie said, as they approached Pamela's table.

'Where else would I be?'

Nearby, three tables had been pushed together by a group of young men talking together at volume in foreign languages. They looked and sounded from the Middle East.

'As far as I can see,' she said, 'they meet here regularly.'

'You didn't get much work done then,' her mother suggested, with a sly wink at Frank.

'That's life.' Pamela shrugged. 'Forgot my ear plugs.'

Flossie wondered where the other chairs had gone.

'I could hardly say someone was using them, could I?' Pamela said. 'I'm just glad they didn't want mine.'

Frank rounded up two chairs from other tables while Flossie went in to buy more coffees.

'So what did you make of her?' Pamela asked, now they had a minute to themselves, 'your worst fears made flesh?'

'She seemed quite nice to me.'

'Quite nice? It doesn't come more analytical than that! Why don't we try a bit harder here.'

'Well,' Frank said, 'she strikes me as an amenable person.'

'For God's sake!' Pamela shook her head in disbelief. 'Right, Frank, do you think you could get on with her?'

'Yes.'

'Do you think you might even come to like her?'

'I think so. I mean,' he said, spreading his hands helplessly, 'it's early days yet.'

'I know I'm pushing my luck here, but did you get any

impression of her reaction to you?'

'I think she likes me. It's hard to say, she keeps coming right out with things.'

'Very direct.'

'To put it mildly,' Frank said, sitting down. 'You might like to know . . . I couldn't believe it . . . she asked me if we take precautions.'

'She just wants to know there won't be an accident.'

'A bit ahead of herself, wouldn't you say?' Frank asked. 'Why's she so concerned? It's not as if we're complete idiots.'

'Ah,' Pamela said, with a knowing look, 'that would be because . . . how best to put this . . . she doesn't consider you suitable material, not for the long haul. Look at it from her point of view, a professional woman, a hospital administrator, whose only daughter is teaming up with a maintenance man. A come-down to say the least.'

Frank was appalled. 'So that's what this is about.'

'Oh yes. Mother's a total snob. Tries to conceal it, but there we are.'

'Strange,' Frank said, 'she didn't come across that way to me. What are you smiling at?'

'I'm wondering what I could get past you if I really tried.'

Pamela reached out and waved her hand in front of his eyes.

'Forget the distractions, Frank,' their neighbours were ramping up the noise, 'what's wrong with me, what's my condition?'

'HSP.'

'And what does the 'H' stand for.'

'Hereditary.'

Flossie was concerned because any child they had, planned or unplanned, might inherit Pamela's condition. Until now, this thought hadn't entered his mind. Having children hadn't entered his mind either.

'Well,' he said, 'she can relax, she's nothing to worry about, we have it covered. As for the job . . .'

'I haven't asked her, but I'm sure she's okay with it. She's probably drawing up a list of tasks even as we speak.'

Pamela saw her approaching with a tray but Frank didn't.

'So what are you saying now,' Frank asked, 'your mother's not a snob?'

'I certainly am not. Whatever gave you that idea?' Flossie asked, putting a hot chocolate down in front of him.

They had nearly made it to their cars when Pamela and her mother decided to visit the shop. Given the number of hours Pamela spent in a shop every week, Frank was always amazed by her interest in visiting them in her few precious hours of freedom.

'So,' Flossie said, when they finally emerged, 'what's the plan?'

'We go back to the flat. Relax. I cook a meal. Frank goes home. You go home or stay over. Whichever.'

Frank had a problem with that. He had to go to his sister's, water the plants and feed the cat. Flossie offered to take him to Roseburn, then bring him back to Pamela's. But Pamela needed a few items from the supermarket. She produced her notebook, tore out a page and handed it over. Flossie read through the list: vinegar, cloves of garlic, salt, sprinkling chocolate, toilet roll (yellow not honey), washing up liquid, milk, profiteroles.

'So now we know what your report was about,' she said, with a smile, 'I knew that was baloney at the time.'

18

Frank advised her to move out of the bus lane. He couldn't drive but he could navigate.

'Are we getting near it now?' Flossie enquired.

'Just drive through Haymarket and head out of town, I'll let you know.'

Following his directions, she drew up near his sister's flat but couldn't find a space. Events were conspiring to prove Frank's case: there were too many cars on the road. Maybe she should wait in the car till he finished his chores. If a warden came she could drive round the block a couple of times, pointlessly burning more fuel. But just then someone left and she reversed into the space.

'You're very good at that,' Frank said.

'It's a skill acquired by practice. You could do it too.' She looked around. 'I've always liked this part of town,' she said, 'unpretentious. Good solid tenements.'

As they were going up the stairs, Flossie stopped on the half landing and put a hand on his arm.

'I think you incline to what is sometimes referred to as blue-skies thinking. And if the skies were always blue that would be fine. But you're just one well-meaning young man standing half way up a dark stair. You won't constrain the world to your point of view.'

'I know. I can't help thinking though.'

'I have no problem with that.' She took his arm. 'Shall we proceed?'

As they entered Flora's flat they both noticed a strong smell of incense.

'You sister's a flower child, I take it.'

'My sister isn't at home. She hasn't been here for several days.'

A black and white cat with magnificent white whiskers appeared out of nowhere, its tail erect in greeting. Then it spotted Flossie and ran for cover.

'Dear me,' Flossie said, 'I'm not that fearsome surely.'

'She's errs on the cautious side, always hides from strangers.'

Flora kept the doors open so Whiskers could wander freely from room to room, visiting her favourite napping spots as the mood took her. She found Flora's duvet attractively snug. When he'd last dropped in, the bedroom door had been open but now it was shut. When he opened it the curtains were drawn so he opened them too. The smell of incense was strongest in the bedroom and a stick was burning itself out in a small container on the window ledge. The man in Flora's bed sat up when the light streamed in. Perhaps he was a creature of the night.

'Who the hell are you?' Frank asked.

'I could ask you the same question.'

'Frank Figures.'

Flossie walked in and the stranger, who wasn't wearing anything, pulled the duvet cover up.

'You were telling us who you were,' she said.

'Henry, a friend of Flora's.' At least he knew her name, though he might have picked it up from several unopened letters on the hall table.

'Strange,' Frank said, 'she hasn't mentioned you.'

Henry looked slightly shifty. 'I haven't been long on the scene. If you could give me a minute to get some clothes on here.'

As they left, Henry got out of bed so quickly he stubbed his toe – he'd forgotten Flora kept it at an eccentric angle to the wall. Frank and Flossie went to the kitchen. Opening the airing cupboard Frank could just detect a bulge under the towels. The cat was betrayed by her tail, which was hanging down temptingly, like a bell-pull. He reached under the towels and scratched her behind the ear.

'Poor cat,' he said, 'what a life.'

'You weren't expecting a resident, were you?' Flossie asked.

Before Frank could answer Henry appeared in jeans and a T-shirt: he'd pulled them on so quickly he looked flustered.

'Mind if I make myself a coffee?' he asked, filling the kettle, 'I've been out for the count for a couple of hours.'

They gathered round the kitchen table, Henry sitting on the chair he'd hung his leather jacket on before hitting the sack. Short, dark-haired, clean-shaven and unusually white of face he didn't smell of drink or tobacco, but he clutched his mug as if it contained medication his life depended on.

'Any ID?' Frank asked.

Henry reached into his jacket pocket, took out a wallet, opened it and handed Frank a credit card.

'Henry W Clement.'

So his name really was Henry. Then he noticed, darkly discreet against the platinum background, an image of the Houses of Parliament. Easily missed, unlike the yellow bird in the top left hand corner.

'What's this?' he asked, but he already had his suspicions.

'If you must know,' Henry answered, 'it's a Lib Dem platinum card.' He looked slightly sheepish.

Frank handed the card back. As Henry put it in his wallet, Frank noticed several others. Maybe this was a man who hedged his bets and supported other parties as well.

'As you probably know,' Henry said, 'Flora's away for a few days.'

'I know alright,' Frank said, 'that's why she asked me to drop by every day to feed the cat and water the plants.'

Henry swallowed some coffee, black. 'Makes sense.'

'Not to me it doesn't. If she knew you were going to be here she'd have asked you to do it and saved me the trouble. 'Do you realise,' he asked, looking significantly at Flossie, 'that we've come all the way from Errol?'

'Errol,' Henry said, 'that's quite a distance! She must have forgotten to mention I'd be here.'

'I don't think so, Henry,' Frank said, leaning on the name, 'I think she doesn't know.'

'Let's discuss this reasonably. I'm not a criminal,' Henry said, looking aggrieved. 'I didn't break in.' And it was true, there were no signs of forced entry. The door was sound, the locks were functioning normally and the glass panel above it was intact.

Frank took his mobile from his pocket.

'There's an easy way to find out.'

Henry looked agitated. 'Let's not be too hasty here. There's no need to bring the police into it.'

'The police! Who said anything about the police? I'm going to phone my sister.'

If Henry really knew Flora he would realise that this was a much greater threat than the boys in blue. Flossie reached out and restrained the hand with the phone.

'You have keys to this flat,' she said, 'but Flora doesn't know that, does she?'

'Not exactly.'

'Not exactly?' Frank shouted, 'you've copied her keys!'

'I wouldn't do a thing like that!'

Frank went back to the airing cupboard and checked the hook where Flora kept her spare set. They weren't there. Why was that? Henry admitted he was having temporary cash-flow problems, he'd borrowed them when he realised Flora was leaving for a few days. He'd be going back home soon. He knew he shouldn't have done it but money he'd worked for hadn't been forthcoming. It was a short-term problem. He could only apologise.

'You expect us to believe that a man with a platinum card has cash flow problems?' Frank asked.

'I could use it to withdraw money but that costs an arm and a leg.'

'So what line of work are you in, Mr Clement?' Flossie asked.

'I'm a musician,' he replied, 'bass guitar.'

'I see,' Flossie said, as if that explained his strange behaviour.

Frank was curious. Had Henry fed the cat? What cat? Henry had been there since late last night and hadn't set eyes on a cat. Frank pointed to the bowls on the kitchen floor, one for food the other for water. What did Henry think those were, offerings to the Gods?

'Right enough,' Henry admitted, he'd wondered about that.

'And what about the litter tray in the corner, what did he think that was?'

Henry didn't know, but he'd noticed an unpleasant odour from that direction which he'd put down to dodgy drains. He had the solution to it though. Incense not only calmed the nerves it masked offensive smells.

'The thing is,' he explained, 'we agreed to play for a percentage of the takings, and the takings were less than expected. That was his story anyway.'

Whose story, Flossie wanted to know?

'The manager at the Pomegranate Club. We complained to the owner, Mr Bryce, but he knew nothing about it. He hadn't made a deal with anyone so it wasn't down to him. You could almost hear the washing of hands. From now on,' Henry stated firmly, 'it's a set fee or nothing.'

'And what,' Flossie wondered, 'if it's nothing?'

'Then it's back to the day job, isn't it?'

Flossie naturally wanted to know what the day job was.

'I'm a dentist,' Henry said, not looking for a round of applause, 'but I'm taking time out from that to see if I can make it in music.'

'So you have two ways of inflicting pain on people,' Frank suggested.

'I'm generally considered a competent player,' Henry replied.

'So what sort of group are we talking about here,' Frank asked, 'an ABBA tribute band?'

'Do me a favour,' Henry said, with a pained look. 'Christian rock,' he said. 'Well, not so much rock, more light metal.'

'Platinum even.'

'Very funny.'

Henry was impressed by his own line-up. 'Bill Thorburn, lead guitar, the Brian May of Leadburn; Andy Cruickshank, percussion; not to mention our vocalist, Tina, once heard never forgotten. And me, of course, providing the harmonic foundations.'

'Tina?'

'Antonia Weir. Looks the part when she puts on the gear but loses her voice too often. Tries to be husky the whole time and loud with it. Not an easy trick to bring off without knackering your cords. She's prone to tonsillitis.'

'Why doesn't she get them out?' Frank asked.

'We've asked her that. It can be very inconvenient. Lost us a gig or two.'

'So what does she say?'

'The Lord giveth, the Lord taketh away.'

'He's hardly going to come for her tonsils!' Flossie said. The stories she would have when she got home. 'When the others aren't playing . . . they don't perform for a living, I take it?'

'Bill's a quantity surveyor, Andy's a solicitor . . . you don't want to know about Tina.'

'Yes we do,' Frank said, sensing juice.

'She's a minister.'

'Goodness gracious!' Flossie was astounded. 'In the church?'

'She's not available on Sundays, well, not to us she isn't. A big drawback that. We're thinking of replacing her with someone more conventional.'

'Young man,' Flossie said, 'you could hardly be more conventional than a minister of religion.'

'You could if you're into metal.'

'What are you called?' Frank asked, 'collectively.'

With so many bill posters active in the city he was sure he'd recognise the name.

'The Altar Egos.'

From Henry's account of the personnel this was an excellent name, Frank thought, and possibly the best thing about them. Flossie liked it too, so that was all right then. What was it with metal, Frank wondered, what was the attraction? Some liked the profane lyrics, but a Christian band would surely deprive them of those. He couldn't see the Gnome beating a path to the venue but if, by any chance, he found himself at an Altar Ego gig he'd soon be barracking from the front row. It would have to be the front row, Frank thought, or Tina wouldn't see his indelicate gestures. Nor, for that matter, would the Brain May of Leadburn. Then there was the joy of being deafened, and though that was the norm these days a good up-standing man like Mr Gibson wouldn't wear it. The Messiah was more in his line. So where, Frank wondered, would a Christian metal outfit get its audience? One of life's unanswered questions.

Frank rose from the table, filled a jug and went through to the front room to water the plants. Flora was into spider plants which sprouted offspring on tendrils. Where other people replanted the progeny, Flora delighted in placing the parent plant on a shelf and allowing the youngsters to trail. They remained perfectly healthy but, since their fresh young roots were never in soil, they depended on their parents in perpetuity which, according to Flora, was becoming increasingly popular among the young of the human population. She cited social trends as reported in the press. She was always up on that sort of thing.

As he went from plant to plant he overheard Henry asking Flossie who she was, and was astonished to hear her claim to be his mother-in-law. This was either a sensible way to avoid a lengthy explanation or he was more popular than he'd thought. Then he came to the cactus. He never knew what to do with it. Being a cactus it wouldn't expect rain every day. Or every week, or even every month. He assumed it must be possible to over-water a cactus and he'd made this point to Flora, but she'd been remarkably vague.

'What type of cactus is it?' he'd asked her, hoping to track down advice.

But she hadn't known. She'd bought it two years ago because it looked nice in flower, but she couldn't remember what it was called and since it hadn't flowered again she was losing interest. When Frank returned from the kitchen, Flossie was at the sink working her way through unwashed dishes and mugs.

'Could you let me see that card again?' Frank asked. 'Just for a moment.'

'Surely we've established who the gentleman is,' Flossie suggested.

'It's not that,' Frank said, without saying what it was.

Henry retrieved the card and gave it to him.

'I hope you're not memorising my account number and expiry date.'

He tried to sound casual but failed. He was worried.

'I thought so,' Frank said, 'this bird of yours has three wings on the right and two on the left.'

'It has?' Henry said. 'I never noticed.'

'Which would mean,' Frank suggested, 'it's doomed to fly in circles, always veering to the left.' He handed the card back and Henry checked it out.

'Well, well, I'd never noticed that,' he laughed. 'Our opponents would say it's a pretty fair description of our policies.'

'Your opponents would be right,' Flossie snorted, turning from the sink, 'legalise cannabis indeed!'

It may have been the sound of running water draining from the basin as Flossie emptied it that opened Henry's ears to a call of nature. He hadn't gone since he'd got up and he'd been in bed for several hours.

'What are you going to do?' Flossie asked when she heard the lock on the bathroom door. 'He seems to be telling the truth. I mean,' she continued, 'if he was going to make something up he would have done better than that.'

'But he shouldn't be here, should he?'

'No,' Flossie said. 'And your sister has a right to know what's going on in her own house.' She dried her hands absent-mindedly on the dish towel. 'You have an opportunity here. Phone her while he's in the toilet, explain the situation, then hand him the phone when he comes back. Let them sort it out between them. It's not your problem. Well it is, but it shouldn't be.'

This seemed excellent advice to Frank so he took it. Unusually, his call wasn't picked up by her voicemail but the minute she heard him she asked him to ring off. She was expecting an important call. Shouting to make himself heard over what sounded like a crowded public bar Frank pointed out that his was an important call. She had a visitor, was she aware of that? Actually, more of a non-paying guest.

This news got her attention and she walked outside to hear him better. What did he mean, a visitor? He told her about Henry.

'In my bed,' she bellowed, 'what a bloody cheek!'

Frank held the phone away from his ear and smiled at Flossie, who smiled back.

'She doesn't sound amused,' Flossie said.

'Is there someone there with you?' Flora asked.

'Henry W Clement.'

'Apart from him.'

'My mother-in-law,' Frank said.

'Your who! Your what!'

Henry came back in and Frank handed him the phone. 'Flora called,' he lied, 'she wants a word.'

'I bet she does. Oh well, here goes.' He took a final swig of coffee even though it was cold. 'Hi honey-bunch, how's it going?'

In Flora's living room, with the door shut behind them, Frank sat on a chair rocking with laughter.

'Honey-bunch!' he said, 'no one calls my sister that and lives.'

'If Henry gets away with it that will tell you something,' Flossie said.

'It will?' Frank said. 'What?'

'Our Henry has the key to the door in more ways than one.'

Frank considered this a moment. 'Mrs Ross, on that subject, I have the key to the door too, and I'm not talking about this flat.'

'Yes, I believe we've established that.' She walked to the window and looked down into the street, checking her car wasn't under attack. Her shoes were loud on the laminate, quiet on the rug. 'Frank, if I hadn't turned up today, where were you going to sleep? At Pamela's?'

'Yes.'

'I'll head back home after we've eaten. The journey's not as bad as I make out.' Frank tried to talk her out of it but she insisted. 'I'll tell her I'm on tomorrow, she can't argue with that.' She walked back into the room and sat down. 'About the mother-in-law thing . . .'

'No problem,' Frank said. 'I can live with it if you can.'

In fact he liked it. Increasingly he felt he belonged, first with Pamela, now with her mother, and the feeling was warm and nourishing, like home-made soup.

The door opened and Henry burst through it handing the phone back to Frank.

'It's okay for me stay tonight. When I leave tomorrow I've to lock the door and post the keys through the letter box. She said she'll phone you later. Oh, and someone by the name of Pamela rang,' he said, 'she wants her groceries.'

19

Preston made his way from the lift to his office. Though he hadn't seen Anita for a day or two, he'd handed her his concoction and was confidently awaiting results. Was it his imagination or were there fewer customers these days? He'd given his mother a quick whiff and she'd approved. It reminds me of something, she'd remarked. He opened his door to find Alice working at his desk. He could tell at a glance she'd switched nothing on: she wasn't snooping, she was waiting. His phone rang and Alice picked it up. She was expecting the call.

'No, that's right, two extra chairs. Thank you, Alastair.'

'Good morning, Miss Mowatt.' Preston said, as she replaced the receiver.

'Good morning, Preston.' She closed a folder and looked up. 'We'll be convening in my office at twelve. That's Gemma, Astrid, and yourself. I'll be there too.'

Preston was alarmed. 'A bit of notice wouldn't have gone amiss.'

Alice rose to leave. 'At our last meeting we gave you a month to sort things out. Since that month is now over today's review can hardly come as a surprise.'

'This is the crunch, then,' he said, stowing his Pro Tour sports bag behind the door. It looked even better now he'd bought a renovating cleaner for black leather and lovingly buffed up every square inch.

'Crunches come to us all.'

'Not to you they don't, you're the owner. You don't find someone in your office when you arrive waiting to put you through it, holding you to account.'

She could tell from his tone he was aggrieved but she no longer cared. Life was too short. Starting the clock now, and she couldn't start it earlier, hers would be shorter than his.

'The fact that I'm the owner doesn't mean my performance goes unexamined. Quite the reverse.'

'Oh yes,' Preston said, with the hint of a sneer, 'and who examines it, Hector?'

'Yes actually, since you mention it, my father still takes an interest. As do bankers, accountants, and Her Majesty's Revenue and Customs, to name but a few.'

'But when you come right down to it Miss Mowatt, no one's going to show you the door, are they – it's your door?'

What a neat formulation, Alice thought. Put the right way, things sounded simple whether they were or not.

Preston was on the point of giving up in the face of life's unfairness, assuming that however well he performed he was on his way out. He was tempted to go before he was pushed, exiting in a torrent of righteous indignation which would make him feel a lot better than he felt now. But a small voice in an American accent was telling him to hold back. As recently as last night, Janice had warned him that impatience would be his downfall, bringing about what he most feared. Sure, he could take control right now, burst the bubble and be free. But – there was always a but – they might decide in his favour, and they couldn't do that if he'd already left.

'It may be my door, Mr Blair, but I have to keep the wolf from it like anyone else.'

Preston was perplexed. 'What do you mean?'

'Tax, business rates, utilities, staff. These things have to be paid for.'

'Oh, right,' Preston said, 'that goes without saying.'

'I'm afraid it would have done,' Alice said sharply, 'if I hadn't said it. We look forward to seeing you at twelve. Oh, and I'm much impressed with your office, it's improved out of all recognition. Alastair has done you proud.'

As she left, Preston realised that Alice, like a chess player, was thinking several moves ahead. The board was in three dimensions, and difficult though chess on several levels was, Alice always won because she had written the rules. Here he was, a pawn, and Alice was moving him from level five to level six, her bony fingers meeting round his waist. He could refuse to go, but that would mean breaking the rules. He'd be removed from the board leaving the other pawns to take the strain, the little people like him who, though they bore the burden of the work, were always the first to be sacrificed for the greater good.

Alice was looking ahead alright. If he took his case to a tribunal he could no longer claim she'd failed to provide what he needed: hardware, software and, not at the outset maybe but over time, an adequate environment. And she wasn't his only problem. What had got into that awful man Gibson, bursting in the other day without so much as a knock, complaining bitterly about interlopers crawling all over his systems?

'I'm absolutely fulminating,' he'd shouted, whatever that meant. But before Preston could ask him he left as abruptly as he'd entered.

As for the site there was little more he could do to improve it. His sole objective now was to relax, to avoid being too tense to talk up his achievements in a coherent manner. He left his office, took the lift to the ground floor and strode to the food hall where he bought an alcopop to promote relaxation and a packet of mints to mask any odour of alcohol which might otherwise be detected when exhaling in Miss Mowatt's office. The cash-out girl was an undistinguished creature and Preston, to whom looks meant a lot, paid her no attention till she spoke.

'If that's your lunch,' she quipped, 'you're some way off a balanced diet.'

'Do you normally speak to customers like that?' he asked.

'Not unless they work here.'

She knew who he was, she'd served him before.

'I don't think I'll be working here much longer,' he replied, taking his change.

At that moment, Avril was better aware of his negative state of mind than anyone else in the building.

As he left the food hall and headed for the lift he saw Kathy Reid in the distance. He gave her a cheerful wave and she quickly turned away. Nothing mattered more to her than her cover. Really, the woman was ridiculous. And she was putting on the pounds. Preston had noticed that some women as they aged accumulated fat in unexpected places. In Kathy's case he'd observed an increase of flesh on the upper arm resulting in an unsightly bulge directly above the elbow. He was sure her legs were the same but she kept them well hidden. He could think of a turnstile or two she'd have trouble getting through. If Mowatts could retain a dough-ball like her they could certainly keep him on the books.

The lift doors opened and he entered. Finding himself alone with no external targets, he realised his thoughts were running wild. He was in an unusually febrile condition, even for him. If he didn't calm down he was doomed. He knew there were tablets for that and he wished he had some, but he didn't. He wasn't into drugs. What would be the point working out if he ingested noxious substances?

On his way to the meeting, suitably fuelled, a mint in his mouth and another in his pocket, Preston tidied himself in the men's room. As always, he presented an agreeable exterior to the world. There was no reason for lack of confidence on that score.

'Come in,' Alice said as he knocked and entered.

She was pleased to see him. Not so much the kiss, more the smile of death. And Gemma was there, of course, and Astrid Bonthrone, who imparted a new meaning to the words cutting edge. He had to admit, though, that when it came to legs she was in a league of her own. Being old, Alice didn't have any. Gemma was attractive in an absent-minded way but deficient in glamour. She had legs alright, but failed to profit by them. Astrid's were part of the package. Beautifully presented, Preston thought, taking in the elegant black wrap-around dress which, having arranged herself artfully on her chair, allowed the observer a useful glimpse of one leg well above the knee while obliging him to derive the other from the gentle curve of the material covering it. Synthetic, he noted, but you couldn't have everything. The Astrid Bonthrone sheer leg experience.

She was seated in front of Alice's desk on a peculiarly cheap and cheerful stackable plastic chair, one of two which Alastair, with his instinct for the appropriate, had brought from the meeting room. The other was waiting for him.

'So,' Preston said, 'you want to look at my new improved web site.'

'Actually, no,' Alice replied. 'Following our previous meeting, Gemma, Astrid and I agreed that none of us had sufficient expertise to evaluate your work so we engaged a firm of consultants.'

'Abercorn Associates,' Gemma said, 'you may have heard of them. They've analysed your site within the context of wider our operation.'

'They've worked for prestigious clients,' Astrid assured him, 'high-street names.'

High-street names, that was all right then. Burger King? Woolworth's?

'They subject what they find to rigorous analysis,' Alice explained. 'If no problems are detected, they say so. If problems are found which may be solved by judicious modification – tweaking, was the word they used – they identify those problems and recommend solutions.'

'But surely, Miss Mowatt,' Preston said, 'it will be in their interest to find problems where none exist? That way they can rake in a fee for solving them.'

Astrid moved the visible leg just a little, took off her glasses and placed them on her executive briefcase. This woman, he thought, was not above giving you an Indian head massage with an axe, an impression reinforced by her hair which, dark anyway, had today an almost metallic sheen. Commercials played in his mind, trade names. This had to be the last word in advanced conditioners.

'As Miss Mowatt will confirm, Mr Blair,' she said, 'Abercorn are fee-based consultants. Their involvement ends when their report is delivered. They have no pecuniary interest in finding fault where none exists.'

'We hope that puts your mind at rest,' Gemma said.

'So what we propose to do,' Alice continued, lifting the report from her desk, 'is summarise their findings.'

'Do I get a peek?' Preston asked, noting with distaste the graphic of two interlocked capital A^s on the front cover. Did these people need roadside assistance? He didn't think so. Did they have an alcohol problem? Probably not.

'We see no need for that,' Alice said. 'This report was commissioned to assist non-specialists such as ourselves and we will appraise you of its contents . . . unless you feel we might misrepresent them.'

'Of course not, Miss Mowatt, though I still think I might be vouchsafed a sight of them,' he said, in what he took to be a parody of her style, 'out of courtesy, if nothing else.'

'If I bought a morning paper,' Astrid asked, reaching for her eye-ware, 'would you have a right to read it – out of courtesy?'

A feeling of unreality was creeping over him now, as if there was a hurricane out there but he was in the eye where conditions were unnaturally calm and all the chaos was swirling some way off. His eye was attracted by a picture on the wall, a portrait. Not especially large but remarkably well executed, the subject was none other than the founder of the store, Archibald M Mowatt. Painted, as he later discovered, by Robert Scott Lauder, it showed the great man standing beside a desk on which were placed a number of documents, a paper-weight and a quill pen, which the viewer would take to be the tools of his trade. The pen troubled Preston till he remembered where he'd seen it before, attached to Hector's uniform headgear. Could it be one and the same? Unlikely but possible. Entitled 'The Merchant Prince', the picture portrayed its subject looking the observer straight in the eye, with confidence but without hauteur. A man secure within himself. Yet here he was, Preston Blair, summoned to judgment by one whose sole achievement was inheriting her ancestor's wealth.

Alice took him through the report's conclusions point by point, and although visual impact was well down the list that was where she started since it gave her an opportunity to be positive. The consultants were impressed by his layout, use of colour, typography, arrangement of images, and ease of navigation. Alice looked up at Preston and smiled. Preston smiled back. Their second main finding, she said (in fact it was their first) was that there was no tie-up whatsoever, even attempted let alone achieved, between these pages and existing systems within the store. By existing systems the consultants referred, inter alia, to the software used by Mowatts for raising orders, invoicing, and recording payment. The consultants found that as a consequence of this fatal shortcoming a customer could, without knowing it, place an order for an item which was out of stock. And even if the item were in stock and successfully ordered through the site, stores would be unaware of the fact and would make no attempt to deliver it. Which, the report continued, was just as well because, if they did deliver it, accounts would be unaware of the credit or debit card details provided and so would make no attempt to charge for it.

'I could go on,' Alice said.

'Please do,' Preston replied, a dead man talking.

The authors of the report had looked in vain for any mechanism by which the data the site contained, or the data on which it relied, could readily be updated. Already, they observed, three items listed were no longer available. There was little point in using a web site to sell if it were not continuously up-dated. That was, after all, a main virtue of e-commerce.

To sum up, the authors appeared to be dealing with a designer who had no understanding of standard commercial principles, and none whatever of the systems upon which e-commerce depended. This being the case, they recommended that the work be transferred to a person or persons properly qualified to do it.

'So there we have it,' Alice said, laying down the report.

'Sorry Preston.' She probably was, but Gemma's sorrow didn't help.

'Astrid?'

'These conclusions are unequivocal,' Astrid said, uncrossing her legs to promote circulation, though that was not how Preston interpreted it, 'so much so that legal fall-out may be safely assumed if you continue down this route.'

'Thank you, Astrid, we appreciate your input.'

'Not at all,' she said, rising to leave in one flowing movement.

What a dress! What a figure! Preston had never liked poetry, except for the occasional arresting image. Now into his mind, from nowhere, came the words, 'the liquefaction of her clothes'. He'd liked it at the time. Textiles could flow on a body, like running water photographed at a slow shutter speed. The author had Astrid in mind, or someone very like her. She put her glasses back on and picked up her briefcase. As she walked past him he caught a whiff of scent, but despite his hours of research he failed to identify it. If it bore any relation to her salary it would be very expensive indeed. Then he noticed the folder she'd left behind.

'I see your brief has prepared my severance in advance,' he remarked, feeling a short-lived detachment now that his ordeal was drawing to a close. 'So,' he added, rising to go, 'a month's notice, I believe it was.'

Alice realised he'd be upset. That was quite understandable. However, there were matters she wished to go over with him, but if he'd prefer another time . . .

Matters? What could they possibly be? He was shafted, impaled.

Alastair knocked and came in. 'I'm sorry to interrupt, Miss Mowatt, but the man from the Planning Department has arrived.'

Preston knew what was going on: this interruption was pre-arranged, an easy way to extricate herself from a tricky situation. The man from the Planning Department was a fiction, an invention. He didn't exist.

Alice rose. 'I'll leave you in the capable hands of Miss Laing,' she said to Preston and left the room. 'What do you think the outcome's likely to be?' she asked in the corridor, no doubt for his benefit.

'Don't ask me, Miss Mowatt,' Alastair said, 'I don't have a crystal palace!'

Gemma smiled despite herself, what would the man say next?

'What's that about?' Preston asked.

'We're supposed to ensure wheelchair access, which we want to do. But this is a listed building. Every suggestion we've made has been knocked back by the Planning Department. It seems we can't do anything right.'

'Know the feeling,' Preston said, 'so where do we go from here?'

'I'm really sorry about this, Preston,' Gemma said. She was always sorry about something. 'I realise what a setback it must be, but we do have a suggestion to make and we hope you'll consider it seriously.'

From his point of view, she said, it was important to recognise that all was not lost. Mowatts took staff welfare very seriously. In cases such as this, fortunately rare, the first port of call was redeployment within the company after any retraining which might be deemed necessary or desirable. Provided, of course, the member of staff was happy with such an arrangement. He might have noticed a plaque on the wall near the main entrance? He had, though he'd never read it. Investors in People, Gemma explained, they'd achieved it last year. A major strand in our thinking, she said, is to play to people's strengths. In his case, he had an eye, he definitely did, and a talent for graphic design. The report was glowing in that regard.

'Where's this leading, Miss Laing?' he asked.

'Do you know Louise?' The name didn't ring a bell. 'Louise da Silva. You've probably seen her about. Jeans and a T-shirt. She married a Portuguese cabinet maker. They're leaving the country at the end of the month.'

Preston had now caught up with this human resources suprema, this investor in people. Louise was a window dresser, of no great talent that he could see. Competent but unimaginative. Come autumn the public could expect a display of raincoats, leather gloves and umbrellas strewn with autumn leaves and pine cones. Christmas would be even worse: reindeer, sleighs, cotton wool masquerading as snow. A step to the side was one thing, two steps down was another. Gemma produced a book and handed it to Preston. The thing was, she told him, not to make a rash decision.

'Take time. Think about it. Talk to Louise.' The phone rang. 'No, I'm afraid Miss Mowatt isn't available right now . . . Mr Mowatt? I believe he's popped into his club . . . That's right, Picardy Place . . . Any time, glad to be of assistance.'

Preston left Alice's office, went to his own and dropped the book on his desk: Window Displays of New York. He didn't open it. He wanted to talk to someone, but who? He went to the restaurant and bought a coffee but the women at the next table started getting to him. Well dressed, dripping with rings and necklaces, they were well-turned-out chatting machines without a care in the world. And gesture, boy did they gesture. Forget the semaphore handbook, refer to the girls. He hoped and prayed Bertrand wouldn't spot him, there was only so much he could take, and for once his prayer was answered.

Preston had often heard the line 'I need to get some air' in films and TV dramas. It had always struck him as odd because the person saying it was usually breathing at the time, but over the years he came to realise what it meant. Inside they were trapped, outside they were free. But this was the first time he'd felt that way himself. He took the lift to the ground floor hoping to meet none of his colleagues on the way, and again he was in luck. Leaving by the main doors, he was about let out a sigh of relief when he walked into Alice, Alastair Geddes and a gentleman with a white short-sleeved shirt and clip-board who looked like an airline pilot who'd seen better days.

'Preston,' she said, 'this is Mr Armstrong from the Planning Department.' Then turning to Mr Armstrong, 'Mr Blair is our graphic designer.'

He liked the use of 'our', very cosy, very inclusive. He wasn't falling for that.

'I was just reminding Miss Mowatt,' Mr Armstrong said, 'that this is a listed building. I'm afraid, much as we'd like to, we can't go along with this plan.' He waved it grandly in the air as if he'd just descended from an aircraft to the tarmac with evidence of good intentions. Conservation in our time. 'As I'm sure you will appreciate,' he said, 'the proposed ramping would completely ruin the period character of the front elevation.'

'May I have look?' Preston asked. Plainly the answer should be no, since he hadn't paid for the plans.

'By all means,' Miss Mowatt said, without a hint of embarrassment. Mr Armstrong spread the sheet against the wall. He'd left his jacket in his car and two large, expanding sweat marks were visible under his arms. Preston helped him out by holding down the left hand side of the sheet.

'As you can see, 'Mr Armstrong said, 'we have one lengthy ramp coming in from the left and another from the right.'

'But if they weren't so long,' Preston said, 'they'd have to be much steeper to meet the top of the steps. That would defeat the purpose, wouldn't it?'

'Exactly my point,' Alastair said, though it hadn't crossed his mind. 'What do you think we're dealing with here, Mr Armstrong, para-Olympians?'

'Yes, well however that may be, and I don't wish to seem unsympathetic to the plight of the disadvantaged, we have certain standards to adhere to. We are, after all, as I'm sure you know, in the middle of a Unesco World Heritage Site here!'

Alastair was astonished. 'We are?' he said. 'No one told me.'

'Oh yes,' Mr Armstrong declared, 'and with privilege comes obligation.'

'So let me get this straight,' Alice said, 'the only way to meet our obligation to you is to flout an Act of Parliament?'

A group of young men sauntered past, the worse for drink and loud with it. The more inane a remark, the more people had to hear it.

'Ah now, Miss Mowatt,' Mr Armstrong said, 'you didn't hear me say that.'

'So what's your solution?' Alastair asked.

'Regrettably,' Mr Armstrong answered, 'I'm not in a position to advise on legal matters where these fall outwith my remit. If push came to shove the Department might be deemed liable for any error made, in good faith or not.'

'And we couldn't have that,' Alastair said, shaking his head.

Mr Armstrong, finding his arm tiring faster than his tongue, removed the plan from the wall. It seemed to Preston there was an obvious solution.

'What,' he asked, 'if the ramps weren't permanent?'

'In that case,' Mr Armstrong replied, 'there would be no alteration to the structure so we wouldn't have a problem.'

'You wouldn't but we would,' Alastair said. 'We couldn't leave temporary ramps in position overnight. They'd walk. They'd disappear like snow off a dyke. We'd come in the next morning and find them on the floral clock. You know what drunks are like in the small hours. They're bad enough now as you can see.'

'Not if we took them indoors at close of business each day,' Alice said.

Alastair wasn't happy. 'They'd be heavy, Miss Mowatt. And where would we put them? There's that to consider.'

'That's true, Alastair, so I suggest we consider it. What do you think, Mr Armstrong?'

Mr Armstrong folded the plan and slid it under the clip on his board.

'Well, yes,' he said, 'at first blush it does appear to have something to commend it. Worth investigating certainly.'

Here was a man, Alastair thought, who must have permanent imprints on his bum from sitting on the fence.

'There we are then,' Alice said, and quite unexpectedly clapped her hands. 'Isn't it amazing what can be accomplished when persons of good will work together!'

Preston explained to Alice that he was going for a short walk to clear his head and think things out. As she must know, he had a lot to mull over. Alice understood, of course she did. He could take as long as he liked. What, Preston thought, a month, a year? With no destination in mind, he turned the corner and walked towards the square. So many people. What did they all do? Resisting the rarefied retail draw of Multrees Walk, he took the escalator down to the bus station. Reassuringly lower level, ordinary people going about their business. He strolled along the concourse. Gate A, Gate B, Gate C. He was tempted. All these buses went somewhere and each one away from his troubles. He read the screen above Gate D. Service number 55, Melrose. Near though it was he'd never been there.

He walked the length of the station and out into Elder Street, his route taking him a few hundred yards down the road to Picardy Place. And so he came to the Nevis Club, where old Hector Mowatt would be out for the count in an easy chair or refreshing himself in the bar. On a day when he had nothing left to lose he let impulse be his guide and walked in. He didn't make it farther than reception, which struck him as more expensive than grand. As for the ebony veneer desk, if that was good taste he was a pumpkin. Of the two members of staff, the man was checking something on a screen, but he couldn't see what. From first to last he didn't look up though he was taking in every word. He'd already judged that Preston didn't rate eye-contact which, coming from a man with a large bald patch, was a bit much. Did he really believe that combing a few strands of hair over it made any difference? Preston had the impression he wasn't a permanent fixture at reception, unlike his younger colleague.

'Yes sir,' she enquired, 'can I help you?'

'I happened to be passing,' Preston said, 'wondered what it was like.'

Apparently there was an easy way to find out: a joining fee of £200 plus an annual membership of £500. He'd have to be proposed and seconded by existing members of course. Did he know any? He could tell from her tone how unlikely that was so he mentioned Sir Hector Mowatt. Having bestowed a knighthood on the old boy the week before he'd been unwilling to deprive him of it since. It suited him somehow. He noticed a concerned look on the receptionist's face. She hadn't realised Sir Hector had a title, she'd been addressing him as plain Mr Mowatt.

'Oh, I wouldn't worry about that,' Preston said, as if he lived in the old man's pocket, 'he doesn't make anything of it. He's a member of the Royal Company, you know.'

'The Royal Company?'

He had the woman on the back foot now.

'The Royal Company of Archers,' her colleague said, still intent on his task.

'I see,' she said, but he knew she'd never heard of them, so there was something to be said for her after all. 'I could give the gentleman a quick look round,' she said, 'some of the public rooms anyway.'

'By all means,' the man said, 'I'll be here five minutes at least.'

Either he was checking the credentials of would-be members or he was hooked by on-line gaming.

The tour was necessarily brief, and though he made appreciative noises Preston didn't care for the modern antiseptic feel of the décor. The bar looked expensive but didn't feel welcoming to him. However, he was struck by a panel in the dining room.

'I see you're admiring our famous mirror display.' The receptionist was observant. 'Each of these mirrors,' she explained, 'can be angled independently on its own ball and socket joint.'

As if that wasn't enough to impress him, she also let it be known that designers had come from far afield to admire this unusual feature. As had a clinical psychologist investigating the effect of reflected light as a trigger for migraine in a self-selecting group of sufferers, though she didn't mention that.

'Where are you from yourself?' she asked.

'Melrose,' he replied. The mind worked in mysterious ways but he knew where that one had come from. 'I'm a graphic designer.'

'Really!' She was starting to warm to him, he could tell.

He left the club knowing he was above all that, and was pleased to note that Sherlock Holmes no less had turned his back on the place as well. A statue maybe but of a man who, as everyone knew, always drew the correct conclusion. What a gulf there was, he thought, between rich and poor, between the life of the ordinary working man and that of the affluent, made easy by the privileges money and contacts could buy.

He crossed the road to the Theatre Royal Bar, liking to think that the four heralds above the door were sounding their trumpets for him. This was more his scene. You couldn't let the chandeliers fool you, nor the ornate woodwork – ordinary people came to a place like this, concertgoers whose transactions were straight up, transparent. They bought their tickets and came. If they were poor they bought cheap tickets. Simple. He ordered a beer. It gave him something to toy with as he considered his position.

His hand was weak, he'd have to play it well. Preparing the ground would make all the difference and, like it or not, he'd have to demonstrate cooperation every step of the way. They were making him an offer. Derisory though it was, throwing it back in their faces might not be the best way forward. Better to register his view that the new position was a demotion while appearing to give it a try. He would find it unequal to his talents, as it plainly was, and then he could make his move.

20

Apart from a few smokers there were no staff outside the main entrance when Preston returned to the store: no Alice, no Alastair Geddes, and no gentleman from the Planning Department. But as he climbed the steps to go in, who should he see in a window but Louise at work on a summer display. She was draping textiles in horizontal swathes to suggest the ocean – a blue band, a white band, a blue band – and her mouth was full of pins. What would Louise add to the scene when she finished her ocean vista: palm trees, buckets and spades? A hammock, perhaps? He entered the store and located the access to the window.

'Hi,' he said.

'Hi yourself. I take it you're Preston Blair.'

'That's me,' he replied.

'I'll be happy to help you, if that's what you want. We could work together till I leave.'

'I could learn the ropes,' Preston agreed, believing there were very few of them and they were all very short.

'Only if you want to,' she said, securing another band of blue. 'You work with computers, I believe.'

'That's right.'

'Well,' she said, 'you never know, you might take to physical media.'

He noticed two cans of paint, a roller and brushes in the corner of the display area. Physical media? He didn't care for paint. Despite his best efforts he never applied it well. Still, as long as it wasn't gloss or varnish he could handle it.

'You're not leaving because you can't stand it?' Preston asked.

'Oh no. Joao and I are moving to Portugal. Actually,' Louise said, 'I love getting covered in paint. Even Mr Gibson accepts it as a credential, like an ID tag for artists.'

'Good God,' Preston said, 'that's an achievement.'

'There's a lot to get round,' she said, 'more than you'd think: eleven windows to the front, ten to the side. And that's not counting interior displays.'

This girl wouldn't be a problem. Even if they didn't get on, which wasn't likely, she'd be leaving soon. His eye fell on two mannequins which she'd moved to the front of the window as she worked on her backdrop. It seemed to him their nipples were larger than life, as no doubt they had to be to protrude suggestively through the costly garments they were supposed to move.

'I thought the custom was to cover them with cloth between changes.'

'I used to, but now I can't be bothered. Can't see the point.'

Preston couldn't either. 'So this is Here Comes Summer?'

'We have new swim-wear coming in,' she said. 'You wouldn't believe so little material could cost so much.'

He became aware of noise through the window and when he turned round saw a group of schoolboys ogling the mannequins. Some of them were making suggestive gestures and one shouted 'Get a load of that!' A thick-set looking boy, his shirt half out of his trousers, was jumping up and down in front of the window uttering strange noises and scratching his armpits. He was a chimpanzee.

'I get this from time to time,' Louise said. 'Occupational hazard. Don't worry, they have short attention-spans. Give them five and they'll be off.'

Preston thanked her for her time. He still had some thinking to do but he'd let her know as soon as he'd made up his mind.

His route to his office took him past cosmetics, and as he approached the glittering realm of polished glass and chromium he noticed a man talking to two of the girls. One of them, seeing him approach, pointed him out and spoke. The man looked in his direction. The girl nodded, that was definitely him. And as he made to pass them he turned and spoke.

'Preston Blair?'

'Yes.'

'This is for you,' he said, punching him in the face, 'special delivery!'

Preston was rocked on his feet, and seeing the man making to hit him again, turned his head to the side to protect his nose. The second blow caught him off balance and he fell to the floor. Believing his attacker would kick him, he covered his face with his arms. The sales assistants were screaming, which wasn't helping much but might attract assistance if he didn't die first. He felt a painful blow to the back. He was curling himself up against the next kick when someone came to his aid.

'Fuck you, fucker!' she yelled, and felled his attacker, who landed heavily on top of him.

Witnesses later stated that even then his attacker continued in his attempts to rain further blows on him but was prevented from doing so by a Britney Spears look-alike with street-fighting skills who did a passable imitation of a windmill in a tornado, so many blows did she land on his assailant in such a short time. But she wasn't heavy, tipping the scales at under eight stones. Finding her blows had too little weight, she reached for a vase and broke it over the man's head.

Two uniformed security men arrived from opposite directions. The first, at great risk to himself, restrained Chloe, whom he believed to be the cause of the trouble. She'd been rude to him in the past, addressing him as Pig and Filth because uniformed security was The Force by another name. The second detained the attacker, suddenly subdued, and sat him on a chair behind the nearest counter. The man had achieved what he'd come to do and was now more preoccupied with the blood flowing from a wound in his head. Two of the assistants, fragrant creatures both and glamorous in their sashes, helped Preston sit up and lean his back against the Clinique display cabinet. Blood was coming from his lower lip and nose, and it was clear a nasty bruise would develop on his cheek. The pain in his ribs was intense. He was winded, but nauseous as he was he knew he wouldn't throw up.

Kathy Reid ran over, breathing heavily, and spoke to Chloe. The guard had her arms pinned behind her, but that didn't stop her stamping on his foot.

'Fuck off, wanker!'

'Watch your lip, young lady,' the guard said, tightening his grip, 'I don't have to take that from you.'

'Who are calling a lady!' Chloe was outraged. She wasn't prepared to be insulted.

'Chloe,' Kathy said, 'if you promise to calm down, Jim will let you go.'

'But Mrs Reid,' Jim said, 'we saw her attacking that gentleman over there.' He pointed to the customer under the charge of his colleague, who was now holding a powder puff to the man's head and pressing down hard.

One of the girls left Preston in the care of the other and joined in the discussion.

'I saw the whole thing, Mrs Reid. That man assaulted Mr Blair. He came here looking for him. That's why she did it. Chloe was defending Mr Blair.'

Kathy hadn't noticed Preston, but she did now. She felt no sympathy for him since he had it coming, whatever it was. She approached him and leant down to speak.

'Why did this man attack you?' she asked, knowing full well that Preston had been sleeping with his wife.

'How the hell would I know?' Preston said. 'I've never set eyes on him before. Oh, and by the way, I'm still alive. Thank you for asking.'

Kathy told Jim to release Chloe, and as he did so she caught him in the guts with a well-placed back elbow.

'Chloe,' Kathy said, 'you know Pamela and June?' Chloe smoothed her hair and nodded, and her top, already brief, rode up even farther, the stone in her navel giving off a dangerous glint. 'Good. Go up to their office. One of them will be in. Tell them exactly what happened and ask them to write it down. Don't make anything up, don't leave anything out.'

'Boring!'

'Chloe!' Who should have to deal with a girl like this? 'It's for your own protection.'

Chloe left and Kathy turned her attention to the attacker who, she realised, now that she looked at him more closely, was of Asian appearance. Blood was seeping freely through the powder puff. It didn't look good.

'My name is Kathy Reid,' she told him. 'I'm going to order a taxi. One of our security men will take you to A and E.' She took out a notebook.

'Your surname?'

'Rangar.'

'First names?'

'Vijay.'

'And what does the V stand for, Mr Rangar?'

'What?'

Vijay couldn't cope. His mind was full of blood, as was his left eye.

'I think you'll find,' Preston said from somewhere approaching knee level, 'that Vijay is a name complete in itself.' He had the benefit of the Samita's Guide, which Kathy had not.

'So that would be?'

'V_ I _ J_ A_ Y.'

'You're sure you don't know why he did it?' she asked. It was hard to believe.

'As God is my witness,' he said, 'I haven't a clue. Why don't you ask him?'

Kathy intended to do just that but events conspired against her. She had to phone the police, phone for a taxi, and summon Frank to escort Preston to the medical room. 'Use the service lift,' she suggested quietly, 'we don't want the customers seeing him in this state.' Since a considerable number of customers had already gathered to enjoy the action, this was damage limitation at best.

To Preston's consternation, Frank arrived with a wheelchair, helped him into it and took him away. Better safe than sorry, he said, as he waited for the lift, risk of concussion and all that. Kathy assured Mr Rangar that a taxi had been ordered and would arrive any moment. In the meantime, noting that blood had now seeped into his shirt collar and jacket, the best thing he could do was remain seated, keep calm and wait.

The policeman arrived at the same time as the taxi, so he radioed his colleagues at the Royal Infirmary to be on the lookout for the new arrival with a view to taking a statement and ensuring he didn't do a runner after treatment. In the meantime, he said, he wanted to speak to anyone who had witnessed the incident.

'I see you have cameras.'

Kathy nodded. 'You're welcome to check the footage.'

Believing everything was under control, Kathy left the policeman to it and took the lift to the sixth floor. She expected to find Chloe in June's office giving an account of what had happened, from which June would delete the expletives.

'That was quick,' she said, seeing Chloe wasn't there. So quick it hadn't happened yet and June knew nothing about it. Luckily, Kathy decided to take the stairs to floor seven, a route which took her past the restaurant. And there was Chloe, deep in conversation with Sarah and talking ten to the dozen on her mobile phone at the same time. Amazing, she thought, that a brain so small was capable of division. The story would be round the peripheral estates by electronic jungle drum before she had the official account she required.

'Chloe,' she said firmly, 'come with me. This is something we can't put off any longer.'

'But Mrs Reid,' Chloe wailed, 'I haven't finished my coke!'

'So bring it with you.'

If only other problems were solved so easily. Leaving Chloe with June, Kathy headed up to the control room where Pamela was watching the monitors.

'You saw that?'

'Exciting or what!'

'We have it on tape?'

'Probably. I'd have to stop recording to be sure.'

Kathy drew up a chair and Pamela rewound the tape to the point where Vijay made his appearance.

'The police will want this,' Kathy said. 'You could make a copy while we watch it.'

Reviewing the footage it was clear to them both that Vijay had been seeking someone out, whom they now knew to be Preston, and that when Preston appeared he'd attacked him. It was totally unprovoked. It was also clear from the tape that Chloe, perched somewhat incongruously behind the Givenchy counter, had tried to stop Vijay inflicting further harm on Preston, not so much by restraining him as by taking him apart. The vase which did the damage had contained artificial flowers. Was everything fake in cosmetics?

Kathy knew what the problem was, she hadn't been far from the mark. Vijay was plainly of Asian origin, ethnically speaking. So was Anita. Vijay was a relative of Anita's who, discovering by intercepted text messages that Preston was getting his leg over, had come to his place of work to duff him up. Family honour and all that.

'Where's Preston now?' Pamela asked.

He was in the medical room with Pamela's fancy man, as Kathy insisted on describing him, and he wasn't happy.

'I've cleaned you up as well as I can,' Frank said. 'The bleeding's stopped.'

'Have you a mirror in here?' Preston asked. He could see one over the sink but didn't feel like getting up just yet.

'So what was that about?' Frank asked.

'Would you believe I don't know?'

'I think you could do with a drink and maybe something to eat. How would that be? You need to sit still and relax for a while.'

When Frank left Preston struggled up and looked himself over. Not a pretty sight, and it would get worse before it got better. If he'd known what sort of day this would be he wouldn't have got out of bed. He sat down again with too much backward force, rolling his chair across the floor till it hit the bed. What was the score so far? He'd just been the victim of an unprovoked assault. He'd lost his job. He'd been offered a new one. Big deal! They'd say it was a move to the side, a horizontal redeployment, but really it was a demotion. He could hear Gemma now 'upgrading' his designation from window dresser to window designer, but the work wouldn't change. They'd still be looking for witches and broomsticks at Halloween, and a pumpkin or two. Not to mention a crescent moon. And Gibson would be breathing down his neck, muttering darkly about idolatry and pagan festivals. Who needed it? Not him.

He felt his jaw. It ached where Vijay had hit it and, strangely, on the opposite side as well. As his dentist would explain to him later, this was to be expected. None of his teeth were loose but no doubt he'd sustained some chipped enamel. And his ribs hurt a lot. His ribs were painful. Pulling up his shirt he noted clear signs of impact. Maybe a rib was cracked. Maybe two. And how was it, he wondered, that the attacker was taken by taxi to the Royal Infirmary while he, the innocent victim, was patched up on the premises by an electrician! That said something. That told him how little he was valued. His way ahead was clear. He'd reject their ridiculous window dressing offer, insist on working his month's notice unless they bought him out by giving him a month's pay in lieu, and in the meantime he'd pull down the whole sorry edifice, the whole house of cards. He'd attack this bastion of privilege on two fronts, through the courts and through the media. They'd take him more seriously then, when it was too late.

A police officer knocked at the door and came in.

'They said I'd find you here,' he said, looking round. He drew up a chair. 'Not exactly attractive, this place.'

How right he was, Preston thought. Talk about industrial first aid! This place was the pits. No one with a brain could stand it for more than five minutes.

21

Alice cycled to the new premises of Henderson McQuarrie LLP. Her last visit, three years before, had been to their fine old building in Queen Street where Astrid's office looked the part, spacious and long-established, giving the impression that documents from decades before would be available if required, together with precedents going back to the Declaration of Arbroath.

Arriving at the new building, very high and purpose-built, she discovered the purpose did not include making life easier for the client on whom their profits depended.

'What do you mean,' she asked the attendant in the underground car park, 'what do you mean you have no facility for bikes?'

'No one comes here by bike. The people who use this place are big earners. I'm talking six figures,' he said, confidentially.

'I've come here by bike,' Alice pointed out.

'So I see,' he replied. 'Listen dear, this isn't a recreation area for the elderly and infirm. It's a car park.'

'For clients of Henderson McQuarrie. I have a meeting with Astrid Bonthrone in five minutes.'

'Never heard of him,' the attendant said. 'I don't work for them myself, of course, so I wouldn't.'

Alice was struck by the man's face: too much flesh on the bone and rather too pasty, as though he'd eaten out of a frying pan all his life.

'You don't?'

'Management of the car park's a separate operation entirely. We manage car parks all over the country.' He pointed to the name on his cap, Comet Carparks. 'We're a significant player.'

'That's very reassuring. It seems I have no alternative but to take my bicycle with me in the lift.'

'Bit of a problem there, I'm afraid. You need a security key to enter a lift from the basement. Only employees of Henderson McQuarrie have those. I mean, it's obvious when you think about it. If anyone could enter, anyone might – drunks, vagrants, bag ladies. You name it.'

This last was clearly aimed at her but she let it pass. If she wished to meet Astrid Bonthrone she'd have to walk up a flight of concrete steps, cross a paved open yard then enter the building again by way of a large rotating door.

The lady at reception was none too pleased to see her.

'You can't bring that in here,' she said.

By this time Alice didn't care. 'Watch me.'

She wheeled her bike into the lift and pressed the UP button. Behind her, she could hear the receptionist calling for security, but she was heading for the seventh floor before anyone arrived. There she found another reception desk and another receptionist behind it.

'As I explained to your colleague on the ground floor, I have an appointment with Astrid Bonthrone.'

The receptionist ran a pencil down her diary.

'Please take a seat. I'll let Miss Bonthrone know you're here.'

Alice had noticed before that while independent-minded women such as Astrid liked the indeterminate 'Ms' in their correspondence, saying it was another matter. It was difficult to stand on your dignity sounding like a bee.

Astrid and the security man arrived at the same time to find her recovering in an armchair, her bicycle propped against the wall, crash helmet resting on the saddle. The security man told her that bicycles weren't allowed in the building. Astrid set him straight, there was no law against it, he was exceeding his authority. He backed down but he wasn't happy.

'On your head be it,' he said, as if the machine might explode at any moment.

Astrid showed Alice into a meeting room dominated by a wooden table large enough to seat twelve comfortably. At one end someone had thoughtfully provided three flasks – one tea, one coffee, one hot water – a bowl of sugar, a jug of milk and some chocolate fingers. Corporate profits wouldn't last long at this rate, Alice thought wryly. She saw a document folder too: Astrid was prepared. Over a calming cup of camomile tea (she'd brought her own bags) she rehearsed her experience of the basement car park. Not a problem for you, she said, thinking of the staff key. That's true, Astrid replied, my taxi drops me at the door. But she was dismayed by Alice's treatment in the car park, she'd take it up with one of the partners.

'So what do you think?' Alice asked.

Astrid opened the folder. 'The obvious starting point is the letter.'

Preston had sent it several days before. 'Dear Miss Mowatt,' it began, 'I write this note from my bed of pain'. Alice found this amusing, calling to mind a dishevelled Preston Blair stretched out with his bruises on a camp bed covered with an old blanket or a patchwork quilt. What a capacity for self-pity the boy had. She didn't find the rest of the letter so entertaining.

> *To begin with, I can only consider your offer of a window dressing position as tantamount to constructive dismissal. In addition, I feel that Mowatts has failed in its duty of care to this employee on two counts: it allowed a vicious attack to take place against me on its own premises and then afforded treatment for my several*

injuries which fell far short of what would be regarded as medically appropriate.

I am currently taking legal advice on these issues. However, realising that defending any legal action could be costly, and also that adverse publicity would reflect very badly on a prestigious store such as yours, I am willing to consider a reasonable settlement.

'What do you make of it?' Alice asked.
'He's bluffing,' Astrid replied, 'and I would construe his reference to publicity as a threat.'
'So would I, and I don't take kindly to it either.'
'However, it could be also taken as fair warning so there's no mileage in pursuing that.'
It had not been a good afternoon for Alice, who reached for another chocolate finger. Comfort eating, she knew, but you took your comfort where you could.
'I'll deal with his grievances in turn and tell you what I'd advise.' Though human warmth wasn't her forte she tried to be reassuring. 'We can handle this, Miss Mowatt.' It was as close as Astrid was likely to get to a comforting pat on the arm.
Before he could claim constructive dismissal Preston would have to resign. Had he done that? Evidently not. In which case, Astrid concluded, he would first have to do so, setting out his reasons. At that point Alice would have twenty-eight days to respond, during which time there would be nothing he could do since he couldn't know whether or not she might chose to revert to the status quo ante.
'But Astrid, he hasn't been dismissed, not from the company. We've offered him an alternative position.'
'Right, so if he goes ahead with this, which I very much doubt, he'll resign. He'll claim you forced him into it by demoting him, by redeploying him in a role which might be considered demeaning or humiliating.'

'I hardly think window dressing . . .'

'I agree, he doesn't have a hope of making it stick. He'd never reach a tribunal with what he's got here. May I speak frankly, Miss Mowatt?'

'That would help.'

'I don't know why you employed him in the first place, but if he offers to resign get it in writing before he changes his mind.'

Alice already knew that Astrid thought Preston Blair was all mouth, forever promising and never delivering. But she couldn't help wondering what sort of person Astrid was. Unlike Preston, she worked in a purposive way, and to judge by her standing within Henderson McQuarrie she was counted a success. But was it possible, Alice wondered, that she had, by sheer concentration on her career, left little room for the personal, reducing herself to a meeter of targets, an attainer of goals? Was it possible that her appearance, always so well contrived, gave her no pleasure at all and certainly nowhere near the pleasure it gave Preston? Astrid had caught him looking her over and clearly didn't like it. But she wouldn't: Preston wasn't in her league.

'I believe you have a tape.'

Alice went to her bike, took a tape from the basket, returned to the room and handed it to her. The footage appeared on a wall-mounted monitor. Alice had seen it once before, Astrid not at all. The relevant section lasted less than three minutes.

'Well,' she said, 'it's clear to me that this attack came out of the blue. No one but a psychic could have foreseen it.'

'Does that matter?' Alice asked.

'I would say so, yes. Okay, you owe a duty of care to your employees but how far does that extend? You've employed uniformed security guards, you've employed a store detective, you've installed CCTV surveillance cameras, and you're part of a retail intelligence-sharing network. Short of machine-gun emplacements and Dobermann Pinschers I can't see what more you could have done.'

She stopped the tape and re-wound it.

'Do we know why Mr Blair was attacked?'

Alice believed she did. Mr Blair had given Mr Rangar's sister a gift, a perfume of his own manufacture. Shortly afterwards, Miss Rangar had come out in a rash. Mr Rangar attributed the rash to Mr Blair's concoction. He was very angry about it, especially as his sister was a girl of great pulchritude regarded by many as a walking advertisement for her wares.

'So he came to the store to exact retribution.'

'Exactly.'

'Well Miss Mowatt, I fail to see how anyone could have foreseen such an improbable sequence of events. Mr Blair knew much more of the background than you and he failed to see it coming himself!'

'Yes,' Alice said, 'but to be fair to the boy, he was unaware of Miss Rangar's allergic reaction. When the rash appeared she rang in sick.'

'Miss Mowatt,' Astrid said, in a slightly admonitory tone, 'we're not in the business of being fair. We're in the business of winning which, in this case, means ensuring that Preston Blair cannot proceed against you and hope to succeed. What an idiot he was,' she added, 'dabbling in perfumes.'

'Well,' Alice said, 'yes and no. We have since received a medical note from Miss Rangar's doctor. It appears her rash was caused by an allergic reaction to something she ate. Shell fish are suspected. The perfume had nothing to do with it.'

'Still and all,' Astrid said. A remarkably incomplete formulation from someone so capable of great precision, Alice thought. 'Anyway, we may be on weaker ground in the way his injuries were dealt with. I'm concerned that we have no accident report. There's no sign of one here,' she pointed out, riffling through the contents of her folder. 'Completion three weeks after the event won't wash. It has to be done at the time.'

'It was. Frank completed it that same afternoon. I asked him for it yesterday.'

'In which case it should be here, but it isn't.' Astrid was clearly suspicious.

'That's down to me, I'm afraid. When I asked him for his report I could have been more precise. He sent it to me as requested, all forty-seven pages.'

Astrid was astonished. What had this Frank person conducted, a full account of the patient's internal wiring?

'Good God,' Astrid said, 'this is serious.'

'Not really. Some weeks ago I asked him to write a draft environmental policy and he thought I was asking for that. I don't know if you have a view on disposable polystyrene cups, but Frank has. And his thoughts on Teflon are unprintable.'

'Teflon?'

'Don't go there Astrid, please,' Alice said. 'Unlikely as it sounds, dead parrots are involved.'

She produced her mobile phone.

'I'll ask him to fax it through. It's the only document we're missing.'

They were standing together looking out the panoramic window on the seventh floor, surveying the city spread out beneath them. The plate glass went all the way to the floor and Alice had a slight sensation of vertigo. What was to stop her falling to the ground below? She wondered if Astrid, gazing out, felt as if she owned all she surveyed, the narrow streets, the road works, the temporary traffic lights. Probably not. The door swung open and a secretary entered with a fax.

'Thank you, Rachel.' A quick glance was enough. 'Excellent. Alice, this is Frank's accident report.'

They resumed their seats at the table and reviewed it together.

'So,' Astrid summed up, 'a cut to the nose, another to the lower lip, a badly grazed cheek, discomfort in the area of the ribs. The patient reported no difficulty breathing. One chipped tooth.'

'Photographs?'

'No.'

'Too bad.'

'The thing is,' Alice said, 'Gemma phoned Preston at home to find out how he was and got an earful. She was actually quite upset wondering whether there wasn't something in what he was saying.'

Astrid smiled. 'Gemma's such a softie.'

'Preston claims his assailant got proper medical attention in a casualty department while he was patched up in a cupboard by a maintenance man.'

Astrid wanted full details, which she got.

'This is a tricky one,' she said. 'Frank's a trained first-aider?'

'He is.'

'And his qualification hasn't lapsed?'

'Not yet, though it will soon. He's very good. Very calm.'

'I'll want a copy of his certificate for the file.'

'Of course.'

'Well I would say that provided Frank's assessment of Preston's injuries was accurate and no internal injuries were overlooked then you're fine. Wait a minute though,' she said, picking up the remote control and replaying the concluding section of the tape. 'I thought so, we have a possible problem here.'

'And what would that be?' Alice asked.

'You'll notice it's Kathy Reid who makes the decision to send Mr Rangar to the Royal Infirmary and Kathy Reid who decides to have Preston looked after in house. What gives her the competence to draw a distinction like that? Is she a qualified first-aider too?'

'Actually, no,' Alice admitted, 'and she can't stand Preston either.'

'Well he might make some headway with that, though I wouldn't lose much sleep over it.'

'So we wait.'

'We do, and we have experience of waiting for Preston, don't we.'

'But what if he approaches some of these people who advertise on television? No win, no fee? Ambulance-chasers?'

'They'd be the only people who'd take him on, and only if they thought there was a chance of success. In this case there isn't.'

Astrid ejected the tape, closed the folder and looked out the window.

'We haven't mentioned Chloe.'

'Good thing too,' Alice said. 'Actually,' she continued, 'you might like to know that Chloe embodies the gritty reality of life.'

'She does? Who says?'

'Who else.'

'Gemma.'

'Mr Gibson set her straight.'

'What did he say?'

'That polite people are every bit as real as those who curse and swear and rain down profanities upon the world. And he was right, of course.'

'My diary's free for the rest of the day. What would you say to a break, in convivial surroundings with real coffee and home baking?'

The place Astrid had in mind was run by Italians who, she said, came up with the goods every time. Alice was taken with the idea. She had heard Astrid refer to her sister's children and sensed a kindred spirit, a woman destined to have none of her own. She wanted to take up the offer but had a problem. Her bike.

'Oh,' Astrid said, 'that's easily solved. Our courier service will deliver it. Someone can sign for it when it arrives and take it up to your office. Why don't I call a cab?'

22

Frank liked the store most in the evening, when the last customer had gone and he and the cleaners had the place to themselves. At this time of night it seemed more spacious. And it was certainly more orderly, like a large library from which the staff had wisely excluded borrowers, the stock where it should be, in its various categories, undisturbed.

Sometimes during the day the store was overpopulated to the point where people, too close together, generated friction and behaved badly, arguing among themselves, jostling, pushing other customers aside, shouting at assistants, jumping the queue in the restaurant, allowing their children to use beds as trampolines and lighting cigarettes in the toilets. Frank believed that bad behaviour was a consequence of over-population, that this was true on a global scale and that the store demonstrated it in microcosm. He had shared this opinion with Mr Gibson who, though inclined to agree, was trapped by the Biblical injunction, 'Be fruitful and multiply', into withholding his assent.

'But Mr Gibson,' Frank had said at the time, 'most of them can't even add!'

'Very witty I'm sure,' Mr Gibson replied, concealing his sympathy well.

Each night, when the store closed to the public, the escalators were switched off to save energy and reduce wear and tear, so Frank was obliged to take the stairs or the lift. When the doors opened on the ground floor he was always struck by the transformation which had come over the building. Shadows cast by lights extended to their full lengths, no longer cut off by customers. But the most noticeable change was in the sound, much less of it and mostly originating from the activity of cleaners, which was now free to travel from one wall to another, to bounce off floors and ceilings and to return by multiple routes to the ear with pleasing complexity. The building sounded larger now, the increased reverberation more reminiscent of a church or cathedral which, in a sense, it was.

People shopped on Sundays now and they couldn't be in two places at once. But in the store they were, in the main, more generous with their offerings, expecting in return not the satisfaction of supporting the church roof or the pastor in his ministry but food and drink, tangibles, manufactured goods to take away. And anyway, who was to say which was better for the soul, religion or retail therapy. It was, in its way, a cargo cult, Frank thought. Was there really such a difference between the hapless Melanesian looking to the heavens for a parachute descending on the breeze with a radio or a fridge, and the shopper heading for the exit with plastic bags and boxes. They both wanted the same things. The Melanesians couldn't pay for them of course, but neither could many of the customers with cards.

On the night of the annual deep clean, Frank's route took him past the chill compartments and he felt the drop in temperature at once. His draft report to Alice pointed out how inefficient this was. Surely the public wouldn't object to opening a glass door to remove their carton of milk or packet of butter? And even from a distance he could see that consumer electronics left a lot to be desired. Banks of televisions, CRTs, LCDs and plasmas, had all been left on. He'd complained about this before, but Colin was more interested in himself than the environment. Technology was moving at breakneck speed, so fast the public had trouble keeping up. That was where he came in, making these developments understandable to the man in the street, though in Colin's case the man was often a woman.

Frank made his way round the shelves switching the sets off one by one. Tuned to the same channel, they were showing contestants competing for a modelling job, their support of each other no deeper than their make-up. As he switched the last one off and made his way to the lift a phone rang. This did not happen on the shop floor at night, all incoming callers hearing a message to the effect that the store was now closed but it's opening hours were . . . He tracked it down to the gift section, a mobile left by a customer or a member of staff. It was radiating sound in all directions, a weak signal made strong by reflection.

On his way to the kitchens he called in at the medical room, his home from home. He smiled a little as he walked in, seeing through the closed locker door to the rolled up sleeping bag behind it. Though it wasn't the most restful night's sleep, he'd worked the trick many times now and no one was any the wiser. The bed might have orthopaedic properties but it wasn't comfortable, and there was always the worry that someone would surprise him in the night and the game would be up. An irrational fear, perhaps, but one which kept him closer to the surface of consciousness than he would have liked and consequently less rested when the new day dawned.

And the fact that his belongings were scattered over the city didn't help much either: a change of clothes in a locker here, another at Pamela's, books at his sister's, redirected mail at Archie's. He wondered what a shrink would say. Something clever no doubt, something which wouldn't help. Just as your physical possessions are spread across several locations, Mr Figures, so too is your personality. The one representing the other, you are clearly a man in two minds at least.

Annie and the girls were pleased to see him. It was one of those occupations where middle-aged women were girls regardless, the only perk of the job. And now their banter had a focus. Complaining about men was one thing, doing it to their face was more fun. Here he comes, Mr Management himself, Mr Time-And-Motion Study. Check the butt on that, Trudy, you could do worse. Oh, I don't know, he seems a bit wet behind the ears to me. Lacking experience, if you see what I mean. Where's he been all my life?

'We're well on target, Frank,' Annie assured him, 'we'll be finished by nine, half nine at the latest.'

It took them some time to tidy up, put on their coats and jackets and make their way out. They always used the stairs when they left, never the lift. Annie assured him they didn't mean anything by their wisecracks, but Frank already knew that. Anyone doing a boring job would try to liven it up. Alastair had it worse than he did, subjected as he was to hints that, being so old, he couldn't get it up. It was all done in a roundabout way, but it was clear that Mrs Geddes was less than happy with his performance. He sometimes failed to deliver the goods. He was having trouble with his gear stick. Being stuck in neutral was no joke. Never mind neutral, what about reverse! The current topic was Mr Mackay, furniture, known to be boffing Lynn Marshall, though whether he was fit for her was another matter. Just as well he had so many beds to choose from!

Frank wasn't comfortable with words like 'boffing' and 'shagging', though he was equally ill at ease with 'making love'. In the economics of sex boffing was surely deflation, though he couldn't deny that, as in the real economy, deflation occurred. Selfish people existed, out for all they could get. Instant gratification, as Mr Gibson put it. On the other hand, to judge from conversations overheard in bars and restaurants, 'making love' was inflation worthy of the Weimar

Republic, a phrase used happily by the promiscuous and serially unfaithful, not to mention his sister. A spot of deep cleaning there wouldn't go amiss.

As the sound of their departure faded down the stairwell Frank did a turn round the kitchens. The girls had done a good job, everything was as ready as they could make it. His phone rang. The team from Catering Hygiene had arrived: could someone please let them in.

23

Preston had a problem with vanity. He wanted a doctor to check him out as soon as possible, when the damage was at its most visible, but several days passed before he could present an acceptable face to the world and until that time he wouldn't venture from the house. I'm afraid Dr Duncan's list is full for today, the receptionist told him. How about tomorrow, Preston asked?

'You can't make an appointment for tomorrow, Mr Blair, we have a same day appointment system now.'

However, if it was urgent, she could offer him an appointment with a locum. Since that didn't entail phoning at eight the following morning he accepted.

'It doesn't make sense,' Preston said. 'It's ridiculous.'

'What is?' Mr Braunschweig asked, laying down his fork. He had a liking for kalbsleverwurst and coleslaw and kept supplies of both in Ada's fridge. Preston explained the situation and Mr Braunschweig listened, occasionally glancing at the kitchen clock. It was now twenty to one and Preston was filling a bowl with breakfast cereal. This did not impress Mr Braunschweig, it did not augur well.

'There have been complaints in recent times,' he explained, 'that patients were waiting two or even three weeks for an appointment. Doctors were therefore given a target. Don't quote me on this, but I believe the nomenclatura have decreed that no one should wait more than forty-eight hours. So,' he continued, 'by the simple expedient of insisting that all appointments be made on the same day, your doctor is able to claim not only that this target is being met but also surpassed. And thus,' he concluded, 'do statistics make fools of us all.'

Preston joined him at the table and poured milk over his Frosties. Mr Braunschweig hoped that the boy did not have a lactose intolerance.

'But everyone will phone at the same time. The line will be jammed!'

Mr Braunschweig smiled. 'A very pertinent point.'

'I thought the health service was run for the patients.'

Mr Braunschweig found this so funny he laughed, something he rarely did. His shoulders heaved under his cardigan, a lived-in Harris Tweed affair with leather buttons.

'My dear boy,' he said, 'a doctor's surgery is run entirely to suit the practitioners. Patients come a distant second. Perhaps if they were called customers, or clients. Or tax-payers?'

Noting that he was having an anaesthetic effect on the young man Mr Braunschweig changed the subject.

'Given the unfortunate events at your place of work, it occurred to me ask whether you have considered going into business on your own account? After all,' he quipped, 'you are unlikely to sack yourself.'

The idea had its attractions. He could get up as late as he liked and save a small fortune in travel time working from home.

'Strange you should mention that, Mr Braunschweig,' Preston said. 'Mum suggested the same thing.'

'She did?' Mr Braunschweig was surprised.

'Something along the lines of mighty oaks from little acorns grow. She didn't put it exactly that way, but you know what I mean.'

'My goodness!'

If Ada was thinking that Preston might develop into a mighty oak she was doomed to disappointment. As he was preparing to depart Mr Braunschweig noticed Preston was too.

'I have an appointment with a locum.'

'I see,' Mr Braunschweig said. 'You are aware that most doctors are impostors?' he asked, by way of a parting shot.

'I find that hard to believe.'

'Then I suggest you subject their qualifications to scrutiny. Most of them are bachelors of medicine, some are bachelors of surgery as well, but very few are doctors.'

Mr Braunschweig knew what he was talking about. Having completed a doctorate in the chemistry of proteins many years before, he was a doctor himself.

Preston was confused. 'So why don't you call yourself Doctor Braunschweig?'

'I used to,' Mr Braunschweig admitted, 'but I grew weary of students knocking on my door with hiccups, nosebleeds, asthma, sprained wrists and in-growing toenails. Reverting to plain Mister Braunschweig has saved me a great deal of trouble.'

The receptionist pointed Preston to the waiting room, Dr Watson would be with him shortly. It was quieter than usual, two other patients reading magazines. He sat himself as far as possible from the old man with the slippers and hacking cough, his chest had enough to contend with already. Five minutes later the door opened and a young woman called his name. She looked almost as young as he was, short with mousy brown hair.

'Mr Blair, if you could come with me.'

She showed him into her consulting room and indicated a chair. Well, Preston thought, this is a turn-up for the books, a female doctor. It was a development he welcomed: being a woman she'd be more sympathetic. So, what was his problem?

He described the assault, dramatising it so well that Vijay sound every inch the professional hit-man. Looking at his face and the healing graze on his cheek, Dr Watson asked when all this had happened and, on finding out, why he had allowed a week to pass before making an appointment. Since he could hardly admit the real reason he cited pain in the ribs and chest.

'We'd better have look then, hadn't we.'

Preston removed his jacket and shirt and Dr Watson checked him out, pressing gently at the various locations indicated by the patient as giving him grief. When she'd finished, she asked him to put his shirt back on, which he did remarkably easily for someone in so much pain.

'So what's the verdict, doctor?' he asked, though thanks to Mr Braunschweig the word 'doctor' stuck in the craw.

'The attack,' she said, 'and I'm sorry to hear about that, has bruised at least one, possibly two ribs. The muscles in that area – you may have heard of the intercostal muscles – have also taken something of a hit. On the plus side, there's no reason to believe you have broken a rib. And even if you had,' she admitted, 'there's not a great deal we could do about it.'

Preston was flabbergasted. 'What, is that it?'

Dr Watson sat back in her chair and sighed.

'As I'm sure you appreciate, Mr Blair, we can't put your ribs in a sling.'

'So what am I supposed to do? What do you recommend?'

'Live with it, as you've clearly been doing, and it will heal itself. All it needs is time. A week or two from now and you'll be fully recovered.'

'That's all very well, but what about the pain, the discomfort?'

'Your analgesic of choice will deal with that, paracetemol, aspirin, both easily obtainable over the counter.'

'I'm not convinced you're taking this seriously,' Preston said. 'You don't seem to realise your notes could be cited in legal proceedings. So could you,' he added as an afterthought.

Dr Watson suddenly became brisk and businesslike, swivelling away from her desk to look him in the eye. The fact that they were both seated removed Preston's height advantage. She was more imposing now.

'Your condition is straightforward, your symptoms unambiguous. Suing me will get you nowhere.'

'No, you don't understand,' Preston said too loudly, the consultation wasn't going well, 'that's not what I meant!'

He explained where he was when the attack occurred, how negligent his employer had been. Dr Watson heard him out in silence.

'Well in my opinion, and that's what you're here for, your injuries are genuine but far from severe. I don't think litigation is a route I would go down.'

On his way home, Preston dropped into the local leisure centre because it had a café in the foyer. He needed time to think in a neutral environment. He ordered a coffee and an iced doughnut and sat down at the one of the metal tables. His visit to the doctor had not been productive. Not only did she make light of his injuries but there was little evidence he could produce to back up his claim since a photograph of his chest would show nothing at all. The bruising was at a deeper level.

Perhaps he should have insisted on an X-ray, but that would only have helped if a rib was fractured and Dr Watson believed this was not the case.

Two teachers emerged from the swimming pool with a class of nursery children. Water wings were much in evidence, yellow and blue, and they chattered incessantly like sparrows in a bush. One of the teachers did a head count before they left. Wise precaution, Preston thought, they didn't want to leave one of their charges at the bottom of the pool. The other asked them to pair off and hold hands as they left the building, which left an odd one out, though she didn't seem to mind holding hands with a teacher. That would change.

Preston took a bite from his doughnut, admiring the almost perfect crescent left by his teeth. Maybe it would have been totally perfect before the attack. Maybe his dentist would confirm when he saw him in two weeks that his bite was no longer what it had been. Mr Anderson would testify on his behalf, or at the very least supply an affidavit.

A group of pensioners appeared in loose pants and tops complete with rolled up mats. This would be the sixty plus yoga group no doubt, working on their creaking joints. Nothing strenuous, gentle movement, flexibility the watchword. Now that was interesting, Preston thought. At the other end of the age-range, forming an orderly queue at the exit through which there was no return, self-consciousness was plainly falling off. Not to nursery level, perhaps, but no one twenty years younger would have paid such scant regard to style. They weren't out to impress. Why would they be, he thought? What would be the point?

Preston decided he'd put it off long enough – he'd have to visit Mowatts to collect his personal effects. As he walked to his car he noticed a large A4 notice under his wiper advising him that he had parked in a bay reserved for blue badge holders. His number had been logged. If it happened again his vehicle would be clamped. He couldn't believe it. Was there no escape from cripples like Pamela or officious oafs like Alastair Geddes?

He was sufficiently provoked by the incident to head for Mowatts and drive straight into the bay reserved for Hector. The letters HM were painted in front of it: Hector Mowatt or His Majesty, Preston thought wryly, delete as applicable. He saw a parking attendant heading towards him, but the old man was too far away to intervene. He walked round to the front entrance, smirked at the caryatids, sneered at the coat of arms, sniggered at the Investors in People plaque – what a joke that was – ignored Louise labouring with a staple gun in one of the windows and strode in. Everyone would know his situation but he had nothing to be ashamed of, neither his eye-catching website nor the fragrance he had given to Anita. His route took him past cosmetics and there she was, the sultry one, the dusky beauty who had recovered entirely and was now gracing her counter as she always had, elegantly, impeccably. What skin tone! What a body! What a star!

'Preston,' she said, venturing out into the aisle, 'I can't tell you how sorry I am. Vijay is a bit of a hot-head, I'm afraid.'

'I wonder if his head will be so hot when his case comes up.'

Anita was on the point of wringing her hands, so great was her concern.

'The papers are with the Fiscal. We don't know what will happen.'

'Oh, that's easy,' Preston said, 'he'll be charged with assault. Unless he's an illegal. In that case he'll be deported.'

'My brother has lived here all his life!'

'Doesn't give him the right to assault complete strangers though, does it.'

Seeing that Anita was sufficiently shocked, he turned on his heel and walked to the lift. So concerned was he to let his body do the talking he didn't spot his saviour, Chloe, who had now progressed to the Garnier counter. Thanks to the ministrations of the ladies and even though she didn't think so herself, she was looking marginally more chic. The girls had persuaded her to abandon the pink beret – quite the gamine, as Bertrand liked to say – and don a white lab coat. Makes you look more professional, they told her, more of an expert. It also made her more anonymous, easier to miss, but that was no excuse for Preston. Chloe spotted him and she wasn't amused. She didn't expect a medal but she was surely entitled to a word of thanks. Looking through her as if she wasn't there, that was out of order. She'd put herself on the line for him. Where did this bastard get off?

His office was unlocked, empty and dark. He switched on the light. To his relief all his belongings were where he'd left them, which was just as well: none of them came cheap. He was looking through his drawers when the door opened. The parking attendant had phoned Alastair, and Alastair had phoned Alice. Word had got round. Preston was in the building.

'Good afternoon, Preston,' Alice said. She had a letter in her hand. 'How are you bearing up after your ordeal?'

Before he could answer June knocked and entered. That couldn't be coincidence, she'd always given him a wide berth before.

'Which ordeal would that be, Miss Mowatt, being assaulted or getting the bum's rush at my place of work.'

Alice knew Preston would be difficult. He could bristle at the best of times, but since receiving his letter she expected the worst.

'The assault, Preston. We were all very sorry about that.'

Feeling he had the upper hand and possessed of a certain moral superiority, he sat down behind his desk as if he, Preston, were interrogating Alice. The feeling didn't last long. Alice handed him the letter she was carrying and sat in the other seat. As she did so, Preston noticed how well she was turned out for a woman of her age: light brown Georgette top with matching light brown slacks. Well, matching to the casual glance. There was a slight but discernible difference in shade and it wasn't down to lighting. Quite good, Miss Mowatt, but could do better. Having a scoop neck, it left a suitable area of skin to display her necklace against, a large amber pendant in a silver setting, a gift from Hector on her birthday.

'I was on my way to the mail room with this,' she said, 'but since you're here it seems only sensible to hand it to you personally.'

'That way you can't deny receiving it,' June said.

'Thank you, June,' Alice said, in a warning tone. The last thing she wanted was unnecessary confrontation. 'It's my response to your letter. You don't have to open it now, of course, not unless you want to.'

Preston accepted the letter, but he had no intention of conducting his business in public. It could contain a reasonable offer but if it didn't he might, in the heat of the moment, say things he would later regret. His position would be weakened by reacting badly in front of witnesses. What he needed was a locked room where he could study the letter without fear of interruption. A toilet cubicle would probably be the best bet, ensuring privacy but offering the chance to respond appropriately.

Alice turned to June. 'I wonder if you could do me a favour, June, and fetch Mel. He doesn't know his way around yet.'

June looked uneasy. 'Are you sure you'll be alright, Miss Mowatt?'

'Oh I think so, June,' she said, 'I have a black belt in country dancing.'

'Is that woman off her head,' Preston asked as June left, 'does she really think I'd attack you?'

'You have been known to lose your temper,' Alice said. 'June can be very protective.'

'Might I remind you that I'm the only person here who's actually been attacked. If anyone needed protection it was me!'

'And we're genuinely sorry about that. It came as a shock to us all.'

'And while we're at it, who the hell is Mel?'

Melville Armstrong worked for the Web Design Partnership, the company Mowatts had retained to sort out the site.

He'd started the day before, acquainting himself with accounts and stock control, and riling Mr Gibson in the process. It would obviously be helpful if he could talk with Preston too.

'Call me simple, Miss Mowatt,' Preston said, 'but surely all the information he needs is in the report. Why don't you let him read it and have done? Of course, silly me, I forgot,' he said, indulging in a spot of ham acting, 'he didn't pay for it, did he? That'll be it, I expect.'

'They have a philosophy, Web Design Associates, that's what they call it anyway,' Alice said, ignoring Preston's sarcasm, 'though I would classify it more as a working practice.'

Preston toyed with his unopened letter. 'You don't say.'

'They believe you only really understand a system if you use it. So after spending some time with Mr Gibson, Mr Armstrong's been working with June preparing customer accounts. As he so graphically puts it himself, you have to get your hands dirty.'

Preston snorted. 'Working in an office!'

'I believe he was speaking metaphorically. And I must say,' she added, 'I have some sympathy with his point of view.'

Looking at her sitting there, an old woman by his standards, he found this conceivable. When she was a girl goods would have been delivered by horse and cart. She had probably helped load and unload, stroked the horse, given it sugar cubes and assisted with its nose-bag. How old was she, he wondered? Seventy-five at least to judge by the liver spots on her chest, which came close to competing in a small way with her amber, duller than normal in the poor light of his office, not a glint or sparkle to be seen. He felt like reminding her that a lot could be achieved by laser treatment or, if she didn't want to go that far, concealed by cosmetics. But she didn't seem to care so why would he?

With the briefest of knocks, June showed Melville into the office and Preston immediately had the impression he was too big for it, not because of his size but his energy. He strode up to the desk where Preston was sitting and stretched out his arm. According to him it was a good afternoon. As they shook hands, Preston knew he was up against it. Despite his artistic talent he had never dressed accordingly, preferring to display himself as a well turned out young man who might, if he had so desired, have made a name for himself as a male model.

Melville, on the other hand, seemed hell bent on proclaiming his artistic credentials. Why else would he be wearing green corduroy trousers, a country style shirt with a mild lumberjack pattern, open at the neck, and a yellow waistcoat? All that was missing was a bow tie! But what struck Preston most was his head. He had thick straight brown hair, combed back, and a moustache as impressive as Zapata's though with more of a vertical droop. Both his hair and his moustache, Preston knew, were carefully styled with a mousse or gel. This was a man with an image which inclined, Preston thought, to the Mexican of days gone by. What a poser, he thought, as he added, in his mind's eye, a sombrero and an ammunition belt.

'Melville Armstrong,' he said, 'Web Design Partnership.'

'I believe you,' Preston said, and invited him to take a seat knowing full well both the seats were taken.

'I'll get back to the office,' June said, glad to escape.

'Thank you, June.'

'If you'll excuse me, Miss Mowatt,' Melville said, 'won't be a second.'

Left to themselves for a moment, Alice explained that Mel had an MBA.

'It's a post-graduate qualification as you know.'

'So what did he do before that, fine art?'

'Computer Science, I believe.'

'He covers most of the bases then.'

'So it would appear.'

Preston was struck by her reply. She was reserving her position till she saw how he performed. That this might have something to do with her experience of him didn't cross his mind. But if Mel had no art background at all, why did he dress as he did? It came close to giving a false impression, a visual breach of the Trade Descriptions Act. Melville wanted to appear the creative type while, as his qualifications showed, he hadn't a creative bone in his body. After all, creative people didn't study computer science. It would drive them to drink or despair.

'Sorry about that,' Mel said, coming back in with a chair. He sat down in the small space there was beside Alice. 'You have my full attention.'

'It would help Mel a lot,' Alice explained, 'to have access to your computer.'

'I bet it would,' Preston said bitterly, 'and why would I agree to that?'

'To help a colleague,' Alice replied.

'But he isn't a colleague, Miss Mowatt. I don't work here any more.'

'Dear me, where to begin?' Alice wondered aloud. 'You're entitled to work one month's notice or to receive one month's pay in lieu. Either way, you're still on the payroll.'

'So that makes Mel here a colleague? I don't think so. No offence Mel,' he said, 'but I don't know you from Adam. This is a mere technicality,' he assured her, 'desperate stuff.'

'So you don't consider it matters.'

'Of course I don't, I'm not a fool!'

'In that case, since you're not a colleague we can safely bid you goodbye and save a month's pay. I'll have security escort you from the premises.'

'Now wait a minute,' Preston spluttered.

'You said it was a mere technicality,' Alice pointed out, 'but actually it's a right. Something you, as an employee, are entitled to.' Preston nodded. 'Well,' Alice said, 'you may not like it but employers have entitlements too, and one of them is the labour they pay for. In this case, the work you did for us in return for the money we paid you.'

Preston was thinking with resentment of the dreary hours he'd spent taking photographs of stock, scanning illustrations and diagrams, converting copy into text files.

'So what am I supposed to do, just hand it all over?'

'That would be appreciated,' Melville said.

'I'm sure it would,' Preston said, wishing now that he'd opened the envelope and knew where he stood. If it contained an acceptable offer, continued lack of cooperation might queer his pitch. 'But you must understand, given my treatment here I'd be doing it with the utmost reluctance. Under duress.'

'To construe a polite request as coercion is hardly reasonable,' Alice said.

'Okay,' Preston said, 'perhaps duress was over-stating it a bit, but I'm sure you knew what I meant.'

'Mr Blair,' Alice said, 'this has gone on long enough. Would you kindly tell me whether or not you will give Melville the password to your computer. Yes or no.'

Preston decided he had little option but to comply but couldn't bring himself to say it, so to avoid losing face he wrote it down. As far as he could tell Alice's arguments were sound. The law, he was sure, would side with her on this one and he couldn't fight her on several fronts at once. Hitler's big mistake, Mr Braunschweig had assured him, was opening a second front. Not that he had anything in common with Hitler, but he wasn't going to fall for that one.

Seeing him search his desk drawers for a pen, Alice reached up to her hair and removed the wooden skewer, her signature adornment, which Preston had assumed kept it up. Wrong. Her bun remained in place and the skewer turned out to be a quality HB pencil of Finnish manufacture, polished wood, which she handed to him with a smile. Taking the unopened envelope he wrote the password on it and passed it to her. ANITA. Of course, she thought, who was more full of grace than Anita? Why hadn't she thought of that? She passed the envelope to Mel, who read it and stuffed it in his inside pocket.

'Just hang on to my future as well, why don't you,' Preston said.

Melville looked abashed and handed it back to him. 'Sorry,' he said, 'I didn't realise what it was.'

'Thank you, Preston,' Alice said. 'It's always good to see people deal with each other in a civilised manner, don't you think?' She rose to leave. 'I want you to know that you can always talk to me one-to-one, in confidence and without prejudice to any decision you might reach.'

'Quite a character,' Mel said, when Alice left.

'Oh yes,' Preston agreed, 'her door is always open.'

Mel was uncertain what to do next. Preston, who seemed to be thinking about something, was sitting at the desk with the relevant monitor on it, but he could hardly lift him bodily from his chair.

'So, Mel,' Preston said, 'you seem a bit light on the graphic design front.'

'I am,' Mel said, 'but I've never found that a problem. Not so far, anyway,' he said, making no concessions now that he had the password and didn't have to. 'What matters most is that it works. If it looks good too, that's a bonus, no denying that. But if it looks good and doesn't work . . .'

Preston didn't like the sound of this. Mel had clearly been briefed and believed he was describing his work. He'd also swallowed the conventional wisdom that appearance was cosmetic only, having no deeper function.

'Look,' Preston said, 'apart from anything else there's such a thing as house style. And it's not just a question of being easy on the eye and using the same two colours on every page. I mean,' he added, 'we've all met people who talk nonsense.'

'That's true,' Mel agreed, wondering where this was leading.

'You listen, you hear a lot of words, but it's just so much noise. Afterwards you're none the wiser.'

'Know what you mean,' Mel agreed, sensing that Preston was making his point by example.

'Well the same can happen with visual images, layout, typography. You see them but they don't communicate anything, or if they do they communicate confusion. Visuals can be incoherent too, you know. That's all I'm saying, and it takes skill to make them work effectively. It's an art. And you know what?' As he was the first to admit, Mel didn't know what. 'I'm not sure it can be taught,' Preston explained. 'Teaching hasn't had much effect on me, or so my mother says, and she should know.'

Interesting as all this was, Mel was keen to make progress; the Web Design Partnership wasn't being paid by the hour, so he opted for flattery.

'Far be it from me to disagree with your mother,' he said, 'but you seem to have learned a great deal. Anyway,' he added, rising to leave, 'I'd better let you get on with it. I'm sure you have things to do.' Like gathering his things and leaving.

Finally alone in his office, Preston surveyed his equipment. There was a time when it had made him feel secure, just knowing it was all there, available if he needed it. His eye fell on Window Displays of New York. He hadn't opened it yet but he did now, aware he was putting off dealing with the letter. According to the ex libraria sticker inside the cover it belonged to Alice. As he looked through it he had to admit some of the designs were striking. Creative even. His eye was taken by shots of window displays at Macy's. Eat your heart out, Louise! Maybe he should not have been so hasty. It was hard to believe but the store had a Visual Merchandising department. Now there was a forward-looking establishment. Instead of lending the book to him, Alice should be reading it herself.

Though he hadn't been aware of making the decision, he found himself opening the envelope. As he pulled out the letter he glanced at the door to make sure no one was coming in. Alice thanked him for his communication. She was sorry to learn that he felt badly done by. She recognised that he was free to pursue legal action and he could be assured that Mowatts would respond promptly to any representations made on his behalf by his legal representatives. As of this time the company did not intend to make any settlement other than that to which he was entitled by statute. Due to the traumatic circumstances surrounding the assault, the company intended to give him one month's salary in lieu since, given his injuries, it would be unreasonable to expect him to report for work in the usual way. The offer of a position as a window dresser was still open should he, on further reflection, wish to avail himself of it. On an attached 'with compliments' slip Alice had written that she had considered offering him three months in lieu but, acting on advice, was unable to do so as that might mistakenly be construed an admission of liability.

So this was it. No prizes for guessing where the advice had come from, Preston thought. Astrid had told her not to give an inch. One month's salary or a life spent in shop windows being jeered at by pubescent schoolboys making their way home through the city centre. Was that a choice? He didn't think so. Images of a spoof Mowatts web site passed through his mind complete with caricatures: Alice on her boneshaker, June fighting the pull of gravity, Bertrand done up as an Onion Johnny with striped sweatshirt and beret, and Astrid as a legal eagle with painted talons.

But he knew that while it would give him hours of pleasure the project was self-defeating. It would offer his enemies just what they wanted, ammunition. He'd be laughed out of court or, even worse, sued for defamation. Being lost in thought, reality took him by surprise.

'Who the fuck do you think you are?' Chloe asked.

He hadn't heard her come in. Leaving the door wide open, she walked right up to him and did her best to stick her face in his. His desk was in the way but, as it turned out, she had a remarkably flexible waist.

'No one ignores me like that and gets away with it.'

Preston drew back, shocked at the girl's vehemence. In her white lab coat she might have been sent from the asylum to take him back. But this was the asylum, so that couldn't be it. And was that anger or make-up, the redness of her cheek? Women would be his undoing.

'I'm sorry, dear,' he said, 'we've never met.'

'Who are you calling "dear", you piece of shit? I've seen better floating in the pan.'

This wasn't what Preston wanted to hear but he was at a loss to understand it. Chloe had felled Vijay Rangar and he'd noticed her afterwards, but he hadn't seen her do it. Taken up with himself and his injuries, it hadn't occurred to him to wonder who had stopped his assailant, who had inflicted the damage.

'Right,' Chloe shouted, 'well you know what I think? You're so far up your own arse you haven't a fucking clue.'

Alastair appeared in the doorway, red in the face, his glamorous assistant in tow.

'Would you kindly moderate your language, young lady,' he said.

'Who the fuck is this old fart?' Chloe asked, looking past Alastair to Sarah.

'Alastair Geddes, head of maintenance,' Alastair said. 'We could hear your language at the other end of the corridor.'

'Shouldn't have been listening then, should you?' Chloe said, straightening up and looking slightly less murderous.

'We didn't have much choice,' Alastair pointed out.

'You were shouting,' Sarah said and, turning to Preston, 'this is my friend Chloe. She dropped that foreign bloke who attacked you.'

'He knows that,' Chloe said, 'he just walked past me at the counter with his nose in the air. Stuck-up bastard!'

'Excuse me, would you talk to your customers like that?' Alastair asked.

'Course not,' Chloe replied, 'what do you take me for?'

Alastair had a choice: eject Chloe from the premises or negotiate. Out of respect for Sarah he opted for diplomacy, oiling the troubled waters with a layer of fake formality. Heavy crude.

'Mr Blair,' he said, 'allow me to introduce Chloe Devine; Chloe, this is Preston Blair.'

'What's so funny?' Chloe asked, seeing Preston smile.

Anyone less divine than Chloe would have been hard to imagine.

'I didn't see who did it. I'm sorry. I didn't know it was you.'

24

Left to himself at last, Preston felt washed out. Too much had happened in too short a time in this incident-filled day, but the fact remained he was out of a job, out of friends, out of ideas, out of luck. However he cut it, the future didn't look good. They'd called his bluff as they would, having legal advice on tap. For him there was nothing in this building any more, not the dimmest prospect. Who would miss him when he left? No one. They'd be relieved. Given half a chance they'd dance on his grave.

He collected his MP3 player, his GPS handset and opened his Pro Tour bag, releasing the unpleasant smell of stale sweat into the confined space of what had been his place of work. His towel hadn't been washed for two weeks, nor his shorts and sweatshirt. A suitable parting gift he thought, leaving his Lynx in the bag. Why waste body-spray on a hell-hole like this? He stuffed his gadgets into the bag and, as an afterthought, added Window Designs of New York. If Alice wanted it back she'd have to ask.

He knew the smartest thing to do was take the lift to the basement and depart unseen, but the service engineer was working on one and the other, taking all the strain, was stopping for an age at every floor. Impatient to get it over with, he decided to face them out – the little people, the pygmies, the second-rate individuals who didn't know talent when they saw it.

The furniture department was quiet. It was always quiet. Hard to believe they made any money. As he was making his through it he saw Frank in the corridor entering the medical room. There was a man going nowhere fast. Correct that, going nowhere at all. On the off-chance that a patient was there in a state of undress, he knocked.

'Come in,' Frank said. He was replenishing his supplies of dressings and plasters and tidying up his paperwork. All very boring but it had to be done. 'You'll want that copy of the accident report,' he said, when he saw who it was, 'for your court case.'

Preston was surer than ever there would be no court case and no industrial tribunal either, but he went along with the suggestion. Keep them sweating as long as possible, Frank included. Why not, if that was the best he could achieve?

'Alice asked for a copy,' Frank said, 'so I made one for you while I was it.'

Preston thanked him, unzipped his bag and slipped it for safe keeping inside the book. He straightened up and looked round.

'It doesn't improve this place, does it? It's so claustrophobic. I don't know how you stand it!'

Frank didn't know either. What he knew were the long nights he spent there when he couldn't doss down at Flora's or snuggle up with Pamela in her apartment. The temptation was to overnight in the penthouse suite, and dangerous though that was he'd already done it twice when he was sure it was safe. As sure as he could be given Hector's unpredictability and Alice's habit of arriving at the crack of dawn.

Preston left the medical room and walked through menswear, where the noise often dropped to devotional level and lower. There was some activity in the golf shop and that was it.

Stepping off the escalator onto the third floor he was struck at once by the contrast. There were women everywhere taking garments off hangers and holding them out for appraisal, turning this way and that in front of mirrors, disappearing into fitting rooms. Women really worked at it, which meant they were discriminating. So you had to wonder how much of what they looked at they actually bought.

Of all the floors the first was Preston's favourite. Peopled as it was with beautiful girls and stacked with electronic toys, he couldn't have asked for more. As he wandered idly past the television sets he heard a customer bending Colin's ear.

'Mr McCandless,' she complained, 'I can't record one programme while watching another. I could before. Am I doing something wrong?'

Colin could answer this one in his sleep and often did since he frequently arrived at work in the morning the worse for wear and looking as if he'd slept in his suit.

'I rather suspect, Mrs Adebayo,' he said, 'that you've gone over to digital.'

She had, and obviously that wasn't his fault, but how could she solve her problem? No joy from Colin there, not without spending more money.

When he reached the gifts department he saw Kathy Reid before she saw him. An elderly woman was asking her how the detecting was going today and Kathy was trying to shut her up. Sadie came every day, regarding the store as a home from home. Her daily journey got her out and about and helped keep the heating bill down. Kathy wanted to ban her, but she was harmless and Alice wouldn't hear of it. She's a character, Kathy, Alice pointed out. Mr Gibson wanted her banned too, she lowered the tone. There but for the grace of God, Alice replied, and he didn't suggest it again.

On his route to cosmetics, he passed the gift section, which boasted an astonishing array of artificial flowers and plants. He could see the point. They didn't die and the best of them looked amazingly real. But they got dusty and needed cleaning. And who should be there today but a company rep demonstrating before a small but attentive crowd the many capabilities of her hand-held steam cleaner. Making short work of your artificial flowers was easy with this little number, she claimed, restoring to its pristine state an impressive long-stemmed lily.

'Some of you may be worried that the heat of the steam will melt the petals or adversely affect the original colours. Not a bit of it! Prepare to be amazed.'

And then, on his way to the world outside, to freedom and opportunity, onwards and outwards to the bright light of day, he saw Anita patiently explaining the finer points of applying some preparation or other to a middle-aged and careworn female face. As far as Preston could see, the customer was a lost cause who might have benefited more from a rub down with a pumice stone or sandpaper. But people lived in hope – of better times, of better things. Hope gets us out of bed in the morning. He smiled to himself. Some of us earlier than others. Hope was the greatest salesman of them all.

Watching Anita and how solicitous she was, he was visited yet again by the attraction he had felt and waited at a discreet distance till she'd finished.

'Hello,' he said, with understandable diffidence. He glanced nervously across to the Garnier and l'Occitaine counters but there was no sign of Chloe.

'Hello,' she replied. She was wary now, and no wonder.

'I owe you an apology,' he said, 'I'd no right speaking to you that way. It wasn't your fault, any of it.'

Anita inspected him as closely as she would a customer.

'I think you must be suffering from tension at the moment. Your facial muscles are really quite tight.'

'That's hardly surprising,' he said, appalled to learn it showed, 'not when you've just lost your job.'

'I heard about that, I'm very sorry.' She walked over to a section of glass shelving and came back with a plastic bottle. 'Some of our customers swear by this product,' she said, 'it helps to de-stress, to relax.'

'What is it?' Preston asked.

'A shower gel. This one has several ingredients but the active one as far as anxiety is concerned is ylang ylang. Very beneficial, they tell me, though I haven't tried it myself.'

'Ylang ylang?'

'It's an essential oil distilled from a plant. Cananga odorata.'

'My goodness,' Preston said, 'you've done your homework.'

'I have a certificate.'

'I'm sure you have,' he agreed. 'Well, I'd better be going. Don't want to keep you from your customers.'

He handed back the bottle but Anita wouldn't take it.

'On the house,' she smiled, 'it's the least I can do.'

And the smile brought it all back, those eyes, those bottomless pools, the feeling, the weakness.

'You're very kind,' he said.

When Pamela entered the office she had the impression that Mel and June were unduly proximate for two people who hadn't known each other long, thrown together only by a shared interest in billing customers.

'No need to spring apart on my account,' she said, and had the pleasure of seeing June blush. Mel didn't seem in the least concerned, so it was possible nothing was going on as yet but June had her hopes. 'We have access to Preston's files now,' Mel said, 'that's bound to save time.'

June was sceptical 'If the password he gave you is correct.'

'Why wouldn't it be?' Mel asked.

'Preston can be awkward, confrontational,' she explained. 'I can't wait to see him slink off with his tail between his legs.'

'I think you might be too late, he was collecting his gear when I left his office. Well, it might be more accurate to say he was collecting his thoughts.'

'That wouldn't take long,' June said.

Alastair appeared in the doorway. 'Hi there, how's things. Just had coffee with your better half, Miss Ross, and a very good coffee it was.'

'You haven't mentioned pastries,' she pointed out.

'Sadly, no.'

'The good life,' June said, 'it will be your undoing.'

Alastair had come with a story he knew they would want to hear. His habit was to improve on a narrative by adding colour, but in this case he couldn't find a way to do it. Chloe's language could hardly have been more colourful, and he couldn't claim she'd come close to throttling Preston when she hadn't laid a finger on him. If word got out, and it would, he'd be dead meat. He wouldn't last a round with a girl like Chloe. She was probably into kick-boxing with ice skates. Even so, and without embellishment, he had their undivided attention, and by the time he was finished the gratification of seeing his audience doubled up with laughter.

'Careful, Miss Ross,' he said, 'you'll fall off your chair.'

'I haven't heard anything like this in years,' June said, clapping her hands, 'if only I'd been there to see it. Dammit,' she added, checking her face in her compact, 'my make-up's running!'

Preston had no idea where he was going till he found himself in the vicinity of New Register House. The urge to lash out hadn't left him but he was running out of ways. Now here he was outside this building again. Someone was trying to tell him something. He walked up the steps to the foyer, explained his destination to reception, and started up the stairs to the first floor only to find his way blocked by an elderly gentleman with a walking stick who was, as he put it himself, running out of puff.

'You'll have to excuse me,' he said, 'the old lungs not what they were.'

This was also true of his other body parts, Preston thought, his waist having expanded with the years and his hair gone grey. When they made it to the top he paused for a few seconds and introduced himself. His name was Donald Grant. Did Preston have a coat of arms, what was the nature of his interest? Having nothing to lose Preston explained that he intended to lay a complaint before the Procurator Fiscal to the Lyon Court, from which Mr Grant inferred that someone had misappropriated his armorial bearings. And that, he said, was nothing more nor less than theft. A colleague had found his family coat of arms offered for sale by a German the other day. Would you believe it, a German!

'Dear me,' Preston said, 'what's the point of winning the war if that's where it gets us?'

Mr Grant sat down heavily on one of the seats provided and leant his walking stick against a display case. Failing to detect any irony in Preston's remark he felt he'd encountered a kindred spirit. He'd given heraldry a lot of attention over the years, he'd be happy to advise.

'That's very kind of you,' Preston said. 'I've begun to look into it. I had a very helpful message from a chap by the name of Anderson.'

'Ah,' Mr Grant beamed, 'an excellent fellow, John Anderson, very knowledgeable.'

Finding it impossible to explain the situation in general terms, he decided to be specific. The Mowatt coat of arms was there for all to see but it couldn't be authentic since Hector Mowatt wasn't a knight and none of his forbears had been either.

'What you're overlooking here, if I may say so, is that coats of arms are granted to institutions as well: local councils, for example, companies, regiments. Mowatts may be a case in point.'

'But surely . . .'

'I used to be a padre myself: Nisi Dominus Frustra, or again, In Veritate Religionis Confido. As you may gather, we had our regimental coats of arms.'

'That's very interesting,' Preston persisted, 'but the arms of an institution wouldn't include a steel helm with an open visor showing the colour of the lining. How could a company or a regiment be a knight or a baronet?'

Mr Grant scratched his head. 'A very good point, Mr . . .'

'Blair.'

'I see what you're driving at here. It does seem anomalous.' He thought for a moment or two. 'If I might trespass on your patience with a couple of points.'

'By all means.'

'The Lord Lyon will only take an interest if someone is using arms to which he is not entitled and someone else is. So if the arms you describe are simply made up, as many are these days, he'll take no action. If no one's rights are being infringed, you see.'

'So I could make up a coat of arms for myself?'

'You could,' Mr Grant conceded. 'They wouldn't mean anything, but you could. Take the clans, for example.'

'The clans?'

'You'll see clan coats of arms all over the place: tea-towels, mugs, cuff links, key fobs. Absolutely meaningless, but there's a market for that sort of thing so what can you do?'

Preston was getting the message. They had it all ways, these people at Mowatts, he couldn't nail them on this one either. Unless they didn't know that. He'd never get anything past Alice, but Hector was another matter.

'I sometimes think there's too much law and not enough justice.'

'Don't let it trouble you, young man, it's the way of the world. I've learned that the hard way.' Mr Grant gathered his breath. His lungs could no longer sustain the sentence-length of old. 'I'd get out while you can. This country's finished, you know. Manufacturing disappearing down the plug-hole, oil and gas reserves running out fast, balance of payments deficit widening every month, increasing dependence on foreign workers while thousands of benefit scroungers sit on their hands. The nation's in a spiral of decline. Brazil's the place. My son's in Brazil. That country's going places, you mark my words. If I had my time over again . . .'

'You'd go to Brazil.'

'Without a second's hesitation. Ah, Helen,' he said, 'as an attractive middle-aged lady came through the swing doors and joined them in the corridor.

'Good morning, Mr Grant.'

'That's Helen Holt,' Mr Grant explained as she disappeared into the depths of the building, 'Herald Painter and a considerable artist in her own right.'

Until now it hadn't occurred to Preston that coats of arms had to be painted, and he was visited by the thought of the comfortable Miss Holt arriving every day, entering this sheltered backwater in the heart of the city, being greeted like a long lost friend by one old codger or another, and quietly getting on with her business in a roomy studio blessed with good light from generous windows. Good work if you could get it, but he knew he never would.

25

Alice seldom convened a meeting of the top three, preferring to consult Hector and Douglas separately. Her intention was to keep Mr Gibson and her father as far apart as possible. Mr Gibson's philosophy had always been that if you looked after the pennies the pounds looked after themselves. From this simple nostrum stemmed an excessive interest in detail. Department heads grew increasingly resentful of completing their monthly returns and floor staff asked searching questions. What did he actually do up there in that office? Whatever it was it didn't include making money. Only people who sold things did that. They paid his wages, but what did he do for them?

Yet recent events had provided Mr Gibson with ammunition. If Arthur Andersen had paid more attention to detail the whole Enron fiasco could have been avoided. Arthur who, Hector had enquired? And as for WorldComm, what could he say? He rested his case. But Hector understood that these examples of cooking the books, all on the grand scale, had occurred in the United States of America. In the United States, he asserted, everything, including fiduciary malfeasance, was on the grand scale. No wonder their companies collapsed in storms of acrimony and litigation. Fortunately, financial scandals of such magnitude couldn't happen in Europe. Oh yes they could, Mr Gibson had replied, and if it weren't for people like him they probably would.

To hear Mr Gibson tell it an accountant was a cross between an investigative journalist and a private detective, living on the edge while being the ever vigilant custodian of social order. But Hector knew that all the detail in the world was no substitute for strategic thinking. You had to know where you were going, you had to see the way ahead, you had to have Vision. Details mattered, he knew that perfectly well. Why else would he pay for the services of book-keepers, bean-counters, number-crunchers, accountants and the like? But without Vision there would be no beans to count, no numbers to crunch, nothing to account for.

The extremes had come into full contact only once, two years before, when Mr Gibson was provoked by another of Hector's throw-away remarks, this one concerning pen-pushers with their noses so deep in double entry ledgers they wouldn't notice the world as we know it coming to an end. Mr Gibson believed he knew about this subject, having read Cooper's commentary on the Book of Revelation.

Hector rehearsed this incident over the tea table that same night, making it sound like the collision of matter and anti-matter resulting in a cataclysmic explosion.

'And what did you say in reply?' Alice asked.

'Didn't have the chance to say anything. That was the fellow's parting shot. He stomped from the room in high dudgeon. Extraordinary!'

'Not really,' Alice said, 'when you consider his point of view.'

And she did her best to remind the old man of Mr Gibson's biblical perspective.

'But surely,' he said, 'he doesn't take that stuff literally?'

'Oh, but I imagine he does,' Alice replied.

'Good God!'

'That's how he sees it, yes.'

'If I find someone standing at the pearly gates with open hand out-stretched I'll be very surprised indeed.' He poured himself a second glass of claret. 'I'm so old I'm nearly dead, yet I must say, Alice, I've had no intimations along these lines.'

'Well you know what they say, father, some instruments resonate more than others.'

'They do?'

'Oh yes.'

But whatever might have been the case twenty years before, Hector was not the force he had been. His vision had deteriorated, his focus was shot. As he said himself, the only way he could read anything these days was by taking his glasses off, which was the wrong way round entirely. His optician had explained this phenomenon to him but Hector was unimpressed. Look at it like this, Mr Wadee had begun. And Hector had replied that being able to look at it at all would come as a welcome relief.

Feeling an obligation to 'keep his end up', Hector would offer ideas from time to time but Alice knew that, without exception, they were trawled from the financial pages and the old man could no longer tell a cod from a haddock. She always listened politely, promising to give his latest wheeze careful consideration. So Hector was satisfied, but none of his fish ever made it to the table and if he noticed he kept it to himself.

Douglas was the first to arrive. Since he always strove for efficiency he appeared at exactly the appointed time, two o'clock. He had a folder with him which contained the data Alice had requested. Hector was five minutes late, not bad by his standards. A new traffic layout had forced him off course: roads blocked here, rows of bollards there. He'd ended up in Leith! His apologies to all. He sat down heavily in the nearest chair and Alice rose to shut the door. She'd called this meeting in the board room because, given the gravity of the subject, it seemed the appropriate place.

'There's only one item on the agenda,' she said, 'and before we begin I must stress that nothing we say in the next hour should go beyond this room. Nor,' she added, 'should any papers be left when we depart.'

'Really, Alice,' Hector said, 'what are you getting us into here, espionage?'

'It may be,' Mr Gibson said, knowing the contents of the documents he had brought, 'that we will be dealing with commercially sensitive information.'

'Exactly,' Alice said, by her standards a ringing endorsement.

Mr Gibson had always preferred Alice to Hector, she was altogether more businesslike and liked to come straight to the point. But this time, armed with a bombshell, dropping it was the only thing she could do.

'I have received an informal approach from Mr Grant Economides, CEO of the Hope Group. He has expressed an interest in buying our business.'

Both men were astonished, Hector more than Mr Gibson who, having seen the figures, had also seen the first faint writing on the wall.

'The cheek of the man!' Hector said. 'It's breath-taking. Economides. Sounds a bit on the foreign side to me.'

'His father came from Cyprus,' Alice explained.

'Well you know what they say about economists, Alice – they lack the imagination to be accountants.'

Alice was appalled, expecting Mr Gibson to spring to the defence of his profession. But he didn't say a word. He was thinking. Mowatts was a family business. Not being a member of the family he wouldn't stand to gain if the business was sold. On the other hand, he could easily lose.

'Presumably this approach is on the premise that we are finding the going difficult.'

'A very good point,' Hector said.

Mr Gibson acknowledged the compliment with the faintest of smiles and handed round several sets of figures which, being print-outs of spreadsheets, were in very small type. Hector removed his glasses and held one of the papers close to his nose.

'Good grief, I'll need a magnifying glass to read this stuff!'

'If you could perhaps interpret these figures for us, Mr Gibson,' Alice suggested.

'Certainly, Miss Mowatt. As you can see, if we compare the first document to the second, out turnover has shown an improvement compared to the same period last year. It may be only 0.34% but this modest rise should be seen against a less-than-favourable trading environment.'

'But as we know,' Alice pointed out, 'turnover and profit are not the same thing.'

'Over the same period our profit has fallen by 0.76%.'

'But how can that be, Mr Gibson,' Hector asked, 'when your own figures show we're selling more?'

'As you can imagine, Mr Mowatt, I've given that some thought. If we could turn to document three.'

But Hector had no time for document three. He wanted an explanation.

'I can point to several factors, Mr Mowatt. Owing to fierce competition in the high street we've been obliged to pare our margins to the bone, with the consequence that increased sales have resulted in decreased profits.' But he could see that Hector wasn't convinced. 'Perhaps I might compare the retail trade to a treadmill. The treadmill's moving faster every year so we're running harder to stay on the spot. We have no choice. If we don't, we'll fall off.'

'You mentioned several factors, Mr Gibson,' Alice said.

'Our overheads have continued their upward trend. On top of business rates, onerous in such a central location, energy prices continue to rise and there's no side-stepping that. We can't turn off the power.'

'Ah, now wait a minute,' Hector asked, 'what became of my plan for mounting wind turbines on the roof?'

Alice looked round the boardroom, the polished wood of the tables, the many empty chairs, the Mowatt crest on the wall. And a trolley stacked with used cups and saucers from a meeting the day before, stale biscuits still pinned to their plates with cling film by someone who'd forgotten to return and collect them. And the air seemed lacking in freshness. Dead air, dead wood. Even with a meeting of three the discussion was going off the rails. Perhaps the time had come after all.

'If you remember, Mr Mowatt, we commissioned an engineer's report, which concluded that only very large turbines would make a significant reduction in our consumption but that the roof could not support one such device, let alone several.'

'I see,' Hector said, 'so much for that.'

'Then there's the salary bill, which continues to rise. This is not due to any increase in establishment – cleaning, for example, has already been contracted out – but mainly to inflationary pressures. There are other factors I could mention, but these are the most significant.'

'Tricky,' Hector said, 'very tricky indeed.'

'A very clear picture, Mr Gibson' Alice said. What can you tell us about projections going forward?'

Mr Gibson was on the point of referring to document four but changed his mind. What was the point?

'In a nutshell, Miss Mowatt, the trends I've identified so far continue several years into the future. I've factored in the variables as best I can, weighting each according to its impact on the business. If the present situation is challenging the outlook could best be described as bleak.'

Hector started drumming the table with his fingers. 'I trust,' he said 'that in factoring in the variables, as you put it, you've made use of stochastic modelling?'

Mr Gibson had heard of stochastic modelling but that was as far as it went. Alice sighed. She had heard of it too: she'd found an article on the subject on Hector's desk. He'd cut it out of the FT and marked several passages with a highlighter. It was the latest thing or, if it wasn't, Hector thought it should be.

'I used conventional, time-honoured methods, Mr Mowatt, tried and tested – taking data from the last few years and projecting them forward.'

'Very commendable, Mr Gibson, but surely your approach is based on historical information and fails to take into account any decisions we might make in the here-and-now to turn things round.'

'True, Mr Mowatt. But as you yourself have pointed out on several occasions, and with some asperity I might add, I do not occupy an executive role. Any picture I paint can only reflect decisions made by others, namely Miss Mowatt and yourself.'

'You're absolutely right, Mr Gibson,' Alice said, 'no responsibility attaches to you in this matter.'

'I was simply suggesting,' Hector said, 'that stochastic modelling . . .'

'Father,' Alice said, 'do you really believe that providing Mr Gibson with a pointed stick will get us any farther forward?'

According to Hector's article, the term derived from a Greek word meaning a pointed stake used as a target by archers. She could see the attraction for Hector, in full regalia, pheasant feather rampant, solving Mowatts' problems with a few well-placed arrows. The stochastic model was ideal for a member of the Royal Company but of doubtful value to anyone else.

At that point the door opened and Grace entered with a dishtowel over her shoulder. She was half way into the room before she realised it was occupied.

'Oh dear, I'm so sorry Miss Mowatt, I didn't realise the room was in use. I just popped in for the trolley.'

'No problem, Grace,' Alice assured her. 'Feel free.'

And Grace felt free enough to spend a couple of minutes tidying up the trolley before wheeling it from the room.

'I note, Mr Gibson,' Alice continued after she had left, 'that my father may be right in suggesting the picture is not entirely bleak. Our profits may have fallen but we're still in the black.'

'Oh yes, Miss Mowatt, we certainly are. All I would say, on the basis of my projections, is that in two or perhaps three years we will move from making a small profit to recording our first ever loss.'

'I see.'

'A sobering thought, I agree, though as always it comes with a health warning.'

'A health warning, what do you mean, Mr Gibson?' Hector asked.

'Well that should be obvious, I would have thought. None of us, whatever model we adopt, can hope to tell the future.'

'And no one would expect that,' Alice said.

'But Heavens above, Mr Gibson, what about Cassandra?'

'An unhappy creature, Mr Mowatt though, I believe, wholly fictitious.'

'Jeremiah, then. You would surely concede Jeremiah could tell the future? And you can hardly write him off as fictitious.'

Alice now knew her meeting was in serious trouble. The Secular Plate was colliding with the Plate of Faith. She was doomed by the tectonics of the mind.

'Gentlemen,' she pleaded.

'I must point out, Mr Mowatt, that the prophecies of Jeremiah were divinely inspired. The Lord spoke to his people through Jeremiah and indeed, through the other prophets of the Old Testament.'

'That's exactly my point. Are you really trying to tell me that people could tell the future then and they can't now? It's ridiculous.'

'Gentlemen, please!'

'If I might just clear up this important point, Miss Mowatt.'

He appeared to grow slightly taller even though he remained in his seat.

'Mr Mowatt, in the times before Jesus, the Lord communicated with us indirectly as it were, through his prophets. And though some leant an ear, many did not. And so he sent us his only Son who, as we might put it in business parlance, gave it to us straight and, as you know, at great cost to Himself. That having been accomplished there was no further need of prophetic voices and, since that time, the only prophets have been false.'

'I doubt if evangelicals would share your view.'

'Possibly not.'

'Nor the Grand Ayatollah Ali al-Sistani!'

Alice groaned. The case was worse than she had thought, Hector had been reading the foreign pages as well. In what Hector later described as her Kruschev moment, and lacking a gavel, she removed the shoe from her right foot, banged it on the table and called the meeting to order.

'Father, please realise that Mr Gibson has done his level best to describe future trends, which is what he is paid to do. And Mr Gibson, please allow for the fact that my father, though possessed of an enquiring mind, is somewhat eclectic in his references and is not given, if I may so put it, to ploughing a straight furrow.'

After a moment's silence, Hector spoke. 'Look here, Douglas, I'm sorry if I've offended you in any way. Quite unintentional, I assure you. I'm well aware that your work for us is of the highest quality.' He removed the handkerchief from his breast pocket and dabbed his eyes. 'It may be, and I realise this is no excuse, it may be that the thought of the family losing the business is affecting me more than I realised. I feel responsible, you see.'

'Very gracious of you, I'm sure, Mr Mowatt,' Mr Gibson said. 'I'd just like you to know that you can count on my full support in any attempt you may make to fend off this unwelcome approach.'

'Beware of Greeks bearing gifts, that sort of thing.'

'Indeed.'

'I'm grateful to you for your support.' Hector stuffed his handkerchief back into his pocket. 'But one point I don't understand – if our business is so bad why would this Economides chap want to buy it?'

Alice had thought about this. There were two possibilities. The Hope Group would acquire Mowatts with the intention of closing it down, thus reducing the competition to their flagship store at the west end. Since Mowatts occupied a prime site they would also stand to make a considerable sum selling it to a developer. Or the intention might be to run both stores on a more cost-effective basis than either could be run on its own. With two stores at their disposal significant savings could be made on the salary bill which would not otherwise be possible.

'So,' Hector said, 'instead of having two sets of buyers they'd make do with one.'

'Of course they would,' Mr Gibson said, 'their own.'

'And they would undoubtedly turn their attention to back office staff,' Alice continued. 'Ordering, invoicing, payroll. What would be the point in running two separate operations? I'm suggesting they will have identified significant savings in the salary bill which they could make but we can't.'

'And has Mr Economides,' Mr Gibson enquired, 'given any indication as to what he might be willing to pay.'

'I'm afraid not. He indicated that would only occur when he knew what our business was worth. So gentlemen,' Alice said, 'what I'm looking for at this meeting is a little guidance. An informal expression of interest has been made. Mr

Economides tells me that he'll take the matter no further if this interest is not reciprocated. And I should perhaps add that he has given certain assurances which are,' she paused to glance at her notes, 'that the Hope Group would expect to run the business as a going concern and that it would continue under the Mowatt name.'

It was some time since Hector had been asked for advice and he found it difficult to give. His whole family history seemed to pass before him and he had no desire to be the last in the line, the one who sold out. Although Alice ran the business, he considered himself the head of the family and he would be the one to sign it away. Mr Economides said the name would continue. But what was such an assurance worth once the business had changed hands, and even if it were honoured what would it be but an empty gesture? He knew old ladies who still asked bus drivers to let them off at Patrick Thomson's even though the store of that name had stopped trading twenty-five years before. Was that the best he could hope for, the fond recollection of ladies living in the past?

As for Mr Gibson, his position was more delicate. He had noticed that Alice, in her review of back-room posts likely to be lost, hadn't mentioned his own position directly though she had identified most of its functions. Tactfully done, but she had to know he would figure it out for himself. He'd be out on his ear.

'Perhaps we should consider what economides we can make on our own account,' Hector suggested. Alice smiled and Mr Gibson looked down at the table to avoid her eye. The old man's mistake had a certain logic to it. 'We should go away and see what we come up with. We can meet again later in the week and compare notes.' Hector rose to leave, he detested meetings at the best of times but this one had been unusually stressful.

'Perhaps you're right, Mr Mowatt,' Mr Gibson said, realising the old man was too emotional to continue, 'perhaps we should postpone consideration of this matter, give it the benefit of our mature reflection.'

Alice agreed. 'I think I'd go along with that. Just one thing,' she added, 'Mr Economides mentioned a couple of other points in the event that we might be interested in his proposal.'

'Oh yes,' Hector said in a suspicious tone, 'and what might those be?'

'He would wish to be assured firstly, that there are no court proceedings, industrial tribunals or the like in process against us or pending: and secondly, that there is no black hole in our company pension scheme.'

'Black hole,' Hector said, 'what on earth does he mean by that?'

'It's the current parlance for a large deficit, Mr Mowatt,' Mr Gibson explained, 'such that the scheme cannot meet its obligations to existing and future pensioners.'

'I see. And what is the position?'

Mr Gibson was startled but managed to conceal it. Like himself, Mr Mowatt was a trustee of the pension fund and should have known the answer to his own question.

'As far as I am aware, Mr Mowatt,' he replied, 'there is a shortfall but it isn't dramatic. We moved out of shares into bonds before the recent market downturn, which saved us from the heavy losses incurred by many other comparable schemes.'

'For which we have you to thank, Mr Gibson,' Alice said, 'very far-sighted.'

'And to the best of my knowledge,' Mr Gibson continued, 'we have not been notified of any legal proceedings.'

Mr Gibson expected this statement to be confirmed, he did not expect silence. Alice considered running the Preston Blair saga past them but decided against it. They had quite enough to deal with as it was and, like everything else he touched, Preston's threats would come to nothing. But Hector looked grave.

'Actually,' he said, 'maybe I should have mentioned it before, but I'm having a spot of bother with that Blair chap.'

'I beg your pardon,' Alice said in her iciest tone.

'It appears he has spent some of his time, or perhaps some of ours, researching in Register House. Anyway, he's discovered we're using a coat of arms to which we are not entitled. It hasn't been registered.'

'So why don't we register it ourselves?' Mr Gibson suggested, 'that would pull the rug from under his feet!'

'Well yes, exactly what I thought, so I made discreet enquiries. According to Ernest Considine, a contact at the club, we can't go down that route.'

'Why not?'

'He tells me it's the work of an amateur and you know what they say, a little knowledge is a dangerous thing.'

'And what does he know about it?' Alice asked.

'As it so happens, he's the Unicorn Pursuivant of Arms.'

'I can take a joke as well as the next man, Mr Mowatt, but really . . .'

'No, seriously, that's what he is. He tells me the beavers are fine, beavering away and all that, very industrious. But when you look at it more closely you start to harbour suspicions.'

They all looked up at the offending device.

'It looks alright to me,' Alice said.

'Ah, there you have it, don't you, the innocent eye. But take that helmet thing – strictly speaking it belongs to a knight or baronet, you know.'

'Maybe your grandfather?' Mr Gibson suggested.

'Afraid not. Though it wouldn't surprise me for a moment to learn he was behind it. A great one for practical jokes. It's a fake, no doubt about it.'

'Goodness gracious,' Mr Gibson said, 'what are things coming to?'

'You may well ask. Anyway, to cut a long story short, I received a letter from Blair the other day threatening legal action in the Lyon Court unless we agreed to a fair and equitable settlement of his grievances.'

'Really, father,' Alice shouted, 'you should have told me. This is serious. Astrid needs to know about it.'

'Astrid be damned,' Hector replied, 'I will not be threatened by a jumped-up little pip-squeak like Blair! If he does try this tack he won't get past Considine, I have his assurance on that.'

'Good for you, Mr Mowatt.' Mr Gibson was beginning to feel more cheerful. He felt the fight-back was starting at last. 'That's the spirit!'

Hector smiled. He still had access to the levers, and what was the point of that if you didn't pull them while you still had the strength.

When the gentlemen left, Alice stayed on. She wanted to compose her thoughts and in her office she could only attempt such a thing very early in the day before her phone rang and people starting knocking at the door. The boardroom, in its way, epitomised the problem. She had sat there herself listening to Preston's assurances, and what had come of that but wasted time, wasted money and threats of legal action? In this room Frank had agreed to draft an environmental policy, and from what she had seen so far he was confusing a department store with the United Nations. All very worthy, no doubt, but less than helpful. And then there was, as Hector perceived it, the weight of history. Well, Hector was on the point of being history himself and so was she. Having a baton to pass was of little value with no one to pass it to. In any case, no dynasty lasted for ever, and that they had in common with nation states and empires. Alexander the Great, Julius Caesar, Napoleon Buonaparte, The Emperor Economides – why had they bothered? What were these people thinking about? Look on my works ye might and despair. She didn't think so somehow.

Her thoughts were interrupted by a knock followed by a tentative clearing of the throat. The boardroom hadn't been on Alastair's agenda till Grace had offered him some of yesterday's biscuits and told him where they'd come from. Strange. He hadn't been notified of a boardroom meeting and Hector's presence these days was almost unheard of. Something was going on and he wanted to know what. From long experience he knew where to look but on this occasion he was disappointed. There wasn't a single document on the table nor was there anything scrunched up in the waste bin, not even a tea bag. This had to have been the tidiest meeting in living memory.

'Alastair?' Alice asked, with the verbal equivalent of a raised eyebrow.

'Excuse me Miss Mowatt,' Alastair said, thinking very quickly, 'you agreed to check out the medical room with a view to re-decorating. This probably isn't a good time.'

'Oh I don't know,' she replied, 'it's as good as any other.'

Aware that the recent condition of Miss Mowatt's knees made going downstairs harder than going up, Alastair led the way to the lift. His attempts at probing small-talk kept her amused till they arrived. He hadn't been aware of a meeting pencilled in for this afternoon. No, she agreed, it was a very informal affair appraising Hector of recent developments. He always liked to keep in touch. Liked to feel useful.

'Don't we all, Miss Mowatt. Well,' he said, opening the door and ushering her in, 'you'd have to say it could to do with a freshen up.'

Alice agreed. The green/brown colour of the walls was most unappealing. For anyone into holistic medicine, redecoration would be called for on medical grounds alone. And the fluorescent tube was showing signs of distress.

'That flickering,' she said, 'I wouldn't be surprised if it could trigger an epileptic fit.'

'I'm already on to that, Miss Mowatt,' Alastair assured her, producing a replacement starter from his pocket.

'As to the new colour scheme,' she said, 'I think you should consult with Pamela and June. And Gemma,' she added, 'might have certain thoughts on the ambience.'

'Good idea, Miss Mowatt.'

As Alastair stood on a chair to fix the light she wandered round the room. Like a customer in the furniture department, she tested the bed. Hard as a board. Idly she opened the nearest locker expecting to find a white coat hanging from a hook or a pair of crutches for emergency use. But all it contained was a hold-all and a rolled up sleeping bag. As she bent down to take a closer look, her nose told her it had been used, and recently. She looked at Alastair. Perhaps Mrs Geddes had heard about her husband's glamorous assistant, a heated argument had taken place and Alastair, banished from the matrimonial bed, had sought refuge in the cold comfort of the medical room. But it didn't seem likely somehow, Sarah's name rested too easily on his lips. The explanation lay elsewhere.

26

Flora tended to act on impulse. If she decided to pay her brother an unexpected visit it was because the wind was in the right direction, planetary alignment wouldn't be so favourable for another thirty years, or on opening a compendium of oriental wisdom the first thing she had come upon was the saying, 'The follower of the Way does not sleep upon a promise.' The moment she read it Flora knew a hidden hand was at work. Was she not a follower of the Way, and had she not promised to visit her brother before another week was out? Who knew what deprivation he was enduring, what rank squalor? And anyway, how could she report back to her father without inspecting Frank's new accommodation?

Henry W Clement wasn't in favour. It was a Friday morning, he wanted to lie in, he needed to recharge his batteries before heading north for a gig. But the more he protested the more Flora knew he was warming to the idea. You'd rather lie in with me, she said, I realise that. Which was fine by him as long as she let him sleep. The trouble was timing. Given to bedtime reading, she seldom made demands in the evening, which Henry would have preferred, a time of day when, as he said himself, he was up for it. The morning after, when she woke him from his slumbers with a view to gratification, that was another story.

So Henry snuggled up, whispering endearments in Flora's ear and caressing her thigh. It often did the trick, but not this time. She drew the curtains, opened the window and pulled the duvet off the bed. Henry wasn't stupid, he got the point.

And his custom was to play along with Flora's whims in part payment of board, lodgings and affection.

Breakfast was noisy. Flora always had a radio playing. In her business she had to keep her finger on the pulse. She also believed in healthy living, so her breakfast cereal had no additives at all except those provided by herself, of which her favourite was the prune. Prunes kept you regular, she said, you should try them. But being regular wasn't high on the list of priorities for someone keen to make it in the music business. Regular doesn't cut it, he replied. Show me, he challenged her, one person who ever made it to the top without trashing hotel rooms, smashing guitars, snorting cocaine, dating c-list celebs, being a born-again Christian or committing suicide. Since the best she could come up with was Doris Day he knew he was on to a winner.

Henry wasn't keen to take the van, he hated the sound of pot-holes bouncing his gear about in the back. They should have gone in her car. It was only when they were half way there that he asked if Frank would be in when they arrived. I could have phoned, Flora admitted, but if he knew we were coming he'd wash the dishes, make the bed, buy Fairtrade tea bags. He might even borrow a plant. It's a wasted journey if we don't catch him in all his glory.

Frank had already arrived. Clearing Preston's office, he came upon a camera and it occurred to him at once. All he had to do was wait till he had a day off, a weekday when Archie would be at work. Then he could document his new lodgings and provide his enquiring father and inquisitive sister with shots. And Pamela. He didn't like to think about that, but he'd show them to Pamela too. Seeing is believing. The camera never lies.

He sat on the settee in Archie's living room, pondering. Not all problems were easily solved. Archie's was a two-bedroom flat. They'd want to see pictures of his bedroom and he couldn't show them Archie's: that was where he kept his books. He didn't read them any more, but there they were, in a large bookcase: Book-Keeping and Accounting for the Small Business, Tolley's Tax and Accountancy Dictionary, Law for Accountancy Students, Learning to Learn Accountancy and Archie's favourite, The Bluffer's Guide. These would have to be covered up somehow, or removed, as would several shots of Archie's parents, Archie's brothers, Archie graduating, Archie taking part in the Garmisch Bonspiel with Amy, Archie in tuxedo at the annual ball of the Society of Law Accountants. But what choice did he have? A bedroom looking less like Frank's would be hard to imagine.

Fatigued by the problem, he left the camera on the coffee table and went to the kitchen to brew up. And that wasn't helpful either. There was Archie's dart-board at the far end with another picture of Amy on which could be discerned a series of small holes. Archie hadn't been furious when she'd run off with a systems analyst at Standard Life, of course he hadn't, he just liked throwing darts. And then were the magnets on the fridge: a black cat, an owl sporting sun-glasses, and a gingerbread house out of Hansel and Gretel. The trouble with duplicity was it forced you to think things out in the smallest detail. Not for the faint-hearted or those with poor recollection.

The bell rang. Expecting the postman with a packet too large for the letterbox, he opened the door and was appalled to see Flora on the landing looking like an overweight jogger in casuals, her latest bag-handler bringing up the rear.

'Surprise, surprise!' Flora said, grinning mischievously.

'If it's not yourself,' Frank replied, trying not to panic, 'and Henry W Clement, of bass guitar fame.'

'I wouldn't say fame exactly,' Henry said.

'You don't get mobbed in supermarkets then.'

'Not yet.'

'So this place is held in trust for the nation,' Flora said.
'What?'
'We don't get in till we've paid?'

Frank had read, or Flora had told him, that rapid eye movement occurred when the sleeper was dreaming, but he wondered whether rapid eye movement during the waking state had also been researched. If his sister was anything to go by, it should be. As she entered the hall and peeled off into the living room her eyes were everywhere, checking out surfaces, furnishings, colours, ornaments, dust. She didn't think much of the furniture which was too utilitarian by far. It had, she decided, a feeling of the flat pack about it.

Frank had one objective, to stop his sister entering the spare bedroom, so he led her into the kitchen.

'What'll it be?' Frank asked.

'The usual,' Flora replied.

'Henry?'

'You don't have decaff by any chance?'

Decaff, and he called himself a bass guitarist, what was the world coming to! This was a man who should be into recreational drugs for image reasons alone. It took him longer than it should have to find the ordinary instant, let alone the decaff, and in that time Flora found her way to the kitchen where she opened the fridge door and had a good look. The interior of a refrigerator told you as much about a person as the books on his shelf.

'Soya milk, you're coming on . . . Good grief, crème fraiche . . . And what have we here . . . tofu! This has got to be Archie . . . . My God, quorn!'

Flora had seldom seen such a politically correct collection of foodstuffs and Frank could tell she was enjoying herself. The longer that continued the better.

'We're out of biscuits, I'm afraid,' Frank said, as they went back to the living room.

'Good. I don't need to put on any more.'

Henry assumed she meant weight. 'I wouldn't say that.'

What was going on here, Frank wondered? Either this pale musician liked having a lot to get round or he was protecting his position. Or both.

'You're not into painted maypoles then, Henry,' he said.

Henry looked at Flora for a lead.

'I believe my brother is referring to models of the wafer-thin, size zero variety.'

'Oh, right. No, give me a real woman any day. That's why guitars are the shape they are.'

'Well,' Frank said, 'they were, till you electric boys came along.'

'Henry likes a bit of flesh on the bone, which is just as well, all things considered.' She was as comfortable with her body as Henry appeared to be.

She picked up the camera and started playing with it.

'I didn't know you had one of these.'

'Borrowed it from work.'

It didn't take Flora long to review the pictures on the card. She'd never seen so many beds and mattresses in her life.

'I could take one of you standing beside the fireplace,' Flora said, remembering portraits of the landed gentry from days gone by, though hounds and dog-irons were nowhere to be seen. 'Dad would like that,' she added, 'you'd be in the shot.'

His rearguard action extended to the corridor cupboard, the door of which, he would claim, led to his bedroom. If pressed he would play for time, showing her Archie's bedroom first. The spare bedroom was, and had to remain, out of bounds. He could further delay the inevitable by introducing her to the bathroom, tastefully decorated in Hawaiian wallpaper by the previous owner, a surfing enthusiast who'd linked a hidden cassette to the string-pull light switch, bathing visitors in the wide vibrato of the Hawaiian steel guitar when they entered.

'So, Henry,' Frank asked, playing for time, 'how are things in the music business?'

Henry and his group were making a name for themselves as supporting artists several point sizes smaller than the headline acts. Everyone has to start somewhere, Frank said, aware that Flora was lining him up in her viewfinder.

'It's not as hard as you might think,' Henry said, 'inasmuch as we're, what you might say, mining a specialist seam.'

Flora took a shot of Frank looking puzzled.

'Right,' she said, leaping to her feet, 'let's do the rest of the house. A photo shoot. We're talking OK or Hello here!'

Before he could stop her, Flora moved into the hall and flung open the door to Archie's bedroom. It only took her a few seconds to conclude that it wasn't Frank's.

'This Archie bloke,' she said, 'a bit of a young fogey if you ask me.' As evidence of this she took three shots of his trouser press from different angles. 'I mean,' she asked, 'who do you know, under the age of eighty, actually owns one of these?'

She picked up the photograph of Archie and Amy at the Bonspiel.

'He's into curling. Probably has linen underwear!'

'When you've finished making a fool of my friend,' Frank said, reclaiming the picture, 'you might remember you've never actually met him.'

'Maybe not, but there's enough evidence here to put him away for years.'

Before he could stop her she was back in the hall and heading towards the bathroom.

'Henry,' Frank said, 'I could do with a hand here.'

'Sorry mate, I never interfere with forces of nature.'

But Flora didn't make it to the bathroom. She came to the spare bedroom first and opened the door. She couldn't believe what she was seeing but knew it was worth recording for posterity and, failing that, for her father. Frank tried to shut the door again but it was too late, her foot was already in it, and where her foot went the rest of her was sure to follow.

'Henry,' she bellowed. 'you've *got* to see this!'

'And why would that be?' Henry enquired from the living room settee.

What a mild fellow he was, Frank thought.

'Just get over here,' Flora shouted, 'now!'

Henry did as he was told. 'God almighty!'

They were standing in the entrance to the spare bedroom. Archie referred to it as the box room: it was so full of boxes the name suggested itself. He bought goods via the internet and was haunted by the fear that any one of them might develop a fault, in which case he'd have to send it back, which would be difficult without the packing. If he'd had the flat long it wouldn't have been a problem, but he hadn't. Most of his purchases were recent and his pile of boxes had grown. Extended warranties didn't help either. He couldn't just jettison some of these cardboard containers and moulded polystyrene packagings after a year, they had to be kept for two or three.

Flora started taking photographs and making sarcastic remarks about the Tate.

'I mean,' she shrieked, 'if you can do it with a pile of bricks or an unmade bed!'

The box for the wide-screen TV was huge, and there were several others: for a PC, a monitor, a printer, a microwave, a popcorn maker, a toaster, a kettle, an electric grill and a Corby Deluxe trouser press with pull out gold-effect tie bar and trim. But it was Henry who asked about the plastic sheeting.

'Oh that,' Frank said, 'yes, we had a leak. Archie covered them up. Nothing worse than a soggy box.'

'Oh, I don't know,' Flora said, looking hard at Henry, 'if it's soggy tending to flaccid we're talking here.'

'I'm sure it isn't,' Frank said. 'Right, Henry?'

'Right.'

Henry reminded Frank of some husbands he had met, but no one in a relationship for such a short time should be so long-suffering. That was supposed to come with time.

None of them heard the key in the lock or the front door opening and shutting, but they noticed Archie when he joined then in the box-room. He needed several documents for a meeting brought forward to that afternoon.

'Not in the diary then,' Frank said.

He strode into the living room and flung his briefcase on the settee. It was marketed as an executive model and required a number to unlock it, or a jemmy if you'd forgotten the combination.

'Archie,' Frank said, conveying the seriousness of the situation with a significant look, 'this is my sister Flora and her friend, Henry W Clement.'

'Pleased to meet you,' Archie said, 'Frank's told me a lot about you.'

'I was afraid of that,' Flora said.

'Nothing too bad.' He pointed to the camera. 'He didn't mention you were an estate agent.' Archie sat down with a sigh, feeling obliged to explain this unexpected appearance in his own home. 'One of our clients has been accused of tax fraud,' he explained, 'very embarrassing for all concerned. Especially us. We recommended his present strategy.'

'Which was?'

'An off-shore trust. A specialised instrument no doubt, but perfectly legal.'

'Anyone we know?' Flora asked.

'Not at liberty to say, though I'm sure you'd recognise the name.'

'You're into tax evasion then,' Henry said.

'Tax avoidance, not the same thing. Why pay tax you don't

have to?'

Archie was plainly distracted, thinking ahead to his rescheduled meeting and how best to tackle it.

'Well,' Flora said, 'I think we should be off. Archie wasn't bargaining for uninvited guests.'

She hadn't noticed exactly when Archie had come in and suspected he'd overheard some of her comments. Better to leave while the going was good. She'd achieved what she set out to, found her brother at home in a state of chaos and had the photographs to prove it.

'You realise,' Henry pointed out on their way home, 'that we never saw Frank's bedroom. It might be fitted out with a heart-shaped bed and a mirror on the ceiling.'

'Excuse me, it's Frank we're talking about here. You'd be lucky to find him with sheets! Still,' she said, 'at least I can send dad some pictures. That'll keep him quiet for a while.'

'And how can you do that,' Henry asked, 'when you left the camera in the flat?'

Despite trying to keep his eyes on the road, Henry noticed Flora's self-satisfied smile. She released her seat-belt, reached into the pocket of her jogging bottoms and wriggled, the flesh of her upper leg fighting her hand every inch of the way. Which was only a problem because of these low-slung seats, she assured herself. It would have been easy standing up. Then she held a small, flat object in front of his nose. She'd left the camera but removed the card when Frank wasn't looking.

'That was your sister then,' Archie said when Flora and Henry had gone, 'quite a handful.'

'Henry seems to think so.'

He went to the drinks cabinet and selected a single malt. He raised the bottle enquiringly but a man who never drank alcohol before sundown wasn't going to indulge before noon.

'Anyway,' Archie said, 'what about you? What are you up to this morning?'

'I was going to take some pictures of the flat, show them to Flora and Pamela and send some to dad.'

'But your sister decided to do it for you.'

'She showed up out of the blue. Not a word of warning.'

'And she chose one of the few times you were actually here. Astonishing!'

'Not according to her. She says she knew I'd be here.'

'What did she make of the fact you don't have a bedroom?'

'You arrived before she realised.'

Archie looked at his glass, now empty. 'You don't mind if I bring this up do you?' Archie asked. 'It's not that I'm unhappy with the arrangement, if you want to pretend you live here it's fine by me, but I can't see it's for the best. Relationships are built on trust, you know.'

He was right. Getting one past Flora gave him pleasure, a feeling of achievement, since it was usually the other way round. But there was no pleasure to be had deceiving Pamela, only feelings of disquiet and unease.

'I mean,' Archie said, 'you have to ask yourself why you're doing it, don't you, what lies behind it?'

There was something irritating hearing about trust from a man into deception on a professional scale, concealing his clients' true financial arrangements from the authorities.

'You don't have to tell me of course,' Archie said, 'but you do have to know the answer to the question.'

Where did it come from, this reluctance to share his thoughts and feelings with someone else? Some of them, okay, he could handle that, but all of them? Give everything away and you had nothing left. Not that Flora seemed to mind. For her, opening up was a virtue. Maybe she had the right idea.

'The trick,' Archie said, in a definitive tone, 'is not to bottle it up.'

Frank looked across the room to the bottles in the drinks cabinet: Archie couldn't be accused of that, not one of them was full.

27

Choosing a night to retire to the comfortable bed in the penthouse suite involved ticking a series of boxes in a checklist which couldn't safely be written down. So Frank remained on the alert for any sign of Hector, cast an eye over the timings on the cleaning rota, checked that the last of the cleaners had left and waited an extra half hour just in case. But of the items on his checklist the most important was a rusty bicycle. If it had gone, Alice had too. Alice was the one he had to watch, equally capable of arriving at the crack of dawn or staying at her desk till no one else remained in the building.

As for rising in the morning, that had to be done early, before anyone else arrived and leaving enough time to cover his tracks. However careful he was, the glasses, cups and cans he drank from left their mark on the coffee table or the kitchen worktop. The sponge in the basin under the sink proved useful in wiping such marks away, but with every pass it left a trail of its own, little smears of water saying someone had been this way. Not many people would notice a thing like that, but a cleaner would. As a cleaner might notice that though the cups and plates were dry, the dish-towel used to dry them was suspiciously damp.

His biggest problem was the bed. Sleeping between the sheets was asking for trouble. However carefully he made it, creases remained which hadn't been there before. And he was well aware that no one, whatever precautions he might take, could sleep between the same sheets for several nights without leaving behind a residue of epithelials and dried sweat. So the farthest Frank went was to spread his sleeping bag on top of the bed and sleep in that. Then it was relatively easy to smooth things out when he got up and the question of dirty sheets didn't arise.

At first these evenings in the penthouse suite had been pleasant. He had the place to himself, could make tea or coffee and dip into whatever food he'd brought along – sandwiches, biscuits, fruit. Alastair would have called it the life of Reilly, and so it was. Or should have been. But lacking the criminal mentality, Frank was always on edge. Before retiring he'd watch some television, but unless the programme held his attention his mind would wander as he watched, mostly to Pamela but also to his strangely double life. What he had seen as indecision, he realised now, was the colourful flower, the eye-catching leaf. It wasn't the root. And though examining that might damage the plant, what choice did he have? He didn't know what he was doing or where he was going. He was living in a self-imposed limbo until he figured it out.

And in the meantime he'd learned a lot from Pamela and June, and now had a handle on IT and the local intranet, but useful as all this was, for him something was missing which, he now knew, was physical skill. Okay, typing was a physical skill, and so was moving a mouse, but they were skills akin to using a knife and fork with no potential for satisfaction – not comparable, say, to marquetry or print-making. Not even to wiring, plumbing or gas fitting. Computing wasn't his thing.

As he rolled out his sleeping bag on the bed, he looked forward less and less to these nights. Lately, too, he'd been troubled by fear of cramp, realising that an attack in the foot or the calf would be very difficult to deal with trapped in the bag. Perhaps he should be on a course of quinine? Since he hadn't yet felt a twinge of cramp he laid his fear like a parcel at the door of his subconscious, hoping that if he rang the bell and ran away someone would take it from him. But the only someone who could do that was himself. He might think he wanted to live this way but it was there to tell him he didn't.

Any deception, any attempt to be what he was not, required energy, and the longer the deception was maintained the more energy it took. Recharging from the mains wasn't an option and his cells were depleting fast. Was that why doctors prescribed lithium, to recharge their patients' batteries? So after a few weeks, though he still passed the time with the television in the penthouse suite, he stopped sleeping there and returned to the medical room where his chances of discovery were vanishingly small.

Frank put it down to the hardness of the bed that sleeping on it inclined his thoughts towards Pamela, especially if he'd been with her the night before. Her mattress was altogether more comfortable and so was she. Lying in bed with Pamela was becoming a habit. He hadn't come across a single survey of sexual mores which suggested their behaviour was atypical, but it probably was. Because on those days when they finished work at the same time, their custom was to return to Pamela's flat, prepare a meal, eat it, watch the early evening news and retire to her bed shortly after. The early evening, Frank maintained, was a time for pair-bonding – a term Pamela banished from the house since it reminded her of gannets, guillemots, cormorant and shag. The concept had come to his attention in a biology unit, though Pamela had no way of knowing that yet.

Anyone overhearing Frank referring to bonding might have taken it as a euphemism for sex, but sometimes they just lay together, snuggling up and talking. The habit, while endearing, was not without its down sides. If they retired too early the horizontal position, so soon after eating, inclined Pamela to dyspepsia, which took the form of stomach ache and acid remarks. And if they had sex Frank tended to fall into a deep sleep afterwards, which made him restless during the night if he was staying and reluctant to leave if he wasn't.

The previous evening Pamela had been unusually talkative. Preston had sent her an e-mail, as if she was a long-lost friend and he'd never miscalled her for anything. He'd even asked after June. And guess what, she said, he was in the States!

'If I'd known he was going I'd have tipped off the FBI,' Frank said. The thought of Preston being hauled off to a secret location and being subjected to a Mutt and Jeff routine as a possible terrorist appealed to him. 'He'd look quite fetching in an orange jump suit.'

Pamela took this for what it was, a piece of childishness with no connection whatever to the realities of life. There was something not completely grown up about Frank, which meant he retained a proper sense of wonder at the world but also lived in a state of naivety well beyond his years.

'He's gone over to be with his girlfriend,' Pamela said.

'So much for the beauteous Anita.'

'Apparently they met on the net,' Pamela said. 'Her name is Janice.'

Preston's message had been remarkably up-beat. They'd been communicating for several months, latterly by webcam. Janice had advised him in his time of trouble when everyone else was doing him down. They were on the same wavelength. She was involved in research, clinical trials. Had Frank heard of West Chester? He hadn't. It was in Pennsylvania, Pamela told him, near Philadelphia. Preston felt sure the outlook was good. He was staying in the girl's apartment, which was small but very nice. Her parents didn't seem to mind.

When the door opened he didn't notice. The little noise it made was masked by music, and the increase in light from the corridor didn't penetrate his shut eyes and wandering thoughts. Ever since checking it with Alastair, Alice had wondered if someone was over-nighting in the medical room. She hadn't imagined that tell-tale smell of sleep.

The more she thought about it, the more she thought of Frank. He was the one who'd been burned out of his flat and he was the only one, other than Alistair, with easy access at any time of the day or night. Her theory was all very well, but it had to be tested and she couldn't have a camera installed in the medical room. Certain rights to privacy could not be infringed.

Her first port of call was Gemma, who turned down her Pacific swell and confirmed that staff contact data was up-to-date. Yes, she had a new address for Frank, who now resided in a flat in Sighthill. His mobile number hadn't changed, he didn't have a landline. Not so unusual these days. Several people she knew saw little point in paying for both.

'Take Melville Armstrong,' Gemma said, by way of an example.

'If it's all the same to you, I'd rather not. There's only so much yellow a woman can stand.'

Alice's debate with herself didn't last long. If Frank was sleeping in store Gemma should be told. Perhaps she could help in some way.

'Oh no, it can't be Frank,' Gemma said. 'Haven't you heard? The Sighthill location's an address of convenience, a mailing address. It has to be. Everyone knows he's moved in with Pamela. It has even been suggested by you know who,' Gemma said, 'that they're really going at it these days.' She looked apologetic, this was too suggestive altogether. 'If you know what I mean.'

'I thought Preston had gone.'

'He has, but Colin hasn't, and you know what he's like.'

'I do indeed,' Alice said, 'though he sells electrical appliances he has yet to be persuaded by the steam iron.'

Alice ran her concerns past Hector, who was greatly entertained by the thought that hanky-panky might be occurring in the building.

'Set up a concealed camera in the corridor,' he suggested, 'or, I tell you what, just pop down whenever you have a minute. Chances are you'll catch the blighter red-handed. Just a matter of time.'

The first two occasions she appeared at the medical room door in the early morning or late evening nothing had been untoward. This time, though, Alice knew someone was there and felt a momentary surge of fear. What if whoever it was attacked her? She wouldn't stand a chance. The skull of an old woman would crack like an egg. But the shadowy bulk in the bed didn't move. Then she heard a noise she'd often heard before on buses and trains, the sound from headphones spilling out beyond the ears of the user. It couldn't be good for them, could it, all those decibels? Someone ought to tell them.

She removed her shoes and walked into the room round the top of the bed. The light from the corridor was enough and no more – Frank Figures, his head sticking from his sleeping bag, his feet hanging over the end of the bed. It was only five past ten, but Frank started work earlier than most so he retired earlier too. She switched on the lights but Frank didn't notice, he was out for the count. His radio was playing and he didn't notice that either.

'Frank,' Alice said. He moved a little but he might have done that anyway.

'Frank,' she said again, prodding him through the bag, 'I don't have all night.'

Frank had no difficulty falling asleep, his problem was staying that way, so if anything woke him he didn't like it one bit. An unexpected burst of noise in his headphones might do it, or his own incessant mental activity.

'Mr Figures!'

She was about to prod him again when she realised that, through the bag, she couldn't be sure which part of him she was prodding. So she removed the headphone lead from his radio and pulled the cans from his ears.

'For Christ's sake!' Frank said, rising with reluctance to the surface.

'Let's keep religion out of this, Frank.'

Realising for the first time that he wasn't alone, he opened his eyes.

'Miss Mowatt!'

'Yes, well at this time of night I'll settle for Alice.'

Frank propped himself up on one elbow, the most he could do without unzipping the bag. He had no idea what to say.

'I have some coffee brewing in my office, I suggest you join me.'

He wasn't going to do that without putting his clothes on, which he couldn't do without clambering from the bag and going to the locker. But all he was wearing was a tired-out sweat-shirt so he was trapped till Alice left.

'That's very good of you, Miss Mowatt. I'll be right up.'

'I can't offer you any biscuits, I'm afraid,' Alice said, turning to leave, 'I wasn't expecting guests.'

As soon as she shut the door, Frank wrestled the sleeping bag to his waist and wriggled out. He padded to the locker and opened it. There they were, his shirt and trousers in a heap on top of his hold-all, which contained clean socks and underpants and the fresh shirt he should have hung up but hadn't. Since the day wasn't over he should put today's clothes back on, keeping his change for tomorrow. But about to join the managing director in her office, putting his tired clothes back on didn't seem such a good idea. As he wondered what to wear he considered the line he should take: he'd lost track of time; he'd worked on so long it wasn't worth going home; he was going down with a virus.

He rejected them all. Miss Mowatt would be offended by any attempt to put one past her. Standing in front of the open locker he didn't know what to wear or what to say. Multitasking, Alastair had told him the week before, that's what it's all about these days. Coming from Alastair it was highly entertaining. Then, but not now. He quickly applied some roll-on deodorant, put on tomorrow's shirt and left for the lift. He'd take his cue from Alice, follow where she led.

'Come in,' she said, as he appeared in the door.

Frank looked round the office as he entered. He'd hadn't made a mistake, her bike wasn't there. He wasn't to know, and would never find out, that she'd come to work by taxi because her brake blocks awaited replacement in Tom Scott's repair shop. Alice rose from her chair and made for the cabinet where she kept her supplies: breakfast blend for herself; Earl Grey for Hector; camomile tea for Gemma and ground coffee for everyone else. She wouldn't hear of granules, freeze dried or not.

'I can't remember what you take. Milk? Sugar? I only have UHT, I'm afraid,' Alice said, displaying the pack.

'Some milk, thanks, Miss Mowatt. I don't take sugar.'

Frank walked over to the cabinet as Alice was pouring the milk and offered her the packet of shortbread he kept against surges of hunger.

'We are fortunate indeed,' she said.

Alice was being sarcastic, using the tone of someone saying grace. She sat at her desk with her tea and two fingers of shortbread balanced on the saucer. Were the two fingers sending him a signal? Probably not, he was being too clever now. She set a plate with the remaining pieces on the corner of the desk nearest Frank's chair. She thought of him as a growing lad.

'So,' she said, 'to what do we owe the pleasure?'

Having emptied his mind the better to go with the flow, Frank found the river was dry. Wadi Figures. He remembered an incident the previous year when he'd been working with Alastair and absent-mindedly attempted to wash his hands. You can hardly expect to empty the tank and still have water coming out the tap, Alastair told him.

'It's a long story.'

'Let's not lose perspective here, Frank. War and Peace is a long story, Remembrance of Things Past is a long story.'

'It's hard to explain, it just sort of happened.'

'After the fire in your flat.'

'That was the start of it. I looked for another place for several weeks.'

He'd checked the ads, called numbers, visited possible locations in several parts of town. He'd even signed on with an agency. He'd almost settled on a furnished room when the landlady said, out of the blue, 'no lady callers after ten o'clock', and asked him if that would be a problem. He wouldn't have been happy in a place like that. Show him the moral high ground and he walked the other way.

'Nothing suitable, I take it.'

'A couple of out-of town places were fine, but buses don't always suit the hours I work. You know how it is, Miss Mowatt, they're more geared for seven in the morning till six at night. And don't even think about Sundays.'

'That person in the flat below you . . .'

'The Gnome.'

'Was that the name?' Miss Mowatt doubted it, but continued nonetheless. 'He has an exhibition coming up in the City Art Centre, Men of Metal I think it's called. A series of panels. If the brochure's to be believed, some of them are quite good.' She opened her desk drawer and produced a magazine. 'There's an interview here with Lesley Wilson.'

Frank took the magazine. He hadn't heard about the exhibition, nor of Lesley Wilson, but found it hard to believe the organisers could afford the security. There was no interim interdict protecting the Gnome at the City Art Centre. Strange how one person's misfortune could be someone else's good luck. The Gnome was obviously doing well while he, Frank, was having to explain himself to management. Life being what it was, he was probably subsidising the author of his misfortune through social security payments and an Arts Council grant.

He glanced through the article, which included a photograph of the artist posing beside one of his panels. It depicted an older woman, her long hair artfully braided and led over the shoulder to her groin, leading a man towards a bed. The caption below the photograph read 'Queen Gunnhild Seduces Hrut'. Miss Wilson had asked the Gnome what had aroused his interest in this subject. Complimenting her on her use of the verb 'arouse', the Gnome cited the episode as further evidence, if any were needed, of the predatory nature of women.

Was Miss Wilson aware that Queen Gunnhild had said to Hrut at the time, 'You shall lie with me tonight in the upper room.' Miss Wilson hadn't been aware of that, no, but so what? Gunnhild and Hrut had only met that day, the Gnome explained, for the first time. She was pulling rank to pull a bloke! Apparently women would stop at nothing. And in fact, Frank noticed, as he handed the magazine back to Alice, there was in the face of Gunnhild a passing resemblance to Barbara, the author of his misfortune, whose picture had since appeared in the Evening News as she left the Sheriff Court.

'Keep it,' Alice said, 'I'm sure you'll find it interesting.'

For a brief moment it occurred to Frank that Alice had given him the article for a reason. She was Queen Gunnhild, he was Hrut, and the penthouse suite was the upper room. Like Gunnhild, she was pulling rank to get him into it. But that was ridiculous of course. Miss Mowatt was a civilised individual and, in any case, well past the age where such a proceeding would hold any attraction.

'My view, for what it's worth,' Alice said, 'is that the artist would be better employed depicting Jon Johannesson with a full set of horns raiding the high street in a longship with wheels and heavy gearing.'

Since Frank paid no attention to mergers and acquisitions, he had no idea what she was talking about and kept his mouth shut.

'So, Frank, you're sleeping in the medical room.'

'Sometimes,' Frank said, 'till I sort myself out.'

'I would find the bed rather hard,' Alice said. 'I'm surprised you don't use the penthouse suite. Much more comfortable.'

Frank knew danger when he heard it. If Alice had reason to believe he'd used the suite she'd expect him to admit it. If he didn't, his credibility would be shot.

'To tell you the truth, Miss Mowatt, I've watched television there once or twice.'

Alice smiled. 'I believe you. So,' she asked, 'does your sister know? I believe we have her listed as your next-of-kin.'

'No.'

'Where does she think you're living?'

'At a flat in Sighthill when I'm not cat-sitting for her.'

'And that would be your official address.'

'Yes.'

'Your mailing address.'

'Yes.'

'Do you cat-sit a lot?'

'Not as often as I used to.'

He explained about Henry W Clement. Alice smiled.

'Life's rich tapestry,' she said, 'it never ceases to amaze me. Perhaps we should introduce your sister's boyfriend to Mr Gibson. They appear to have a lot in common.'

'I wouldn't recommend it, Miss Mowatt. Appearances can be deceptive.' He shouldn't have said this but he'd no way of taking it back. 'I realise this might apply to me.'

'Don't let it worry you, Frank. It applies to everyone. It applies to me, and I'm too old to bother putting on an act. I sometimes think,' she added, looking out the window and getting nothing back but weak background radiation from city lights, 'that we aren't so much what we are as what we appear to be.'

'I'm not sure what you mean, Miss Mowatt.'

'Well it could be argued, couldn't it, that we are the sum of the perceptions of those who know us.'

This was an alarming idea. It was obvious to Frank that if two friends or colleagues had different views of a person then, in the act of summation, those views might be cancelled out. In theory it could happen that summing everyone's perception of a given person would result in that person's non-existence.

'I suppose it could,' he said.

'Your sister will perceive you in a certain way.'

That was only too true, he conceded.

'And then there's Miss Ross.'

Frank looked as if his face had been slapped.

'You know about her?'

'Of course I do, and so does everyone else. People talk to each other. Much though I discourage it they even talk to me. It's out there. It's common knowledge.'

'We don't let it interfere with our work.'

'I'm sure you don't. But she doesn't know either, does she?'

'If I tell her she'll ask me to move in.'

'And you wouldn't want to do that.'

'If we're going to live together it shouldn't be because she's taking me in off the street.'

Alice, who didn't normally snack a great deal, reached out for another piece of shortbread. Why did young people make life so complicated?

'You want to bring as much to the table as she does.'

'That's it exactly, Miss Mowatt. That's very well put.'

'A partnership of equals.'

'Yes.'

'Well in that case, Frank, you've got some thinking to do, and not just about where you spend the night.'

Pamela was a girl of character and considerable abilities. She was coming on by leaps and bounds while Frank was at a crossroads, both in his personal life and his professional. Alice knew that attempts had been made to broaden Frank's range, and his green credentials were second to none. She'd read his report with interest and agreed with much of his analysis, but his main recommendations could only be met by an agreed course of action adopted in concert by the major nation states. And when had the major nation states done anything in concert?

'From where I'm sitting, Frank, you appear to be drifting, both in your professional and your personal life. Which is all very well if you don't mind washing up in one of life's many backwaters but really, you need to take charge.'

'Life is a serious business.'

She thought of how he'd been living and smiled.

'But not without its laughs along the way, wouldn't you say? Tell me, Frank, how do you see your career developing?'

'That's a tricky one, Miss Mowatt. Things are changing quickly right now.'

'Okay, let's come at this from a different direction – how do you see my career developing?'

'I don't think it's my place to have a view on that.'

'Young man, I thought we'd just established that you don't have a place.'

'Okay, if you're pressing me for an answer I would say there's nowhere left to go when you've reached the top. I would expect you'll carry on as you are.'

'For how long – till the end of the fiscal year? Till I drop? This is a family business. As I'm sure you're aware I never married. I don't have children. I know he shows up from time to time but the truth of it is my father retired years ago. Have you considered what will happen when I follow him into retirement to concentrate on my begonias?'

Which might be sooner than anyone realised. A second approach had been made directly to her since Grant Economides had come to suspect that she was the one who made the decisions. Of the two documents remaining in the bottom drawer of her desk one of them testified to that. On top lay a copy of Frank's environmental policy and below that, seen by her alone, an impenetrable paper on the subject of business re-structuring. The title page bore the words 'Shells, Holding Companies and Other Arms-Length Corporate Vehicles', and anyone rifling through Alice's desk would have read it vain for any reference either to Mowatts or to the Hope Group. If the document had not met the criterion of total and complete anonymity Mr Economides would never have sent it.

'You have to face the fact that life won't go on for ever as it has in the past. I might be felled by a massive stroke the week after next.'

Frank was about to protest but Alice raised her hand.

'It's simply an example. I might run off with a bishop. But if something like that were to happen the business would assuredly be sold and the new owners might, as they so delicately put it, let you go. Why would they do that? Because you're a poor performer? Of course not. They won't know you from Adam. Their sole intention from the outset, however they disguise it, will be to make money, perhaps by redeveloping the site, in which case they won't have the slightest interest in the business or its employees. And if you're sitting there thinking that the old girl's good for a few years yet, well, you might be right, let's hope so, but there are no guarantees in this life. None. In any case,' she asked, 'why would you assume I would want to carry on? Can't you imagine that after forty-five years doing much the same thing my motivation might not be what it was?'

Frank noticed that despite uttering several consecutive sentences Alice showed no signs of breathlessness. That had to be good. On the other hand, the sudden stroke scenario wasn't so funny.

'Your colleague Alastair, in all the years I've known him, has been very impressed by his permanent contract. For the life of me I can't imagine why.'

'One month's notice.'

'That's all it means. Security's a reassuring fiction.'

'If I lose my job here . . .'

'You'll look for another one, that's what people do. As for where you might live, we both know the answer to that. Talk to her. Negotiate. She must know by now you're not on the make. Who cares if she contributes more in the early years? I'm sure *she* doesn't. No doubt the pendulum will swing the other way at some point.'

It wouldn't be a pendulum if it didn't, Frank thought.

'You've met her mother?'

'We get on well.'

'There you are then. So,' she continued, 'where does that leave us? Where do we go from here?'

'Out the door in my case, I would think.'

'Don't be ridiculous, Frank. You'll continue to sleep here for the time being, but in the penthouse suite if you don't mind. The medical room is entirely inappropriate.'

'Mr Mowatt won't take kindly to that.'

'You can safely leave him to me. However, she added, 'there are angles you'll have to cover for yourself. If word gets out your life won't be worth living. People will accuse you of getting special treatment. Why does he get to stay in the penthouse suite, nobody else does? I can hear them now. And I have no intention of sitting in the board room fielding questions from Mr Gibson concerning your sleeping arrangements. As for Pamela, what she would make of it I don't like to think.'

'Neither do I.'

'So we put a limit on this understanding because the longer it lasts the more likely it is to unravel. Shall we say one month? Four weeks from now? Ample time to sort things out with Miss Ross.'

'That's very kind of you, Miss Mowatt, I must say.'

'Oh I don't know,' Alice said, 'for sheer entertainment value it beats the television hands down.'

Frank was struck by an after-thought. 'What about the cleaners?'

'I'll bring in some odds and ends of Hector's: braces, a shaving kit, a spare set of teeth. I shall also invent an electrical job requiring your attention. In the event that a cleaner finds you in the room that is why you are there – though you wouldn't have to be in bed at the time.'

Alice rose to leave and as Frank followed suit she caught him glancing regretfully at the plate of shortbread. She picked it up and gave it to him. Together they walked to the penthouse suite. Though it wasn't far from her office Alice hadn't been in it for some time. It was really quite nice, she thought. Why Hector sometimes spent the night at the club was beyond her. Better breakfasts, Frank wondered? Yes, Alice agreed, that would be it. Anyway, it was his for the next few weeks. Well, she said, I'll leave you to it: you'll have your things to collect from downstairs. Which would have to include his thoughts, such as they were.

Back at her desk, Alice wondered what the future held for Frank, a slightly feckless young man but not pretending to be what he was not: as Hector said, he was totally lacking in side which, he explained, had something to do with billiards or snooker. Or was it bowls? She also wondered what the future held for herself and her father, but there at least matters were in her own hands. She opened the drawer and took out Economides' document. A heavy read, it implied a way forward involving the setting up of two additional companies and the creative transfer of assets between them. It was so complicated she had sketched it out on a sheet of paper, making several corrections along the way. But then, she reflected, what great artist gets it right first time?

Alice suddenly felt tired. The wheelers and dealers were knocking at the door. But even as it was, going through the same routine year in, year out was losing its shine and she realised now, for the first time, that she would sell. Not next week nor the week after, but finally the end was in sight and what a relief it was. Would she feel the same way about life? Probably. When the time came, yes, she would.

28

From the comfort of his pocket-sprung mattress Frank began to surf. When Alice had given him a month to sort things out it had seemed generous, but time had a way of passing. And the closer he came to owning up the more some Ohm's Law of the emotions impeded the current of honesty when it started to flow. Not a problem faced by raccoons. Despite that bandit look about the eyes they weren't into deception, they had no explaining to do. They colonised chimneys, raided bins, relaxed and had a good time. And what was he doing watching a documentary about raccoons anyway? Where was that getting him? Thinking those thoughts he fell asleep, the television still on, the remote control in his hand.

The following morning was one of the few when weather played a part in his life. Heavily overcast, it was threatening rain. On a sunny day the light might have wakened him, but not today. His mobile phone, doubling as an alarm, lay silently by the side of the bed, its battery flat. The first he knew another day had dawned was when he realised he had company.

'Sorry to disturb you, mate, didn't know anyone was here.'

The woman made to leave but there was something he wanted to know.

'What's the time?' he asked.

She checked her watch. It was nearly half past six. Did he need fresh towels? No? She was sorry she'd disturbed him. But Frank didn't want her to go. He had to find out who she was and get her on side. Anything to buy a little time.

'We haven't met,' he said, sitting up.
'Alison. They call me Ali.'
'You're from Australia, right?' he asked.
'Rainbow Beach.'

Alison gave him an enquiring look. 'So what are you doing for brekkie?' She glanced at the mini-bar. 'Nothing appropriate in there.'

She was young, with a fresh face, and her bronzed skin suggested the outdoor life. Light on make-up, Frank took her for a straight-forward, down-to-earth individual. A person he could talk to. She was taking two years out, working her way round the world.

'You must be the grandson.'

She'd obviously met Hector at some point.

Frank smiled. 'There isn't one. The Mowatts are a dying breed. Alice is the last of the line. She's letting me use the place for a while.'

'So who are you then?'
'Frank. Maintenance. I work here.'
'Only I don't see your ID,' she said.
'I don't wear it in bed,' he replied.
'From where I'm standing you don't wear that much.'

Frank pulled the bag up a bit, though nothing of note was exposed.

'Don't see yours either,' Frank said, checking for the beaded chain and tag.

She plunged her hand into her pinny, reached down and hauled it out.

'Gets in the machinery if you leave it dangling.'

When Alison left, promising to return in an hour with her vacuum cleaner, Frank knew he had very little time to tidy up and leave. And he was still in the bathroom when the cleaning supervisor arrived. The door was open and she walked right in.

'Well, well, well,' she said, savouring the moment, 'what have we here? Wait till the girls hear this!'

Frank eyed her in the mirror. 'It's legit. Ask Alice.'

'You're her blue-eyed boy alright.' She peeked out of the bathroom towards the bed. 'Anyone else in residence we should know about?'

What did she think he was, a two-timer, a double-dealer, a sewer-rat, a sleaze? Annie eyed him up and down, unimpressed by the long grey T-shirt covering most of his off-white underpants. A little bleach in the pre-wash wouldn't go amiss. He was trying to remove soap from his armpits with a face cloth, splashing all over the place like a dog just out of the water.

'You've met our Alison then.'

Frank nodded. An unusually forthright person, he thought.

Annie agreed, but she was smart with it, that girl. She had a college degree. Frank was surprised to hear that.

'It's true,' Annie confirmed. 'Sports science. She's so well qualified we thought twice about giving her the job. You know how it is with these educated types,' she explained, plainly believing this was a problem which didn't face Frank, 'they get bored and move on. Nothing you could lift with two hands she can't lift with one. Been with us five weeks and I'll tell you what, Frank, without a word of a lie that girl can drink the rest of us under the table. Checked the tattoos?'

'No,' Frank said, 'she had her clothes on.'

'You should. Start with the arrow on the small of the back and work your way down. Could prove instructive for a retiring lad like you. Bring some colour to your cheeks.'

Frank knew it was over. Alison had told Annie and Annie would tell everyone else. That's how it went. When Alastair arrived his number would be up, he'd never hear the end of it. But later, when the great man walked into the office, he dropped his paper on the table and made straight for the kettle. He was unusually bad tempered this morning, partly because he'd failed to trace the origin of water seeping through a wall in the basement, but mostly because he was expecting Mr Gibson. If he'd been younger his mobile would have rung, or someone would have texted him with the gossip. But Alastair never got texts and didn't miss them.

His tea thick with sugar, he sat down at the table, took a swig, sighed in satisfaction, leaned back and opened his paper. Frank looked up from the work-in-progress folder. He was sure Alastair wasn't stringing him along, he wasn't that good an actor. He hadn't heard yet.

'It says here,' Alastair said, 'that our native ducks are in danger from the American Ruddy Duck. Apparently,' he read, 'it's over-sexed and over here!'

Mr Gibson was polite enough to knock but not so polite he waited for an invitation to come in. As part of his annual audit he had come to cast an eye over their paperwork. He had an unnerving ability to bury his nose in documents and conduct a conversation at the same time.

'What branch of the navy did you say you were in, Mr Geddes?'

'The silent service,' Alastair replied. 'Above us the waves and all that.'

'Well I think it's high time you surfaced,' Mr Gibson said. He'd found a few errors already. 'I see you have added an additional ring binder to your already formidable array.'

Only Mr Gibson could make a set of ring binders sound like an advanced weapons system. Alastair was quite relaxed when Mr Gibson reached over to have a look. The new folder logged equipment borrowed by other departments, duly signed out and signed back in.

'I can't stand that man,' Alastair said when he left, 'he's so bloody sanctimonious! Thinks he knows it all.'

But Frank began to rest a little easier. Gibson was gone and he had breathing space till the news broke, time to decide what he was going to do. Since Alastair had asked him to help in the basement he felt even safer. Apart from the car park, the basement wasn't frequented by women, and it was women he had to worry about.

'It's obviously coming from a pipe,' Alastair said, looking for the source of the leak, 'the question is which one?'

They inspected the breeze blocks, their texture looking rough in the raw light from the overhead tubes. There were pipe runs everywhere.

'I always meant to colour code these,' Alastair said, wishing now that he had.

They didn't see her coming.

'Danger, men at work. Morning boys.' It was June faking good cheer. 'Pamela needs to see you, Frank,' she said.

'I'm sorry dear,' Alastair said, 'it'll have to wait.'

'I don't think so, Mr Geddes, not this time. Something's come up, hasn't it, Frank.'

'Frank?'

'It's nothing, really.'

'Will you tell him or will I?'

'So I dozed off in the penthouse suite, big deal!'

'So you dozed off overnight,' June said, 'in the bed.'

Alastair gasped. 'What were you thinking about, lad?'

'Where he was discovered in the early morning by our Ozzie friend with the risqué tattoos. Or maybe she'd been there all along.'

According to the story, Alison had found him in bed with a beer in each hand and someone's bra, pants and tights scattered across the floor, the tights replaced later in the day by a suspender belt and fish-net stockings. When Annie had gone to investigate, the underwear had disappeared but Frank was in the bathroom, still in the buff.

'She's in the office,' June said. 'I'll stay out the way for a while.'

He ran to the nearest lift and took it to the sixth floor. Mr Gibson spotted him through his open door and tried to detain him 'on a matter of some urgency', but Frank sped past with a quick wave of the hand. When he reached Pamela's office he went straight in and shut the door. Her tied-back hair made her look severe, matching her mood completely, though the sole intention was to keep it out of her eyes as she worked.

'The phones are on divert,' she said, 'we won't be disturbed. So,' she said, staring at her screen to avoid looking at him, 'tell me about the underwear.'

'Embroidered.'

'What!'

'The story. It's been improved on. There never was any underwear. There weren't any beer cans either.'

'But you were there with Alison.'

'I was there by myself. My mobile didn't go off. I slept in. Alison woke me when she came to check the room.'

'You told me you were going home last night, to your flat in Sighthill.'

'That's true. I did.'

'Well I would say you've some explaining to do.'

Frank did his best to account for what had happened in the days and weeks after the fire, how he'd looked for somewhere suitable and failed to find it. Sometimes he'd stayed at his sister's when she was away, but since she'd taken up with Henry W Clement these opportunities had been few and far between. Then Archie phoned and they met for a drink. That's when the idea occurred to him: a home address he could give to Gemma, who kept asking where he was staying; a mailing address he could give to everyone. The only trouble was he couldn't actually stay there till Archie cleared his junk from the spare bedroom. So on those nights when he'd nowhere else, he'd taken to sleeping in the medical room. Sometimes he stayed over with her, of course, quite often in fact, but only when she suggested it. He didn't like to ask. He didn't want to take advantage. And if he'd told her his predicament she might have felt obliged to offer even if she didn't really want to, and he didn't want that either.

'You're not saying anything,' Frank said, after some of the most difficult minutes he had ever lived through.

'The medical room,' Pamela said.

'That's right.'

If ever there was a room where mischief was out of the question the medical room was it. But if Pamela's instincts were worth anything, Frank would never be unfaithful anyway. For a start, he wasn't that way inclined, and when it came to getting close to people he was disabled by a combination of inhibition and lack of interest, either of which would have done the job on its own. They both knew they wouldn't be together if she hadn't nailed him. He had responded, but she had made the first move.

'You look in very bad shape, has anyone told you that?'

'I didn't have time to tidy up. I haven't eaten.'

She reached into her desk drawer and took something out, a small tube.

'Close your eyes.' She sprayed his face with instant boost skin tonic spritzer. 'That should help,' she said. 'Refreshing?' He nodded. He would have nodded anyway. She wasn't the only one trying to save his skin.

'Good,' Pamela said. 'We should go to the restaurant. I don't know about you but I'm starting to find this place claustrophobic.'

Unfortunately, their route to the restaurant took them past Mr Gibson, who made a second attempt to intercept Frank, only to be saved by Pamela's assurance that he was far from well. But when he bent down to thank her, she told him that if he didn't need medical attention now he would when she was finished with him, which wasn't so reassuring.

'I can handle this, you know,' Frank said, and Pamela assumed she was referring to queuing for coffee at the counter. But as he waited for their lattes, which always took an age, he overheard remarks from the back shop which made him reconsider: playing away from home, taking maintenance a bit too far. When Bertrand realised who was there he duly appeared, the very soul of joie de vivre. Had monsieur appreciated the service d'étage? Frank hadn't a clue what he meant and said so. All he wanted was a couple of coffees, was that too much to ask?

'Pas du tout,' Bertrand replied, and finding Frank wasn't playing, made to return to the kitchen.

'I see you're preparing your dreaded haddock again,' Frank said, pointing to the specials menu.

'Very funny,' Bertrand said.

'That's what it says,' Pamela said. Bertrand looked at the board.

'For Christ's sake Angela,' he shouted through the swing door, 'pardon my French,' he said to Pamela, 'how many times do I have to tell you!' He looked downcast, a man fighting a battle he couldn't win. 'The girl's dyslexic,' he explained. Lovely person but she won't admit it. I've told her to check her spelling every day this week.'

'C'est la vie,' Frank said.

Bertrand shot him a reproachful look. He could take a joke but stealing his Gallic clothing was something else again.

Frank felt happier sharing a table with Pamela in the restaurant than he had in the office. Other people were there, all getting on with their lives. They had problems too, and the few that didn't would have soon. So he wasn't alone and he felt safer. Pamela had been known to shout when provoked but she wouldn't do that here.

'Maybe,' Pamela suggested, 'you have a problem with commitment.'

'What makes you say that?'

'Remember you told me about Archie splitting up with his girlfriend?'

'Yes.'

'Maybe you were more affected than you thought.'

'I don't think so.'

'Two people getting on really well till they start living together. Then it all goes pear-shaped and he has to buy a new flat. Makes you think, doesn't it?'

'I suppose.'

'Oh come on, Frank. They walked right into it, they didn't see it coming.'

Frank considered the suggestion and rejected it.

'You're not scared of commitment.'

'No.'

'So, and I'm speaking hypothetically here, if a registrar of births marriages and deaths, a ship's captain, a minister of religion or some other authorised person walked in here right now and offered to marry us . . . in front of witnesses, a legally-binding contract . . .'

'I'd say yes.'

But Pamela wasn't so sure, and wasn't likely to be till this business was sorted out. Her mother had wondered as recently as the previous night whether he was good enough for her. He was a nice enough lad, totally harmless, wouldn't hurt a fly and all that, and on the credit side he had certain practical skills – but when you came right down to it her daughter's boyfriend was sadly lacking in drive. I'll just leave you with that thought, dear, she'd said, before hanging up, a little something to ponder. Gee thanks mum, Pamela had replied, have a good night's sleep yourself!

Frank wondered if Pamela agreed with her and found that she did, up to a point. The facts spoke for themselves. How had he ended up in this mess? He left his flat and he had good reasons for that, but when he couldn't find another after a week or two, what did he do? He took the line of least resistance and ended up in the medical room. The medical room! So yes, she felt he tended to the passive sometimes, quite frequently, in fact. She toyed with her spoon. Inertia. That was a legitimate concern.

'Maybe,' she said, 'you've sat on it all this time because saying nothing was easier than talking it through. It could be,' she said, 'that all this stuff about not wanting to take advantage, maybe that's just so much crap.'

Frank found this an upsetting suggestion and it showed in his face. He tried to explain how he'd wanted to tell her but couldn't bring himself to do it. He didn't know why that was, but he wasn't making it up. Pamela reached out and took his hand.

'You can look at me, you know, I'm not going to kill you.'

They became aware of noise rising above the general background hum of talk and the clink of knives and spoons on plates and saucers. Colin McCandless was buying a coffee and joking with the girl at the till. You weren't having a good time if you weren't making a noise. As they knew he would, he pulled up a chair and joined them. He'd just bumped into Mr Gibson, who'd told him Frank was far from well. Maybe, he suggested, Frank needed to lie down for a while. There was an excellent bed in the penthouse suite or, as everyone was calling it now after last night's goings on, the pantyhose suite.

'Reports of your wit have not been exaggerated,' Pamela said.

'What's that supposed to mean?' Colin asked, suspecting that Pamela was insulting him.

'Irony isn't Colin's strong point,' Frank said.

'Irony,' Colin laughed, 'tell me about it. They're ironing the sheets up there even as we speak. Rumpled beyond recognition!'

'A bit like your shirt,' Pamela said, casting a deprecating eye on the creased lilac number he was wearing.

'No need to be personal,' Colin said, 'it was just a bit of a joke.'

'That's what they always say,' Pamela observed to Frank, 'it was just a joke. The last refuge of people like our friend here who give it but can't take it.'

Frank agreed. 'You've got him sussed.'

'Excuse me,' Colin said, in an offended tone, 'I'm present. I'm here.'

'Yes,' Pamela said. 'Why is that?'

Never one to stay where he wasn't wanted, Colin rescued his coffee and went to another table.

'That man skims the surface,' Pamela said, 'always has, always will.'

'Well,' Frank said, 'that's his niche. You know, in the human environment. That's what suits him best in the struggle for existence.'

'That's how you see it?'

'Well,' Frank hesitated, 'yes.'

They sat quietly for a moment in a sea of noise, an ocean of inconsequence, Pamela thinking that existence was all very well but not worth much if it lacked significance. But you couldn't reach up and pluck significance from the nearest tree. You had to create it, adding value to the item before it reached the market.

'You want to know what I think?' Pamela asked.

'Yes.'

'You should move in.'

'That's what I've been trying to avoid.'

'I know, but from where I'm sitting your reasons don't make sense.'

'I told your mother I wasn't using the fire as an excuse.'

'That was then, this is now. What's the alternative?'

'Finding another place.'

'You've tried that.'

'I'll try again. Harder. Convince you and your mother I can do it.'

'So what's it to be, spend the rest of your life doing things you don't really want to just to convince other people? Unless you're motivated to do a thing on your own account it won't work. Not over the long haul. I'll explain the situation to mum. She might not like it but she'll understand.'

She was speaking quietly, looking him straight in the eye, noting his reaction to every word. Her eyes were blue, attractive but not strongly coloured. A little short of pigment, Frank had thought at first, another area where genes hadn't dealt her a strong hand. He didn't think so now. Now he just looked at them, knowing he could tell her from the crowd on iris recognition alone.

'And believe me, this is the long haul we're talking here,' she said.

'If I move in because there's no alternative you'll end up resenting me.'

'That's true.'

'There you are then.'

'But if you move in because you want to . . . Frank, you have to ask yourself, you have to know what you want.'

He thought for a moment, of how relaxed and happy he was in the time he spent with her – cooking, eating, washing up, watching TV. The simple things people did.

'I want to live with you.'

Pamela smiled, reached over and rumpled his hair.

'That wasn't so difficult, was it?'

'Want a bet?'

He was delighted. Delighted and relieved. Whatever the barrier had been he'd shattered it, he'd finally broken through, though no doubt the bricks were still in there somewhere, waiting for a chance to wall him in.

Pamela sat back and smiled. 'There's hope for you yet.'

When Alastair appeared, looking breathless, he came straight to their table and sat down.

'You've been gone so long I thought something had happened.'

'We had a lot to discuss.'

'Well all I can say is don't let the bastards grind you down. The rumours, you know how it is, they'll go the rounds for a few days and then they'll fade away.'

'Glad you think so,' Frank said.

'I don't think so, son, I know. You two may find this hard to believe, but you know Sarah?'

'We do, don't we Frank,' Pamela said.

'Your glamorous assistant.'

'Well as I say, you'll find this hard to believe but there were rumours going round about her and me.'

'No!' Pamela said, feigning shock. Frank tried to kick her under the table but barked his shin on her chair by mistake.

'And some of them were pretty colourful I can tell you. They even reached the ears of my lady wife, that's how bad it got.'

'These people are unbelievable!'

'And that fellow there in the poncy shirt,' he pointed at Colin chatting to a couple of young stylists from the salon, 'he was the worst.'

Back in her office Pamela began checking a print-out of out-going calls while fielding a stream of questions from June. One in particular exercised her. If Frank had taken to sleeping in the medical room, how come he was found in the penthouse suite?

'There'll be a reason. I'll ask him tonight.'

'Tonight?'

'He's moving in.'

'No pets allowed,' June said with a smirk, 'except guide dogs for the blind.' She was citing a policy which had caught her eye when Pamela first took up residence in her flat.

'I'll come clean. I'll tell them. I'll renegotiate the contract.'

'Will the rent go up?'

'Haven't a clue.'

'If it does his nibs will have to chip in.'

'He'll have to chip in anyway.'

'To preserve his self-respect.'

'There is that, but I was thinking more of my bank balance. Anyone living with me pays his way.'

'Two mouths to feed.'

'I'll say this for you, June, you can count.'

'Or are we talking three?'

'Not if I have anything to do with it.

29

'Come in, Frank.'

As he entered Mr Gibson's office he was struck yet again by how austere it was. Apart from the yearly calendar from a supplier of office sundries there was little by way of adornment: neither his accountancy qualification on the wall nor a family photograph on the desk.

'Do have a seat,' Mr Gibson said without looking up, 'be with you in a moment.'

Alastair had made much of Frank's invitation to meet with Mr Gibson in the inner sanctum. As he saw it, this unusual request could only mean one thing: Mr Gibson had discovered a discrepancy.

'You'll have seen this, no doubt,' Mr Gibson said, handing him an A4 sheet of paper.

The drawing portrayed Frank as Paddington Bear with a placard round his neck inviting passers-by to give him a bed for the night. He was shown shivering on a street corner selling the Big Issue.

'One of these has recently been found in a lift. We shall have to discourage this sort of thing. It shouldn't be in the public domain.'

Frank was about to say 'Amen to that', but decided not to.

'It's none of my business, of course, but I hear you're living with Miss Ross.'

'For the time being, that's correct.'

'I have the highest opinion of Miss Ross,' Mr Gibson said, 'a girl of great integrity and strength of character. Have you considered regularising the position?'

Frank didn't want to go into that with anyone, and certainly not with Mr Gibson.

'There may be some difficulty with her mother,' he said, as an easy way out.

'She doesn't approve.'

'She has reservations.'

'She may,' Mr Gibson suggested, giving Frank a hard look, 'consider you a man of limited prospects.'

'She might be right.'

'And she may not. It's all about perception wouldn't you say? Consider the time women spend in front of mirrors, the sums they expend on cosmetics and jewellery, the treatments they lavish on themselves in salons and beauty parlours.' He opened a manila folder. 'According to recent research,' he said, reading from his notes, 'your average woman spends £36,903.75 on her hair in a lifetime! And lest we feel complacent,' he added, 'there is reason to believe that expenditure by the male of the species is increasing too.'

'I see you're looking into this,' Frank said.

Mr Gibson indicated his collection of cuttings. 'I propose to venture into print, hence the research. My thesis will be that as we spend increasing amounts of time and money on our bodies, we devote less and less attention to our souls. And of the two which, would you say, is the more important?' Frank was about to answer but Mr Gibson forestalled him with a dramatic gesture of the hand. 'There can only be one answer, I'm afraid. And if things continue as they are at present the outlook is dire.'

Frank was mystified. Mr Gibson had a case, but why was he running it past a maintenance man? Was he wearing a green visor? Had he mistaken him for an editor?

'Your recent little escapade in the penthouse suite . . .'

'Not my finest hour,' Frank admitted.

'It is not my intention to criticise or poke fun, far from it. But if you could bear with me for a moment or two I have some questions.'

Mr Gibson wanted to know what the experience of living in the store had been like. What had he done for food? How had he dealt with the question of personal hygiene? Frank began to feel like an astronaut quizzed about natural functions by visitors from primary five, who naturally wanted to know how bladders were emptied without incident in zero gravity within the confines of a space suit.

'Put it another way,' he said, 'if I were to ask you to live in this store for a month – without leaving the building and without anyone supplying you from the outside world – do you think you could do it?'

'Oh yes,' Frank assured him, 'no trouble at all.'

'All your needs would be met.'

Frank could think of one which wouldn't, but even though Mr Gibson was married he didn't like to mention it.

'They would.'

'Thank you, Frank, you've confirmed my suspicions,' Mr Gibson sighed. 'It has come to such a pass that the large store, mall or retail park meets all our physical needs while the spiritual dimension is entirely absent from the bill of fare.'

'Well,' Frank said, recollecting thoughts of his own along similar lines not so long ago, 'you certainly have a case.'

'I realise that, but it's good to hear you say it nonetheless.'

Mr Gibson thanked Frank for his cooperation, and after he had the room to himself again returned to his figures. There was wastage everywhere he looked. Take photocopiers. In recent weeks these had produced fliers for an amateur opera company, sets of minutes for a bowling club management committee, and fifty copies of a poster concerning Misty, a grey and white cat last seen in the Morningside area of the city. Since Mrs Rattray (ladies wear) had included her phone number on the poster, identifying the culprit had been easy. Shall we say, he'd said to her among the pastel tones of the slow-moving autumn collection, fifty copies at ten pence per copy? She handed over the five pounds with ill grace, off-loading as much small change as possible.

'How do I know it won't go straight into your pocket?' she asked, aggrieved.

'That's exactly where it will go, Mrs Rattray, till I get it to the safe. Good day!'

Mr Gibson was especially scathing about computers, which had been oversold not only to Mowatts but to several branches of government at an ongoing and unacceptable cost to the tax-payer. Given his attitude to technology, Mr Gibson wasn't best pleased when Hector arranged for a contact of his to call in and see him. Mr Enderby had the solution to all their problems.

He was neatly turned out and Mr Gibson saw from his grey business suit, white shirt and dark tie that there was nothing showy about him, an impression which quickly faded when he flashed his cufflinks and opened his mouth.

'As I'm sure I don't need to tell a man of your experience,' he began.

'Glad to hear it.'

It soon became clear to Mr Enderby that his only hope was to state his case and leave Mr Gibson to mull it over. His RFID system wasn't dependent on line of sight. The data on the tag could be read through a door, a cabinet, a customer, a member of staff or other obstacle which would defeat a bar code reader. And data was captured much more quickly.

From the fact that Mr Gibson stopped furtively checking columns of figures on his desk, Mr Enderby assumed that he had at last secured his attention. Companies employing RFID in their supply chain were noting marked reductions in cost.

'Name one,' Mr Gibson said.

'Well I might cite Debenhams, not to mention the John Lewis Partnership. They swear by it, as do R&P.'

'R&P?'

'A niche chain but growing fast. They concentrate on the youth market, what we might term the young and trendy.'

Known to its clientele as Rape and Pillage, R&P was favoured by Goths for its coffin handbags and wide variety of black patent leather footwear. Their victim boots were walking off the shelves.

'Yes,' Mr Enderby said, reinforcing his point, 'they have tapped into the considerable buying power of the youth demographic.'

'Have they indeed.' Mr Gibson paused, he was thinking. 'I take it that RF stands for radio frequency?'

'Correct.'

'And the tags you referred to earlier contain radio transmitters.'

'They do. Astonishing really, when you think of it.' Mr Enderby looked genuinely impressed by his own technology.

'So how many tags are we talking about here, Mr Enderby – hundreds, thousands?'

'Oh, in a business of your size hundreds wouldn't begin to cover it.'

'So if I understand you aright, we'd have thousands of tags transmitting radio signals to receivers concealed, for example, in doors.'

'Low frequency signals, that's right. That's how it works.'

Mr Gibson opened a desk drawer and withdrew a report.

'You'll see I'm about to fall back on paper, Mr Enderby, but I make no apology for that.'

'Nor should you, Mr Gibson,' Mr Enderby said in an emollient tone.

Mr Gibson was holding a copy of Frank's draft environmental policy. Mr Enderby had unwittingly reminded him of Appendix B, which had actually been written by Flora. The Scientific Basis of Feng Shui was a book whose slimness artfully disguised its breadth of reference. She had taken a particular interest in electro-magnetic radiation, believing that Henry W Clement's bass guitar might, over a period of time, have an adverse effect on his gonads. Look where he holds it when he's playing, she wailed, fearful of future pleasure – just asking for trouble! And Frank couldn't deny that the instrument was dangerously close to the organs of procreation. But that, he assured her, was simply to show that Henry was less a musician, more a sex-god making music. Guitarists had been doing it for decades.

'I have here,' Mr Gibson said, 'a summary of research findings concerning the adverse effects of electro-magnetic fields on public health. And now you propose to add to this electro-magnetic soup in which we are already obliged to swim, not hundreds but thousands of additional radio transmitters!'

'Low power transmitters, Mr Gibson.'

'Transmitters nonetheless,' Mr Gibson replied. 'And if I might just say, in my capacity as an accountant, a value may be a small, but that value multiplied by thousands becomes large. We are talking here, surely, of a cumulative effect.'

Mr Enderby had been trying to catch the title on the front cover of Frank's report, but because it was bound in transparent covers had been foiled by reflections.

'If I might ask,' he said, 'what document is that?'

'As of now this research is classified,' Mr Gibson said, not wishing to reduce its impact by admitting its local provenance, 'but I can assure you that its findings are referenced, primarily to sources in this country, the United States, and the People's Republic of China.'

'It's just that there have been, as I'm sure you're aware, a number of scare stories . . . the popular press . . . you know how it is.'

Mr Gibson looked up from Appendix B. 'I am not given to reading the popular press. Life is too short.'

Accepting that he was getting nowhere with this industrial antique of a man, Mr Enderby handed him a high gloss, high impact marketing folder the contents of which covered the subject in detail.

'My card's inside. If there's anything else you wish to know, please don't hesitate to call.'

Having seen off Mr Enderby, Mr Gibson turned his attention to reconciling figures from the food hall. After two hours he had still failed to do it, so when his phone rang he picked it up with some relief, by no means his usual reaction. The caller was his wife, who rarely contacted him during working hours but was making an exception in this case.

'Douglas, have you seen today's News?' she enquired, breathlessly. 'I'd get hold of a copy if I were you.'

'And why would that be, Doris?'

'Mowatts, it's being sold.'

Since Mr Gibson was one of three people in the store who had known this was on the cards he wasn't unduly surprised, but sworn to secrecy by Alice he hadn't informed his wife. At first he attributed her breathlessness to her beta blockers, but in this case it was clearly evidence of distress. He couldn't but feel concern.

'You really must relax. Have a seat with some herbal tea.'

'Never mind me,' she shouted, 'it's your pension you should be worried about!'

Without knocking, June burst into the room. Mr Gibson had always felt physically intimidated by June and her unexpected arrival, in a state of high excitement, affected him like a sudden detonation of the flesh. He felt enveloped, and where some men might have found the sensation comforting, Mr Gibson didn't care for it at all.

'Have you heard?' she gasped.

'My wife is just off the phone.'

'I can't believe it.'

'I would say that's for the best, wouldn't you? It may be just a rumour. In any case, as we have good grounds to realise in this establishment, the fact that something is for sale doesn't mean anyone will buy it.'

Mr Gibson knew that if the family decided to sell there was no way of stopping them but he also knew, whatever it might say in the papers, that it was far from a done deal. He had read many such stories over the years and knew that in no sector of commercial life was speculation more rife than in mergers and acquisitions. He also knew that if the family had decided to sell, provoking a bidding war by a leak to the press would do them no harm at all.

But that didn't sound like Alice to him. No, more likely it was a lapse by someone in the Hope Group or their financial advisors, someone who had spoken out of turn, left a document on a copier, or been overheard discussing the matter in the washroom.

'The only thing we can do is try to establish the facts, and that may take some time.'

Following a sharp knock at the door, Gemma came in. Her face was whiter than usual, though it might have been the light.

'I'm sorry to intrude, Mr Gibson, but my phone's going non-stop. Alice did warn me but I didn't expect so many calls. I mean, what can I say to them? I know they don't believe me, but I haven't the faintest idea what's going on.'

An envelope appeared on Mr Gibson's screen. June noticed it before Mr Gibson and willed him to open it, which he did. The document was in italic type, a failed attempt to add the personal touch: a memo from Alice up-dating the staff. As they scanned its contents Mr Gibson, with June on one side and Gemma on the other, felt like an ageing quiz-show host with two young sidekicks who, unlike him, did not have the answers to the questions.

'What do you make of it, Mr Gibson?' June asked.

'It seems quite reassuring to me,' Gemma said, 'we'd continue trading.'

Mr Gibson looked at her in amazement, though he had to admire her trusting nature: it had an innocent, childlike quality which he found appealing. If everyone shared those attributes the world would be a better place. But they didn't. Far from it. The woman was a lamb to the slaughter, easy meat with letters after her name.

'Miss Laing,' he sighed, 'where have you been all these years?'

She looked alarmed. 'What do you mean?'

'After a business is bought the buyers can do what they like. They might not get round to it for a year or two, but the sheep's clothing will gradually be shed and we will see the wolf in all his glory.'

'But surely,' Gemma protested, 'if a business is sold on the strength of certain undertakings the buyer could be pursued in the courts for failing to honour them.'

'I'm with Miss Laing on that,' June said.

'Well that's all right then, we can rest easy in our beds tonight. The favourite exit strategy,' he explained, 'is to claim a change in market conditions. We meant what we said at the time but now – what with cheap imports from the Far East, soaring energy prices, and unexpected fluctuations in the exchange rate – conditions have changed to the point where our assurances, given in good faith, are no longer sustainable.' Mr Gibson slipped back out of character. 'Or words to that effect.'

'So you think it's a con,' Gemma said.

'Without access to private discussions in the Hope Group boardroom we have no way of knowing.'

'Sounds to me like an argument for bugging them.'

'Anyway, ladies, there we have it,' Mr Gibson said in a summary tone, 'all we can do is wait and see.'

'Fair enough, Mr Gibson, but we don't have to wait here.'

Easy for June to say, he thought. She was young. Moving on might be desirable in her case since it would add to her range of experience. Miss Laing's position, too, was relatively strong. Human resource vacancies were advertised every week and she was well qualified, if too well-meaning for her own good. When it came to himself, however, the outlook was bleak. He was competent, and his record would attest to an impressive lack of days off through illness. But however artfully concealed, his age – fifty-eight – would surely be held against him.

No one would want to know. Alice would write him an excellent reference, but word got round. It always did. People talked. He would have a reputation as stickler for accuracy, an admirable quality in an accountant you would think, but there were people out there who didn't like questions they couldn't answer. There were even a few who knew the answers only too well and had reason to conceal them.

However, as he would later point out to his wife, his pension looked safe and would start paying out in less than two years, in addition to which, if push came to shove, there was some prospect of a package. They would get by.

'Well, if you'll excuse me, people,' June said, rising to her feet with unusual vigour, 'I'd better be off. The place must be buzzing by now.'

Hoping it was, she headed for the first floor. Colin had tuned a radio to a local station and was hovering nearby in the hope of breaking news. He was clearly frustrated by an older customer trying to pin him down.

'You say it comes with a one year guarantee, young man, but it won't be worth the paper it's written on if the business folds!'

'I hardly imagine it will come to that,' Colin said, inwardly cursing the old goat for interfering with his listening.

'Oh yes?' the gentleman said. 'It did when Powerhouse went down.'

'I can see where you're coming from on this one, sir. Perhaps I could direct you to my colleague Andrea,' he said, pointing to a girl who'd only started the week before, 'she specialises in the legal side of things.'

Colin was shameless, he'd say anything! But if he imagined Andrea would end up ironing his shirts he had another think coming. It was then June noticed his shirt wasn't creased. That was a turn-up for the books. She didn't know it was down to Hilda, she of the honeyed tones and practised demonstration skills. Colin had heard her pitch several times before he finally succumbed and purchased one of her hand-held steam cleaners, taken with its resemblance to a cute yellow penguin. Now each night before retiring, Colin hung a shirt from the handle of his bedroom door and steamed out the creases, knowing that any moisture absorbed by the fabric would dissipate by morning.

June noticed Kathy examining a set of silver tea spoons, each one topped with a clan crest. She was keeping an eye on someone in the gifts section when June sidled up behind her.

'Good morning, madam, can I be of assistance?' she asked.

'You could start by keeping your voice down,' Kathy suggested.

'You must be lost without Preston to keep an eye on.'

'You think so? I'm glad to see the back of him.'

'Pamela got another e-mail from him. Apparently he's taken up with an older woman, a Polish seamstress by the name of Radwanska. Something like that. Anyway, according to him she's very bed-worthy. I kid you not, that's the word he used. They're so happy together he's not coming back!' June paused for breath. 'You couldn't make it up.'

'Why not? He did.'

'You don't believe him?'

'Of course not. He has so little in his pathetic little life he has to invent it.'

'This place is so quiet,' June said, looking round. 'Where is everyone?'

'Conferring in the store room,' Kathy said, 'God knows why.'

'You haven't heard?' June asked. 'The store's being sold. Mr Gibson's trying to find out what's going on.'

Kathy was shocked but determined not to show it.

'It wouldn't surprise me if he was behind it.'

'You're so cynical, Kathy.'

'Comes with the territory, dear.'

'I'll get you a copy of Alice's memo.'

Kathy sighed. 'That will make my day.'

As soon as she was free to do so, Alice made her way to Mr Gibson's office.

'I've done my best to allay people's fears' she told him, 'but the rumour mill's in overdrive right now.'

'I'm sure your memo will have helped. But come now, Miss Mowatt, you didn't beat a path to my door to tell me that.'

'No, Mr Gibson. Since you know the background the least you're entitled to is an accurate update.'

She wanted to assure him that nothing had been settled since their previous meeting. And though she couldn't mention it, this was true even of the complex plan by which the family might maximise its profit on selling, still lying dormant in her desk drawer.

Mr Gibson was eating a chicken sandwich made by his wife, with a flask of rooibos tea beside him. It contained no caffeine, his wife had assured him. Good for high blood pressure. Which was just as well. The more he examined the latest set of figures the more exercised he became.

'It's possible,' she said, 'that one of their corporate accountants may wish to pay us a visit.'

Alice's way of reminding him that the books should shortly be available for due diligence auditing by the Hope Group.

'Of course,' Mr Gibson said. 'That's only to be expected. No one in their right mind would buy a pig in a poke. In any case,' he added, 'they would want to arrive at a reasonable price. I know I would.'

'I value your support, I hope you know that Douglas.'

The question was how much. As he knew from long experience, golden opinions were all very well but you couldn't cash them in at the bank.

30

'Have you read the literature I gave you?' Flossie asked.
'I have.'
'What do you think?'
'It's certainly a possibility.'

They were sitting on the bench behind her cottage on a pleasant autumn afternoon, the yellows which had been there all along starting to show through the fading greens. It was warm with a light wind, a relaxing place to sit if the person you were with wasn't intent on planning your future. The garden caught the sun from the south, its boundary marked from the footpath on the other side by an old drystane dyke colonised by ivy-leaved toadflax.

Seeing these lovely little flowers Frank felt that nature did it best. Flossie disagreed. She had planted a clematis against it, but the wall was only five feet high and for some time now it had tried to climb higher. Some of its tendrils spilled over to the other side where she couldn't see the flowers. The rest were falling back on themselves. Just like people did, Frank thought, when their backs were to the wall.

'I see you're admiring my Nelly Moser. It's come on very well. Quite a display when the flowers are out.'

They were out now, a profusion of two-tone mauve and white flowers.

Flossie was reconciled to the fact that Pamela and Frank were serious. Whether they'd get married was something else again. As she'd said to her daughter the day before, she knew he had his good points but they needing sharpening somewhat. They liked each other. Okay, they loved each other, but so what? That was no guarantee of success and she was speaking from experience. In many respects they were well suited, yet it seemed to her a marriage of convenience. They happened to meet at work and got on well, but if Pamela had gone about it more actively, put herself about more, surely she would have met someone who suited her better. A more dynamic individual with a better sense of himself?

Pamela listened to her mother's concerns without surprise. What she hadn't heard before she'd guessed, though she was dismayed by Flossie's marketing approach to mating. Put herself about more – what was she, a commodity! Granted, Frank wasn't a compendium of the social graces: when they were alone together, that's when the real Frank appeared. But Flossie knew when her daughter was trying too hard. My goodness, dear, she said, you make him sound like a hermit crab!

'So what's your thinking at the moment, Frank?' she asked.

He wasn't sure, but he'd narrowed his options to three. He could stay where was, carrying on as before, perhaps taking over when Alastair retired. Modest advancement there, though not if the Hope Group closed the store. Then there was Archie, who was trying to recruit him. His property portfolio was taking off, he really needed a practical man like Frank, not just as an electrician but a project manager. But Archie liked nothing more than talking big, some of his grander claims accompanied by a flourish of the air cigar. My advice to you, he'd said, is get in on the ground floor. Or what, Frank wondered, buy a set of ladders? Then there was Flossie's idea, which had much to commend it.

'I suppose you'll tell me in your own good time,' she said.

'I am considering it,' he told her. 'I've read your leaflets through, I'll read them again. I just need to let it lie in my mind for a while.'

'And you'll wake up one morning knowing what you think.'

'That's about the size of it.'

Flossie couldn't help feeling that if that was the size of it, it wasn't very big. There he was, a lad with a sufficiently enquiring mind to be halfway through a BSc in Natural Sciences, so the subject should appeal to him. Particle acceleration, just the thing for a dark winter's night. And laser technology, how up-to-the-minute was that! And after he'd qualified the job would be every bit as practical as the one he was doing now. Given the shortage of radiographers he'd have no trouble getting work. A hands-on job and doing good in the world while he was at it. What more could the boy want?

Flossie looked over at two large plant pots on either side of her back door. 'Something's been eating my hostas.' The dark blue flowers were standing up well but some of the leaves were badly chewed.

'Snails,' Frank said. 'Slugs.'

'Someone advised putting out a saucer of beer. Can't remember who it was. Apparently they like it so much they drown themselves in it by mistake.'

He was about to point out that snails could procreate without the need of a partner, but decided not to in case Flossie took it as a sign of an overly self-sufficient cast of mind. How simple life would be if you didn't require a partner. You wouldn't need to negotiate all the time. You wouldn't have to talk to her mother and answer her questions. On the other hand, the next generation would be clones, losing the possibility of advance through mutation. But would that be so bad? If Pamela had been a clone of her mother she wouldn't have HSP. But she wouldn't be Pamela either, she wouldn't be herself.

'Are slugs just snails without shells?' Flossie asked.

'They're both gastropods,' Frank said, 'but don't quote me on that.'

'Oh Frank,' Flossie said coyly, 'I wouldn't dream of it.'

Why was it, he wondered, that Flossie so often adopted a sardonic tone when talking to him? Was she trying to put him down, or was that her way of addressing someone who was down already? And also, as now, he sometimes detected a sexist attitude behind her questions. She brought up his intentions at regular intervals but he had yet to hear her cover the same ground with Pamela. The assumption was always that he would be supporting Pamela, never that she would support herself, let alone him.

'So tell me,' he said, waving one of her leaflets, 'who would be paying the bills when I'm doing this? It's a full time course. I couldn't hold down a job and study at the same time.'

Flossie was aware of that, but in her mind, behind all the good intentions, there was a bargain, a quid pro quo. Pamela would pay him through the course, but that was a debt he would repay several times over if her condition worsened. It might not happen for many years but somewhere down the line Pamela would need looking after. Flossie wasn't a mercenary person, but she did have legitimate concerns.

'I take it you have no savings.'

'A little. Nothing to speak of. Might get me through the first month.'

She considered running her scenario past him but couldn't bring herself to do it. It would come over as remarkably hard-nosed, an impression she didn't want to give, and it smacked of tempting fate. She had known couples who'd had an arrangement like this, the woman – it usually was the woman – sacrificing her own career, the husband or partner getting the qualification and, on the strength of it, going on to better things. Which, it turned out, included a better woman. Then there was a bitter and acrimonious parting of the ways. He left her for someone younger, more glamorous, someone less tired, less worn out. Someone to whom he owed nothing. Thoughts like this troubled her a great deal. Though her instinct told her Frank wasn't like that, it was no consolation. These women had instincts too and where had that got them? Into deep trouble, emotionally and financially. She didn't want that for her daughter, who had enough on her plate as it was.

And now she came to think of it, this was the man who'd assured her he wasn't using the fire as a pretext for moving in. No doubt he meant it at the time, but look where he was living now. And it was all very well Pamela saying she had to twist his arm, but what if he'd been angling for it all along?

'Pamela would be working,' Flossie said. 'I could help out. Maybe your father could too.'

He realised when she said this that he had no idea of his father's finances, though he always had food on the table and his house was warm on a cold night.

'I suppose I could do homers, that would bring in some cash.'

'It would,' Flossie said, 'but where would you find the time? As you said yourself it's a full time course.'

'Evenings and weekends.'

It didn't sound realistic. Flossie knew he'd need time to work on his assignments. He'd also need time with Pamela. Quality time, as they put it these days. The relationship wouldn't last if all he did was work. But work was by no means guaranteed for either of them.

'Will the sale go ahead?'

'Pamela thinks so, and she sees more of management than I do.'

'What do you think, Frank?'

'I think Miss Mowatt's getting tired. She's had enough.'

'Pamela told me what she said the night she found you snoozing in the shop.'

Flossie liked cutting things down to size and frequently referred to the store as a shop and to Frank, in his absence, as 'the boy'.

'I didn't realise at the time,' he admitted, 'but looking back on it now I can see she was handing out hints. It's almost as if she was trying to warn me.'

'Is that so surprising? Pamela says she likes you.'

'Could be, I suppose. It has been said.'

'Maybe you're the son she never had.'

'I don't go in for that psychological stuff.'

'You should,' Flossie suggested, 'if you want to get a handle on people.'

Frank didn't agree. He took people as they were in the here and now. How they had become that way was immaterial. It wouldn't change anything.

'Pamela has a suspicion,' Flossie said. 'She ran it past me last night, straight out of the conspiracy-theory handbook.'

Which handbook would that be, Frank wondered, the one in which JFK was murdered by the mafia at the request of the DAR or the one where Neil and Buzz took a wrong left turn at Albuquerque and the moon landings were shot in Hangar 18?

'It wouldn't involve Mr Gibson, would it?'

This was an educated guess: Pamela had run it past him as well. Mr Gibson was trying to put a spanner in the works. If there were serious gaps in the books the Hope Group wouldn't proceed to a formal offer. They'd have no way of knowing the true value of the business. In her opinion, and June had evidence of this, Gibson had been going over every last shred of paper with unusual thoroughness, even for him.

The errors in maintenance he'd already discounted as mistakes – just what you'd expect in a section run by Alastair Geddes. But major questions had arisen in some other parts of the store. Where the sums involved were larger and staff handled plastic and cash there was always the possibility of fraud. His audit was still underway, but in just over a year Mr Gibson could retire and in the meantime, Pamela believed, he was doing everything possible to delay the sale. His objective was clear, security for himself and his wife in their twilight years.

'I know it's an explanation,' Flossie said, 'and it accounts for the facts, but surely he wouldn't do a thing like that?'

Probably not, Frank thought. But if he wanted to he could, and with a clear conscience, simply by being thorough. That was his natural inclination and that was what he was paid for. He could even do it by mistake, an unintended consequence of his painstaking approach. Which would fit the facts too, though it didn't seem likely.

'But Flossie,' Frank said, 'you could just as easily turn this argument right round. The family can't sell *unless* the books are in order. Mr Gibson is doing his best to expedite the sale.'

Flossie stood up. 'Would you care for a glass of wine?'

'Thanks,' Frank said, anticipating some relief from the question and answer session while Flossie went inside to pour it. 'And a slice of Selkirk Bannock?'

'Now you're talking.'

He watched as Flossie, the compleat gardener, walked into the house in her baggy cords and flapping checked shirt. He heard her ask Pamela through the closed bathroom door if she was alright. Apparently she was. Soaking in salts and enjoying it. Frank didn't mind Flossie's questions, her constant search for clarification, it struck him as entirely natural. What he minded was not knowing some of the answers. She returned with a glass of wine and a generous slice of bannock.

'Try that for size.'

He did, it was delicious, but when he tried the wine it was less to his taste. A closer look revealed it wasn't as clear as your average white and were there traces of sediment in the bottom of the glass.

'What's this?' he asked. She hadn't brought the bottle.

'That,' she told him, 'is elder-flower wine. Chateau Ross Grand Cru. I made it last year so it's fully matured.' She smiled. 'Like me.'

Okay, he thought, so if I agree I'm saying she'd old, but if I disagree I'm saying she's immature. This woman would take some watching.

'Very nice. Very distinctive.'

'Frank!' Pamela was calling him from the bathroom.

'Excuse me. Duty calls.'

Flossie smiled but she didn't feel like it. Duty used to call her but now she was being replaced. Given a few more years she'd be totally unnecessary. Or worse, a burden.

Frank regretted leaving the bannock but had the presence of mind to take the wine, seeing an opportunity to dispose of it without offending his host. Flossie might suspect but she was hardly going to say anything. He found Pamela wallowing in a sea of suds which seemed to be multiplying with a view to world domination. Her head was resting on a towel against the end of the bath, her hair wet and bedraggled. He could see it needed rinsing, no doubt why he'd been summoned. As Flossie put it, summoned to The Presence. Pamela had a glass too, but she'd had years to get used to it. An acquired taste he could get by without. Elderflower. Straight from nature's larder. Flora would be into that. He'd ask Flossie if he could take her a bottle. He smiled to himself. That would get them both on side in one neat move.

'Shut the door.'

'Why, what are we planning?'

She sighed. 'Nothing. I'd like to keep the draught out, though. If that's alright with you.'

Frank considered perching on the edge of the bath but the last time he'd done that she'd pulled him in, so he sat in her chair instead. Pamela's bubble bath filled the air as well as the water. There was a strong citrus twang about it. Flora had bought it because it had 'karma' on the label. Typical Flora. The smell would linger on for hours after the last drop of water had drained from the tub.

'Relaxed, are we?'

'I am. Don't know about you.' She looked at his glass. 'Pour it down the sink.'

As Frank had guessed, Pamela wanted him to rinse her hair. She could do it herself but it was easier if someone else did it for her, someone who would spot any surplus shampoo still lingering behind the ears. Frank got up, rolled the chair out of the way, switched the mixer from taps to shower and lifted the head.

'You'll have to sit up and lean forward – the hose won't stretch that far.'

Frank had suggested installing a riser on the wall, but Flossie was happy with her bathroom the way it was and Pamela pointed out that while the present arrangement was basic she could reach the shower without standing. The subject never came up again.

Pamela grasped the handles on the sides of the bath and slid herself forward.

'That's great.'

He held his hand under the spray until he had the temperature right.

'Eyes shut.'

'Fine by me,' she said, 'you look better that way.'

Her hair was so wet it was almost brunette, which he didn't like. Pamela was blond. If she'd died her hair chestnut or brown he wouldn't have cared for it at all.

Flossie knocked. 'Hello people. Mind if I come in?'

'Of course not,' Pamela said.

She entered and shut the door. 'My, this is cosy. I was wondering what you two might like for tea.'

'Oh, we're not fussy, are we Frank? Whatever you've got.'

'Well,' she said, taking a towel from the rail, 'you could have venison and cranberry sauce, or Swedish meat balls. There's always fish, of course.' She placed the towel on the toilet seat and sat down.

'I'm fine with venison,' Pamela said, 'how about you, Frank?'

Frank was fine with it too. Pamela offered to help with the cooking but Flossie told her to relax. That's what she was here for. A break.

'Oh,' Pamela said, 'and there I was thinking it was to have you organise my life with the hairdresser here.'

'Over more years than I care to remember,' Flossie said, 'I have learned to attempt only manageable tasks.'

'I don't know how to take that, do you?' Pamela asked Frank. 'Don't worry, mother. We'll get by. We'll muddle through.'

'I'm sure you will.' That was what concerned her.

Pamela splashed around a little.

'This is nice, the three of us in here. Very cosy. Very happy families.'

'Well, it would be,' Flossie said, looking at Frank, 'if Flora was here, and your father.'

'Flora's here in spirit, check the smell.' It was strong enough to suggest that his sister would stay for another week unless all the windows were thrown open and left that way for twenty-four hours. 'As for dad,' he said, 'he isn't the happy family type. Too much of a loner.'

'There you are,' Flossie said, 'what did I tell you!'

The phone rang in the hall and Flossie excused herself.

'What was that about?' Pamela wanted to know.

'Your mother thinks the past explains the present.'

'Seems reasonable.'

'It is, but it doesn't help. I'm stuck with me the way I am. You have to take me as you find me, as I am now.'

Pamela pulled her hair back from her eyes and gave him a hard look. 'I think you're forgetting something.'

'What?'

'I don't have to take you at all.'

Frank felt a moment of panic. Pamela was stating the obvious, but was there intention behind it too? Probably not. She just liked to keep him on his toes.

'Good news,' Flossie called through the bathroom door. 'That was Flora. She can make it after all.'

Frank turned the water off, tried to lay the shower head down and found the hose fighting him every inch of the way. When it came to coils it had a mind of its own. He sat down on the bathmat, which would shortly absorb the water from Pamela's feet. In an hour from now, two at the outside, he'd be alone in this cottage with three women each of whom had her own take on Frank Figures, each of whom saw him from her own angle. So really, it was all coming down to triangulation. Where the three lines intersected, there he was. Nowhere to hide, no wriggle room.

So much for Preston and his GPS handset, he thought. Kid's stuff. This was the last word in positioning, what he was dealing with now. He'd have to sign up to something. Compared to his wayward life so far, the future would be less indulgent, more constrained. Narrower. Narrower but deeper. Whether he liked it or not he'd have to grow up. Pamela reached over the edge of the bath and ruffled his hair. Looking serious didn't suit him.

'It's not the end of the world, you know. You'll survive.'

Printed in Great Britain
by Amazon